Vicky shook her head a l over-think things. "How long w get to it?"

"I'm the faster of us," Tina declared.

Another shriek of pain echoed around the forest, and all three girls couldn't help the shudders which coursed through their bodies. Vicky couldn't stay any longer and turned back to the two waiting girls, decision made. "I've got to go and find out what's happened, but going on what we're hearing, I've a feeling we're going to need an ambulance."

At this, Sal turned to her friend. "I'll go and wait by the phone. If you need one, come back and tell my mate Tina here. She'll be with me in a couple of minutes."

Yet another howl of pain made up Vicky's mind. "You know where we are?" she asked, getting nods from the two. "Right. Phone for an ambulance anyway. I'm pretty sure the one at the saw mill is out of order," and not wanting to waste another breath, she nodded, hefted her axe over a shoulder, and took to her heels in the same direction as Marcy had gone. The forest they were working wasn't large, but the part where they hadn't cleared the ground made the going slower than she'd have liked, if she didn't want to break an ankle. Brushing aside some branches, she found herself in a very small clearing. Before her was a sight no one and nothing could have prepared her for.

Praise for M. W. Arnold

"A skill of writing portrays the bravery of the women…"
~Nicki's Book Blog

~*~

"M. W. Arnold certainly knows how to grab the reader's attention and draw them into what proves to be one hell of a read."

~GingerBookGeek

~*~

"Overall, it was amazing to go back to this series and see where the story would go next."

~Jess, Bookish Life

~*~

"The friendships and the turmoils faced also pulls you in and it's easy to care about the characters and doesn't overtake the mystery, but enriches it."

~Bookmarks and Stages

~*~

"A perfect series for readers who enjoy historically accurate War time drama, with strong female characters at their heart."

~TheTwoFingeredGardener Blog

~*~

"*I'LL BE HOME FOR CHRISTMAS* is another fabulous story in this saga which made me feel as though I know the characters through and through. I can't wait to read the next one."

~Jera's Jamboree

The Lumberjills

by

M. W. Arnold

The Lumberjills, Book 1

The Lumberjills

Cover Art by *The Wild Rose Press, Inc.*

The Wild Rose Press, Inc.
PO Box 708
Adams Basin, NY 14410-0708
Visit us at www.thewildrosepress.com

Publishing History
First Edition, 2023
Trade Paperback ISBN 978-1-5092-4712-7
Digital ISBN 978-1-5092-4713-4

The Lumberjills, Book 1
Published in the United States of America

Dedication

For Ian Winter.
The best friend I'll ever have.
Miss you, mate.

Acknowledgments

Welcome to the first book in my Lumberjills series! In case you are unaware, the Lumberjills were a branch of the better known Land Girls of WWII Great Britain. Officially called the Timber Corps, this group was formed to take on the tremendous task of felling trees for much-needed timber, a large part of Britain's war effort, replacing the male lumberjacks (hence the nickname) who had gone into the Armed Forces. Out in all weathers, these girls found themselves in a dangerous job from which they were not allowed to resign, so vital was their work. Their contribution to victory should be remembered and honored.

Betty's, for those not in the know, is a well-known café/tea room chain whose most famous establishment is to be found in York, in the county of Yorkshire, north England. During WWII, there was a tradition of patrons "signing" their names on a mirror. That mirror can still be viewed in the York establishment. My thanks to their staff for aiding my research for that part of the story.

Wing Commander Mair was a real Canadian pilot who flew Lancasters and was lost when his aircraft, based at RAF Linton-on-Ouse, was shot down in November 1943.

My thanks, as ever, to my wonderful editor, Nan. You've the patience of a saint!

For all the encouragement I've received over the course of this project from my good, good friends in the Romantic Novelists Association, the words "thank you" can never be enough.

To my Lady Wife—you're my rock and my muse. Love you!

Chapter One

August 1942

The cold north Yorkshire wind blew harder than ever that afternoon and for the umpteenth time since she'd come on site, Beryl "Berry" Chambers wished she'd worn her pullover and long johns.

In between rolling out of bed at ungodly o'clock, stumbling outside to throw some cold water upon her face, and wolfing down a breakfast of eggs and bacon— one of the perks of being billeted on a farm—she'd looked up at the sky and made the wrong decision in wearing a shirt to work with nothing over it. She hadn't even tied a pullover around her waist! She hoped it would be the last time she'd make the mistake of underestimating how cold it got out in the forest. Something else she hadn't been taught at the training camp in Wetherby.

Spitting upon her hands, Berry took up her axe, eyes focused on the base of the tree where she'd made her mark, and swung the axe, then again, and once more before pausing to catch her breath and wipe her forehead. Another ten minutes and her wedge was cut. Stepping back, she was joined by her new colleague Sophie, who waited for Berry to pick up the other end of the crosscut saw. It wasn't anywhere as easy as it had been when they'd been taught how to fell trees, but if it had been easy, then it wouldn't have been worth the challenge, and Berry wanted a challenge.

****

The trappings of inherited wealth had never sat easily on Berry's shoulders, made even heavier by the outbreak of war three years ago. For those years, she'd been the good little girl her mother thought she'd brought up, and she'd played her part well. Even as the country lurched from one crisis to another, the most danger she'd ever found herself in was not being able to obtain a new dress for the next society event which, war or not, there still seemed to be a never-ending requirement for. As the months and then years crawled by, Berry had become ever more frustrated with her mother's assertion that by attending balls, opening village fetes, and generally being seen *around*, she was doing her *bit*. One by one, the younger staff members of the household had either been drafted or volunteered, and with the exit of each, her sense of self-worth had dipped ever lower.

The final straw had come when the house received, as the only point of contact the War Office had been able to find, a telegram notifying the next of kin of the death of an Alwyn Baker. That wasn't the tipping point, though. That came when she'd had to admit she couldn't place the poor man and had been forced to speak to their elderly butler about who this Alwyn chap was, only to be informed, under disapproving bushy eyebrows, that he'd been her father's driver for the past ten years. She'd been further informed he'd only joined the Army six months ago, and now he was one of the innumerable dead. How many times had he driven her to school? To parties? Down to Devon for holidays? And she hadn't even recognized his name! Her shame had been complete.

That night, after a three-course meal she'd never felt less like eating—she'd long ago stopped wondering where all the house's food came from—she'd traipsed miserably upstairs to her room and locked the door. After throwing off her dress, she'd slumped onto her bed and taken out the application form she'd hidden under her mattress. The *Women's Timber Corps*, it advertised, kept as a reminder for if her nerve deserted her, after she'd signed up at the recruiters. With determination emanating from every pore, she pulled her suitcase from the top of a wardrobe, slung it on the bed and, fighting years of training and instinct to fold the items first, threw in everything she believed she would need, including some of her brother's pullovers he'd left behind after joining the RAF. The recruiter she'd seen on the quiet a few weeks ago, had admitted that bringing her own warm clothing would be a good idea, as no one would mind them wearing what was needed to keep warm, if needs be.

After scribbling and then ripping up four versions of a goodbye letter to her parents, each of which did nothing but make her squirm in embarrassment, she gave up the idea of writing a meaningful goodbye note and instead settled for a few lines that told them the basics: where she was going and why. She didn't expect either would understand. At twenty-four, when most everyone else of her age was engaged in some kind of war work, she could only think her father had pulled some strings to keep her at home, and the idea didn't sit well. So far as she could tell, they still thought of her as their little girl, and though she understood this, she could no longer reconcile it with her need to be useful to the country.

So, with her suitcase packed, she'd changed into

outdoor clothes, her hardiest coat which she'd hidden away earlier that day, and checked all she'd need was safely in her shoulder bag—ID card, ration book, and the money she'd squirrelled away and hoped would last until her first payday. Then it had been a long anxious wait for her father, always a night owl, to finally go to bed and for the house to become quiet.

At last, she'd been able to make her escape on her trusted old bicycle, a fourteenth birthday present, to catch the last train to Wetherby, the training station, and her new life.

****

"Tuppence for them?"

"Pardon?" Berry replied, as she and Sophie leaned their shoulders into the trunk of the oak they were felling.

"Your thoughts, I mean," Sophie Baxtor grunted as the tree gave a tremendous creak. "You look like you're somewhere else."

"Not worth that much," Berry told her, as with a final groan and combined, "Timber!" from the two of them, the mighty oak gave up the struggle and crashed to the ground, sending up a flurry of dust, leaves, and brushwood.

Sophie waved her hands in front of her face, coughing in the process, to clear the air, and turned to where Berry was doing much the same. A grimy smile was pasted upon her face, matched by the one on her friend's, though there was also a knowing eyebrow raised which implied she wouldn't be forgetting the haunted look she'd seen any time soon.

Either way, further questions were curtailed by the appearance of Marcy Gagnon, their measurer and site boss. "Finished, girls?" she asked, swinging a tape measure. "It's about time to knock off for the day."

"Thank heavens for that," Sophie said, bending and stretching her back, then leaning forward on her toes to stretch out some of the kinks in her spine. "I don't know about you two, but I could do with unpacking. I hadn't banked on getting to the billet so late last night."

The expressions upon Berry and Marcy's faces matched Sophie's, relief at the end of their first day on the job, tinged with weariness they hoped they'd soon get used to.

Upon leaving the training camp, they'd taken the train as far as possible toward the small forest of oak trees in the Howardian Hills they'd been assigned to, then a couple of buses, and had finally wheeled their heavily laden bicycles up the track to Wipers Farm, just outside of Wiganthorpe, at somewhere past nine the previous night. Though the farmer's wife, Sheila Harker had been as welcoming as it was possible to be in your nightie, the same couldn't be said for her husband. Though not openly hostile, he'd restricted his side of the conversation to indecipherable murmurs and shrugs of his shoulders. Eventually being shown into what was obviously, even in the twilight, a hastily converted barn, the girls had collapsed onto their rickety beds, bags dumped on the ground, the weariness of the day's travelling overtaking them, even as Marcy had vaguely told them they needed to be up at six the next morning to start work.

Further conversation was curtailed by an unearthly whine of mechanical distress, and they all looked up in time to spot a single-engine aircraft pass low overhead. Smoke was pouring from the engine, and as they watched, it pulled into a climb it struggled to maintain, the obviously dying engine coughing louder. With more urgency, the plane clawed desperately for height in the cloud-speckled sky.

"Did you see any markings?" Marcy asked, a hand shielding her eyes. "Is it one of ours?"

"Couldn't make anything out," Berry replied, frustrated.

Sophie shook her head, whilst keeping an eye on the dying plane. "Me either."

As they watched, there was a final cough, a spark of flame burst from the exhaust and crept along the fuselage toward the canopy, and the engine died. Beginning its fall to a fiery grave, the three girls each held their breath as the canopy broke away, the plane rolled onto its back and out tumbled the pilot, his parachute beginning to open virtually as soon as he'd left his now well alight wreck.

Marcy watched for a moment and then turned her head to Vicky, the other girl they shared their billet with, urgency ringing in her voice as she shouted, "Vicky, run! Go use the telephone at the sawmill and get hold of the police. Tell them an unknown pilot's parachuting into the forest and to get here bloody quick! When you've done that, get back to the farm. Don't argue!" Slightly shocked, the girl stood there until Marcy yelled again, "What are you waiting for? Get a move on!"

Only when Vicky had sped off did Marcy turn her gaze back to the sky. "Where's he gone?" she asked.

Berry pointed toward the forest canopy, roughly a hundred or so yards deep into the forest. "I reckon he's going to come down over there."

As they watched, the parachute disappeared into the trees.

Marcy made a decision, saying, "Berry, grab your axe," and earning herself a raised eyebrow. "Don't fret. You won't be chopping him into pieces, probably," she added, earning herself the other eyebrow before clearing things up. "We may need to chop some branches off to get him down. Sophie, take an end of that ladder." She pointed toward a wooden ladder lying against the crude wooden shelter they'd built earlier that day. "We'll likely need that too."

The underbrush made going slower than any of them was prepared to voice out loud. Today had been the first day on site, and the most they'd been able to accomplish, after making sure their shelter was up, was to fell some of the trees at the very edge of the part of the forest they were due to clear. Hence the underbrush caught at their feet with every step as they made their way toward where they'd agreed the parachute had come down. Not much was said as they traipsed determinedly onward. No one voiced their fears that they could be marching toward an enemy—an enemy likely armed with a firearm with far more reach than anything they had to hand. There was a very real possibility they could be in deep trouble at any minute.

After five minutes, they could hear someone yelling, "Help!" and altered their course a little as the shouts grew louder. Berry reached out and gripped Sophie's upper arm just as the other girl was about to break into a trot.

"Steady," she urged, being joined by Marcy on Sophie's other side.

"But he needs help," Sophie pleaded, trying to break out of her companions' hold, keeping her head turned in the direction of the pleas, now so loud they must be virtually on top of their owner.

"And that's why we need to be careful." Berry was firm, keeping her grip upon Sophie. "Germans can speak English too, you know."

When Sophie turned her widening eyes to Marcy and received a nod, she relaxed and the other two let go their grip. She cast her brown eyes to the forest floor before looking up. "You're right. I'm sorry. I should have thought of that."

At the sound of another yell, Marcy checked with Berry. "Keep a good grip on that axe. Right." She took a deep breath. "Let's go and see what's what."

With much more caution than before, the three pushed through a bush until, ahead of them, dangling about ten feet above the ground as his parachute had caught in the lowest branches of a huge oak tree, was a man in a blue-gray flying suit, life jacket, and a black leather flying helmet. Upon spotting them, he stopped wriggling around in a futile effort to free himself.

"Thank God for that. Can you ladies get me down?"

Standing close together, the three women stopped their advance when they were still a good ten or so feet away from the tree. Leaning a little closer so they could speak without being overheard, Marcy asked, "Can anyone see if he's got a gun on his left hip?"

"Why?" Berry asked.

"Something I've seen from the newsreels. The Germans have their pistols on the left hip and draw across the body. Our boys have theirs on the right," she explained, before muttering, "I think."

Sophie, not too subtly, poked her head around the side of Berry, something she had to do as she was a good half foot smaller. "Can't see anything on either, Marcy."

"That's helpful," muttered Berry. "Now what?"

The man hanging around was becoming annoyed. "I say," he shouted, "I don't know what's going on, but it's been a rather crappy day, and I would like to get back to base."

Marcy detached herself from the huddle and edged a little closer toward him. No obvious firearm or not, there was still no reason to take a chance.

"Where's your base, then?" she asked of him.

It's very difficult to look dignified whilst sagging from a tree, not that the man didn't try. "I'm afraid that's not information I can give you, young lady."

Marcy took a step back as her colleagues rejoined her. "I'll give him *young lady*," Marcy muttered when Berry and Sophie could hear.

"He is right, though," Berry pointed out, which earned her a sour look from her elder colleague.

"Of course he's right," Marcy agreed. "Doesn't mean to say I like it."

"Oh, for goodness' sakes," Sophie suddenly blurted out, taking the others by surprise as she marched until she was standing a bare couple of feet from tree. "Look, throw me down your ID card, or we'll be here all night."

"At last," the chap said out loud, eyeing Marcy as he did so, "someone with an ounce of sense."

Upon hearing the expression and the context in which it was used, Berry felt some of the tension in her shoulders start to ebb away. It had been said so naturally that she felt no Nazi could have faked it and fooled them. Bending down, she picked up the card the man had dropped. It said *R.A.F FORM 1250* at the bottom and the picture inside, so far as she could see with the limited light, appeared to be the same as the man now glaring down at them. Dark wavy hair, slightly bent nose, and going by the name of Flying Officer Dennis Grey. Nice name, she thought, looking up at him a little more closely, noting his nose didn't appear quite so bent in person. In fact, it added an air of distinguished mystery about him. She suspected rugby would be to blame.

"Let me have a look," Marcy interrupted her thoughts, and took the card. "Hmm," she mused whilst rubbing her chin.

"Look, are you going to let me down, or do I have to let myself out of this harness and drop to the floor? I'd rather not risk breaking an ankle. I've a game of squash booked for later."

"I think he's English," Sophie put in after looking at the card too. "Shall we get him down?"

The sound of a police siren approaching made up Marcy's mind, and she nodded. "Let's get the ladder up," she told Sophie and, whilst doing so, told Berry to, "Have your axe ready."

Her eyes were upon the captive airman as she gave her last instructions, and a grin split her face as she noted the color had washed from his face upon hearing what Marcy had just said.

Not including the five minutes it took Berry to persuade Dennis to release his final grip on his harness and allow her to hook his feet with the blade of her axe and guide them onto the ladder, the whole rescue was over in barely longer than the previous discussion had taken. However, ID card or not, none of them took a chance, and with Berry standing guard with her axe at the ready, Marcy insisted that he take off his life jacket and open his flying suit to prove that he was, indeed, unarmed. Even then, they made certain he walked a good six feet in front of them as they escorted him out of the forest until they were met by two armed policemen.

"Ladies," he said, turning back toward where his three rescuers were standing after concluding his interview with the police, "I'd like to know who I have to thank for my rescue?"

Before anyone else could speak, Sophie blurted out, ignoring Marcy's look of slight annoyance, "I'm Sophie, this is Marcy, and the one with the axe is Berry."

"In that case," he replied, and Sophie and Marcy noticed he was looking at Berry as he spoke, "I'd like to thank Berry here for being careful with her axe."

No one was given any chance to reply as he was then ushered by the policemen into their car, and they drove off in a cloud of leaves and dust, alarm blaring.

"They do love that siren of theirs, don't they," Sophie commented as the car disappeared up the road.

"Let's get back home, eh?" Marcy suggested.

Marcy and Sophie had mounted their bicycles and were half way down the road when they noticed Berry wasn't with them. Coming to a stop, they turned to find Berry slumped to the ground, shaking from head to toe.

Chapter Two

It had taken all Marcy and Sophie's patience to coax their friend to her feet. The couple of miles back to the farm had seemed like twice the distance because of their desire to watch out for her, despite Berry insisting they shouldn't bother. Sophie's snort informed her what she thought of that idea.

By the time they'd propped their bicycles against the barn, it was getting on for eight in the evening, and all three were nearly out on their feet. The sound of their arrival alerted the fourth occupant of the barn cum lodgings and the door flew open, framing a girl barely out of her teens, with unfashionably short auburn hair and a face that was nearly all freckles. The mouth inside the freckle was set in a line that could mean anything from disapproval to constipation.

"There you all are! I was beginning to wonder if you'd found somewhere better to lodge and hadn't told me."

As she stepped back, Marcy held open the door for Sophie to usher Berry into the barn. "You do remember the little bit of excitement we just had?"

Slapping her head, Vicky threw herself onto a bed in the corner, the creak echoed around the space, and all—bar the girl herself—held their breath anticipating a collapse. When it failed to live up to expectations, Sophie closed the door behind her, and the three of them made their way to their beds and dumped their rucksacks and tools beside them.

"Have we missed tea?" Marcy asked toward where Vicky had her feet in the air and was undoing her boots.

To the accompaniment of a dull thump, Vicky replied, "Sheila popped her head in ten minutes ago, and when she saw there was only me, told me tea would be at half eight. She thought that would be long enough for you all to come back."

"Time enough to splash some water on our faces then," Marcy decided, throwing a glance over at where Berry sat upon her bed, her face framed in her hands. Padding across the rough wooden floor in her bottle green socks, Marcy sat down next to her and placed a hand on her knee. "Want to talk about it?"

Berry looked up. They'd also caught the attention of Vicky, who had turned onto her side, jodhpurs half way down her knees and forgotten in her interest in the conversation going on.

Berry gave her head a small shake, and for the first time since they'd left the forest, actually appeared to be aware of where she was. She sat back, her arms propped behind her, and took a look around the room, becoming aware of the audience she had, and let out a deep sigh.

"It was seeing that RAF pilot up close. I haven't seen or heard from my brother since he joined up last year. No one in my family has, and it's driving me mad! We used to be so close, getting up to all kinds of mischief. It drove my parents wild with frustration, admittedly mostly when we were teenagers, but I miss him terribly."

"Surely you've been around pilots since he joined up?" Marcy asked, leaning her head against Berry's shoulder.

She shrugged, the movement nudging Marcy's cheek. "Done my best to avoid them. Turn around, go out the room, even ignore them."

"Can't have been easy," Sophie added from her bed on the other side of the barn, proving it at least had good acoustics.

"That's putting it mildly," Berry agreed, letting out a small chuckle.

"So what happened?" Vicky asked, kicking off her jodhpurs and then yanking her knickers back up, her blush matching the color of her hair.

Berry flopped back onto her bed, taking an unsuspecting Marcy with her and addressed the ceiling. "Who knows? There's been no letters or…well, no telegrams, if you know what I mean."

Marcy heaved herself upright. "At least that's something." She then stood up, stretched out the kinks in her back, and kissed the top of Berry's head before scratching her own. "Isn't it strange when you come to think of no news as good news?"

"Very strange," Vicky agreed, as she passed them on the way toward the door. "Back in a few minutes!" she told them, her wash bag in hand and towel over her shoulder.

Sophie raised an eyebrow at Marcy, and the two, in unspoken agreement that they weren't likely to get anything else out of Berry about her brother, both got up to change. After a few moments, Berry looked up and smiled. "Thanks, girls." A little hesitantly, she added, "Friends?"

Vicky, demonstrating perfect timing, crashed through the door, strode over to Berry, and wrapped her arms around her. "Goes without saying," she told her with a kiss on the cheek before folding her towel over a piece of string she'd set up above her bed and putting her wash bag on top of an upturned orange crate she was using as a wardrobe. "Memory of a goldfish, yes," she explained, pulling on a pair of shorts and a fresh blouse, "ears as fine as any bat!"

"What she said," added Sophie, also padding over to kiss Berry's cheek, "though without the bat ears."

"Same here," said Marcy, standing over her with a towel over her shoulder. "Only don't forget, I'm also the boss," she added with a grin before going out to wash.

****

"Mrs. Harker," Berry said, "that was the best shepherd's pie I've ever had!" adding a burp behind her hand for emphasis.

"I aim to please," Sheila Harker answered, picking up Berry's picked-clean plate as she passed and depositing it in the butler's sink with the others. "Now, I know it's late, but does anyone have room for some apple pie?" she asked, turning around with a still-steaming pie in her hands.

Opposite Berry, Marcy and Sophie were both slumped back in their wooden chairs, arms over their stomachs. Berry thought she was about to give birth, and from the look of things, her friends were in the same boat. Still, it would be rude to refuse, especially on the first evening they'd spent with their hosts.

"I think I can speak for us all," Marcy began, "when I say how very, very glad I am you're willing to put us up, Mrs. Harker. I can't remember the last time I ate so well, and yes, I'd love some pie."

With a smile as wide as the lady herself, their

hostess placed a piece of pie in front of each of the girls before taking her seat and picking up her own fork. "I'm very happy to help, and don't make me say it again—call me Sheila. Everyone in the village does."

"Sheila it is," agreed Berry, digging in as well.

"Won't your husband be joining us?" Vicky asked around her mouthful, wiping her mouth with the back of her hand.

Sheila stared up at the roof as a creak interrupted everyone's repast. "No, Bob tries to be in bed by ten. He has to be up at five in the morning, so he tries never to waver from that ritual for anything."

There was something about the way Sheila stared at the ceiling, for a lot longer than Berry thought necessary, that made her pat her hostess on the hand and treat her to a smile. Here was someone harboring an unhappy life. "I'm sorry to hear that."

Sitting back, Berry picked up her spoon and started to tuck into her pudding before it got cold. The apple pie was delicious and such a treat. Even with the frequent visits her mother had insisted upon making to London, the likelihood of being able to savor her favorite pudding had decreased as the years had gone by. As well as being a surprise, she was aware it was a huge treat, and from the way her friends were wolfing it down with a smile, they did too.

"If everyone's finished..." Sheila waited as spoons were placed onto empty plates again. "How about we all introduce ourselves? It was so late by the time you'd all arrived last night that we didn't get the chance. Now," she added with a smile Berry noted didn't quite reach her eyes, "who wants to go first?"

Both Vicky and Berry raised hands at the same time;

the younger girl put hers down so Berry could go first. She coughed to clear her throat and swept her dark hair out of her eyes. "I feel like it's the first day of school, especially after putting up my hand!" she added, to small chuckles. "Anyway, my name's Beryl Chambers, but everyone calls me Berry. Actually, only my brother does. I don't know why I said that."

"Berry it is!" declared Marcy, raising her glass of apple juice and was joined by a chorus of, "Berry!" This quickly died down as there was another creak from the ceiling, accompanied by a loud grunt.

A little quieter, Berry went on, "I'm twenty-four and this is my first ever job, though I've always loved the outdoors."

"First job, ever?" Sophie repeated, leaning toward her a little.

Not bothering to sweep her hair away as she shrugged, Berry replied, "Sorry, posh parents, privileged upbringing, you'd say." She then looked out at the others through her fringe, slightly unsure of what her admission would bring.

Her answer was a punch on the shoulder from Vicky, accompanied by a cheeky grin. "If the others don't, then I'll soon knock you into shape, Berry!"

Berry let her shoulders relax and, to show she understood, punched her playfully back. "Your turn."

Vicky gave everyone a small wave. "Explained why you were upset when that RAF chap called you Berry," Vicky announced before immediately saying, "Hi, I'm Vicky Strood, and I'm a few months off my eighteenth. I joined the Lumberjills as I didn't want to end up in a munitions factory. Didn't fancy going all yellow," she finished.

"Lumberjills?" questioned Sheila.

Marcy answered, "It's what people have started calling us. You know. Lumberjacks, Lumberjills."

Sheila clapped her hands in delight. "Oh, that's wonderful!"

"My turn!" Sophie broke in and carried on before anyone could say otherwise. "Sophie Baxtor, at your service." She got to her feet, performed a little bow, then sat back down and continued, "I'm single, though I've a twin sister called Shirley in the Land Army. I think she's at some farm up in Scotland. I've been working as a carpenter for my dad's firm since I left school, but when he was killed by a bomb last month, I had to get away. London holds too many memories for me."

At this announcement, everyone closed their mouths, not knowing what to say. After a minute or so, Berry asked what was probably on everyone's mind. "What about your mother, Sophie?"

By way of an answer, Sophie informed them, her eyes momentarily glazing over before she found the words, "Same bomb."

When no one could think of anything to say, Marcy took a sip of her juice to wet her lips, before clearing her throat. "And that leaves me. My name's Marcy Gagnon, and yes, my surname is strange, but blame that on my Canadian parents. As you've probably guessed, Sheila, I'm a little older than my friends, but seeing as we're all girls together"—she leaned toward the center of the table and everyone unconsciously leaned in with her—"you can all know I'm thirty-five. I'm married." Here she leant back and took out a ring on a chain around her neck. "And I've kept this around my neck since I started this job, just in case I catch a finger. My husband—he's Matt, by the way—is in the Army and, unfortunately, was captured by the Germans, at Tobruk in Africa, in June."

"Bugger," uttered Vicky before anyone else had a chance to speak.

This seemed to be what the room needed to break the tension that had been building up with both Sophie and Marcy's statements, and there soon followed a mixture of tears and laughter, abruptly brought to a halt by a roar of anger from upstairs, a banging on the ceiling, and then the voice of Sheila's husband yelling, "Bloody well shut up down there!"

Just as abruptly, the color drained from Sheila's face, and she put a finger to her lips to quiet everyone down. "Please, please, girls. Don't make him come downstairs. He's been in a temper all day. The Land Girls we were promised didn't turn up, so he couldn't get all the work done he wanted, not even with my help," she added.

Berry went and put an arm around Sheila's shoulders and asked, "You going to be all right?"

"Don't worry about me, love," Sheila told her. "He's all bark and no bite," and when Berry raised an eyebrow, reached up and patted her hand. "Honest, he is! I'm in more danger from the hens when I collect their eggs."

Berry held her gaze for a few moments before squeezing her shoulders and going back to her seat. "So long as that's the truth."

Getting to her feet, Sheila smoothed down her apron, finished her glass of water, and looked up at the clock on the wall. "Goodness! I had no idea that was the time. I really must get to bed myself. Now, since we've all been introduced, what time do you have to be up to get to the forest in the morning?"

Berry, Sophie, and Vicky all turned their gazes upon Marcy who, after a few moments, replied, "We should be on site for eight, so I'll be setting my alarm clock for six. That all right with you girls?" Everyone nodded, so she carried on. "Knock off will be about five, so with luck, we should be back for around six, to be on the safe side."

Sheila clapped her hands together and disappeared into the hall, reappearing a minute later with an armful of blankets and a handful of candles. "Here you go," she said, distributing her load amongst the four girls. "It may be warm at the moment, but you can never tell how cold it'll get at night. Sorry there's no electricity in the barn, but his nibs only converted it a few weeks back when we lost our last laborer to the Navy. Anytime you need more candles, you just let me know. I'll not have you buying your own, not whilst you're in my care. From tomorrow, breakfast will be at six thirty. I'll make you all up some sandwiches to take for dinner, and tea will be at seven. Let me know if you're going to be late, if possible, please."

Sophie went and stood beside the sink and picked up a cloth. "Want a hand with the washing up, Sheila?"

Shaking her head, Sheila took the cloth from Sophie and flipped it over her shoulder. "Ordinarily, I'd snap your hand off, but not tonight. Let him calm down a bit, and then I'll be glad of any help." Sophie nodded her understanding. "Oh, by the way," Sheila went to add, "let me have a word and explain to my Bob about you lot. I think he's taking his temper out on everyone because of those other girls. By the time you get back tomorrow, I'll have him eating out of the palm of my hand. You'll be welcome into the house anytime you wish."

"Does that include the bathroom?" piped up Vicky.

Sheila nodded, and Vicky went up and kissed her landlady on both cheeks. "The heart of my bottom thanks you, Sheila."

Chapter Three

After seeing the girls out, Sheila made her way back toward the kitchen, stopping to lean on the door frame before entering. Whatever lay in store after tonight, at least it was good, very good to hear the sound of happy voices in the house. Head in hand, she wracked her mind to think of the last time—and for the life of her, couldn't. Glancing over her shoulder, Sheila had no hesitation in admitting to herself this was a very sad state of affairs for nearly twenty-five years of marriage.

Upon opening the kitchen door, she wasn't one bit surprised to see Bob waiting for her at the table. He didn't look very happy, mind you, she couldn't remember the last time he had. Before taking a seat, she filled a glass with water and sat down opposite him.

"Go on," she told him after taking a sip to wet her lips, "say what you must."

He may have been a professional grouch, possibly an award-winning one; however, he was also nothing but honest and provided her with as good a life as a farmer's wife could wish for, albeit one in which there was little love, or at least it seemed like that since they'd got married.

During his two weeks on leave from the torture of the Great War, they'd sworn undying love to each other, very likely as hundreds, thousands of other couples who met in similar circumstances had done. Bumping into each other as they'd come out of a West End cinema had seemed like fate, and for the rest of his leave, they'd spent each waking moment together—walks in the park, sharing a drink down the Dog and Duck, and Whitby's famous fish 'n' chips had never tasted better! On their last evening together, waiting at the station for the train to pull in that would take him down to London, thence to the south coast to catch a channel packet back across to the hell that were the trenches of the Western Front, he'd dropped to one knee and proposed marriage to her. Her heart fuller with love than she'd ever believed possible, she'd promised him that, no matter what, she'd wait for him and they'd marry as soon as he returned. He'd promised to come back safely to her. The words had nearly stuck in his throat, as too many other love-struck men and boys in the trenches, who'd told him the same story he'd just enacted, had never fulfilled their promise. Nevertheless, he'd said them, and part of him had even meant the words, he'd explained to her once she'd dragged out the reason for his hesitation.

"Explain to me again why we've got to have those…those girls here?" he demanded, waving an expansive hand in the general direction of the barn.

Even though she knew it was what he was going to ask, it didn't mean she couldn't help but let out a groan of exasperation. How many times had they been through this?

When Marcy and the others had come knocking on their door trying to find a place to stay, a billet, they'd looked all in. They'd been forewarned by somebody from some government office she could no longer remember about a month back, that they were sending some people up to begin felling oak trees locally and it was heavily hinted that it would be good if they could fix up some accommodation for four or five; no mention had been made that the people in question would be women. It had fair taken Sheila's breath away when she'd opened the door, and her first instinct had been to ask if this was someone's idea of a joke. She'd worked on the trolley buses herself for the last six months of the last war, but she'd had no clue there was such a thing as a female lumberjack! Her second instinct had been to say they couldn't stay. Bob had converted the barn himself, but— and she couldn't blame him for this—he'd naturally had men in mind when he'd done so. Spartan didn't begin to describe it. However, Marcy had said she'd seen worse, and the others had been too tired to disagree. By the time Bob had arrived on the scene, the new arrivals were all fast asleep.

"Do you really want me to explain again, Bob?" she began, snapping out of her thoughts.

"But they're girls!" he exclaimed after a wait.

"Why are you being like this? You know women worked in the last lot."

Bob opened and closed his mouth a couple of times before finding the words he was searching for, though that didn't mean they were very eloquent. "Well, yes, but I thought they were with the Land Army. You know, to help out on the farm. We're going to need them before long. I don't think we'll be able to manage the cows on our own for long without help, now the farmhands have joined up."

Sheila thought for a few minutes before replying. "I suppose, when they turn up, they'll just have to find somewhere else for their billet."

"I don't want this lot here!" Bob stated, pounding

his fist down on the table for emphasis.

Sheila leant forward and matched him gaze for gaze. "Tough. We've no choice. They're here to stay until their job is done, however long that may be, and no amount of belly-aching's going to make any difference," she told him. "Tell me how these girls are different to the Land Girls?"

"They're not working on the farm!" her husband shouted.

Getting to her feet and shaking her head in disbelief, Sheila made for the door that led to the stairs and their bedrooms. Turning her head, she regarded her husband, sitting there in his confusion and unresolved anger, and advised him, "I agreed to marry you, Bob. I agreed, and in spite of how things have turned out, I still believe in those vows. However," she added, placing a foot upon the first step, "times are changing, and I'm changing with them."

Chapter Four

After all the girls had feasted on a wonderful breakfast of bacon and eggs, with toast on the side and tea to wash it down, Sheila presented them each with a packet of sandwiches, wrapped in newspaper, and filled up their flasks with more tea.

"Sorry, there's no sugar left," Sheila apologized as she waved them off on their bicycles.

"Don't be silly," Marcy told her, climbing onto her saddle. "We'll get our ration cards sorted out tomorrow so we can pitch in."

"Thank you, my dear." Sheila beamed, then added, a little twinkle in her eye, "If there's one thing we haven't figured out how to make yet, it's sugar."

"See you later!" Marcy waved over her shoulder.

****

Berry leant back against the tree trunk she'd finished stripping of its branches and took out the packet of sandwiches Sheila had given her that morning. Fifteen minutes later, she was slumped across the trunk, her hands across her stomach as she uttered intermittent sighs of pleasure.

"You know," she said out loud so her three friends could hear, as they were in similar positions, "I don't know for sure, but I think I could give up sex, so long as Sheila would keep making beef-dripping sandwiches for me."

"Amen to that!" Sophie muttered, punctuating her prayer with a belch that brought forth a snort from her friends and another look of envy from the two men who were there to help connect the stripped logs to a tractor and then take them on to the timber mill.

"How long are we due to be here?" Vicky asked.

"Somewhere around six months, I think," Marcy answered. "There should be more of us, but apparently they can't spare anyone else yet."

"Don't quote me, Marcy," Berry advised, leaning on an elbow, "but if you can swing it so we stay with Sheila for the rest of the war, you can have my firstborn."

Marcy cupped her chin in a hand and pretended to think about it. "Let me get this straight. You'll give me your first child if we can stay here and get fed by Sheila?"

"That's right," Berry confirmed, whilst Sophie and Vicky watched with interest.

Marcy shook her head. "If you'd have bargained a weeks' worth of these sandwiches, I think we'd have a starting point to talk about a deal."

After relaxing for the rest of their lunch hour, Marcy took out her notebook, stood, and stretched her legs. "I'll see you lot in a couple of hours. It's about time I took my measurements."

"Where's she off to?" asked Vicky, taking up her axe and joining Berry and Sophie in walking back toward where they'd been cutting down a group of mature oaks before lunch.

"I don't know how much attention you paid in training, Vicky," Berry tutted, watching as Marcy disappeared through the underbrush, "but Marcy's a Measurer. That means she works out how much useable timber we can cut down. Clear?"

Whether she was listening or not, Vicky merely hefted her axe onto her shoulder and trotted off.

Spitting on her hands and cursing herself for forgetting her gloves, Berry lined up her own axe, left hand a short way from the end, right about halfway down the shaft, and swung. The recoil shook her arm muscles as it always had in training, though she had the satisfaction of seeing plenty of wood splintering off only an inch from where she'd aimed. Not too bad. From a short way behind her, she heard Sophie curse from the shock of her first blow of the afternoon.

Soon her cut was ready for the two young women to bring in the crosscut saw, and she yelled across for Sophie to come and join her.

"You know," Sophie puffed out between hefting the saw back and forth, "I know this isn't the biggest copse of trees in the world, but it'd sure speed things up if there were more than the three of us doing the felling."

After a few minutes sawing, both straightened up to stretch the kinks out of their backs and rub the knots out of their muscles. "Very true," Berry answered, "and I dare say we will get more girls before too long. In the meantime, I say we make the most of the luck we've had."

"Luck?"

"You know what I mean," Berry said, reaching down to take her end of the saw back between her hands. "We've got a very good billet, the lady of the manor"— Sophie raised an eyebrow at her friend's expression, though neglected to make any comment—"seems nice, and she's an excellent cook."

"What about her husband?" Sophie asked.

Berry shrugged. "Too soon to say. I mean, all we've heard was him yelling for quiet last night."

"Do you really think Sheila can handle him?" Sophie asked.

Berry gave the question a few minutes thought before answering. "I really couldn't tell you. She seems strong and certainly says the right things. I suppose we might find out tonight. I will tell you something, though. Did you notice the way she looked far away when she heard the ceiling creak for the first time?"

"Actually, I did," Sophie admitted. "What do you think that's about?"

"I don't know," Berry told her. "But she seems nice enough, so how about we keep an eye on her? See if anything comes up that we can help with."

Sophie patted her stomach and grinned. "Hey, anyone that can make a sarnie like she does, I'll do pretty much anything for."

"What're you two gabbing about?" Vicky asked, as she appeared next to them wiping a rather grubby handkerchief across her brow, merely moving dirt from one spot to another.

"Did you notice how Sheila was, well, a bit lost at one point last night?" Berry asked her.

Vicky stood staring into space for a minute or two before answering. "I think so," her face screwing up in concentration as she thought back. "No idea why, though."

Sophie shook her head. "Us either, but we're going to keep an eye on her. We think it'll be a good idea to keep our cook fit and well. Besides, she seems a good sort."

"Hmm. You don't believe she'll think we're putting

our noses in where they've got no business?" Vicky asked.

"So long as we don't make it too obvious," Berry suggested.

An hour or so later, the three of them had managed to fell a couple of large oaks and were taking a rest to have the last dregs of tea from their flasks when Marcy reappeared. She had twigs in her hair, which was wayward to say the least, dirt and leaves on her jumper, and a nasty scratch on the back of the hand that wasn't holding her notebook.

"Bloody good idea," she stated, going and getting her own flask before coming to join them and sitting down on a tree stump.

"All done?" Sophie asked.

Marcy took out her notebook, opened it, and frowned a little before nodding to herself and putting it away. "I think so," she replied, looking at her friends.

They were joined by one of the men, his mate having driven off with a load to the sawmill set up on the other side of the copse. With no sawing or chopping going on at the moment, they could easily make out the noise made by the machine saws, their buzz cutting through the calm of the day.

"Marcy?" he raised his voice to get her attention.

"Yes, Bill."

"Sam should have been back by now. D'you mind if I borrow your bike? I want to go and see what's happened to him."

Marcy pointed over toward the shelter where all the bikes leaned against one wall. "Help yourself. Mine's the one with the blue saddle."

Once Bill had pedaled off, Vicky lay back on the

ground, picked up a thick stick, and started to whittle away at the wood.

"Come on, Vicky," urged Marcy, getting up and going to give her boot a nudge with her toe. "It's not quite knocking-off time. There's still enough light to work on for a bit."

"Aww…do we have to, Marcy? I'm knackered! And it's nearly the weekend." She suddenly bolted upright and fixed the older woman with an urgent expression upon her face. "We're not, um, working tomorrow, are we?"

"I'd love to tease you and say yes, we are working tomorrow morning. Only we're not. At least not yet. We met our quota for the week, so tomorrow's your own."

"Yes!" Vicky punched the air.

"Or it will be when you and I've brought down one more tree, so…" She turned, strode quickly over to the hut and picked up her own axe, and made her way back to Vicky's side. "So get to your feet and put that knife away."

Marcy leant down as if to take the knife from the younger girl's hand, yet as soon as her hand made to curl around the handle, Vicky shuffled backward until she bumped into a tree stump, the knife held up menacingly in front of her, its point aimed up toward Marcy's throat.

"Don't touch my knife!"

Berry and Sophie, innocent bystanders of this bizarre scene, moved until they were either side of Marcy, the three of them a good number of paces away from where Vicky was now waving the knife back and forth.

"Easy there, Vicky," Berry said in what she hoped was a soothing tone of voice. "Marcy wasn't trying to take your knife."

"She's right." Sophie backed her friend up. "No one wants to harm you. Can you hear me, Vicky?" she asked after a very short wait as Marcy looked to be in a state of shock at the proceedings.

"My…knife?" Vicky stuttered out, her eyes briefly dropping to the instrument in her hand before flicking back up to her three friends who were patiently watching her.

Marcy recovered her ability to talk at last. "They're right, honey. I don't want to take your knife. So why don't you put it away, and we can all have a nice, quiet chat."

It must have been the combination of the soothing voices and smiles that all three were displaying. Slowly, the knife started to droop until it finally lay in her lap. Looking closely one more time at the three girls before her, Vicky tucked it back into a sheath tied to her leg. None of the others had noticed the hidden blade before.

"That's better," said Marcy, lowering herself to sit on the forest floor, still a few paces away from where Vicky had leant back against the tree stump. "Now, if you're up to it, would you care to tell us what just happened?"

"Please do," Berry urged. "No one's angry with you. Honest!"

Vicky's gaze flicked back and forth across her friends, searching their faces for any signs of lying. She found her voice and said with wonder, "Really? Marcy, you're not angry with me?" The disbelief was plain for all to hear.

"Cross my heart," Marcy told her, though she then added, "but I am very curious as to why you reacted like you did."

Before she replied, Vicky looked again at her audience and then, after taking a deep breath, untied the sheath and slowly, reverently, laid it on the ground before her. Only then did she look up at her friends, the unshed tears in her eyes only being kept at bay by sheer effort of will.

"This is…was…my brother's knife. It's all I have left of him."

Slowly, Berry got to her feet and, with baby steps, came and stood beside Vicky. When she showed no signs of stopping her, she then crouched down and sat beside her. "What happened? I mean, to him?"

Vicky looked up into Berry's eyes and, for the first time since she'd met her, Vicky seemed to be her age rather than acting like someone who was ten years older. Her lip was trembling with the effort of keeping her emotions in, and Berry, acting with empathy she hadn't known she possessed until that moment, opened her arms and gradually, slowly and carefully so as not to spook the girl, pulled her until she was nearly in her lap, her head resting upon Berry's shoulder.

"No one's angry with me. Really?" she half muttered in some disbelief into Berry's neck, before pulling a hand across her nose and wiping the snot away.

Unbeknownst to either Berry or Vicky, both Sophie and Marcy had joined them and were crouching down beside the pair. Marcy ran a hand up and down Vicky's arm. "Of course not," she reassured the girl before adding, "now, if you want to tell us about your brother, go ahead, but if you've changed your mind, that doesn't matter. We'll be here when you're ready."

With a loud sniff, Vicky sat up a little straighter,

easing her posture a little until she was more leaning against Berry than sitting in her lap. "It'd probably be for the best." She took a deep breath, coughed a couple of times, and began.

"My brother, Gary, was killed on the beaches of Dunkirk. A Stuka bomb got him, and this knife is all his mates found. They took the trouble to come and pay their respects when they got back, and they gave it to me."

Berry, Marcy, and Sophie exchanged looks. Words would have been totally inadequate.

After searching around in her pockets for a while and failing to find what she was looking for, Vicky scooped up a handful of leaves from the ground, blew her nose and then threw them behind her. "It's all right, girls," she told them with a weak smile. "I don't know what to say either. If it makes you feel any better, that's the first time I've spoken about Gary to anyone other than family since I found out."

Ray chose that moment to cycle up and, once dismounted, stood staring down at the confluence of women, scratching his head, before finally clearing his voice. "Er…Marcy? Sam said the tractor's broke down and he won't be able to get the part he needs until Monday."

Marcy didn't bother getting up from the ground, merely glancing up at the rather confused and embarrassed-looking chap. "In that case, do me a favor, Ray. Gather together anything that needs locking up in the hut, and then you can get yourself off. Tell Sam I'll see him on Monday too."

After glancing down at the huddle, Ray doffed his cap in a general type of way and then busied himself as Marcy had asked.

In a short time, Ray had made himself scarce, and the only sounds to be heard were the birdsong and what was likely the bark of foxes. As for the girls, Berry was convinced she was getting cramp in her left leg from the awkward way she sat, Sophie was cursing as she'd managed to kneel in the only patch of water on the ground in sight, and Marcy still wasn't sure if she could say anything that would make Vicky feel better.

As for Vicky herself, she was finding it difficult to accept that she did, indeed, have real friends. She remembered a saying she'd always felt applied to her— once a loner, always a loner. For the first time in her young life, and discounting her dead brother, perhaps that was no longer the case?

Chapter Five

"Have you noticed we've got a shadow?"

Both Marcy and Sophie dismounted from their bicycles at the rail station, leant them up against the wooden fence, and stared behind them as a solitary figure puffed around the corner and then, upon seeing the audience, jerked to a halt while still a good hundred yards away from the trio.

"Do you think we should wait for her?" Sophie asked, untying her head scarf and narrowly avoiding elbowing the solitary porter as he came unexpectedly around the corner from the platform.

"I'll go and get the tickets, whilst you two keep an eye on her, okay?" Marcy told the others and marched off.

For the next couple of minutes, there occurred a strange Mexican stand-off as Berry and Sophie secured the three bikes, pretending not to know Vicky was there. Vicky merely stayed where she had stopped. This was a little awkward, especially for the youngest girl, as she stood slap in the middle of the road. Though no longer very busy with civilian traffic, the road still had the odd car and military vehicle which sped along without a care in the world. This was also the road that led from the sawmill to the station, and Berry was a little surprised to see the tractor Ray had reported to be broken down neatly parked up at the far end of a dead-end lane opposite the train station. She nudged Sophie and pointed, upon which Sophie's eyebrows shot up.

"Marcy's not going to like that."

Berry shook her head and then turned back toward where Vicky had now wheeled her bike to the pavement and half-turned her back on them. If anything, it only served to make it even more obvious she was pretending not to be there, though heaven alone knew why.

Both Berry's and Sophie's attention had been so fixed upon their young friend that neither heard Marcy coming back from buying the tickets, and they jumped out of their skins when she spoke. "She's still not moved?"

It took a few moments before she got an answer. "Sheesh, Marcy! You could scare a girl out of a year's growth! And"—she swept her hand up and down—"it's not like I can spare any inches!"

"Sorry about that," apologized Marcy, laying a hand on Sophie's shoulder, though not without letting out a chuckle and a wink toward Berry. More seriously, she told them whilst moving her gaze on to Vicky, "I don't think there's anything to be gained in going and forcing her to come with us." She added, upon seeing Berry open her mouth to object, "We made it as plain as we could yesterday that she's a friend. Who knows?" She shrugged. "Perhaps she's simply having a hard time accepting that?"

"Not that we were talking about it, but tear your gaze away from our young friend and cast it over yonder." Berry pointed toward the tractor.

It didn't take long for the significance of what she saw to get through to Marcy, and she turned her back on the tractor to face Berry and Sophie. "Remind me to have a word with Ray and Sam on Monday, will you?" The look of ferocity on Marcy's face almost took the two girls' breaths away before she softened her face, probably upon seeing the expressions upon her friends' faces. "Come on, the train'll be here in a few minutes."

"What about Vicky?" Berry asked, pointing at where Vicky was mounting and then dismounting her bike, obviously caught in two minds.

Marcy cast one final glance at Vicky before making her mind up. "If she wants to come, she knows where the train is."

****

It wasn't until they were halfway to York that Vicky finally opened the door to the carriage they were sitting in. Back, forth, and back again her head went, as if she were caught in headlights, before she finally found her voice.

"Um, mind if I take a seat?"

In reply, Berry pulled her down by the waist to sit beside her. "You are a silly sausage. What are you?"

Vicky, with her chin upon her chest muttered, "I'm a very silly sausage."

Marcy leant against her other shoulder. "And a daft haporth as well!"

"That as well," Vicky agreed, raising her chin and treating them to a wry grin.

Sophie undid the leather strap and let the window down slightly so she could blow the smoke and tap the ash from her cigarette out. As the only one of the three who smoked, she was remarkably conscientious of her friends. To be fair, they had made it plain on their first night in the barn that they'd very much appreciate it if she didn't smoke around them.

After a few minutes she threw the cigarette stub outside and secured the window, saying it may have been a nice morning, but the wind and smoke from the train that blew in hadn't been very nice to endure. "So why were you playing silly buggers this morning?"

"You, er, noticed that?" Vicky replied, blushing.

"I think everyone noticed," Marcy told her with a smile.

"And?" Berry prodded.

"And...I was being stupid," Vicky admitted, going on to add, "I wasn't sure if you wanted me along."

"But you were there when we were all talking about it and agreeing to go into the city this morning, weren't you?" Berry asked, puzzled.

"I didn't say anything, though," Vicky told them. "I was reading a magazine whilst you were talking, and then I fell asleep."

Marcy slumped back into her seat with a grin. "Girls, what we have here is a misunderstanding. Young lady," she addressed Vicky, "we assumed you were listening and would be coming. I'm sorry, we should have made it clear. Mind you, you did start off with us this morning and...and...what happened to you? One minute you're behind us, the next time we see you, you've pulled to a stop in the middle of the road!"

Vicky began to run her hands through and through her hair until Sophie reached, took her hands, and placed them in the girl's lap. "Hey! You'll muss up your hair!"

Vicky smiled, finally, her thanks. "Can we put it down to being silly? Finding it hard to believe that you three...like me?"

"You know what she needs," stated Marcy and was rewarded with equal grins from the other two. "Girl sandwich!"

They were a very happy bunch of friends who got off at York station, though as they walked toward the center of town, the smiles on their faces faded. Wandering over Station Road Bridge, they turned right into Lendal Street, then onward into Coney Street and stood outside the remains of the Guildhall, burnt and blacked.

"Come on," Berry urged. "We knew we'd see this. There's no point in depressing ourselves. Anyone know the way to Betty's?"

"Betty's?" Vicky asked.

Sophie smacked her lips. "If you've not heard of Betty's, then you're in for a treat, Vicky. It's the best place to come for tea in York, despite the war."

Vicky's stomach gave a loud rumble. "I think you'd better lead on then," she replied, laying a hand over her belly.

Unfortunately, a queue of substantial size had already formed outside of Betty's by the time the girls found the Tea Rooms.

"Bugger," Sophie exclaimed.

"Couldn't have put it better myself," Marcy muttered, looking in through the tape-crossed windows in envy.

After waiting in the queue for ten minutes and not moving an inch, Berry suggested, "Shall we just move on somewhere else? I don't want to waste my day standing in a queue. Even for somewhere like Betty's," she added upon seeing that Marcy was about to protest.

Circumstances, however, chose that moment to intervene, and all four looked up as they became aware of an insistent knocking coming from the other side of the window from where they stood. Inside, grinning like a lunatic, was an RAF officer whose slightly bent nose rang a bell with both Marcy and Berry.

"That's never…" began Marcy.

"You know, it might be?" finished Berry for her.

Sophie took a little longer to recognize him. "I think you're right."

In the meantime, Vicky stood with her hands on her hips and when none of her friends seemed in a hurry to fill in the gaps, elbowed Berry gently in the ribs. "Are you three going to keep whoever this dishy officer is to yourselves, then?"

"Oh, sorry," Berry replied, rubbing her ribs in a slightly exaggerated way. "This is the chap we cut down from the tree the other day."

"The parachutist?"

"That's the one!" agreed Sophie, waving to him.

A moment later, the door to Betty's was pulled open, and he'd appeared by their side. "Flying Officer Dennis Grey, at your service, ladies," he informed them with a small bow before turning to Berry, taking her hand in his and raising it to his lips. "Miss Berry Chambers"—he added a kiss to the back of her hand—"what a delight it is to see you again." He turned to the others. "Ladies, my friends and I would like to invite you to join us."

Marcy looked around. There were about ten people in front of them, and four more had arrived since they'd queued up. "I'm not certain I could do that. Won't everyone object?"

With confidence typical of the image of the dashing RAF officer, Dennis merely grinned at the ladies before striding to stand at the front of the queue and holding up his hands. Rapidly everyone, from a couple of schoolgirls who'd been pulling at their mother's hands in impatience to a pair of men in Home Guard uniform and (presumably) their wives, gave him their attention.

"Ladies, and gentlemen." He acknowledged the pair of Home Guards with a touch of two fingers to his forehead. "I know this is against all rules of decorum, but my fellows inside and I shall be immensely grateful…"

"Laying it on a little thick, isn't he?" Vicky interrupted, not bothering to keep her voice down and getting a chortle from the schoolgirls for her trouble.

"…if you would allow me to bring them in as my guests," he added, not missing a beat. "Why should you allow this? I hear you ask. This lady"—and here he beckoned Berry forward to join him until she eventually and with head shyly bowed did so—"and her companions rescued me when I was stuck up a tree after I'd had to bail out of my plane."

The little old lady at the front of the queue immediately took it upon herself to speak for everyone. "If that is the case, then I don't believe anyone here would have any objections. Would they?" she added, a surprisingly steely glint in her eye that would brook no argument.

Upon hearing this, Dennis raised a thumb to his comrades inside. Berry saw they immediately got to their feet and proceeded to round up, she knew not where from, four chairs and jammed them around their table. Dennis opened the door to allow the girls in before him. Making certain everyone in the queue could hear their thanks, the fivesome entered the establishment, passed a slightly flustered elderly maître d', and were greeted, very enthusiastically, by his three friends. Dennis remained standing to make the introductions.

"Ladies, I want to introduce you to the biggest lot of reprobates you'll ever come across." He added, raising his voice as they started to protest, "Though they also happen to be the best bomber crew you'll ever meet!"

"We'll let you sit back down for admitting that, Dennis!" the one to Berry's left told him.

"I guess we'll start with Pilot Officer Jimmy Dunn, Master Bomb Aimer and Front Gunner, or so he'd tell you. The only thing he's ever shot down was the airfield's windsock when I made a bit of a bumpy landing last week."

The one called Jimmy pulled his fingers down a rather bulbous nose, his defining feature, so far as Berry was concerned. "Bumpy landing? Skipper, the rest of us were convinced we had liquid kangaroos for fuel!"

Vicky burst out with laughter, and seeing as she was on his other side, that had the effect of drawing his attention onto her. Shortly after, the two of them had their heads close together, totally ignoring everything and everyone else.

They were introduced to a Flight Sergeant Ginger Baker, their Rear Gunner. "There's always a *Ginger* in the RAF, it seems," Berry observed, which caused said Ginger, who was actually more of a strawberry blond, to roar with laughter and lean a little closer toward her. This was noticed by Marcy and Sophie, who raised their eyebrows at each other, confusing Dennis, who they'd noticed only had eyes for Berry.

Dennis hurriedly said, "Ginger, I need you to swap seats with me." Somewhat to Berry's surprise, he did just that, though not without receiving a very knowing smile from his gunner. "And as you're in such a good mood, old chap, this is Sophie. She's a dab hand with a ladder!"

This earned him a death glare from her.

In the meantime, Marcy and the chap Dennis had introduced as the *old man* of the crew (at twenty five), a very weird name of Pilot Officer Archie (his last name slipped past Berry's attention) were diving into the rock cakes and arguing over who should have the most butter.

After naturally splitting into pairs, whilst still sitting at the same table, Berry nudged Dennis and asked, not bothering to keep her voice down to see if she got any reaction, "Is it my imagination, or is Archie entranced by my friend?"

"I think he is."

Berry raised her eyebrows, as it was Marcy who'd answered, rather than Dennis.

"So long as he knows what he's getting into," Berry replied.

Whilst Dennis was engaged in ribbing his mate, Marcy leant in and whispered into Berry's ear, "It's okay. I'm having a bit of fun." She then looked around and, as the two men were still chatting and nobody else appeared to be paying them attention, quickly pulled a chain from around her neck and showed her the bright gold ring that hung from it, then winked. "Don't tell him yet!"

****

After a very enjoyable few hours, as the time approached four in the afternoon, Dennis announced that they had to be getting back to base. He said this with obvious reluctance, reaching down to take one of Berry's hands. She, much to her own surprise, allowed him to do so. When Vicky stated it was a shame they had to leave, his crew agreed, and all were sorry they couldn't say why.

On the way back to the railway station, Dennis asked for and received permission to take Berry's hand again. "I am sorry we have to go," he told her as they crossed the bridge.

Tucking a stray hair back around an ear, Berry squeezed his hand. "I think I have a pretty good idea why you lot have to go. Don't give it another thought."

They waited for Archie and Marcy to catch them up. "Come on, you two!" yelled Vicky, her arm through Jimmy's, as Marcy had stopped to peer into a haberdasher's shop. Eventually, they came to the train station.

"When's your train?" Sophie asked, peering at the timetable.

"We've got a car back in town," Ginger answered.

"Though a train may be safer, what with your driving, Ginger!" Dennis told him with a grin.

Berry let go of Dennis's hand and immediately felt a sense of loss. Sensing a flush start to spread up her face, she wafted a hand in front of her face a few times, before turning to face him. "That was silly. You shouldn't have walked all the way back with us."

"I think at least four of us would argue with you about that," he told her and with an expansive sweep of his hand, pointed her in the direction of where Sophie and Ginger were locked in an embrace. Behind them, Jimmy seemed to be writing something down in a little notebook that Vicky had given him. Marcy was stood in front of Archie shaking her head at him, though he didn't seem to be taking much notice of her.

"I see what you mean," she agreed, laughing.

Dennis stepped closer to her until he was nearly nose to nose, satisfied that Berry hadn't backed off. He reached out and took her hand in his once more, rubbing his thumb back and forth across the back before looking up into her eyes. "I'd like to see you again, Berry." Upon noting the rise of her eyebrow, he also noted that she hadn't said no straight away, nor taken her hand back.

"You don't waste any time, do you?" she said with a tinkle in her voice.

He shrugged his shoulders, and it may have been her imagination, but when he next spoke, his voice seemed lower, forcing Berry to lean in to hear what he said. Suddenly, the heat between them was palpable. "These days, there's no point."

She could only agree with him there, and when she nodded, he brought her hand up to his lips and, keeping his blue eyes locked with hers, kissed it. The station was pretty crowded, yet for a few moments, Berry could imagine they were the only humans within sight.

"You're a pretty smooth talker, aren't you," she told him when she could trust her voice not to waver.

Keeping hold of her hand he slowly, in case she didn't let him, moved that one last step closer and wrapped his arms around her, whispering into her ear so that only she could hear, "More than you know. Do you think that queue of people would have allowed you lot to join us if they knew I'd only bailed out of a Magister training aircraft?"

Chapter Six

By the end of August, the girls were able to finally have a good sit-down meal with Sheila. Busy did not come close to describing how things had been for them up at the site, as still headquarters hadn't been able to send them any extra girls. By the time they got home each evening, all they felt up to doing was eating and sleeping. They even had to work a few Saturday mornings due to the orders they had to fill. For four days of the week, including Marcy most days, they chopped down trees, and on the Friday and Saturday mornings they all helped out at the lumber mill, cutting and shaping the logs into railway sleepers along with the men who worked there. If anything, that was harder, as they were using a different set of muscles, not to mention even more dangerous. They needed to concentrate every moment, as the risk of losing a finger or even a hand was present each and every second.

That last Friday, Berry and Vicky were working away with a crosscut saw at a particularly stubborn oak. "Is that wedge in right?" Berry asked her friend, and upon getting a nod, the two of them soon had the tool free, and they finished sawing through the trunk.

With a somewhat muffled crash, it came to rest on the forest floor, and Vicky took the chance to whip off her cap and take off and wring her scarf before replacing them both. "Do you think we could bribe Marcy to call it a day?" she asked.

Berry looked up at the sky. "If you ask me, it's darker now than when we woke up."

A crash of thunder shook the air, immediately followed by the murky sky lighting up as two bolts of lightning smashed into the ground a mere ten yards away from where they were resting.

"What the hell!" Vicky let out, whilst Berry simply stood there, frozen to the spot.

As thunder continued to hammer and continuous lightning flashed around the wounded sky, Marcy and Sophie, accompanied by Ray and Sam, came running up.

"Are you two okay?" Marcy asked, grabbing the two of them and crushing them in an embrace. "We saw how close that was!"

Once they'd been released, everyone stood there eyeing the sky. Sophie was the first to voice what everyone was thinking. "Marcy? I don't have any problem with rain, you know that, but I don't really want to be electrocuted." She was stopped in her tracks by another crescendo of thunder punctuated by a bolt of lightning striking a tree stump twenty yards away and setting it alight. "That's it, if the rain doesn't get us, we'll burn to death!" she added watching as the two men trotted over and kicked dirt over the stump to help the rain put out the small fire.

Berry wiped her watch clean. In the few moments she could see the dial clearly, she saw the time was only eleven, very early to contemplate knocking off for the day. However, none of them had experienced chopping down trees in these conditions before; she suspected even Noah hadn't!

In the meantime, Marcy had been making up her

mind and, with a layer of water coating her face, now announced to her audience, "This is getting way too dangerous. Those last two strikes were no joke," she pointed out, not that either Berry or Vicky would need persuading otherwise. "I'm calling it a day."

To the accompaniment of various soggy whoops and cheers, Marcy elaborated a little. "We're ahead of our quota, so losing a half day won't do any harm, and because of that, and as my thank-you for all your hard work lately, including this morning, don't bother to come in tomorrow morning. Have a good weekend, everyone."

As they all hurried to gather up and put away their tools, barring their axes, which went home with them, Marcy grabbed Sophie by the elbow and pulled her to one side. "I'm going to take a ride over to the lumber mill. I've got to tell them my decision and also phone up Sheila and explain things. I'll meet you all back at the farm."

Sophie nodded, kissed her friend on the cheek, and told her, "Be careful in this weather. I'll tell the girls, and we'll see you shortly."

****

The rain was even too heavy for Sheila's husband to be out on his tractor, very much to his annoyance, especially as this was supposed to have been the first day he'd have his Land Girls helping him out. He'd been so looking forward to having someone to boss around, as he'd been telling anyone who'd listen as he prowled around the house, jerking aside the curtains in annoyance every half hour or so in the vague hope it would have stopped.

"Much longer, and they needn't bother coming at all!" he muttered to the world at large before stalking out of the kitchen.

The clock on the wall indicated slightly after midday. Sheila had been instructed by Marcy that she should stay seated and enjoy being waited upon. This had taken a lot of persuasion.

"But surely you all must be very tired," she protested as Vicky kept a firm hand upon her shoulder as she made another attempt to get up from her seat and do something for them, "and just because you can't go to work, it doesn't mean to say that you have to wait upon me."

"Yes it does," Sophie countered, holding up her cup for Vicky to refill it with a cup of her specialist builders-strength tea. "You just haven't read the contract closely enough."

Sheila turned her head toward where Berry was leaning back in her seat. Without opening her eyes, Berry told her, "Don't look at me for support."

Glancing over her shoulder, Sheila focused her attention upon the range oven.

"There's nothing to worry about," Berry admonished without opening her eyes. "If it starts smoking, we'll put out the fire."

"And that's supposed to put my mind at rest?" Sheila asked, her eyes wide open.

"Please try and relax," Marcy advised, taking a seat next to her. "It's only shepherd's pie. I used to make it all the time."

Sheila sniffed the air, not appearing to hear what Marcy had said. "I think dinner may be ready."

Sophie went and opened the door of the range whilst Vicky, hands wrapped in tea towels, took out a steaming hot shepherd's pie. "Dinner is served."

In short order, six plates were loaded with pie, peas, and carrots, and Sheila had yelled up the stairs for her husband to come down, but five minutes after, he still hadn't turned up and she was starting to look embarrassed.

Seeing this, Sophie laid a hand upon her arm. "Leave this with me," she told her, putting her serviette back onto the table and getting to her feet. "I think I saw him go past the window a few minutes ago. I think he's heading down toward the stream."

Before anyone, let alone Sheila, could protest, Sophie had disappeared outside, telling everyone, "Don't let it go cold," on her way.

****

Sure enough, Sophie found Bob Harker sitting on a low-hanging branch whose end dipped into the fast-running stream. He didn't see her until she stepped on a twig, upon which his head snapped around.

"What do you want?" he snapped.

Sophie let his tone slide off her shoulders. Like the water flowing before them, its coldness couldn't harm her, and she promptly sat down next to him. He was unable to keep the surprise from his face.

"What do you want?" he repeated, though without quite so much animosity in his voice as before.

"Nothing, other than to let you know dinner's ready and will be getting cold if we wait much longer."

"Don't let me hold you up," he told her, pulling his cap down lower over his ears.

Sophie in turn pulled her coat tighter around her neck, trying to keep the rainwater running down her neck from making a move down her shirt.

"I'm not going unless you join me," she said and,

anticipating him, "and there's nothing you can say that will make me change my mind. Oh, by the way, don't try and scare me off. I've got your number, Mister Bob Harker—your bark is much worse than your bite." She promptly grinned at the perplexed expression upon his face.

When he didn't say or do anything other than to turn his head down to stare into the rain-speckled water, Sophie inched closer to him before saying, "Why do you pretend to be a monster, Bob? You don't fool me, you know."

"Oh? I don't, do I."

"No, you don't. So why the act? Who made you this way? I can't believe someone as nice as Sheila would have stayed this long with you if you were really as bad a man as you make out to be."

After she'd finished talking, poking her nose in where it hadn't been asked, Sophie braced herself. He hadn't asked her to analyze him and, especially considering they'd barely exchanged more than a few words before, this was very bold of her. A small fish poked its head up beneath her booted toe. Noticing this, Bob snapped out of his reverie.

"You remind me of my old Sergeant Major."

It wasn't what she'd expected to hear, and with no idea what he meant or where he was going, she kept quiet. Sometimes being the nosey one in a family meant you found out things you wanted to know, sometimes things you didn't want to know. And sometimes it got you chased around the yard by your brother waving a cricket bat. Sophie contented herself that at least the latter was a very unlikely scenario.

"He watched over me from when I arrived in the

trenches in January 1917, right until the end of the war. Like a mother hen, only a lot uglier, and meaner, but he kept most of our platoon in one piece for over eighteen months, more or less," he added and held up his left hand. For the first time, she noticed that the two fingers on the outside were missing. "We were like family," he continued, not that Sophie had intended to enquire about his damaged hand, "louse-infested, dirty, usually hungry, but a family. Then my little brother, Jack, turned up."

Upon telling her this, Bob Harker took a deep breath, wiped his hand across his nose, and Sophie could have sworn she saw a tear in his eye, but she sensed that if she interrupted him now, he'd never open up, to anyone, ever again. After gathering himself, he continued.

"Don't ask me how he managed it. Just dumb luck, I expect, turning up in my platoon of all places. I wasn't happy with him at all. I'd hoped the war would end before he was called up." Bob turned, a wry smile on his weather-beaten face. "The stupid bugger lied about his age. He wasn't even seventeen! He always had been a hothead, especially at school, and he hadn't changed at all. I told him I'd tell the company commander his true age and get him sent back, and he threatened to go over the top on his own if I did. What could I do? So, I told the sergeant major, and the only thing we could do was to try and keep him safe. We did too, right until the beginning of November."

Though not knowing if she should, Sophie took out a handkerchief, slightly sodden, and passed it to him. Bob took it and blew his nose, and she insisted upon him keeping it. She'd witnessed the explosion that had come out of his nose.

"Thanks," he muttered, before telling her, "We were in a battle to take a French town called Valenciennes when Jack copped it, four days before the Armistice! Four bloody days."

"Oh, Bob," Sophie said quietly, feeling something break in her heart for his pain.

"And that wasn't the worst of it," he added.

Sophie frowned, wondering what on earth could be worse.

"He lingered," Bob managed to get out after a few tries. "Archie lingered until the sixth of November, and then died one bloody day after the end of the whole flaming war!"

"You must miss him," Sophie told him, unable to stop herself, though knowing how crass the comment sounded.

"The whole family did," he admitted. "Then me and Sheila married a month after I got back in January nineteen-nineteen."

"Did that help?"

He let out a bitter laugh at her question. "You'd have thought so. But a promise is a promise. We'd met when I was on leave in Blighty for Christmas 1917 and had wanted to get married straight away, only we decided to wait until after the war, just to be on the safe side in case, you know, I didn't make it."

"And?"

"And? And I turned all my resentment at losing my brother upon her. Yes, we're married, but it's in name and on paper only. I've no idea why she's stuck with me, I really don't. There's no way I deserve her."

"Have you told her any of this?" Sophie asked,

knowing the answer but also knowing that he needed to say this out loud.

The words, when he was able to speak, were harsh, but his tone of voice wasn't. "You think we'd be in this mess if I had?"

Sophie offered him her hand. "What say we go and speak to Sheila?"

****

"Wash your hands, Bob!" Sophie instructed him as she followed him through the kitchen door.

Sheila opened and closed her mouth, her eyes flitting to and fro between her husband and her house/barn guest, obviously not knowing what had happened. She settled upon piling peas upon her knife as her husband studiously, much more studiously than she's seen in many a long year, washed and scrubbed his hands before taking his seat at the head of the table. If she'd been surprised before, what he did next totally took her breath away.

He held out his hands to where, on one side, Marcy unwaveringly took hold, whilst it took a few moments before his wife did the same on his other side.

"Shall we say grace?" he asked her with a smile that totally transformed his face and caused her to drop her knife. Peas scattered all over the tabletop, though no one noticed, as everyone's attention was upon the strange scene unfolding before them; except Bob who had started to speak, "Bless us, O Lord…"

Chapter Seven

Sheila stared at her husband and wondered what was happening with the world.

For one, he was whistling, in tune. He'd never whistled in tune before that she could remember. He had no interest in music that he'd ever shared with her either, so any whistling he'd ever done before had been whilst he'd been working. Even more confusing, he was helping her with the washing up, certainly something else he'd never done before. If she asked him to chip in, he'd mutter, "Housework's women's work," before stalking off. Now, she hadn't even asked.

"Here you go, love," he told her, offering another dinner plate to be dried.

And he was calling her "love"! Whilst accepting the plate, Sheila pondered if he'd ever called her anything other than, "The missus," or "The wife," or on rare occasions, "Sheila." She couldn't remember the last time he'd said any term of endearment to her, let alone using the L word.

Carefully placing the plate in its place in the dresser, she crossed back to stand by her husband's side. Now he was smiling at her as he shook a cup dry. When she didn't return his smile with anything other than a curious glance, the smile slowly slid from his face, and he turned back to the butler sink to fish out the last few pieces of crockery to be washed.

"I don't blame you for being confused, Sheila," she heard her husband say as he once more dipped his hands into the soapy water. "I don't really know what to say myself."

"What do you want to say, Bob?" Sheila eventually asked him.

Since she'd essentially told him he'd have to like it or lump it when the Lumberjills had turned up before his expected Land Girls, conversation between the two, always stilted at best, had ground to a halt, or as good as. They didn't communicate by note, though that was mainly because they were both strict followers of advice on conserving anything, including paper, for the war effort. This was also why he'd failed to put a log burner in the barn cum billet the girls lived in. His argument of the weather being warm at present wouldn't hold up for much longer, and she was determined to have something done about it before the girls had the chance to freeze. However, it was rather difficult to get her husband to do something when they weren't talking.

Now, somewhat out of the blue, he was not only talking to her, but the smile she vaguely recalled from when they'd first met, which had been sadly lacking since he'd come back from the Western Front, had also made a reappearance. It had awakened something in her that she'd thought had long since died—hope.

Whatever he wanted to say, it waited until he'd finished cleaning the last piece of crockery. Only after she'd shut the utensils drawer and, wiping her hands on the drying towel, turned to face him, did he speak up.

"I'm sorry," he began, his back leaning against the basin and his head down.

Still confused, Sheila pulled out a chair and, sitting,

steepled her hands before her on the table. "You're going to have to help me. What, exactly, are you sorry for?" Sheila really didn't know what he was saying, but she wasn't going to make it easy for him.

What would once have annoyed him—her asking a question—now didn't have any effect, as he merely held up the tea caddy, waited for her to nod a confused yes, and then put on the kettle. Whilst it began to boil, he took a seat opposite her after preparing the teapot and mugs.

Bob held her gaze, and Sheila was struck, for the first time in a long while, with how vividly green his eyes were. She could only compare it to staring into the depths of the ocean, with the seaweed that for so long had clouded them now swept away. "For everything," he began, and before she could ask him to explain, he willingly did so. "For the last twenty-odd years, for not being the husband you deserve."

He reached, tentatively, for her hand, and when she didn't move it away, took a firm yet gentle grip upon it and drew it toward him. Leaning forward, all the time maintaining eye contact with her, he slowly drew her hand toward his lips. His calloused hands suddenly felt soft and untouched by years of hard work in the fields and, before that, the years he'd survived in the trenches. His kiss when it came was soft and warm upon the back of her hand, his lips staying there for a few seconds before he placed her hand back on the table, though he didn't let go.

Who was this in front of her? Closing her eyes, Sheila could almost imagine he was the same young man she'd met all those years ago, not the weather-beaten man she'd come to know. Could he really mean what he said? She'd love to believe so as, despite everything, despite the loveless marriage she'd come to accept, she would still like to believe that what they once had, a love that had carried them both through two hard years of war, could resurface and help to bring them both through this one. Words were one thing. The reasons behind them were completely another.

"What's brought this on, Bob?"

Before answering, he got to his feet, made the tea, and placed a mug in front of her. Lifting it to her lips, she was surprised to find the tea it held wasn't builder's strength, exactly the way she liked it. It had been years since he'd bothered to make a cup, let alone one that was as good as this!

He waited for her to put her mug down. "I've had a wake-up call. Something you can thank young Sophie for."

Sheila raised her eyebrows as she took another sip of tea. So something had happened between them earlier. She'd thought it had taken a while for her to come back, and Bob certainly wasn't the same man she'd been used to.

Bob took and released a big breath. "You never met my brother Jack, did you?"

Her eyes widened in an instant, and her hand automatically clenched her husband's. The power of speech failed her, though, so she could only shake her head.

"Silly little bastard joined up when he didn't have to," he began, his eyes still locked on hers and with more than a little surprise, she noticed there were tears in them. "We kept him safe, not even a stubbed toe, right up until four days before it all bloody well ended."

"He was…" She gulped to get control of her voice.

"He was killed that close to the end?"

Bob snuffled and took out a dirty handkerchief to wipe his eyes before continuing. "Not quite." His voice had gone quiet, and she had to lean in to hear what he was saying. "He was wounded, badly. We thought he was going to make it when we managed to get him to the aid post still alive. They patched him up and sent him down the line to a hospital. He was still there on the day the war ended," he added, now ignoring the tears, the first tears she could recall him shedding in front of her, "so me and my sergeant major got permission to go to the hospital to see how he was the next day. We were…too late. Ten minutes too bloody late," he spat out, and he stopped his confession to take a long sip of his own mug of tea. "He made it through so much, only to die then!"

Bob looked up into Sheila's eyes, and there she saw in his eyes, for perhaps the first time, the look of a man who'd let a world of pain build up inside. Was this what had changed him?

"Why did you never tell me?" Sheila asked, her own voice as low as his. She watched him fight the urge to slam his mug down on the table.

"What could you have done?" Though the words were harsh, the tone in which he said them was far from it. If she had to describe a word, she'd use "resigned." Seeing the confusion in her face, Bob made a visible effort to gather himself and lean forward so he could take both her hands in his. "I'm sorry, so sorry. There wasn't anything anyone could have done. He was everything to me, to me and my mum and dad."

"So why did you marry me?" Sheila asked.

Bob shrugged and then made another effort. "I'd

made a promise to marry you, and marry you I was going to do."

"And look how that turned out," she told him before she could stop herself.

Somewhat to her amazement, he let out a small laugh. "Yes, and that's my fault entirely. I'm amazed, so amazed, that you haven't thrown me out," he told her, wiping his eyes on his shoulder. "Heaven knows no one could have blamed you, including me."

Somewhat hesitantly, Sheila raised his hand to her lips and kissed it, the surprise registering on his face. "I have thought about it," she admitted.

"Perhaps you should have acted upon it," he suggested. "God knows you'd have been happier."

"For better, for worse, Bob."

"Well, it's certainly been the latter," he admitted. "And that's all down to me. I let my anger at the world prevent me from seeing what a beautiful thing I have in front of me, and that's prevented me treating you…loving you, as you've deserved all these years."

The declaration of his love was enough to take her breath away, again. It had been so long since she'd heard anything of the like. It took her a few moments to find the words to say, "And Sophie got this out of you? Persuaded you to say all this?"

"Not quite," Bob admitted. "Mostly, she got me to admit that my anger at Jack's death had got in the way of giving you the love you deserve…and I do love you," he went on to say, ignoring the tears still dripping from them both every now and then. "I love you just as much as when I first met you, and if you'll somehow forgive me, I'll spend the rest of my days telling you, showing you, how much I love you. I can't promise I won't make any mistakes, or lose my temper when I shouldn't, but I will never stop trying."

Sheila physically felt the chain binding her heart break and was leaning across the table when the back door burst open and Sophie fell in upon her knees.

"Are you two going to be all right?" she burst out.

A changed Bob got to his feet and, chuckling away, he helped her to her feet. "And just how long have you been listening at the keyhole?"

"Since your wife shooed us out," Berry replied, as Marcy and Vicky both popped their heads around the door too.

Sheila could do nothing but laugh, causing everyone to join in.

The happy scene was rudely broken by the piercing scream of a child's voice!

Chapter Eight

"What the hell was that?" Marcy cried, her head swiveling, trying to find the source of the unexpected cry.

"I've no idea," Bob replied as he bounded out to the hall, returning a moment later with a coat each for him and his wife. "All the village school kids should be home by now, and besides, that sounded like it came from the woods behind the house. Come on," he grabbed Sheila's hand and joined his lodgers outside.

Once there, they all stood stock still, keeping as quiet as possible, every ear as pin sharp as possible, straining to hear anything out of the ordinary.

Vicky was the first to break the silence. "Are we sure we heard what we heard?"

Berry groped out a hand whilst keeping up her scanning of the horizon. "I don't think it can be anything but a child. You're sure it can't be any of the locals, Sheila?"

She shook her head and answered in as quiet a voice as she could, "Positive. There aren't that many children in the village, and there's nothing else I know of around here which could scream like that."

"Aye," agreed Bob. "They're made of strong stuff around here."

Marcy and Sophie reappeared and handed out jackets to both Berry and Vicky, and also their torches, a good idea as it wouldn't be long before the light would begin to fail. She'd just finished when the silence was broken once again.

"Help! Help, please!"

There could be no denying the voice was a child's this time, and they were deathly afraid.

"Where did that come from?" asked Berry, her head cocked to the side.

Nobody replied straight away, though everyone sensed the tension had ramped up a notch. Suddenly, Sheila pointed toward the small woods that Sophie had found Bob in. "I think it came from in there," she said and matched actions to words by striding off before anyone could stop her. Bob took off after her, and both were soon lost amongst the dark bark of the woods.

Berry grabbed hold of Vicky, who was about to follow them. "Vicky, someone needs to stay here."

"Why should it be me?" the younger girl pouted, crossing her arms.

"Because if whoever we find needs some medical attention, then someone has to call for an ambulance. You're the youngest, with the biggest ears!" she added with a grin.

Vicky opened and closed her mouth a few times, obviously trying to find fault in Berry's suggestion. When she couldn't, she plonked herself against the back door, obviously not very happy but willing to do her part for the greater good.

"Go on then," she told them, waving her hands. "You'd better be off."

Marcy nodded, not wasting time on any words, and set off at a trot in the direction Bob and Sheila had disappeared. Once they'd all got out of view of Vicky, she stopped and addressed her friends. "There's no point in us all going in the same direction. Spread out, keep your ears pricked and eyes peeled, and be careful. I don't want anyone getting hurt. Am I understood?" she asked, making certain she got a nod from everyone before she allowed everyone to make off on their own. "Back here in an hour!" she yelled at their departing backs.

****

Berry had been making her way, more slowly than she'd hoped because of the difficult underbrush she had to fight her way through, when a bendy branch whipped back and caught her across the bridge of her nose. "Buggeration!" she exclaimed as tears sprang to her eyes.

She was just wiping her eyes dry and checking if she were bleeding when the cry came again, "Help! Someone!" only much closer than before.

Ignoring the pain in her nose and not noticing the streak of blood across the back of her hand, she turned around and around on the spot. Still nothing could be seen, so she made an educated guess and ploughed off in the direction she thought the voice had come from, this time yelling out, "Hello! Can anyone hear me?"

Turning around in a circle once more, she carried on in the same direction as before, detouring around a large bush of bracken, until she nearly stumbled over the remains of a crumbling wall. Clambering over it, she found herself in the ruins of what could have been an old barn, only it must have been ancient, as only one wall was still mostly standing, with the remains of another at right angles to it. Something in that corner didn't look as if it should be there, so she carefully picked her way across to it, having to heave away the remains of a couple

65

of wooden beams on the way. As she came to a stop, she could see that what she'd thought had been a strangely shaped shadow was actually a lean-to made out of a canvas sheet. She bent down, peeled a flap away, and took a look inside.

Laid upon the ground were a couple of coats that had seen better days. Upon them, a tatty rucksack and a case, a small case such as a child would carry, together with some apple cores and plenty of old newspapers. Standing up once again, she got the impression that someone, or someones, were camping rough and, if she was right about the case, those someones were children.

"Hello!" she yelled at the top of her voice again. "Is anyone there?" The latter felt as if she were at a séance and made her feel silly. However, it did get a response.

"Over here!"

Berry cupped her hands to shout out again, "Where are you? Keep yelling! I think you're close!"

"We're down here!" came the reply and then, "Please hurry! She's hurt!"

"Keep yelling!" Berry instructed again, as she made her way slowly across the ground inside the barn's footprint before she went out what had been the door. "My name's Berry! What's yours?" she shouted.

From much nearer this time came the reply, "Harriet. Please hurry! Lucy's hurt, and she won't wake up!"

The voice was much, much closer this time, in fact, nearly at her feet, and so Berry slowed her pace, caution ringing in her mind. Carefully placing one foot in front of the other, she moved slowly toward where she thought the voice was coming from. "Over here!" was being repeated over and over. About ten feet slightly to her left, she saw what looked like a low brick wall, circular as though it may have once been a well.

Being very careful, she kneeled down on the ground, placed her hands on the crumbling lip of the well, and stared down. The moment her head was over the wall, she was answered by a cacophony of yells from the same young voice, "Berry!"

She couldn't see anyone—the woods were quite dark by then and the view into the well was pitch black. In the hope her face could be seen, she summoned up her best smile, hoping to calm whomever she'd found.

"Harriet?"

"Yes!" was yelled back.

"It's okay," she replied in a normal voice, hoping to calm the panicking girl down. "Tell me what happened, Harriet. Are you hurt?"

Berry's tone of voice must have worked. Though she could hear the girl's reply was strained, at least she'd stopped shouting. "I'm okay, but I think my sister's broken her ankle, and I can't wake her up."

"Bloody hell," Berry muttered under her breath. More loudly, she asked, "Do you know how deep this well is? I assume you can't climb out?"

"What do you think?" was the snapped reply.

She suppressed an impulse to snap back. It had been, she now realized, a very stupid question. "Sorry," she told the well. "Look, I'm on my own, and I need to go get a rope or a ladder. How deep do you think the well is?"

The well's occupant must have given the matter some thought, though eventually the answer came, "I'm not sure. About ten or twelve feet?"

"Good. Now, I want you to keep quiet, but I'm going

to have to get my friends to help me get you out."

"Don't go! Please, don't go!" Harriet yelled again.

Berry leant back over the well. "I won't go anywhere," she tried to reassure her, before adding, "but I do need to shout for my friends. Now, before I do, I'm going to throw you down my coat. You must be cold, so wrap yourselves up and we'll have you out of there in no time. All right?"

After she'd dropped her coat down, the answer came back shortly after, "Okay."

"Good girl. Now, hold on."

Standing up, Berry moved away from the lip of the well before raising her head to the sky, mustering all her strength and shouting at the top of her head, "Marcy! Sheila! Bob! Sophie!" She waited a few moments, though no reply came so she tried again. Only upon the fourth yell did she think she heard her own name being called and so shouted once more. This time, she received the definite reply of, "Berry! Is that you?"

"Over here!" She yelled over and over until she heard the sound of someone stumbling over the ground to her left. Fighting the urge to move farther away from the two girls down the well, she waved her hand until the figure saw her and made its way over to her.

"What've you found?" Marcy asked after releasing her from a quick embrace.

"Down here." She took hold of her friend's hand and quickly pulled her over to the lip of the well. "Harriet! My friend Marcy's here, so hang on a while longer, and we'll soon have you out."

"All right," came the reply echoing up the well to them, "but please hurry!"

Without wasting any more time, Berry turned to

Marcy. "I'll stay here. Would you go back and bring a rope—or better, a ladder. I'll be surprised if Sheila and Bob don't have one around."

Within ten minutes, Marcy came back leading Sophie, a ladder over their shoulders, whilst Marcy carried a coil of rope over her shoulder in case it was needed also. Once they'd lowered the ladder carefully into the well, Berry clambered down and, with Harriet's help, hoisted Lucy over a shoulder As soon as she was certain she wasn't going to drop her, she climbed slowly back up.

By this time, Sheila and Bob had joined them. Not wasting time, Bob wrapped Lucy in a blanket he'd brought along, and with her elder sister hobbling along at his heels, he strode off toward the farm.

Sheila held out a hand and pulled Berry into a hug whilst Sophie and Marcy marched off with the ladder. "Well done, dear, so very well done! Now, let's get back home. Vicky has called for an ambulance, but there weren't any available, so Doctor Oxford's on his way to check her out."

Berry made her way over toward the lean-to. "Hang on a minute." She ducked inside to gather up the case and rucksack, the coats from the ground. Anything else she didn't think was rubbish, she stuffed inside the rucksack. "I think this is where those girls were staying and that this stuff is theirs."

By the time they got back to the farm, the doctor had arrived and was leaning over the smaller girl, who had been laid on the sofa. Sheila immediately went and stood next to her husband, taking him by the hand. In fact, when the doctor heard the door close behind Berry and her friends, he looked up and surveyed the room before announcing, "It's a little crowded in here."

Harriet's head jerked up, and her eyes sought out Berry. "Her," she said. "I want her to stay."

No one said anything as they filed out of the room, though both Sheila and Sophie winked as they went into the kitchen.

Berry came and sat down on the arm of the sofa above Lucy's head, and Harriet came and stood next to her. A little hesitantly, she snaked an arm around Berry's shoulder, whilst Berry, sensing the girl needed some adult reassurance, simply sat and let her. Meanwhile, the doctor got on with his examination.

As he took Lucy's feet and laid them across his lap to examine, the girl groaned and her eyes snapped open.

"Lucy!" Harriet exclaimed, and Berry had to keep a firm grip on her to prevent her from interfering with the doctor's examination.

"Let the doctor do his work," she told her.

After a moment, Harriet reluctantly nodded, though she did reach down to stroke her sister's auburn hair until the girl stopped wildly looking around. "Shh, it's going to be all right, Lucy. He's a doctor," and when her sister then twisted her head and took in Berry, Harriet added, "This is Berry. She found us, she helped."

This must have been enough to calm the girl, as she stopped trying to get her foot out of the doctor's grip and let him proceed, letting out only the odd small whimper at his ministrations. The quietest she became was when he inspected her head and peered into her eyes.

She was braver than she had a right to be at her age, Berry thought, as when the doctor pushed down a dirty, once-white sock, that ankle was black, blue, and swollen so much the doctor had some difficulty removing the shoe. Finally, the doctor gently laid Lucy's legs upon the sofa before he rose and went into the kitchen, returning with a towel upon which he was drying his hands. He stood over the little girl, and the smile that he treated her to not only seemed to calm her down but also had the same effect upon her sister.

"You've been a very lucky little lady, my dear," he began, addressing Lucy directly. "You could have done yourself some serious harm falling down that well." He walked over to his bag and came back with a big bandage, some sticky tape, and a bottle of pills. He cleaned a small cut under Lucy's fringe and placed some tape over it. Then, sitting on the edge of the sofa, he proceeded to wrap her ankle tightly in the bandage before taping it up and getting back to his feet. "As for your ankle? There's no break, but you have badly sprained it. You won't be going anywhere very soon on that, my girl."

At those words Lucy, who'd shuffled up until she was sitting up more, turned her head to look up at her sister. "Harry?" Her voice was decidedly worried.

Harriet, or Harry—it seemed Berry wasn't the only one with a nickname—was worried too. Berry could see the blood had drained from her face as Harriet looked up at her.

Though she didn't know for sure what was going on with the two girls, she could also make a very good guess, not that she wanted to voice that in front of the doctor, in case he had a duty to report such things. Whilst she was pondering what to say, the door, not for the first time that day, burst open, only this time Sheila had the first word.

"Don't you worry yourself about anything, Doctor,"

she told him in a voice and with an expression that would brook no argument whilst she took out her purse in readiness to pay him, "these two aren't going anywhere. We'll be looking after them."

Chapter Nine

Later that evening, Sheila and the girls sat around the kitchen table enjoying a cup of cocoa before retiring to bed. Sheila's bedtime had already passed, at coming up to ten o'clock, but with the unusual adventures the day had brought, she didn't think she stood a chance of getting to sleep. All the girls were in the same state, except Vicky, who'd long ago fallen asleep in her chair—how she hadn't fallen out was anyone's guess.

"You know," Sheila mused, her eyes on the ceiling where the usual creaking noises could be heard, though not from the usual location, "I never knew he had it in him. I didn't even know he knew any stories children would like."

"It certainly looked like he had them eating out of his hand," Marcy agreed, taking a deep gulp that left a foamy moustache on her upper lip. She licked it off with relish.

"I don't know about you lot," Sophie added, "but I wouldn't have minded hearing the end."

Marcy laughed. "You can't tell me you've never heard the story of the Three Little Pigs!"

Sophie's cheeks went as red as the mug she was holding. "Not for a few years I haven't."

"How many?" Berry asked, joining in the teasing of their friend.

"A few," Sophie admitted after a short wait.

"Let her be, girls," Sheila advised and let out a sigh of deep contentment. "I'm in too good a mood to even put up with polite teasing. I seem to have back the man I married, for which I believe I have you to thank, Sophie. Whatever you did or said, I can't begin to thank you."

Sophie blushed to the roots of her brown hair, made shushing movements with her hands, and busied herself with her cocoa rather than trust her voice to speak. Eventually, she managed to fill in a few blanks. "I didn't really do anything. All I did was get him talking, and once he started, he didn't seem able to stop."

Sheila leant her head briefly on the younger girl's shoulder. "Well, whatever you said, we had a longer, more intimate talk than we've had since, well, since he came back from the Western Front. I don't know if it'll last, but at least we've now got a chance."

Sophie was saved from further embarrassment by the appearance of Sheila's husband, who managed to appear in their midst without anyone hearing him come down the stairs. The first thing he did after shutting the door that led upstairs was to move behind his wife, lean down to brush aside her hair, and kiss her on the top of her head. He then took the free seat on her other side and picked up his cup.

"Lovely," he announced, smacking his lips.

Berry decided to fill the awkward silence by asking Bob, "Did you find anything out about the girls?"

Contrary to the contented smile he'd been wearing, Bob revealed a worried frown as he turned to face her. "No," he said with a shake of his head, "they wouldn't tell me anything. However," he added—Berry's head perked up—"Harriet would like to talk to you, now."

"About what?" Marcy wanted to know.

Bob shrugged. "I don't know, but maybe you'll have more luck getting out of her how they ended up here."

Berry took up her mug and emptied its contents before getting to her feet. "I'll see what I can do."

"Left at the top of the stairs and they're in the spare room, second door on the left," Sheila informed her.

Berry knocked on the door she'd been told and waited for an answer.

"Is that you, Berry?" came Harriet's voice.

"Just me," she answered.

The door was pulled open, and Harriet stood there in a nightdress that looked about twenty years out of date, though was at least clean, even if it also dragged along the floor. Standing before her, the girl looked smaller than when she'd been found in the forest, though perhaps that was because Berry had only seen her completely down the well and as she was climbing up the ladder before her. Bob had spirited her away before she'd had a chance to speak to her, and when her sister had been examined by the doctor, she'd been stood behind her and Berry's attention had been more on Lucy.

"You wanted to see me," Berry stated, being careful not to make a move without being invited.

Harriet stood back to allow Berry into the sparsely furnished bedroom, there being only a battered chest of drawers and a single bed for furniture. Lucy was tucked up to the chin by a layer of blankets in the bed and appeared fast asleep. Her sister waited until Berry was inside before shutting the door and going to sit at the head of the bed. After stroking her sister's hair for a few seconds, she looked up at where Berry was studying her and, with a shy yet wary smile, patted the bed.

Making certain to keep her movements slow and

deliberate, Berry did as she was bid and then waited for Harriet to make the next move.

"I never had a chance to thank you for saving us," the child began.

"How long had you both been down there?" Berry asked.

Harriet shrugged. "Maybe an hour or two. It seemed much longer at the time, though."

"I expect it did," Berry agreed, hoping the young girl could see her smile. The light was still off, and there were no curtains in the room, confirming her thoughts that this was a room little used, if at all. When she received a smile back, Berry decided to take the initiative. "What were you doing in the woods, and how did you end up down that well?"

Harriet began to play with her long, dark pigtails whilst her other hand lay upon her sister's sleeping form, making it obvious she was torn between wanting to tell the truth and wanting to protect her sister.

"Harriet?" Berry prodded.

The girl let go of her pigtails, though she left her other hand on her sister. "Harry. My friends call me Harry," she told Berry, her chin jutting up, defying the elder girl to make fun of the manly nickname.

Berry held out her hand, and Harriet took it. "Pleased to meet you, Harry," she said with a wide smile.

The acceptance of her preferred name seemed to relax Harry, and she tucked her legs beneath her bottom and leaned back against the pillows, careful not to disturb Lucy's slumber.

"It was silly," she began, "falling down the well. Lucy needed to go to the toilet and stumbled out when I was asleep. Neither of us knew the well was there, and for some reason, she went off in a different direction to normal. I heard her yells for me, and when I found her, I removed a lot of the bracken she hadn't seen."

"So how did you end up down the well too? Why didn't you yell or go for help?" Berry asked, hoping her questions wouldn't make the girl clam up.

It took Harry a moment to answer. "I guess I wasn't very clever," she said, a definite tone of sheepishness in her voice. "I didn't think. When she stopped yelling, I lowered myself down to her. I couldn't just leave her!"

"Of course you couldn't. Now, don't think I didn't notice you didn't answer my question. How did you end up in the woods? The truth of that as well, please," she added, keeping her smile on her face, as she needed the girl to trust her.

Harry turned back to her sleeping sister—who looked so young, especially as she chose that moment to put her thumb in her mouth—then again to Berry, and once more back to Lucy. Berry kept quiet, knowing the young girl was going through an internal conflict. Berry needed the outcome of that conflict to go her way, and the best way to make that occur was not to interrupt. Fortunately, this didn't take long.

Harry took a pigtail in hand, an obvious nervous habit Berry was beginning to recognize, and began. "We ran away. We were put with this horrible man and his wife up near Berwick. He smelt of whiskey and she did nothing all day but sit around and smoke. They tried to make us do everything around the house and barely gave us any food. Then," and Berry noticed the child's eyes had lost their focus, as if she was recalling some very bad memories, "she started to beat us, especially Lucy. I wasn't going to let her do that," she continued, her chin jutting out in defiance. "Mum made me promise to look after her. So I did."

Berry reached out and, as she'd hoped, Harry allowed her to take her hand. "I thought you were runaway evacuees…"

"Do you blame us?" Harry interrupted, her raised voice, evidence of her agitation, causing her sister to stir slightly.

"Of course not," Berry hurried to reassure her. "Go on, what happened next? What did you do?"

"The next time she raised her hand to us, I hit her on the shin with the poker, and then, when she fell to the floor, I broke a vase over her head. We knew we couldn't stay any longer then, so we hurriedly packed our things, and I stole all the money I could find in the house, and we began to hitch a lift back to London. Only thing is, we couldn't risk trying to get a room for the nights, and it'd look strange, two young girls on their own, too, so we've been sleeping rough. Don't look like that," Harry told her at seeing the frown appear on Berry's face. "We're tough. But then we woke up in a barn two days ago, and I couldn't find my purse."

After waiting a few moments, Berry surmised that Harry didn't know how to go on. "You ran out of steam, didn't you? That's why you were camping in the woods, right?"

Harry nodded, and Berry noticed that, for the first time since she'd got involved in the whole ordeal, there were tears in the child's eyes.

"How old are you?" she asked.

At first, Berry feared she'd gone a little too far, as she felt a slight pull to the hand in hers. "You don't have to answer, if you don't want to," she hastened to add.

"No, that's all right," Harry replied having quickly thought it over. "I'm fourteen and Lucy's eight." Her brow then furrowed together as a thought hit her. "You're not going to send us back, are you?"

Even though she knew full well she didn't have any authority to do so, Berry immediately shook her head, which had the desired effect of calming Harry down, whilst making a mental note to talk the situation over with her friends the first chance she got.

With her free hand, Berry reached up and tucked Harry's pigtail behind her ear. "Now, you climb in next to your sister and get some rest. I'll be here in the morning, and we'll have a proper talk then. No running away, mind," she made certain to tell her.

Harry took her hand back, pulled back the blankets, and lay down, her sister automatically turning onto her side and laying her head on Harry's chest. "We won't. Promise," she said, her eyes already closed.

By the time Berry was closing the door, she could already hear a soft snoring sound coming from the elder sister's lips.

****

"What a horrible tale!" Sheila exclaimed, her hands flying to her mouth.

Next to her, her husband didn't say a thing, though judging by the furrow between his brows and by the way his hands were curling and uncurling into fists, he was working hard to keep his anger inside. This was matched by Vicky, who had taken out her brother's knife and was using it to clean dirt out from underneath her fingernails.

"They're not Germans, but they'll do," she was muttering over and over to herself, which caused Marcy's and Sophie's brows to furrow with concern.

"We'll have to have a talk with her soon," Marcy leant over to whisper to Sophie and Berry. Both nodded.

Berry stood up and shortly had everyone's attention. "Look, it's only my opinion, but there's no way I can see those girls go back to that couple. We do only have their word for what happened, but I trust her…Harry, that is—"

"Harry?" Marcy asked.

"Harriet. She told me it's what she prefers to be called. Anyway, what say we go and speak to the local police on Monday, have them phone London, and find out if we can get them taken back to their parents? Would that be all right, Marcy? I'd like to be the one to take them to the station, so I'll need to be a little late into work."

"Take your time," Marcy told Berry. "We need to get this right."

Bob stood up, stretched, and let out a huge yawn. This had, as is usual when anyone yawns, the effect of setting off a chain reaction. "I think now's a good time for bed, everyone."

Chapter Ten

Sergeant Elias Duncan was one of those fellows who looked like they'd been policemen all their lives, including when they'd been at school. According to Sheila, he'd been coerced out of retirement in the summer of 1941 when the last bobby under thirty had been called up to the Army. He was nearly as wide as he was tall, with a silver-gray and extremely bushy moustache that he had a habit of twiddling between his fingers as he spoke. What was left of his hair was silver and combed over to cover a bald spot that threatened to take over his entire head.

"Harry," Berry whispered, nudging the girl in the back, "it's rude to stare."

"It's not my fault that his neck's spilling over his collar," she replied.

Berry discovered how difficult turning a laugh into a cough was and found herself under the intense and worldly-wise intelligent gaze of the sergeant.

Fortunately, Sheila had insisted upon accompanying the two of them to the police station that morning and had known Elias for donkey's years. With a glance, she was able to defuse any anger the policeman may have felt. Bob would have come as well, only he was engaged in knocking up some wooden beds for their lodgers and, he'd muttered, for when the Land Girls eventually turned up. He'd been very apologetic to the Lumberjills about it all at breakfast, but Marcy had said she couldn't see any problems, and the rest of them had agreed that there was plenty of room, and more bodies would make it warmer in the cold evenings ahead.

"Now we've resolved that I need to lose a little weight," the sergeant said, leaning over the counter to look Harry directly in her eye and completely spoiling any attempt at telling her off by winking. "What can I do for you, Mrs. Harker?"

Sheila gently took the little girl by the shoulders and pushed her so she was standing in front of the two women. "This is Harriet…Harry," she quickly added as the little girl's head started to turn, "and we came across her and her little sister Lucy in the woods behind the farm last night. She's back home by the way, with one of Berry's," here, Berry canted her head to the left and gave Elias a brief smile, "friends. They're evacuees and ran away from where they'd been placed, as they were being beaten."

It hadn't taken long for the girls to be convinced that honesty was the best policy when they'd talked over everything at breakfast that morning. They actually hadn't done that much talking, as they'd been too busy stuffing their faces with toast and marmalade, but they had agreed with the suggestion. Sheila in particular had been very pleased to agree with Berry when she'd told her she believed that at least Harry was an honest girl. She hadn't actually been able to speak to Lucy, though she believed the younger girl likely worshipped her older sister.

"Are you really?" Elias replied, his strangely dark eyebrows making a move toward the ceiling.

"We haven't done anything wrong," Harry told him

in no uncertain terms. It had also been decided no one needed to know exactly what she'd done before they ran off.

"I didn't say you had," he replied, adding a smile that transformed him into more of a homely uncle than an authority figure. "Sheila, do me a favor and put the Closed notice in the front door, and let's all go through to me office. We can be much more comfortable in there."

Berry busied herself with making tea, and after being given the okay, used up the last of Elias's milk for Harry. Sheila and the girl were sharing a chair whilst the policeman perched on the edge of his desk.

"Thanks very much. Berry, was it?"

"That's right," she replied, pulling up another wooden chair for herself.

"I don't know," he said, picking up and blowing on his mug. "You girls with your names these days."

"Don't take any notice of him, Harry," Sheila chided him as she handed Harry her glass.

"I won't," was the defiant reply.

Elias let out a great big belly laugh that, more than anything he could have done, made the child relax and sit back to sip her milk. "Now, Harry," he began, "I don't think there's any point in asking you to go into any detail about what happened up in Berwick, as you're not going to tell me, are you."

"No, sir, I'm not," Harry admitted, meeting his gaze.

"In that case, suppose you tell me if your parents have a phone?"

Harry shook her head and put her milk down on the floor. "No, we don't have one. But mum made me memorize the phone number of the butchers' just around the corner. It's a Mr. Waller, and he's a good friend of my dad's. She said he wouldn't mind if we had to call, and he'd send his errand boy to find them."

Taking his seat, it took the sergeant a while to be put through, and when he did, as soon as he'd confirmed he was speaking to this Mr. Waller, he asked how he could get hold of Mr. or Mrs. Dunn. As he listened, all the color drained out of his face, and he almost dropped the phone before recovering his composure enough to end the call politely. He slumped back in his chair, shaking his head. When he was able to look up, his gaze was fixed upon Harry. Berry didn't think she'd ever seen anyone look so sad in all her life.

Sheila stretched out her hand but couldn't reach his. "Elias. What's wrong?"

Before he found the power to speak again, he took up and finished his tea. Then he got up and moved around his desk until he could sit on the edge, right next to where Sheila and Harry sat.

Observing this, Berry felt a chill settle around her stomach. She hadn't had any experience with death personally, but she didn't need to be an undertaker to know that something terrible had happened. She looked at Harry and knew the little girl too knew something very bad had occurred and her life was about to change forever. At almost the same time, though, Berry sensed more than saw her steel herself and sit up straighter next to Sheila. She didn't have long to wait.

Elias tried and, in Berry's opinion, nearly succeeded in softening his natural expression. "Harry. I'm sorry, I really am, but there's no way to say this that'll make the news any easier."

One of Sheila's hands flew to cover her mouth

whilst the other gripped Harry tightly around the waist. "Oh, Elias. Surely not!"

"That was Mr. Waller. There was an accident last night. Some fool of a lorry driver hit your parents in the blackout. I'm sorry, but they died at the scene."

****

Elias insisted upon driving them back to the farm. "It's only ten minutes," he'd mumbled and then told Sheila, after he'd helped them out of his car, "I'm going to see if I can track down any relatives, but can you see if you can get any names out of her? I don't know, at this moment, what to do if there's no one."

Berry didn't need to look at Sheila's face to know what her friend was thinking. Sure enough, she heard, "I'll ask her, and her sister, as soon as I think they're up to it, but don't worry. If there's no one, they can stay with me and Bob."

This received a look of astonishment from the policeman. "Since when did you start calling your husband by his first name again? I wasn't aware the two of you were even talking!"

Berry held Harry against her. She hadn't said a word since being told the news, nor had she shed a tear. Consequently, she got to see Sheila go beetroot red, which confirmed her suspicions, based on Elias's reaction, that their previous estrangement had been widely known in the area.

"Let's say that one of our Lumberjills had a word with Bob, and we're giving it another go."

"Well, I'll be," he exclaimed, slapping his forehead. "At least that's one bit of good news today. You must thank her for me. I've known for years he hasn't been the same since we got back from the trenches. How you've put up with him, I've no idea, but if you're sure you're not making a mistake, then I really do wish you all the luck in the world."

"Nothing's certain, Elias," she told him, shaking her head sadly at where Berry was rocking Harry back and forth. "If nothing else, today's taught us that."

There really wasn't anything anyone could say to that, so the friendly policeman kissed Sheila on the cheek, smiled at Berry, and with a last sad shake of his head toward Harry, got back in his car and drove off.

Waiting for them in the front room were Sophie and Lucy, listening to some classical music on the radio, though it became obvious neither was paying much attention, because as soon as she caught sight of her big sister, Lucy heaved herself out of her seat and hobbled over to her, the strapping supporting her ankle making walking difficult.

"Harry!" the smaller girl cried out, wrapping her arms around her sister and burying her head in her chest.

Harry, with a quick glance at where Berry stood leaning against the kitchen door, hugged her sister tighter than it looked possible for anyone to withstand before taking her by the hand and taking her upstairs.

"What's that all about?" Sophie asked as Sheila went to put the kettle on. After Berry had told her what had happened, Sophie could only shake her head, mutter something about, "This bloody war," before she made to follow the two girls upstairs.

Berry gripped her by a shoulder. "No, let them be. This is something Harry has to sort out herself."

"But she's so young!" Sophie uttered, her hand flying to her mouth.

"Aren't we all," Berry agreed.

No one could think of anything else to say, and the three of them all sat in silence around the kitchen table until Harry came back down. Without a word, she took a seat. Eventually, Sheila got to her feet, went to the larder, and came back with a carrot cake.

"It's not as good as before the war," she told them with a shrug. "Still, what is?"

As Harry was finishing off a large slice, Bob burst through the door and was immediately admonished by his wife. "Sorry, sorry," he told the room at large, before pulling a chair around so he could sit next to Harry. To everyone's surprise, he immediately placed an arm around the girl's shoulders, neither noticing its urgent need of a wash. Gently, he drew her unyielding head onto his shoulder.

He brushed the fringe from her eyes before planting a kiss on the top of her forehead. "I'm so, so sorry, Harry. I ran into Elias, and he told me what happened."

Where she hadn't shown much emotion when only Berry, Sheila, and Sophie were present, Harry chose to break down and cry in Bob's embrace. At first, he appeared not to be comfortable with what was happening, but it only took a reassuring nod from his wife for him to get up from his seat, kneel in front of her, and allow the distraught girl to sob her heart out.

A little hesitantly, Berry got to her feet. "Come on, Sophie, we'd better get to work."

****

A short while later, Berry and Sophie leant their bicycles on the ground and trudged over to meet Marcy and Vicky.

"You both looked more tired than we feel!" Vicky declared.

Berry and Sophie exchanged glances before answering. "It's been an…emotional morning," Berry settled on.

"Come over to the hut. You both look in need of one of Vicky's builder's brews," Marcy told them, not giving either a chance to object. Grabbing each by the hand, she dragged them over to where Vicky was already lighting up their hexi-stove.

"What happened, then?" Vicky asked them as she dug out the tea leaves, keeping an eye on the boiling water.

Her gaze focused on the ground, Berry filled them in. "Their parents were killed in the blackout."

"Nazi bomb got them?" Vicky asked, breaking a twig between her fingers into tiny pieces.

Berry snorted. "Nothing of the like. They got run over."

"Bloody hell," Marcy uttered.

Vicky stirred the tea leaves a while before looking back up. "Never rains but it bloody pours. So what's going to happen to the little blighters?"

"For the meantime, they're going to be staying with Sheila and Bob whilst they try to find some relatives. If they can't find any…"

"Sheila told the police she'd take them in," finished Sophie, when Berry couldn't go on.

"And Bob's all right with that?" Marcy asked, unable to keep a note of incredulity out of her voice.

"I don't think he's going to be a problem, and I think you need to blame Sophie, here." Berry added, "Whatever she said to him in the woods, he seems a changed man."

"Well, bugger me!" Vicky put in.

Chapter Eleven

"I think I may need to wash these," Vicky stated, lifting an arm and sniffing gingerly at her overalls.

Berry let her axe fall to the ground and came over to where her friend stood waving a hand before her nose. A moment later, she fell theatrically to the ground, holding her nose, amongst the flotsam of the forest floor. Leaning back on her elbows, she told her young friend, "If you leave it any longer, those could walk here and do your shift for you!"

"They're not that bad!" Vicky protested, though all the same, she didn't perform another sniff test.

Unseen, Marcy appeared behind her, finger and thumb also pinching her nose and clapped her on a shoulder. "The foxes have sent in a complaint, so yes, believe us, it's that bad."

Sophie trotted up to help Berry off the ground, but before she could put in her tuppence worth, Vicky had held up a hand. "Okay, I get the picture. I'll wash them tomorrow afternoon. Satisfied?"

"More than," Berry agreed, accepting Sophie's hand up.

"Now we've established that Vicky does have cleanliness standards, perhaps we can get back to work?" Marcy suggested, hands on her hips, a smile on her face.

For the next two hours, the girls worked hard to make up time. The sun peeked out from behind a cloudy morning, making the air warm enough for them to work with their sleeves rolled up for a change, and Marcy had decided the clearing they'd made needed the brushwood burned out to make it easier to get to the unfelled trees. They were watching to make certain things didn't get out of control, especially as they'd just finished packing the last load, when Vicky had interrupted things with her discussion on her whiffy overalls.

Marcy wiped the soot and sweat from her brow with her sleeve and pondered the irony for a minute as she finished with the clean-up. Her Matthew wouldn't even let her stoke the fire in the grate at home, let alone start a forest fire. If he could see her now, he'd have a heart attack! Things had certainly changed, and whether for the better, time alone would be the judge. As she surveyed her girls, arms linked as they strode toward her, each sporting a grin that showed white teeth against soot-darkened faces and hands, she didn't think she'd ever been happier. In fact, the only way she could be happier was if her husband was once more by her side. Before the others reached her, she wiped a tear from her eye.

"Ready to call it a day?" Berry asked as she came to stand by Marcy's side.

Surveying the burnt ground in satisfaction, Marcy nodded. "The saplings will be here Monday morning, early, so we'll have another busy day and," she added with a wince, "a back-breaking one, too."

"All the more reason for a bit of fun tonight then!" Berry stated.

"You have plans then, titch?" Vicky asked.

Berry swatted Vicky's bottom for the jibe. "Less of the name-calling, you, and yes, I do have plans, as it happens. Jimmy's coming over to take me out for a drink this evening."

Berry looked her friend up and down. "You may want to get changed and perhaps have a wash before he comes. He could easily lose you in the blackout, otherwise."

****

"Oh, my word!" exclaimed Harry as the four girls cycled up the lane, past the farmhouse, and toward their barn. "What happened to you lot?"

In the week since she'd learned of her parents' death, Harry had taken to following Bob around the farm and, in her opinion, helping him with his work, Lucy trailing behind. The way Bob put things, he spent most of his time stopping her from getting tangled up in various pieces of machinery. Mind you, he always had a smile upon his face when he spoke about their little adventures, as he called them. Sheila had taken to teasing him mercilessly about how close he was becoming to the young girl, though everyone could see she'd never been happier than now, playing the role of mother, and her husband also, in that of an unlikely father.

Harry had seemed to shrug off her loss, or at least no one had seen her shed a tear since she'd cried on Bob's shoulder, though every time anyone asked her about any relatives—Elias down at the police station had drawn a blank so far—she instantly clammed up and went up to bed to lie down, dragging her little sister behind her. Berry had tried the first two times she'd done this to get her to talk, or to at least come back downstairs, but she refused, and the two of them would stay in their room until the next morning, not even coming down for supper. Despite this behavior, everyone in the household was determined to keep trying until they got an answer out of her.

Slightly more worrying was Lucy. Yes, she wasn't letting a sprained ankle prevent her from traipsing around the farm, though Sheila was getting tired of having to clean the bandages each evening, but apart from her sister, she wasn't speaking to anyone but Berry. To Berry, she would chat happily about anything that came to her mind, be it the crow that she thought was teasing her each morning to the fact that she didn't like porridge anymore now that sugar was hard to come by. However, ask her about her parents or any relations, even if it were Berry doing the asking, and she would go silent; though Berry was convinced she was on the point of telling her something each time it happened. She didn't run off to her sister, so Berry persisted.

Leaning her bicycle against the barn, Marcy turned and pasted a tired smile on her very dirty face before answering. "Making sure we don't burn the whole of the wood down, sweety."

"You look like Uncle John," Lucy told her. "He gets black as pitch from the coal, mummy used to say."

Her words had an effect like lightning striking on her elder sister.

"Lucy!" she hissed, before grabbing her sister's hand and attempting to drag her off before anyone could react.

Fortunately, Berry was too quick for her and headed the pair off before they could get to the farmhouse's kitchen door. Standing firm in the doorway, she folded her arms to show she meant business, yet kept a friendly smile on her soot-smudged face, "Harry, would you and Lucy care to help me get cleaned up?"

Letting go of her big sister's hand, Lucy jumped up

and down, clapping her hands together, seemingly unaware she may have said something she shouldn't. "Let's go to the stream in the woods, Berry," she decided. "The water's lovely and fresh. Me and me sister used to wash there."

Shooting a look back at where Marcy, Vicky, and Sophie were struggling to stifle their laughter, Berry had little choice but to allow herself to be led into the woods, with a reluctant Harry traipsing behind.

As they disappeared from view, via the barn so Berry could pick up a towel and her washing kit, the back door opened and Sheila stood there, a potato in one hand and a knife in the other. "Where's Berry going with the kids?" she asked.

Feeling that as the eldest she should show the most control, Marcy found her voice. "Well, Lucy let something slip about an Uncle John, and Harry tried to drag her off, but Berry managed to distract her by asking Lucy to help her wash."

Sheila scratched her hand with the potato. "So why are they heading into the woods?"

Sophie joined her friend and wrapped an arm around her waist. "Lucy decided it would be good for Berry to wash in the stream."

With a look that plainly said she thought the idea was ridiculous, Sheila turned back toward the kitchen before turning her head to look over her shoulder at her very mucky lodgers. "Normally, I'd say she was mad, but seeing the state you three are in, I think you should all traipse off and do the same."

"Hey!" protested Vicky, reaching out with a grubby hand. "I've been looking forward to a hot bath after today."

Sheila stopped and rubbed her chin with the potato before deciding, "Tell you what. Scrub off the worst of that in the stream, and then—and only then, mind"—she pointed the sorry potato at them for emphasis—"you can all come in for a bath. There isn't much hot water, so I suggest you hurry."

****

As Lucy promised, the water was indeed clear and clean. What she'd failed to say was anything about its temperature, and Berry was unable to suppress the shudder that went through her from her hands to the tips of her toes. Hoping she wouldn't embarrass the two children, she took advantage of the remoteness of the location and rapidly stripped off her clothes, piling them onto a rock next to the clean skirt, jumper, underwear, and shoes she'd brought. Lucy didn't appear fazed by her nakedness, though Harry had turned her head slightly away as Berry stepped into the stream and knelt down.

"Bloody hell!" she couldn't help but let out, which at least brought a laugh from Harry whilst Lucy decided she'd sit on a rock and dangle her feet into the running water.

Taking up her cloth, she dipped it and her bar of soap into the water and started to wash off the grime of the day. As she washed herself down, Berry kept an eye on her companions. Lucy seemed to have forgotten the tense situation back at the farmhouse, whilst Harry, still a stiffness about her shoulders, also seemed to have relaxed a little. She was also now watching her as she finished up her ablutions.

Stepping carefully onto what looked like a clean-ish rock, Berry quickly set about drying herself before she caught a chill. The afternoon was drawing in, and though she hadn't planned on doing anything this Saturday, she'd prefer to be in the warmth of the farmhouse rather than where she was. The wash had been invigorating, but she'd really not have to do it again, if possible. Mind you, if Marcy decided they needed to do another burning, she might very well find herself down here again. She doubted Sheila would be very happy with the four of them if they made a mess of her bathroom.

Judging the girls, specifically Harry, were relaxed enough, Berry pulled on her last shoe and addressed her, carefully. "Harry, I know you don't want to talk about it, and we really don't want you to feel we're pressuring you, but who is this Uncle John? Is he a miner?" she added, hoping the extra question would prove to the elder of the two that she was still her friend and not just after finding out if there were any other relations.

A multitude of emotions flickered across Harry's face, and all Berry could do was to stand there, running her fingers through her hair, working out the tangles, not daring to say anything in case she frightened her again. Finally, she saw Harry take a deep breath as she plonked herself down on the rock next to her sister. Before answering, Harry threw an arm around Lucy's shoulders and brought her head to rest on her shoulder.

Pushing her glasses back up her nose, she held up her free hand, and when Berry took it, Harry pulled her down hard so she had no choice but to sit next to the young girl. "I know what you've all been asking us, and I'm sorry for being such a rotten so-and-so. Uncle John, he's not a real uncle, he's my…he was," she altered, "my father's best friend from school days."

Berry squeezed Harry's hand and glanced across at Lucy, who simply shrugged her shoulders in agreement of what Harry had just said. "So," Berry decided to ask straight out, "let me get this right, because it's important. You don't have any relatives? There's no one?"

When Harry replied, be it bravado or simply that she had no emotion left to give, Berry believed what she said to be the truth more than she'd ever believed anything else before.

"Mum and Dad told me their families were very hard hit by the flu in 1919, and that all their brothers and sisters—I forget how many now—died during it. We buried our last Nanny the year before the war started."

"Will we have to go back?" Lucy had squirmed out of her sister's grip and stood before Berry, squeezing her hands together. The bandage around her ankle was soaked and half hanging off.

Berry knelt down before her and retied it before placing her hands on her waist and looking up at Harry. "Do you remember what Sheila said at the police station last week? What she told the two of you?"

It took a moment for Berry's words to become clear to Harry, and when they did, Berry was rewarded by the smile that took over the girl's face.

****

"Sheila!"

Everyone sat around the kitchen table awaiting the return of Berry and the girls when Harry shouted, "Sheila!" again. The happiness in the voice was a surprise, especially when its owner followed into the room and threw her arms around the farmer's wife.

"Harry?" Sheila only just managed to get out, as Harry had thrown herself at the plump woman and was now hanging around her neck. Reaching up, she untied the hands, which took some doing, before setting the girl onto her feet. Though only fourteen, she was nearly of the same height. "I take it there's nothing wrong, then?"

"Not now," Harry replied. "That is," she amended, taking a small step back, yet making certain to look the older woman in the eye, "if you meant what you said to that policeman?"

It only took a moment for Sheila to realize what Harry was referring to and then the biggest smile overtook her—before disappearing as she comprehended what it meant. She turned toward Berry. "Does this mean Harry here has finally spoken up?"

Harry herself answered. "It does, and"—she looked around the table, making certain to lock eyes with all Berry's friends and Sheila's husband Bob too—"I'm sorry I've been such a rat this week to everyone."

"She is!" piped up Lucy, who began jumping up and down next to her big sister in excitement. "And she's been a rat to me too, so I think I should get an apology too!" she stated, nearly jumping onto her sister's foot.

Harry grabbed Lucy by the shoulders, and once the child had stopped bouncing, hugged her to her chest and ruffled her hair. "Gerrof!" she said, before adding, "I am sorry for being a rat to you as well."

Sheila, though, still had to check with Harry, and everyone could see her emotions were tearing her every which way. "Harry, does this mean you don't have any other relations?"

Berry decided to speak up, not wanting Harry's emotions to be tested any more than necessary. "I'm afraid it does, Sheila. I'll give you the details once these two ruffians have had tea and gone up to bed. Will you be able to let Elias know tomorrow?"

"He's not on duty on Sundays, but Bob'll pop

around to his cottage in the morning and fill him in."

Whilst everyone was talking, Lucy took a place at the table between Marcy and Sophie. Vicky had gone to wait outside the village pub for Jimmy, and now Lucy looked on the point of banging her knife and fork on the tabletop.

Bob reached across and laid his huge, calloused hand upon her tiny one. "Patience, little one," he told her with a lopsided smile. "The sausages aren't going to get cold yet."

****

Later that night, after two over-excited girls had been persuaded to go up to bed, everyone—except Vicky, who wasn't back yet—was lounging around the sitting room, humming along to a band on the radio. Bob had broken out a few bottles of his '38 cider and a muted mood of celebration had been present all evening, though the spell had nearly been broken when Sophie and Marcy had tripped over the poker and nearly ended up on the floor. Marcy just managed to stop her friend from falling into the fire grate.

Sheila had only finished asking out loud to no one in particular, "You really think we'll be able to keep them here?" when the sound of the back door opening and being banged shut was heard. The next minute, Vicky stumbled into the room. Contrary to her immaculate coiffure when she'd gone out, her mascara had run and her hair was disheveled. There were very obvious tear tracks down her cheeks, too, and tears swam in her eyes, on the point of falling.

Berry was at her side in an instant. "My God! What happened?"

"Did this Jimmy lad do this to you?" Bob demanded,

getting out of his chair and looking on the point of grabbing the poker.

Vicky gripped his arm, being wise enough to stay his temper. "No, of course not."

"Then what on earth happened?" Berry repeated. "Is Jimmy all right?"

Vicky allowed herself to be helped to the sofa, where Bob pressed a glass of cider he'd nipped into the kitchen to get into her hands. "Jimmy's fine." She looked over at Sophie. "It's Ginger. He was killed last night."

Chapter Twelve

No matter how much Sophie cajoled or pleaded, Vicky refused to say anything other than Dennis and the remainder of his crew would be coming over the next morning. Vicky spent the rest of the evening curled up on the sofa and cried herself to sleep against Marcy's shoulder. Sophie just stared out into the darkness of the night and refused to say another word after failing to get any more details out of Vicky. At some point toward their normal bedtime, Berry went out to the barn and grabbed a handful of blankets, tucked them around Vicky and Marcy, and took Sophie by the hand to guide her back to bed. Berry would have bet good money Sophie wasn't aware of what was happening.

Upon reaching the barn and helping her friend to undress and put on the tatty pair of pyjamas she liked to wear, she tucked her in and, once clad in her own black-and-white striped set, went to blow out the candle she'd lit. Berry was passing Sophie's bed when her friend reached out a hand and gripped her forearm.

"Don't leave me." Berry had to strain to hear the words even in the quiet of the night, but then Sophie flicked her blankets aside and said, a little more clearly, "I could do with a cuddle."

"Shift over a bit then." Berry slid in beside her.

Though cramped in a camp bed designed for one, with some shifting and not a little laughter, a welcome sound after the day they'd had, Berry found herself with Sophie resting her head upon her shoulder. She figured that as long as neither of them wriggled around too much, they stood a slight chance of not falling out of bed. Berry's eyelids were beginning to droop when Sophie, not asleep as she'd thought, surprised her by speaking.

"I didn't know him well, you know," she began, her words tickling Berry's shoulder. "Hadn't seen him since that afternoon in York, actually, but we were going to see each other next weekend. He had some leave coming, he told me. In this letter," she added, sliding a hand under her pillow and clutching a letter.

This was news to Berry, who didn't know Sophie had been in contact with him. As for herself, despite Dennis Grey making it quite clear he was keen on her, she'd not given him real reason to be hopeful and hadn't heard from him since. In wartime, she was well aware that few people, especially young couples, took the time to take things slow. Berry was struck by the thought that Sophie and Ginger wouldn't have the chance of even a short time together. Whether it had been meant to be or not, no one would ever know. Her friend was certainly cut up about it, though, and she doubted if whatever Dennis would be able to tell them tomorrow would be of any comfort.

Berry didn't really know what to say, so figuring the best thing she could do would be to remain quiet in the hope that Sophie may say something more. After a few minutes quiet, Berry began to snuggle up against Sophie's warm back. She let out a sigh and was about to give in and close her eyes, only Sophie began to talk again.

"I haven't had a real boyfriend, ever. My parents

never told me anything about how to behave around boys. Going to an all-girls school, I could barely talk to men after I left and began to work in that office. I think everyone thought I had a stammer, I was so nervous!"

"What about at dances?" Berry wanted to know. "How did you get on at the dance hall?"

Sophie let out a dry chuckle. "I found excuses to go to the toilet and then escaped back to my parents. Soon, my friends stopped asking me to dances…"

"So you can't dance?" Berry finished for her.

"I don't know if I even have two left feet! It would have been nice to have had a chance to find out, with…Ginger," she eventually added before going quiet again.

"You were keen on him, then?"

Berry could just about see part of Sophie's face from where she was leant on her shoulder, and could make out her forehead wrinkling in concentration.

"I was keen on the idea of him," Sophie allowed. "He seemed so easy to talk to. Much easier than any other man I've ever known. Now, it'll never happen. I think I must be cursed!" she ended with a sob.

Quick as she could, Berry wrapped her free arm around her. "Come on, don't be like that. You're not cursed, or bad luck, or anything of the like. It's the war, and I'm sure there are many other men around who're just as nice as Ginger…was."

"Are you sure?" Sophie wanted to know.

Honesty was the best answer Berry knew. "As sure as I can be of anything at this time. There'll be another. You just need to give yourself time."

Things must have finally caught up with them both, finally, as the last thing Berry could recall was Sophie repeating to herself over and over, "Time. I need time."

****

Something was tickling the top of Berry's head. At first she ignored it. Since it was quite early and a Sunday, she was reluctant to get up earlier than she had to, as Sheila had agreed for breakfast to be pushed back to nine. The tickle made her only half crack open an eyelid before closing it once again. Barely a minute later, the tickle on her head increased, and fighting off her first impulse to scratch herself with both hands, partially because Sophie was still using her shoulder as a pillow, she slowly reached her free hand up and into her hair.

"Argh!" she shrieked and shot upright, knocking the previously sleeping Sophie out of bed and onto the cold floor.

"What the hell?" Sophie groggily muttered as she struggled into an upright position. Turning her head to look up, she saw Berry sat bolt upright with one of her hands on the top of her head—and on top of her hand was a little white mouse.

****

Sheila, Bob, Marcy, and a bleary-eyed Vicky sat around the kitchen table. Bob was slumped back, his face like thunder. "They can't do this to me!" he complained for the second time in as many minutes.

Dipping her toast into her soft-boiled egg, Sheila simply let her husband cool down for a few more minutes before judging it the right time to ask, "What can't they do?"

Bob waved the letter he'd opened that had put him in a bad mood above his head, "Land Girls' bloody what-not people. They're telling us we won't be getting our two girls for another week now."

"That'll give you time to finish the bunks, then," she decided, watching him carefully for his reaction.

Until a few weeks ago, until Sophie had somehow talked back the man she'd fallen in love with, her comment would have caused either a blow-up or him to storm out of the room; probably both. She saw the familiar red tinge start to appear on his ear tips. However, when she saw him look directly at her, he took a deep breath, and the tinge leaked away. Though he didn't exactly smile, he also didn't lose his temper, indeed he actually reached for her hand and raised it to his lips.

"You're perfectly right, my love. Mind you, it still means another week where it'll be just you and me who'll have to milk the cows. That'll mean I'll be very tired come the night," he added with a wiggle of his eyebrows.

Marcy spluttered her tea back into her cup, whilst Vicky's wide-eyed expression made it clear she understood what she'd just heard. Of course, Harry and Lucy chose that moment to pad down the stairs.

"If you need help with the cows, Mr. Harker, I'd be happy to help. I've always loved animals. You'd have to show me what to do, though," Harry offered, as she and her sister took their places at the table.

At least it looked like she hadn't picked up on what Bob had meant.

"Are you always tired at night, Mr. Harker?"

It appeared Lucy had heard enough, though, and Bob promptly bit into his finger instead of the bacon sandwich he was holding.

"I think now would be a good time to pop around to see Elias, Bob. Don't you?" Sheila suggested when it looked like her husband didn't know what to say.

Clearing his throat and then briefly studying his finger, Bob got up from the table and shot his wife a look of gratitude. "I think that's an excellent idea, my dear. I'll take him around a bacon sandwich, butter him up, so to speak."

Harry looked up at where Bob was promptly buttering up some toast and loading it high with crispy bacon. "Can I come with you, please?"

Sheila shook her head and laid a hand on the girl's arm. "I don't think so, my love. They need to discuss adult things."

"But it's us they'll be talking about!" she protested with a pout.

"Who'll be talking about who?" Berry asked as she and Sophie made their way into the kitchen.

"I'll be on my way to talk to Elias about these two troublemakers," Bob filled in for the latecomers, shooting the two smallest members of the room a grin to show them he was only joking.

****

"I come bearing gifts," Bob declared as Elias opened his front door at the second time of knocking.

"Never let it be said I turn down a gift." The stout policeman raised to his nose the square newspaper package dripping grease. "Especially when it's a bacon sarnie. Come in, Bob," he added, stepping back from the door. "To what do I owe the visit?"

Bob followed the older man down the hall and into his kitchen. Markedly smaller than the farmhouse, it nevertheless sported a spotless butler's sink, basic cooker, and a tallboy neatly stacked with plain white crockery. Laid upon the table were a Sunday newspaper and a half empty cup of tea.

"Wouldn't say no if there's any left in the pot," Bob said upon spying this.

Elias took down a side plate and laid out his sandwich, took his seat, and told him, "Help yourself, you know where everything is. If you think I'm going to allow some of Sheila's cooking to get cold, you don't know me."

Bob grinned and took down a cup. "I know you well enough. Tuck in," he advised as he swirled the tea in the still warm pot.

For the next five minutes, the only sounds in the room were of Elias munching enjoyably through his unexpected breakfast together with Bob slurping his tea, watching. With a smack of his lips, Elias pushed his plate away and, sitting back, announced his satisfaction with a huge belch.

"Someone enjoyed that," Bob commented.

After letting out a very satisfied, "Aah," Elias put his hands behind his neck and regarded the farmer. "So what brings you here on a Sunday morning? Shouldn't you be getting ready to go to morning service?"

"I'm sure the reverend will forgive me if I miss it this once. I've something I need to run by you. It's regarding Harry and Lucy."

Elias leant forward, resting his elbows on the table after folding his paper closed. "I'm hoping you've managed to find something out. I've drawn a blank," he explained with a heartfelt sigh. Rubbing a hand through his thinning hair, he looked up again and added, "Well, not quite. You do realize I've had to contact the couple they stayed with, to get their side of the story."

"Mmm," Bob mumbled, his brow furrowing.

"Come on, Bob," the policeman implored, "you

know I had to. We may be friends, but it's my job."

"What did they say, then?"

"First, they claimed they never laid a hand on either of the girls. In fact, they said they treated them as their own and were nothing but kind to them. In fact, they say Harriet stole a very valuable music box from them."

Chapter Thirteen

"I never stole anything from them!"

Harry sat opposite Elias at the Harkers' kitchen table. Lucy was on her lap, and to her left sat Berry. She'd insisted upon Berry being present as some kind of legal counsel, even though she wasn't sure what one was. She'd read it in a Miss Marple mystery book, she'd told them, as if this made a difference.

For Berry's part, on the one hand she was happy to be there for the girl, as she'd grown very fond of her. However, Dennis and the surviving crew had turned up ten minutes ago, and circumstances notwithstanding, she'd been looking forward to getting to know him a little better and, of course, finding out what had happened to poor Ginger Baker. When Bob had run her down, everyone had only just finished saying rather awkward hellos. Still, she'd been reluctant to leave the group until Bob had explained why she was needed, so pushing her curiosity aside, she'd hurried after the farmer.

"Nobody here said you did," Elias assured her.

He'd made the very sensible decision not to wear his uniform, Berry thought. "Just what have those people been saying?" she asked, correctly guessing what his line of questioning was.

If he was annoyed he'd been interrupted, he didn't show it. "The McAlister's claim that Harriet…"

"Harry," Sheila, Berry, and Lucy corrected automatically.

"…Harry…stole a valuable, family heirloom from them."

"What's a familyloon?" Lucy wanted to know, causing Berry to cough.

"It means something that belongs to someone," Harry half-supplied and then jutted her chin out again. "And I never stole anything from that witch."

"What did they say she stole?" Sheila wanted to know, stroking the agitated child's hand.

Elias took out his notepad. "A silver music box with a—" He stopped to read from his notebook. "Small figure of a ballerina on the lid. Do you know what they're talking about, Harry?"

After a few minutes, it became clear that she wasn't going to answer, so Berry gave her a semi-playful prod. "Come on, Harry. The sooner we clear this up, the sooner you can go and help Mr. Harker with the milking," she suggested.

Harry was a very smart girl; this had become very clear to everyone, and so, "Yes. I know what she means. But it's mine…ours," she amended as Lucy shot her a look over her shoulder. "My mum gave it to me for safekeeping when she sent us away. It's all she had left of her dad's family when we were bombed out in the Blitz, and she didn't want to risk it being nicked."

"Why would it be stolen?" Elias wanted to know.

"It wasn't a very nice place they put us in after we lost our house," Harry explained.

"I didn't like any of the kids at school," Lucy added. "They thought we was too posh."

Berry thought that was a bit rich, but kept her

thoughts to herself. "So, she gave it to you for safekeeping."

"Yes," Harry agreed.

Elias took a sip from the perpetual cup of tea in front of him before looking at her again, "That's not what these people say."

"Do you have this music box?" Sheila wanted to know.

"Course we do," supplied Lucy, though all could see Harry was annoyed that this information had been given out so quickly. Lucy, however, didn't seem to be aware of this. "Go on, Harry, show them!"

With little choice in the matter, Harry uttered a small growl and then, after shoving her little sister off her lap and telling Berry, "Hold her," she trudged upstairs and, a minute later, reappeared with her rucksack clutched to her chest. Treating Lucy to a frown, which entirely failed to faze her, Harry rummaged around and shortly produced a small newspaper-wrapped package, which she carefully laid on the table.

"Can I?" Elias asked, nodding toward it.

Harry shrugged, which he took for permission, so he pulled it nearer before untying the string securing it. Inside was a small, rectangular silver-colored box, roughly five to six inches long. The sides were plain, though on the lid was the most exquisite little ballerina, posed up on her points, that you could wish for. Lifting it up, Elias searched for and found a hallmark, confirming the item was indeed silver.

"This is beautiful," Sheila told her as Elias passed it to her and then on to Berry, who could only nod in silent wonder.

"It's my mum's…it was my mum's," Harry

corrected herself, "most prized possession, Mrs. Harker…Sheila."

"Can you prove it's yours?" Elias asked her.

"Can they prove it isn't?" Harry shot back. "Possession is nine-tenths of the law," she added.

"I think the law doesn't quite see it like that," Elias replied, though his smile showed he wasn't too annoyed with her.

Berry wondered if there was anything she could do to help. Taking a closer look at the music box, she turned it this way and that, seeing if there could be anything that only someone who had possessed the box and been around it for years would be aware of, but the plain exterior showed no such marks. The bottom, too, bore only the hallmark, and so, with falling hope, she opened the lid. The inside she found to be inlaid with what seemed like red velvet, firmly affixed and therefore unlikely to yield a clue. Upon turning it upside down so she could look inside the lid, her heart skipped a beat. She could make out, for want of a better description, swirly squiggles inside. Holding it close to her nose, she could read the tiny writing.

"Elias," she asked without taking her nose out of the box, "I suppose these people can prove this box is theirs?"

"They say so."

"And they can describe it? In detail? Do they have a photo?"

"I'll be honest and say that I didn't ask if they have a photo, but they did describe it, and that looks like what they described to me."

"What did they say was inscribed inside?"

"Inscribed inside? There's something written?

Where?" Elias asked. He took up his notebook again and, carefully turning each page, he looked through it once more. "They never mentioned anything about an inscription."

Berry turned to where Harry sat with what could only be described as a huge grin. "I'm guessing Harry knows exactly what's inscribed inside."

"*Love of ages past shall never die.*"

Silence prevailed at Harry's words, and as she looked around the room, Berry knew hers weren't the only eyes that had tears in them. Wiping the back of a hand across her eyes, she cleared her throat and suggested to Elias, "I expect they don't know those words."

Elias got to his feet, took the music box from Berry, opened the lid, and squinted to read the inscription himself before, unhesitatingly, he returned the box to Harry and bobbed down to kiss the tops of her and Lucy's heads before telling them, "You keep this safe, young lady. I've a phone call to make, and afterwards, I doubt you'll ever have to worry about this again."

Once Elias had said his goodbyes, Lucy turned her face up to her sister. "Harry. Stop squeezing, you're hurting me."

By way of an answer, Harry shoved her chair back, still with her arms tightly around her younger sister, and stood up. To the amusement of everyone, including Bob, who'd kept quiet, merely keeping in the background, watching proceedings, she then started to dance around the kitchen, laughing her head off.

Only Bob heard the knock at the door, and when no one immediately entered, he got up and went to open it. Waiting in the porch was an RAF pilot. The chap greeted him with a nervous smile.

"Mr. Harker? Flying Officer Dennis Grey," he introduced himself with an outstretched hand, which the farmer took in his larger one, raising an eyebrow. "Um…I'm a friend of Berry's."

"I'm always pleased to meet one of our brave pilots," Bob told him with a welcoming smile and stepped back to allow him entrance. "Come in and take a seat," he invited, just as Harry, Berry, and Sheila whirled past him.

Making a snap decision before he lost his nerve, Bob reached out for his wife's arm on her next pass and, relying very much on instinct, started to slowly and carefully waltz around the room to a tune he hummed out loud. After the initial shock, his wife relaxed into his arms.

With the loss of one of her dance partners, Harry slowed to a halt, and with Lucy between them, leant against Berry to watch the newly loved-up couple. After a minute, two things were obvious. Firstly, Sheila and Bob were off in a world of their own, and secondly, Dennis had the look of someone who'd rather be anywhere than where he was at the moment.

"Come on." Berry grabbed both Harry and Dennis by the hand, pulled them outside, and slowly, and as quietly as she could, closed the door behind her.

As they made their way over to the barn, only Harry noticed that Berry and Dennis were still holding hands, until she went to reach for the door handle, when she held up their entwined hands. She proceeded to go beetroot red and hastily let go, though not before Harry had helped things along by nudging Berry in the ribs.

Remembering what kind of conversation was likely

to take place, Berry turned the younger girl around and swatted her lightly on the bottom. "Off you go and play for a while, but don't be long and don't go far. Bob'll be after you in a while for the milking."

"Can't we come in and sit with you?" Lucy asked.

Berry knelt down so she could speak at Lucy's level. "Not this time, I'm afraid. We've, er, things to discuss which you're a little too young to hear."

Though it looked like Lucy accepted what she'd been told, Harry had a deeply unhappy frown on her face and merely turned on her heel and marched off back toward the farmhouse.

Straightening up, Berry watched the two girls as Harry pulled open the back door and slammed it behind her. Wincing, she turned to where Dennis stood trying to keep a bemused expression from his face. "Oh, dear," she began, "I think I've upset her."

Dennis grabbed her hand and pulled her toward him, and to prevent herself stumbling, she threw her arms around his neck. His promptly went around her waist. "Well, not quite what I was expecting, but I won't look a gift horse in the mouth," he told her.

"Just as well there's no audience," Berry mumbled, aware that her cheeks were reddening up again, though for a completely different reason. Seemingly of their own accord, Berry's hands went up and she ran her fingers through his wavy hair, making it even messier than normal and eliciting a low purr from his throat.

"I wouldn't care if the world was watching right now," he told her, locking his gray eyes which matched perfectly his name, with her blue ones as he lowered his mouth to hers. Tentatively at first, then with increasing pressure as the pleasure of the moment engulfed them, they held each other as tightly as possible, losing themselves in each other before finally breaking apart.

"Well, I was coming to see what had happened to you, Skipper, but I don't think I need to ask."

Reluctantly breaking the kiss, Berry kept her arms around Dennis's neck and looked over her shoulder to where his bomb aimer, Jimmy Dunn, stood in the barn's doorway, hands upon his hips and a smirk upon his face.

"Nice to see that grin again," Dennis announced, taking one of Berry's hands in his and facing him. "Now, if you want to keep the teeth, a little respect for the lady, Jimmy."

"Ah, young love. It does my heart good to see it alive and well," added Jimmy, quickly ducking away from the swat Dennis aimed at him.

Vicky and Sophie closed the barn door and joined the three of them as they made their way toward an RAF Humber car. Opening the rear door, Vicky pulled Sophie onto the back seat after her and then shouted, "Enough, everyone. It's getting late. Let's go down the pub and you can tell us what happened to Ginger."

A very short while later, by which time Marcy had tracked them down to the village pub, the King's Head, everyone sat around the largest table Brian Lynne's drinking establishment could provide.

As village pubs went, the King's Head was on the large side and took up an entire quarter of the square. Built of red brick, it had black beams criss-crossing its frontage, hinting at Elizabethan origins, something which neither Brian nor his redoubtable wife Muriel did anything to dispel, it being good for passing business. Everyone who'd lived in the village all their life knew Brian was a sharp operator and at least a few of the beams may have been added as repairs. Come what may, even without being the only such establishment within ten miles, you were always assured of a warm welcome.

Though the first time the girls had visited the pub, looking around the group, there wasn't a smile present.

Chapter Fourteen

Whilst Dennis and Marcy went over to the bar to get a round in—by general agreement everyone would have a pint of Ginger's favorite bitter—Berry spied a table large enough for the four girls and the three RAF men. Sophie slumped into her wooden seat with her arms tucked into the sleeves of an overlarge pullover, her face as miserable as the day was long. Berry pulled up a chair, sat down, and hooked an arm through her friend's, and momentarily Sophie leant against her and settled her chin on Berry's shoulder.

"You going to be okay, love?" Dennis asked, placing a tray of pints on the table before shifting it over a little so Marcy could add hers.

After waiting a short while, it became clear Sophie wasn't going to answer, so Berry took it upon herself. "She will be," then, upon feeling her friend squeeze her arm, added, hoping she'd got it right, "but let her be for the moment."

With a little scraping, everyone took their places at the table and pulled a pint of bitter toward them, at which point, Dennis got back to his feet and cleared his throat. With glass raised, he began, "Gentlemen, and ladies, I'll keep this simple. Please raise your glasses to our crewmate and friend, Ginger. Ginger, give 'em hell!"

As if they'd done this before—which, Berry mused, they very likely had—the RAF men raised and sank their drinks in one, banging the glasses upside down back on the bare wooden table. With a nod of her head, Marcy, albeit slower, did the same, though she did immediately let out a huge belch which set Dennis, Archie, and Jimmy roaring with laughter.

"He'd have appreciated that," Jimmy told her.

Though neither Berry, Vicky, nor Sophie were able to follow Marcy's lead, the three did their best, and in a couple of minutes, there were seven empty glasses on the table.

"Our turn for a round," Marcy announced, getting to her feet and laying a hand on Dennis's shoulder as he started to protest. "It's not the time for chivalry, Dennis. You can buy as much as you like afterward, but allow me this one." Before he could say anything more, Marcy motioned for Berry to come and give her a hand, and she did so, passing on the business of looking after Sophie to Vicky and Jimmy.

Looming over the bar was a sparsely-haired man in his mid-fifties, who was built like the proverbial outhouse, though his genial smile negated his somewhat scarred visage. Nevertheless, Berry had to fight the impulse to take a step back when she reached the bar where she was treated to the most lopsided smile she'd ever seen. Next thing she knew, the man-mountain dissolved into uncontrollable peals of laughter. From behind him appeared an extremely short lady in a pinny that could have advertised what was on the menu, so long as the only item was tomato soup.

"Take no notice of my Brian, lovey," she told her and backed up her words by slapping him on the backside, not that he appeared to mind or notice.

"What was that you said, my dear?" Brian asked,

turning his head to look down at his wife. When he looked back at the bemused Berry and Marcy, he asked, "Would you be the Land Army girls staying up with old Bob?"

"I beg your pardon!" exclaimed Marcy, looking for all the world as if she'd suffered the worst of insults.

Much to their surprise, Brian seemed to visually sink into himself, and he actually moved so he was behind his much-smaller wife. "I'm…sorry," he stammered out. As his wife squeezed his hand encouragingly, he managed to ask, though both girls could see the effort it took him, "Did I say something wrong?"

Marcy pasted on her best smile and leaned against the bar. Her relaxed posture had the desired effect, and Brian slowly moved out from behind his wife and took up his previous position, though with one hand resting upon a pump handle in what looked like a comfort thing to Berry and Marcy.

"I'm sorry," Marcy began, "I didn't mean to snap. We do live up in Bob and Sheila's barn, but we're actually what are known as Lumberjills." As both publicans gazed at her wonderingly, she added, "We chop down trees."

"Amongst other things," Berry added.

"By all, that's wonderful!" Brian's wife remarked, clapping her hands in delight.

With the ice broken, Marcy placed the drinks order, and whilst Brian started to pull the pints, they introduced themselves. "I'm Muriel," the little lady said, holding out her hand to shake each of the girls'. "You'll have to forgive my Brian there," she told them, elbowing her husband playfully in the ribs. "I love him to death, but he always forgets about introductions."

"I don't," the man in question protested as he placed the last but one pint onto Berry's tray.

"Going senile, too," Muriel added. At that, Brian broke off from his duties, grabbed his wife in his arms and swept her off her feet, and in full view of the lounge bar, which at that moment consisted of the girls and their RAF friends, kissed her passionately full on the lips. He then set her back on her feet and returned to pulling the last pint. Her cheeks flushed and her ample bosom heaving, Muriel told them, "He does have his moments, though."

Marcy chuckled, paid for the drinks, and left Berry at the bar to await the final drink.

"There you are. Berry, was it?" Brian asked as he placed the final pint on her tray.

"That's right," she agreed before Brian nodded his head and strode off into the back of the pub.

"I'm sorry if we upset Brian," Berry took the opportunity of saying.

Muriel glanced over her shoulder before motioning for Berry to lean down a little so she could speak with a little more privacy. "Don't worry, you didn't. Look, you'll have to forgive my Brian. Since he came back from the Western Front, he doesn't react very well to strangers, mood swings, that kind of thing. I've never asked why, but now he knows your faces, he'll be fine with you. Of course, you're welcome any time and, truth be told, I'm a little surprised that we haven't seen you before," she finished with a raised eyebrow.

Berry glanced at where Marcy was looking back and motioned for her to take a seat.

"Yes," she finally answered. "I'm sorry about that. We weren't being unfriendly, I hope you understand, just tired. We're only just becoming used to not being absolutely exhausted when we get back from this job every day, so I do expect we'll be regular visitors from now on."

"That'll be wonderful!" Muriel replied as her husband returned to the bar.

With a grin, Muriel picked up a cloth and began polishing a wine glass. Taking the hint, Berry picked up her tray and made her way back to her friends.

"About time too," Jimmy said, but with a smile as he helped distribute the drinks.

"Sit back down and drink up," Sophie told him, the first words she'd uttered for a while.

Everyone turned to where Sophie had picked up her glass and was holding it before her mouth, albeit without actually drinking, quite obviously to hide some embarrassment at her outburst. Vicky wordlessly persuaded Jimmy to swap seats, and once next to her, she patted her on the knee until Sophie finally took a sip of her second drink. Berry, recognizing the need to take everyone's attention away from her friend, nudged Dennis in the ribs.

"Right, right. Ginger. Are you sure you want to hear this, Sophie?" he asked, his face full of concern as he addressed her.

After clearing her throat, Sophie gripped Vicky's hand, seeking to leech some much needed courage. "I know I didn't know him all that well," she began, her voice a little over a whisper, "but I'd hoped to, I'd really hoped to. So yes, please, Dennis, I hope I'm not being silly, but I need to know what happened."

Dennis looked briefly at Berry, and she gave him a smile of encouragement. Taking a deep steadying breath, he began.

"We were supposed to be on a milk-run—an easy mission," he clarified for the girls—"if such a thing exists, a mine-laying trip. It started out quiet enough, plenty of cloud, nice and dark, exactly as the Met guys said it would be, so we didn't relax as such, but we didn't have any reason to believe there'd be any trouble. When we got over the target, we took some flak, nothing too heavy and far enough away that we barely felt it. We all dropped our mines and then climbed away from the area and set course for home. All the way back home, our main gripe was that we were parched, as Jimmy there had left the top off the vacuum flasks, so the tea had gone cold."

"He's never going to let me forget that," muttered Jimmy, earning him a clip around the ear from Vicky.

"No, I'm not," Dennis agreed, thanking Vicky with a grin. "Anyway, we were lowering the under-carriage when we got hit. A Nazi night fighter had been tailing us, and before we could do anything, he opened fire. Ginger couldn't have felt anything, Sophie," Dennis said turning to her, his voice soft and soothing. "I'm not trying to butter things over, really I'm not. It would have been over in a second." He turned his attention back to the rest of his audience. "We managed to land, but the kite was a write-off and no one could do anything for him."

After a few minutes quiet whilst everyone mulled over what Dennis had just told them, Sophie rose to her feet and leant over Jimmy and Berry to pull Dennis by the lapels toward her. She kissed him on the cheeks and then sat back down with a sigh and with a slight smile upon her lips.

"Thank you, Dennis, for telling us, for telling me." Taking up her pint, she got back to her feet and raised her glass, "Ginger! We won't forget you!"

Chapter Fifteen

"And you're sure she's a good mouser?"

Berry eyed the coal-black cat Bob was holding out.

"Elias swears blind that she comes from very good mousing stock, love," he informed her, hoping the young woman wouldn't spot that he had the fingers of his spare hand crossed behind his back.

Said cat, to Berry's first impression, didn't look up to the job. She (Bob assured her the cat was a she) was letting herself hang in Bob's hands like a rag doll, four thin paws clawing at the air every now and again. The brown eyes seemed to be concentrating on Berry, whose own face couldn't hide her skepticism.

"Just how old is she?"

Bob turned the cat around so they were nose to nose and was rewarded with a raspy tongue licking his chin. The cat proceeded to purr and grabbed one of Bob's wrists between front paws, and the farmer couldn't help the wry grin that came to his face. He'd just placed the cat upon his shoulder when the kitchen door banged open.

In strode Sheila with what could only be described as a miniature tiger gripped tightly in her outstretched arms. Spittle was spraying from his open mouth, which displayed fangs that belied his size. He was only a little larger that the black one that was now curled around Bob's neck, but his ferocious attitude made him seem much bigger. At seeing the other cat, claws which looked like they could cut air sprang out and he started squirming this way and that, determined to escape from Sheila's hands.

"Aww. 'Oo's a cute liddle puddy cat," Sheila cooed.

Somewhat to everyone's surprise, the ginger tabby stopped hissing and spitting and turned to stare straight into Sheila's face. The kindly woman's face drained of all color, and she promptly dropped the cat.

This turned out to be a mistake, as it swiftly launched itself at a frozen-to-the-spot Bob. Using his claws, he made his way up Bob's dungarees, leaving obvious holes where his claws dug in for purchase, and upon reaching his chest, hung there, eyes blazing and emitting a deep throaty growl that raised the hackles of the little female. She launched herself off Bob's shoulders, aiming for the open window behind him where she disappeared from view, to be closely followed by the tiger as he used Bob's head as a springboard. Then came a loud yelp in a young girl's voice, and a second later, in walked Harry, with a tearful Lucy rubbing her arm close behind.

"Can someone tell me what the hell that was?" Harry demanded as she led her sister toward the sink. "Something landed on Lucy's arm, and she's now got these deep cuts," she added, holding out her sister's bleeding arm where a couple of inch-long parallel cuts were evident.

Sheila's hands flew to her mouth, and she swiftly made her way to the sink and took the arm in her hands. "I'm so sorry, my dear. This is all my fault."

As his wife proceeded to clean the wounds, Bob took a seat at the table and asked, "Forgive the language, but to echo Harry; what the hell was that?"

Sheila kept her head down as she ran Lucy's arm under the tap. "Berry and Sophie mentioned they had a mouse problem, so I asked around the village to see if anyone knew where I could get a good cat."

"Where did you get that one from? The London zoo?" asked Harry, who'd taken a seat whilst Sheila took care of patching up her sister.

Bob laughed at this and nudged Harry in the ribs. "I didn't think they were allowed to keep animals *that* dangerous!"

Sheila pulled up a chair and sat Lucy down on her lap with a towel pressed against the injured arm. Lucy herself hadn't shed one tear, despite the iodine, and gave the impression that she now considered the whole incident a bit of an adventure. Indeed, she was paying close attention to the conversation. "Yes, Mrs. Harker. What was that?"

"Just a cat that Paula said she couldn't take care of any longer."

"Not bloody surprised," Bob declared.

"Could you get me a bandage from the bathroom, please, Berry?" Sheila asked.

"What's its name?" Lucy wanted to know.

"I believe Paula called him Pudding."

Harry promptly fell off her chair from laughter, eventually managing to look up at where Sheila had, likely at having to say out loud the ridiculous name, gone bright red with embarrassment. "There's no way that ball of fur is a Pudding!" She sat for a moment, stroking her chin, before looking up. "Lucy, what do you think he should be called?"

Berry came back in and handed a bandage to Sheila,

who took the towel away from Lucy's arm, revealing that the cuts had stopped bleeding, though they were a nasty shade of red. As she started to bandage her up, Lucy replied, "I like Percy," she decided.

Bob got to his feet, clapped the girl lightly on the shoulder and made for the back door. "You're the one that got hurt, so I don't see why not."

"But why have we now got two cats?" Harry wanted to know.

"Sophie and me woke up to a mouse sitting on my chest," Berry explained.

"They're mousers!" Lucy let out, hopping off Sheila's lap now her arm had been bandaged but not forgetting to kiss the woman's cheek in thanks, which brought a delighted smile. "Thank you, Mrs. Harker."

Bob shook his head. "Well, Percy," he tried out the name, "looks like he's up to the job. Not too sure about mine, though."

"Was that the small black thing Percy was chasing?" Harry asked.

"Aye, got a feeling I've wasted my money there," he muttered, running a hand through his hair and addressing his wife. "Guess it's our own fault for not talking to each other before going to get one, eh? We're now stuck with two cats!"

****

The girls were all curled up in bed early that night.

"So far as our first time down the local pub's concerned," Berry announced, pulling on a tatty pullover she used to keep out the night's chill as she sat cross-legged on her bed, "I don't think we could have given Ginger a better send off. Mind you," she added, kneading her temple, "I don't want to see another pint of bitter for a while."

"Poor Ginger," muttered Sophie to the world at general.

Marcy came and sat down on the end of her bed, feeling the younger woman twitch her toes out of the way of being crushed just in time. "You going to be all right?"

Sophie worked a small smile onto her face and rubbed her nose with a tissue before answering. "Am I being silly?"

"Silly?" Marcy asked.

"It's not like I knew him that well, so, silly, yes."

Before answering, Marcy tilted her head to one side. "Perhaps," she told her honestly, "but let me tell you a little story. I don't know how much it'll help, but it is relevant and may give you some perspective."

"Yes! I love a good story!" Vicky announced from her bed. As normal, even though barely past ten of the evening, Vicky was curled up under her blankets, and so her voice had an echoing quality to it.

"I don't think it's going to be that kind of a story, Vicky," Berry advised.

Vicky paused before replying, "Forgive me if I snore then, all!"

Sophie threw a pillow at her, hitting her somewhere on the bottom, she thought, "What do you mean, *if*?"

"Now the heckler's been dealt with," Sophie decided, turning her attention back to Marcy. "Whenever you're ready."

"I've told you about my Matthew?" Sophie nodded. "Well, how long do you think we've been married?"

"I couldn't begin to guess," Sophie admitted after a moment's thought. "A while?"

With a wry smile, Marcy replied, "Come November

the twenty-ninth, it'll be three years."

"That," Berry declared, "I didn't expect."

"What are you saying? You thought I'd been married for as long as Sheila and Bob!" Marcy declared, though both Berry and Sophie caught the teasing note in her voice.

"Longer!" cried Vicky from her refuge.

"Could you throw another pillow at Trouble there?" Marcy asked Berry, who went one better and instead launched herself at her unsuspecting friend, proceeding to smack her, quite hard, on the bottom.

"Ouch!" the younger girl yelled, squirming to get out from under her blankets and away from the playful attack, though only managing to fall onto the floor and become tangled up.

Berry left her where she was, sat back on her bed, and placed a spare pillow on her lap in case she needed to defend herself.

They all watched Vicky struggle to untangle herself, which, accompanied by much swearing and huffing and puffing, she managed, to be greeted by three sets of identical grins. "Thanks for the help," she muttered, throwing herself down next to Berry, ignoring her paper curlers which were mostly hanging off, or torn.

"Hush you, and listen," Berry told her, ruffling her hair and making matters worse, before pulling her close so Vicky's head was resting on her shoulder.

"Thank you," Marcy told her before settling back onto her bed and making herself as comfortable as possible. "What I'm going to tell you three is something I've not told anyone, not even my Matt. Understood?"

"We do, don't we, girls," Berry agreed, making a point at looking at both Sophie and Vicky, who both nodded, before turning back to where Marcy was waiting.

"This is a love story, Sophie," Marcy began, making a point of addressing her words to the girl who needed them most. "An unconventional love story, but still, a love story. My Matt, he had a brother called Dennis. He was ten years older than me, but whenever he came back for holidays, I'd hang around him like a lapdog. How Matt put up with me, I've no idea." She chuckled. "I was too young to know what love was, but Dennis, unfortunately, knew where my affections lay. When Dennis went back to school, Matt acted like nothing had happened and we became best friends again, or at least I did. Matt didn't tell me at the time, but whilst I was pining after his brother, that's when he fell in love with me."

"Oww! What the hell?" Sophie yelled, breaking the spell Marcy's story had woven over them. "Will you…gerrof…me!"

Everyone's heads snapped around to find Midnight, as they now called the black cat, had jumped onto Sophie's chest and was presently ignoring the girl's attempts to prise her off. Lucy had named her this because, in the dark, she was very difficult to spot. She'd just used that to her advantage to find a nice warm spot to sleep.

"I'd leave her be, if I were you," Berry advised as Midnight closed her eyes and let out a deep sigh. "I reckon she's in for the night."

With one more tug to her blanket, pointless because the kitten had dug in her claws, Sophie nodded. "Sorry about the interruption, Marcy."

"Anyway, back and forth, this went on for a few

years, and then, along came the Spanish flu of 1918. He may have been a big, strong lad, but it didn't give a damn. Old, young, weak, or strong, it took them all. Dennis fought, but once it got its hands on you, it usually never let go. That was the first funeral I'd been to. Somehow, and I'm still not sure how, Matt ended up taking care of me more than I did of him. I don't know if that was when I transferred my affections from his brother to him, but I began to see him in a different light."

"Hold on," Vicky said, holding up her hand. "Did you have a twenty-year engagement?"

Marcy chuckled. "Not quite, more of a very long friendship, which eventually turned into love. Whether this makes it stronger than what you feel for Ginger, I don't know. I can't answer that for you, Sophie. There are many types of love, and despite what you may think now, you will love again. Matt knew what I felt for Dennis and, don't forget, this was his brother, so it wasn't easy for him. Take life one day at a time, especially now, and trust your feelings. When you're ready, you'll know."

Sophie was now leaning over Midnight, and if it wasn't for the fact the kitten's body was moving as it breathed, you'd think the girl had squeezed it to death. "And now? For now, what do I do?"

Unnoticed by Sophie, Marcy had a mischievous twinkle in her eye. "Now? Now, you trust us to look after you," she told her before launching herself onto the younger girl's bed, which gave an ominous creak. "In the meantime, come on, girls," she announced, making a grab behind her. "Pillow fight!"

Chapter Sixteen

"Yoo-hoo!" Sheila cried as she rapped on the barn door. "Everyone decent?"

"Come in!" Marcy cried. "We're all girls here!"

Sheila entered to find both Berry and Vicky standing over Sophie with pillows raised above their head.

"My, can anyone join in?" Sheila asked, her arms full of fresh blankets and sheets.

Putting down her burden on an upturned packing case, she grabbed the pillow on top and leaped with surprising agility at Vicky, raising the pillow as she went and bringing it down with a dull thump on the girl's head. Seeing an opening, Berry and Marcy joined in from either side of Sheila, driving Vicky back toward the bales of hay toward the rear half of the barn, until the backs of her knees hit a bale and she fell flat on her back, shrieking with laughter as pillow after pillow came down upon her.

"A bit of help here, partner!" Vicky managed to shout before taking a well-placed pillow to the face from Sheila.

From behind the four, Sophie prised herself off her bed, made all the more difficult as she'd been laughing so hard she'd lost her voice and tears were coursing down her face, only to fall back, narrowly missing Midnight, who'd taken up residence on her pillow. She managed to crank an eye open to survey the scene and grabbed Midnight into a tight hug against her neck. The kitten let out a single cry of protest before settling in and falling back asleep.

"Not a chance! You're on your own."

"Turncoat!" Vicky yelled as she took a pillow to each side of her head. Collapsing back onto her behind, she fell onto the bale of hay just in time to receive a precisely aimed pillow to the chin from Sheila. Legs kicking in the air were all anyone could see of young Vicky before she tossed her own pillow over the heads of her attackers. "I surrender! No more!"

Leaving Marcy and Berry to help their friend up, Sheila traipsed back to sit on the end of Sophie's bed, reaching out to give the sleeping kitten a scratch behind the ears.

"I wondered where she'd disappeared to. Percy refused to come in when I called him and last Bob saw him, he was chasing what he swears was a mouse across the courtyard."

"Isn't he a bit young to be a mouser?" Berry asked, throwing her pillow back onto her bed and flopping down next to it.

"Well, the people I bought him off said he caught his first mouse at three months. He's coming up to eighteen, so he barely counts as a kitten now. It's more habit than anything else for us to call him that. Same with Midnight there," Sheila informed them, removing her finger from out of the black kitten's mouth as she yawned, nearly snapping shut on the end, "she's about the same age."

"Not sure how much of a mouser she's going to be," Sophie ventured. "She seems to be a very good sleeper, though."

Sheila regarded the kitten that was still wrapped around Sophie's neck and was uttering wee kitten snores as she slept. "You may be right. Still, let's wait and see."

"What brought you to this den of pillow-fight cheats?" Vicky asked, rubbing the slightly red end of her nose and glaring a little at Sheila.

"First," Sheila said, "I do hope your nose doesn't hurt too much. I couldn't resist it. It's years since I've had a good pillow fight!"

"You're very good," Marcy praised the farmer's wife.

"Put that down to beating the odd carpet," Sheila told her.

"But three against one?" Vicky pointed out. "Hardly fair."

"Wouldn't have been half as much fun otherwise," Marcy told her.

Vicky folded her arms and pouted. "Fine, but next time, you get Sophie. She's bloody useless!"

"Hey!" Sophie protested, though not too loudly as she didn't want to wake Midnight, and she was smiling as she said so.

"Anyway, at least it's got you smiling," Berry noted.

Sheila frowned, turning her head toward Sophie, who was smiling as she gently stroked Midnight's head. "Why shouldn't she?"

Marcy raised her eyebrows at Sophie, who shrugged her shoulders and answered for herself, "A friend, someone I'd hoped to get to know, was killed. We," she looked up at all her friends, "only found out today."

"I'm sorry," Sheila told her, reaching out to squeeze and pat her hand. "That's tough. If you don't mind my asking, what happened?"

134

Sophie opened her mouth, and when no sound came out, Vicky answered for her. "He was the tail-gunner of a crew we got to know in York. A Nazi fighter killed him as they got back from a mission."

With a sigh, Sheila got to her feet and kissed Sophie on the top of her head, "I'm sorry. There'll be others, my love. Try not to dwell on it too much." She went and stood next to where she'd left the blankets. "Here are some fresh blankets and sheets for you. Tomorrow's washing day, so leave your dirty ones on the ends of your beds, and Harry and me'll pick them up in the morning. Oh, and you lot, keep an eye on her." She motioned toward Sophie.

"Don't worry," Sophie replied, "they are, and I hope Vicky won't mind my saying, seeing her beaten up by you lot has done me the world of good! Good night."

As Sheila closed the barn door, she had to force herself to keep going, as Vicky was sneaking up behind Marcy with her pillow raised, seemingly intent on exacting revenge.

****

Bob was waiting for his wife when she came back into the kitchen. As she sat down, he reached up and plucked a strange object from her curiously disheveled hair. "How come you've a feather in your hair? Last time I checked, we didn't have any chickens."

Sheila took the feather from her husband's fingers and only then became aware of a smell which hadn't been there before she'd left for the barn. Eyes dancing, she searched the kitchen until her eyes settled on a package wrapped in newspaper laid in the sink. Twiddling the feather between her fingers, she stepped toward it, lowered her head for a closer look, and then jerked back upright as if she'd been shot.

"What, in the name of all that's holy, is that?" she demanded, hastily stepping back to stand by Bob's side and gripping his hand tightly.

"That," he replied, unable to keep a look of distaste off his face, "is a present from a sick mind."

Taking up a wooden spoon from the table, Bob gingerly gave the package a prod before taking his wife in his arms. The rediscovered intimacy between the two was such that he was acutely aware of the slight flinch Sheila gave occasionally when he gathered her in his arms, however since he'd been making a point of doing so at each and every opportunity, he was noticing a decrease in her hesitation. Glancing down into her face, he could swear there were less lines there than before the Lumberjills had turned up. Well, they may have caused him some havoc at first, but he now realized he had a lot to thank them for.

"But why would anyone send us a fish? Let alone one that's gone off!" Sheila asked, moving her head so she could look over at the sink. She felt him take a deep breath, before releasing her from his embrace and gently pushing her down into a chair. His brow furrowed, he took an envelope from his pocket and laid it before her. He took a single piece of paper out and laid it before her. "Read that."

A few seconds later, Sheila dropped the paper onto the table, her face drained of all color. "Oh, Bob. Who'd write such a thing?"

Open on the table before them, in large, messy block letters the letter declared—

You don't deserve children!

Chapter Seventeen

"Has anyone else noticed Sheila's been a bit…"

"A bit, what?" Marcy asked Berry, taking her pencil from between her teeth.

Leaning on her axe handle, Berry wiped the sweat from her forehead and, seeing she now had the full attention of not only Marcy, but also Sophie and Vicky, looked into the distance, even though there wasn't much to see as the fog had yet to lift that morning, before answering.

"A bit, off. These last couple of days, she seems to have lost some of that sparkle she'd had, especially since taking in Harry and Lucy."

Straightening up, Vicky scratched the back of her head with the point of her brother's knife, snapped it shut, and took out her thermos flask from beneath the cat lying asleep in the front basket of her bicycle.

"Do you think that's going to become a habit?" Sophie asked, giving Midnight a scratch behind his ears. The kitten merely leaned into the scratch before turning onto its back and proceeding to snore away once more.

Vicky tucked a gingham tea cloth around the sleeping kitten and unscrewed the lid of her thermos flask. She took a sip of her tea before replying, "Midnight joining us, you mean? You know, I think it probably is."

"Isn't he supposed to be a mouser, though?" Marcy

asked, unable to prevent herself from reaching out a hand and stroking the kitten's jet-black coat.

All their heads turned as the kitten in question chose that moment to open his mouth wide, yawning and half meowing at the same time, before settling back in. Chuckling to herself, Vicky turned to face her friends. "I think Bob and Sheila are going to have to leave that to Percy."

"I hope he's not going to make a habit of dropping what he catches below the head of my bed, though," Sophie remarked with a slight shudder. "I nearly stepped in what I think were some mouse guts this morning."

"Aww, I think that's cute!" Marcy piped up.

Sophie accepted the thermos mug from Vicky, taking a sip of her friend's tea before saying, "Really?"

"He's only bringing you a present," Marcy tried to reason with her.

"It's a little difficult to accept such a *present*, at silly o'clock in the morning, Marcy," Sophie told her friend, shuddering again at the memory. "Now, if it were a pair of silk stockings…" she mused.

Berry gave her a brief hug of sympathy. "Well, I've never been around cats before. Father didn't allow pets," she admitted with a shrug, "but if that's what they do when they love someone, I'd hate to be someone they hated!"

"Do you think she regrets getting the cats?" Sophie asked.

Berry shook her head. "No, I don't think that's it. We had them before she got this way." She was interrupted by the loudest snore any of them had ever heard come from a kitten, and she laughed. "Mind you, she may change her mind if she sees this one's idea of work."

"Speaking of work," Marcy announced, clapping both Berry and Vicky on their shoulders, "break's over. Let's get those axes back to work. Those trees aren't going to fell themselves."

A couple of hours later, everyone had worked up a good sweat. The pile of pine trees lying on the edge of the forest was slowly growing, now that the ground had been cleared enough to allow the real work to begin.

"So," Vicky grunted as she prised her axe free and prepared to swing again, "do you know when you'll see Archie again?"

Taken a little off guard, Marcy let her own axe drop. Strictly speaking, it wasn't her job to help cut down trees, as the Measurer, but the girls were used to her pitching in, as she told them it helped her think. None of them could figure out the logic behind this. The racket the axe head made each time it struck the tree trunk was, in everyone's opinion except Marcy's, more than enough to numb the senses. Still, the help was welcome, as they were short on numbers despite being joined by a new girl that morning.

Marcy spat on her hands, rubbed them together and, hefting her axe, swung it against her mark. "I think," she said once her breath came back, "that's a moot point. Married, remember," she took out the chain she wore around her neck to show her wedding ring.

"But he's kind of nice, and your other half's not around," Vicky pointed out, though when she saw her friend's disapproving frown, she clammed up. "Sorry, sorry. I wasn't thinking."

Marcy struck the tree twice more—with considerable force, Vicky noted, gulping—before replying firmly, "No, you weren't." In a kinder voice, she added, "However, I hope he'll be a friend. We could all do with as many friends as we can get these days. Which lets me ask about you and…Jimmy, isn't it?"

One good thing about all the physical exertion was, as you were red in the face much of the time, no one could tell if you were embarrassed. Vicky was extremely glad of this, though she gave herself away by not being able to meet Marcy's gaze.

"Hark at them! Time enough to chat, rather than work!"

The unexpected comments caused both Marcy and Vicky to look around for their source. Only when they'd both turned around did they find they were about fifty yards from a wire fence, and they had an audience. Leaning upon a fence post was a girl not much older than Vicky, with a colleague leaning upon her shoulder. Both were wearing dungarees, with shirtsleeves rolled up past their elbows.

Marcy laid her axe on the ground and, putting her pencil back behind an ear, strode toward them, Vicky close behind, though she hadn't put her axe down, something Marcy discovered only when she stopped before the two Land Girls.

"Do you two have a problem?" Marcy asked, making sure to lace her voice with as much authority as she could. She wasn't looking for an argument, but she'd become fiercely defensive of her girls. The girl leaning upon the wooden post straightened up, even as the one who'd been leaning on her shoulder took a couple of steps back. Perhaps they recognized the authority Marcy exuded. She concentrated her attention on the one who was now leaning forward, hands on hips, eyes flashing.

"No," said the one who'd stepped back and gripped her friend's shoulder. "Come on, Sal."

It didn't appear Sal was interested in being sensible, though, as she shook her friend's hand off. "No! What makes 'em so bloody posh, eh?"

"Posh. What the hell you on about?" Vicky asked from by Marcy's side, casually swinging her axe back and forth. Marcy gripped Vicky's arm. She'd told her girls many a time, the last thing you should be with an axe is casual. "Sorry, Marcy," Vicky said, though she didn't let go of the handle.

Marcy turned her attention back to where this Sal person was still glaring at the two of them. "Yes, as my friend asked. Can we help you?"

If it were possible, Sal the Land Girl seemed to become more agitated at the calm way Marcy put her question. "Yes, you can bloody help me!" she shouted, making as to step over the fence, only her friend held her back, ignoring the slaps on her hands the action earned her. "Why wouldn't your lot take me, eh? Here I am, stuck on a farm, earning a pittance and working my ass off! Let me go, Tina!"

"I'm sorry about her," Tina told them, not letting go of her angry friend.

"Don't you apologize for me!" Sal snapped, still trying to break free.

Marcy thought for a few seconds. "Let me get this right, Sal, is it? You weren't accepted into the Timber Corps, and so you're taking out your anger on us?"

The logic of Marcy's statement brought Sal up short, or at least she stopped struggling against her friend. Her mouth opened twice without any words coming out. Finally, in a somewhat muted voice, she told her, "Well, yes."

"What a bloody stupid thing to say!" Vicky announced, not really helping matters, as this caused Sal to struggle once more to break her friend's grip upon her.

"I'll kill her!" Sal blurted out. "Let me go! I'm going to bloody kill her!"

Marcy saw Vicky drop her axe and began to breathe a sigh of relief which proved a waste of time before it had barely begun, as instead, Vicky pulled out her brother's knife from a pocket and stepping in front of Marcy, opened it and held it up before her.

Whilst Tina had her hands literally full trying to stop her friend from climbing over the fence, Marcy tried to decide whether she needed to do the same with Vicky. However, an ear-bending shriek of pain brought everything to a stop and everyone's heads turned each and every way to try and find where the disquieting sound had come from.

"Marcy!"

Upon hearing her name, Marcy's head turned toward where she thought Berry, Sophie, and the new girl, whose name she couldn't recall, were working.

"Marcy!"

That was definitely Berry's voice. Without another thought, Marcy took to her heels, following the continued call of her name, certain something very bad had happened. Vicky, with a last glance at the two Land Girls, both staring at where Marcy had disappeared into the forest yet making no further moves, put her knife away and stooped to pick up her axe.

"What's happened?" This was Tina, obviously the more sensible of the two, Vicky thought.

"Not a clue." Vicky shrugged and then, all the while

fighting the urge to take off after her friend, forced herself to stop and think on what could have happened. She directed her words to Tina. "Look, do you have access to a telephone?"

Surprisingly, Sal replied. Perhaps the seriousness in Vicky's voice brought her back to reason. "There's one up at the farm."

Vicky shook her head a little, determined not to over-think things. "How long would it take one of you to get to it?"

"I'm the faster of us," Tina declared.

Another shriek of pain echoed around the forest, and all three girls couldn't help the shudders which coursed through their bodies. Vicky couldn't stay any longer and turned back to the two waiting girls, decision made. "I've got to go and find out what's happened, but going on what we're hearing, I've a feeling we're going to need an ambulance."

At this, Sal turned to her friend. "I'll go and wait by the phone. If you need one, come back and tell my mate Tina here. She'll be with me in a couple of minutes."

Yet another howl of pain made up Vicky's mind. "You know where we are?" she asked, getting nods from the two. "Right. Phone for an ambulance anyway. I'm pretty sure the one at the saw mill is out of order," and not wanting to waste another breath, she nodded, hefted her axe over a shoulder, and took to her heels in the same direction as Marcy had gone. The forest they were working wasn't large, but the part where they hadn't cleared the ground made the going slower than she'd have liked, if she didn't want to break an ankle. Brushing aside some branches, she found herself in a very small clearing. Before her was a sight no one and nothing could have prepared her for.

Lying on the ground was the new girl—Vicky couldn't remember her name—an axe embedded deep into her lower left leg! On either side of her were Berry and Marcy, both trying to hold her as still as possible with one arm, whilst using the other to clamp down either side of a blood-soaked piece of cloth around the axe. Behind her an ashen-faced Sophie had one arm around the stricken girl's chest, with her other wrist clamped between the girl's teeth. Blood was pouring from where those teeth were dug in, yet not a whimper escaped Sophie's lips. Swallowing hard, Vicky dropped to her knees and forced herself to look at the grisly wound. Blood was rapidly soaking through the cloth of what used to be a jumper and spreading around her friends' fingers. Everyone knew better than to remove the axe no matter the pain the girl must be in.

Quickly, Vicky took off her own jumper and, as gently yet as quickly as possible whilst being careful not to touch the axe, she wrapped over the one in place and tied off the arms. Swallowing the bile threatening to burst from her throat, she looked up into the girl's pain-filled eyes.

"The telephone's broken," Marcy muttered through clenched teeth, looking up at Vicky, who gave a nearly imperceptible nod, knowing she could only mean the one at the saw mill and that she'd guessed right.

"It's going to be all right, I promise." She brushed the damp hair from the girl's eyes and leaned close, praying she was right. "Keep breathing. An ambulance is on the way. You're going to be all right."

Getting to her feet, Vicky took a deep breath and looked at her friends. She could see they were quite plainly scared, yet also that they were all determined to stay with their stricken friend and help her through what was a terrible experience.

"Stay with her. I've got to make certain it knows where we are."

With one last look over her shoulder, Vicky took a deep breath and turned and ran as fast as her legs would take her, praying the Land Girls would keep to their promise.

Chapter Eighteen

The ambulance disappeared down the road, bearing to the hospital the new girl, who at least had managed to stammer out her name, Elaine Swallow. The mood of those left in the forest was subdued, to say the least.

'Do you think she'll be all right?' Sophie croaked, absently rubbing her wrist in its sling.

No one answered.

No one was capable of saying anything.

For long, tense minutes, everyone left lying on the forest floor seemed to be concentrating on simply breathing, in and out, in and out, trying to come to terms with the harrowing ordeal everyone had been through. Even the birds were silent, as if they too sensed what had happened and didn't want to upset anyone by breaking out into song. By silent agreement, the remaining Lumberjills and the two Land Girls were as far away from the too-large bloodstain on the forest floor as they could comfortably get whilst remaining in a tight group.

Eventually, someone coughed, and then again, until they were able to find their voice. Typically, Marcy was the first to recover her wits. Running her fingers through her now not-quite blonde hair, she looked around the clearing, taking in where Vicky and Berry were leaning up against each other's shoulders and Sophie was flat on her back, now scratching her bandaged arm. Her gaze passed over Sal and Tina without really seeing them, before she came back to the two.

With visible effort, she pushed herself to her feet and went the few steps until she was standing over them before flopping back down to the ground beside them. Sal moved a little away before coming up against her friend. Marcy put as kind a smile as she could muster on her tired, somewhat blood-smeared face. "From what I can gather, Elaine has the two of you to thank for getting help to us so quickly."

The elder of the two opened her mouth, but the younger of them, Sally, the one who'd berated Marcy earlier, spoke first, quickly, her words almost running into one, as if she believed that if she didn't get them out, she wouldn't be able to.

"I'm sorry! For what I said, earlier, I mean. I didn't mean it—well, I did, or thought I did, until we saw…"

Perhaps the possibility she was about to recount what she'd seen when the two Land Girls, aided by Vicky, had led the ambulance to the scene caused her to stop? For whatever reason, she couldn't continue and instead, buried her head in her friend's neck. The one called Tina cleared her throat and continued.

"She is," she began, stroking her friend's hair as Sal sniffed into her shoulder, "about being sorry."

Marcy waved away her apologies. "I'm sure there's a story there, and perhaps we can talk about it sometime, but now's not that time." She shuffled a little closer, gently laying a hand upon Sal's back and giving her a gentle rub. "Sal, or Sally?"

"Sal," she snuffled, turning her head to face Marcy and mustering a weak smile. "Please, just Sal."

Marcy smiled back. "Sal it is. And, you're Tina?" A nod of confirmation allowed Marcy to take both girls by their hands. "Well, Tina, Sal, thank you for all you've done. I don't like to think what could have happened if you hadn't been around."

Unseen by the three, Sophie, Vicky, and Berry had sidled up to join them. Unplanned, yet all the more special for that, the three Lumberjills flung themselves upon Marcy and their new friends. It proved impossible to tell one voice from the other, as everyone was speaking at once. Finally, and with much sniffing and wiping of noses, everyone gradually broke apart, though more than one pair of hands were still being held.

"Is she going to be all right?" Tina echoed Sophie's earlier words.

By unspoken agreement, all heads turned to face Marcy, who took a few needed seconds before telling them, "The doctor thinks so, though…though he's not certain they'll be able to save her foot."

Vicky let out a squeak and buried her face in her hands. Berry immediately flung her arms around her friend, while Marcy threw a sympathetic look at the pair before addressing Sal and Tina once more.

"Whatever the outcome, your actions have given her a chance, a chance she probably wouldn't have had if you hadn't been around. So let's forget what happened earlier." Marcy looked at her watch. "We're going to call it a day. I don't believe anyone"—she passed her gaze over her friends—"is in any fit state to do any more work today. Girls, put everything away that doesn't need to come back to the farm with us, please." She turned back to Sal and Tina. "And the two of you? You're working on the farm on the far side of the forest. Are you billeted there too?"

"The barn's a little drafty," Tina volunteered, "but,

yes, we're staying there."

"Excellent!" Berry declared, guessing where Marcy was going with this. "That must be the next farm over from where we're staying. Do the names Bob and Sheila Harker mean anything to you?"

The girls looked at each other, before an expression of dawning comprehension appeared between them. "I think the Robinsons have mentioned neighbors called Harker."

"In that case," Marcy said, "perhaps you'd join us tonight at the King's Head? I think we could all do with a drink."

The growing bonhomie was interrupted by a shadow looming over the group.

"Pardon me for being a nuisance, but before anyone goes anywhere, I need a few words."

Looming over them was the portly, kindly visage of Sergeant Elias Duncan, and they scrambled to their feet. Sophie needed Berry's help to stand and indeed required her friend's aid to stay upright, as she'd turned pale and was scratching at her bandage more than ever, where blood was now staining the surface, though she seemed unaware of this.

"What can we do for you, Sergeant?" Berry asked, all her attention on the policeman, idly wondering if he'd been as busy before their little group had entered his no-longer-quiet patch.

Everyone waited whilst he took out his notebook from his top pocket, licked the tip of his pencil as if he were some detective rather than a retired country policeman who'd been called back to the uniform. When he was ready, he wiped his hand across his brow and opened his mouth.

"Sorry to hold up your plans. I won't keep you any longer than needed. Now, I got a telephone call from the hospital when they sent the ambulance out." He briefly glanced around to make certain he had everyone's attention. Apart from one of them scratching away at a slightly bloody bandage, he was satisfied he did. "Right, Berry, you I know, of course. I'll take down everyone else's names shortly. In the meantime, can someone tell me exactly what happened to…" He paused to flip his notepad back a page or two. "Miss Elaine Swallow? I hear she's got some kind of leg injury?"

When this statement was met with silence, Elias cleared his throat, his experience telling him he'd badly understated what had happened. On Berry's shoulder, Sophie continued to work at the bandage, tears were now leaking down her face. The kindly gentleman in him quickly won over his police duties, and he swiftly tucked his notebook away and knelt down before the distraught girl.

"Berry, this is…"

Also aware her friend was in a bad way now, Berry told him, "This is Sophie. She was with Elaine when the axe rebounded off the tree."

"Oh, bloody hell," Elias couldn't help uttering, his imagination supplying the unnecessary images.

All at once, Sophie began to talk, as if the words which tumbled out of her mouth needed to find their way into the world. "It all happened so quickly! I couldn't do anything to stop it. The axe hit the tree and it just…it just…it just rebounded back and hit her leg! There was blood everywhere, and she was screaming…and I was screaming!"

"Sophie!" Marcy appeared next to them and took

hold of the hand which was scratching away at the bandage, forcing her to stop harming herself. "Give me your hand, honey, please. That's it, nice and gentle." Whilst keeping her gaze upon the poor girl, she told the policeman, "Elias, this isn't the time. It's Saturday tomorrow, and after today, we're not working the weekend, so come to the farm around midday."

"But I need to get a statement!"

Vicky stepped in front of him, with the Land Girls taking up stations to either side of the two, as Berry told Elias in no uncertain terms, "Marcy's right, Elias. See this?" She briefly uncovered Marcy's hand from the bloody bandage. "Not only did Sophie provide immediate and possibly lifesaving first aid to Elaine, but she also kept a level head by not trying to take out the axe. She got these wounds by allowing the poor girl to clamp her teeth down upon her wrist, to help with the agony Elaine was in so, no more talking. We need to get Sophie home." She nodded her head over Elias's shoulder. "I see you've got a car. Please take off your policeman's uniform for a while and take me and Sophie back to the farm. That's all right, isn't it, Marcy?"

Unable to find her voice, Marcy nodded and wiped her face with the hand which had been on Sophie's arm, unwittingly spreading her friend's blood on her cheeks and nose.

Realizing this was the right thing to do, Elias helped Sophie to his car, gently guiding both girls onto the rear seats.

"We'll see you in a bit!" Berry called out the window as Elias turned the car around and pulled away.

Once they were out of sight, Marcy turned to those left behind. "Sorry, girls." She addressed Sal and Tina.

"I don't think the pub'll happen tonight."

Sal shrugged her shoulders but replied, "Probably for the best. How about tomorrow evening? We can bring a few bottles over to your farm and, who knows, maybe we'll know more about Elaine by then. You girls need to look after Sophie and, hopefully, she'll be feeling a bit better by then. I also feel the need to apologize to everyone again for my behavior, and perhaps even explain things."

"You don't have to do that—apologize, that is," Marcy told her.

"Yes, I do," Sal objected, "for me."

"Hey," piped up Vicky, "so long as she brings around some bottles, I'll hear her out."

Tina threw an arm around her friend's shoulder, shaking her head, though with a smile on her face for the first time since the accident had happened. "All right, we'll be there about four, but you don't want to let this one here get talking. If she's a drink inside her, she sometimes doesn't know when to stop."

"That's okay," Vicky replied, "if she gets too mouthy, we've a nice cold stream out the back of the farm we can throw her in."

****

"Sophie!"

"Sophie!"

Marcy and Vicky burst through the kitchen door, leaving their axes and other tools in a pile outside, where Percy proceeded to sniff around before deciding there wasn't anything of interest and going off into the fields for an evening's mousing. Midnight raised an eyelid from where she was still sleeping in the basket of Marcy's bicycle, then went back to sleep.

"In here!" Sheila's voice yelled from behind the closed lounge door.

Two seconds later, Vicky and Marcy both tried to get through the door at the same time. The scene which met them was, fortunately, much calmer than either girl had pictured in their minds in the frantic cycle back to the farm. All the way back, they'd had visions of Sophie going into complete meltdown and being a blithering wreck by the time they got back.

What they saw instead was Sophie lying upon the sofa, calmly drinking a steaming cup of coffee. Their attention flew to her wrist, and identical smiles graced their faces to see she now wore a clean, white bandage.

Seeing where their gaze landed, Sophie waved her wrist in the air, nearly taking off Berry's nose as she sat on the edge of the sofa. "Sorry about that."

"You'd better keep that one clean, madam," Sheila told her.

"I will," Sophie barely had time to answer before a thunder of little feet announced the arrival of Harry and Lucy into the room.

"Sophie!" they cried as one before launching themselves onto her lap. "Uncle Bob told us you'd been hurt!"

With her arms wrapped around both of the girls, she looked up into the eyes of her two friends who needed to hear her next words the most. "I'm fine...and don't worry, I won't do *anything* again. You understand?"

Marcy and Vicky both raised eyebrows at Berry.

"Don't worry, she's okay. Aren't you, Sophie?"

Letting the girls go and biting her lip whilst they made themselves—though, not necessarily herself—comfortable as they draped themselves across her,

Sophie made sure to keep firm eye contact with her other two friends before assuring them, "I'm…calmer now. I think seeing what I…saw messed up my mind for a bit. The scratching"—she held up her wrist—"was some kind of reaction."

Whilst Marcy poured two more cups of tea from the pot, Vicky settled herself on the floor against the sofa. "You were so brave, Sophie. Whatever happens, just keep telling yourself this: you saved Elaine's life."

"But what if…" Sophie began to say.

Marcy came back and didn't give her the chance to finish. "Don't go there. What will be, will be." She ended with a gulp. "Concentrate on what Vicky just told you." When Sophie gave her a slight smile and nod in reply, Marcy added, "Now, nobody is going to work tomorrow. I'll ring up HQ in a while and tell them what…happened. We all need a few days to get our minds in order again."

"Quite right, my dears," Sheila put in, getting to her feet and coming to stand over the group. "For tonight, you"—she laid a hand on Sophie's shoulder—"are sleeping in here. I want you where I can keep an eye on you. No arguments," she told her when Sophie opened her mouth, undoubtedly to argue.

Vicky put her cup down and announced, "If that's the case, then we're all sleeping in here too. You don't get rid of us that easily, my friend."

"Fine, fine," Sheila agreed. "In that case, you three go and get washed up and changed, before you make a complete pigsty of my house, then, and when you've done so, tea will be ready. You can bring your blankets in later."

"Can we sleep here too?" Harry asked, Lucy nodding her head vigorously beside her.

"Why not?"

Everyone looked around, no one having noticed Bob leaning against the door. Both girls jumped up, eliciting a huge, "Oof!" from Sophie as the air rushed out of her lungs and they hurried to give the farmer a big hug.

Taking her empty cup in hand, Sheila patted her husband on his slightly rotund stomach as she passed, "Fine. But if this lot make a mess, then you're cleaning it up!"

Chapter Nineteen

As there were now so many people living in and around the farm, Bob had fixed up a shower unit in the corner of the barn the girls slept in. Well, he called it a shower. Everyone else called it the holey bucket on a piece of string, but the sentiment was well received, and once he'd recovered from the hugs and kisses of everyone, he'd walked away whistling happily to himself. It took two girls to work, with one trying to enjoy the cold water and the other constantly topping up the bucket from the rainwater butt outside their barn, trotting up a small ladder to empty it as many times as was needed.

This Sunday morning, Sophie was loading the bucket after the other girls had cycled off to the forest, as Marcy wanted to check they hadn't left anything out they shouldn't in yesterday's chaos. True to her word, Marcy insisted she should stay behind, even though they wouldn't be long and it wasn't a work day. Sophie had sworn she was feeling okay and could help, but she had been overruled by the others. The weather was dry but a little cold in the early morning, so she was in the process of emptying the fifth bucket.

"Aren't you clean yet, Harry?"

"One more, please," Harry shouted from behind the blanket which served as a shower curtain.

Putting the empty bucket down, Sophie twitched the

blanket aside a little and began to say, "It's always one m…"

"No!" Harry cried, making a grab for the blanket, but she lost her footing and fell head first out of the tin bath she stood in.

Chuckling to herself, Sophie told the girl to, "Hold on, I'll get your towel," and picking it up from the tree stump it lay upon, hurried back to where Harry was just regaining her feet. She held it up before her as Harry leant over, gripping the edge of the bath, not quite sure of her bearings. The morning sunlight chose that moment to shine through a break in the clouds, the beam falling upon her back.

Kneeling before her young friend, Sophie laid a hand gently upon her back, tracing the ragged red lines she now saw there, before covering her with the towel and helping Harry to her knees. "What happened, Harry? How did you get those…?"

Harry made sure her towel was securely wrapped around her before turning to face her friend. When she did, the determined set to her jaw defied her young years. "Get those…scars?"

Now the word was out there, Sophie found she'd lost her voice and could only nod.

Harry sniffed back tears and, setting her jaw, she looked Sophie directly in the eye. "Mister McAlister whipped me with a piece of cord when Lucy broke one of his wife's teacups." She then proceeded to dry herself, though Sophie noticed how gingerly she dried her back—the marks were obviously not very old and still rather sore.

Ignoring the fact that they'd discovered the girl didn't like to be treated as someone her age, undoubtedly to do with the protectiveness she felt toward her younger sibling, Sophie knelt before Harry and slowly, ever so slowly, wrapped her arms around her. For a moment, she could feel her body tensing, as if she was going to pull away, but as quickly as it came, it left even before Sophie could really register it. Gradually, Harry let her head fall forward until it leant upon her older friend's shoulder, and then she let her arms follow. Sophie let her hold her for as long as she needed, and when she pulled away, there were no tears upon her face, only a look of concern.

"You're not to tell anyone," she stated, the tone of her voice brooking no argument. When Sophie's brows knitted together, Harry placed a hand on either of her friend's shoulders. Her grip was surprisingly strong for one so young. "Look, Sophie, I'm serious. You can't tell anyone. Not Mr. and Mrs. Harker, not your friends." She looked away.

Sophie opened her mouth to answer, but a male voice beat them to it.

"I'm not supposed to know about what?"

"Mr. Harker! I didn't see you there," Harry cried, stepping as much behind Sophie as she could.

Bob Harker stuffed the rest of the hunk of bread and dripping he'd been eating into his mouth, gave a couple of quick chews, and swallowed. "I know you didn't, lass. Now, was it those red marks on your back I wasn't supposed to see?"

Harry opened and closed her mouth, looking between Sophie, who had taken a fierce grip upon one of her hands and had drawn the young girl against her own body, and the farmer who'd taken them in. You're not…angry with me?" she asked. Sophie tightened her grip as she felt Harry tremble slightly as she spoke.

Seeing quite clearly her fear, Bob knelt down on one knee before her but deliberately out of his arm's reach and pasted one of his rare smiles upon his face. When he answered, his voice was as tender as either girl had ever heard. "At you? Never," and he reached out a slightly grubby hand which, after a moment of hesitation, Harry took as Sophie let go her hold. For such a big man, to watch the farmer draw the slight girl into standing before him, where he took her other hand, brought it to his lips, and kissed the palm, was a sight Sophie would treasure.

"Is there anything else we should know?" he asked, stroking Harry's hand.

The girl turned her eyes toward Sophie, who nodded in what she hoped was an encouraging fashion. "Lucy saw…" She gulped before gathering her courage as both Sophie and Bob smiled at her to continue. "She saw what…happened."

Sophie thanked small mercies that Harry had her face turned down as she finished talking, as Bob's eyes flashed ever so briefly with what could only be rage, before she looked back up into his once again serene face.

"Would that be why she doesn't speak much?" he asked, reading what had popped into Sophie's mind.

Harry nodded her head. "She was a right chatterbox before we ended up there," Harry told them. "Was a right bloody effort to get her to shut up, to be honest!"

With perfect timing, Lucy herself came running around the corner, and close on her heels came the miniature tiger, Percy, as everyone had now grown to think of the ginger tabby. Whether the mouser was actually chasing her or not wasn't clear, but Bob didn't take any chances. Swiftly heaving himself to his feet, he scooped the youngest girl up in his arms as Percy flashed by and disappeared into the underbrush at the back of the barn.

"I think he's hungry," Lucy said, watching him disappear from view before she settled back happily into Bob's shoulder.

"Someone's feeling talkative today," Sophie announced, reaching up and ruffling the girl's hair.

"I'd better go and get dressed," Harry announced into the silence which followed, and with only the slightest hesitation, went up on tiptoes and kissed Bob on the cheek before taking to her heels. "Please don't tell Mrs. Harker," she shouted over her shoulder.

Only as the girl reached the kitchen door was Bob able to find his voice. "Hurry up, then. Those cows won't milk themselves!"

Still carrying Lucy, and seemingly unaware he was gently tickling her under the arms, Bob turned back toward the kitchen with Sophie in tow. "So, how are you feeling this morning?" Bob asked Sophie.

Sophie gave it a little thought before replying, not wishing to come out with the normal, "Okay." Eventually, she shrugged her shoulders. "Getting there, I suppose. If that's the worst thing I see in this war, I should consider myself fortunate." She held open the door for Bob and Lucy as they reached the farmhouse. "I should go back to work on Monday. The longer I stay away, the harder it'll be, I expect."

"The harder what'll be?" Sheila asked.

She was elbow deep in washing-up and so hadn't seen who'd come in. However, as both Sophie and Bob, still with Lucy upon his hip, pulled out chairs and sat down at the kitchen table, she turned around, and whatever she was about to say was left unsaid at the sight before her. She turned back to face the window over the sink, while Bob and Sophie watched without a word as she took a handkerchief out of her apron pocket and dabbed at her eyes before going over to take the seat next to Bob. Sophie suddenly wished she were somewhere else, anywhere other than where she was at the moment, especially when Sheila reached out to rest the palm of her hand briefly on Lucy's cheek.

Carefully choosing his words, Bob asked his wife, "You heard what Harry said?"

She nodded, staying her hand as it made to stroke Lucy's cheek again. "Window's open."

Sophie cleared her throat. "I was telling Bob I should go back to work tomorrow. It's for the best, or it'll only get harder."

Sheila's head whipped around to face Sophie, who could see the farmer's wife's mothering instincts kicking in before her eyes. "So soon? Shouldn't you take a few days? Marcy did say that'd be all right," she added.

"I know she did," Sophie answered with a shake of her head, "but it's for the best."

"She's right, love," Bob agreed, before kissing Lucy on the cheek and setting her down. "Be a love and go and hurry your sister up, will you?" he asked her, and Lucy promptly dashed out of the room. The next thing everyone could hear was what sounded like a herd of elephants thundering up the stairs. He took Sheila's hand. "It's what we did in the trenches. If you had a shock, the best thing we could do was to get you straight back into the fight. Mind you…" He stopped to stroke his chin, seemingly lost in thought, before coming back to himself. "There were some, quite a few, I expect, for whom that wasn't the best thing. We didn't know it at the time. Poor sods," he finished with a bitter shake of his head.

Sophie was, once again, wishing she could be elsewhere. Just as she was thinking it would be best for all if she simply got to her feet and disappeared outside, the back door opened, simultaneously admitting the other three Lumberjills just as Harry and Lucy reappeared.

Sheila kissed Bob on the forehead and got to her feet. "Best get those cows milked," she said. "Are you joining them?" she asked Lucy, who nodded. "All your homework's done?" she enquired with her hands upon her hips and received another nod. "Off you go, then," she told them, shooing the threesome outside.

"Everything all right?" Sophie asked, as her three friends took seats.

"Marcy's an old worrywart," Berry announced, earning herself a playful swat around the head from the worrywart.

"There's nothing wrong with checking," Marcy announced.

"Any plans today?" Sheila asked as she filled the kettle.

"Well," Vicky answered, glancing up at the kitchen clock, "we've got those two Land Girls who helped us out yesterday coming around about four for a drink."

On her way back from putting the kettle on to boil, Sheila stopped to look into the larder and a few cupboards before shaking her head. "I wish I'd have known. I don't think we've got more than a few bottles of stout in."

"That's okay, Sheila," Berry said. "They said they'd

sort the drink out. We wouldn't wish to impose."

"Do you mind if I use the telephone?" Marcy asked Sheila. "I want to see if I can find out how Elaine is."

At the mention of the injured girl, everyone's head turned automatically toward Sophie.

"Stop worrying," she told them, sounding a little annoyed. "I'm okay, really."

"Really?" Berry asked.

"Really, really!" Sophie half-snapped, encouraging everyone to stop asking.

"You know where it is," Sheila told Marcy. "Number for the hospital's on the pad on the table next to it." At everyone's raised eyebrows, she added with a shrug as she got up to make a pot of tea, "I knew one of you would want to."

Marcy went out to make her telephone call, shutting the door behind her. All that could be heard was a one-way muffled voice as Sheila tried to busy herself with making the tea. Almost as soon as she'd left, Marcy came back into the room—she was as white as a sheet.

"Oh, hell," Sophie cried.

Chapter Twenty

"To Elaine!" Marcy raised her glass.

Solemnly, everyone got to their feet from the circle of hay bales Bob had arranged outside the barn, and all raised their glasses. "Elaine!"

Vicky treated Marcy to her best glare. "Right, we're all here. Now, are you going to tell us how she is?"

"Wait, wait!" Tina West exclaimed. The dark-haired Land Girl sat to Vicky's left, running a hand through her hair. "You lot don't know how she is?"

"No," Berry replied, throwing her own glare Marcy's way. "Marcy here refused to tell us what the hospital told her until we were all together."

"Yes." Sheila joined in from the bale she shared with her husband. "She's not our favorite person right now."

"Which is why," Marcy said getting to her feet, "I should share the news."

"About bloody time," Vicky muttered.

Ignoring her friend, Marcy took a quick sip from her glass and then, with a deep sigh and a quick wipe of her eye began, "Firstly, she's alive…"

If they'd been inside, the roof would have been lifted by the cheers that interrupted Marcy's words, as if a cork had been shot from a bottle. The noise only died down when Sheila noticed the bearer of the news wasn't joining in. She quickly got to her feet, waving her arms.

"Quiet, everyone! I don't think Marcy's finished," she ended with a raised eyebrow.

Marcy waited until those who'd stood up reluctantly plopped themselves back down. "Thanks, Sheila." Looking around, she saw that despite knowing Elaine was alive, everyone's face now showed deep apprehension of what else was to come, and unfortunately, Marcy knew she wasn't going to disappoint them. "I'm afraid she's right. Though Elaine is alive, the doctor's aren't certain they can save her foot. They've treated the wound but won't know if she has an infection for a few days."

Sophie asked, "What happens if…"

She was unable to finish the question, but Marcy answered for her, "She'll probably lose it."

"Bloody hell," both Vicky and Sally swore at the same time.

Bob coughed and got to his feet. "Well, I'd better get back to the cowshed. I've left Harry on her own, and quick learner or not, I can't leave her alone for too long."

"I'll come with you, Bob," Sheila told him, getting up and linking her arm with his. "Let's leave these young ones alone."

Once the two were out of earshot, Sally declared, "Well, you lot are much better off than us!"

"How'd you work that out?" Vicky asked as she picked up two bottles of stout their new friends had brought and went around topping up everyone's glasses.

"Well, your landlords don't treat you like you're something the dog's brought in, for a starter."

Vicky put her bottles down and took up a seat next to the young Land Girl. "Shift up a bit," she told Sally. "Come on, that needs some explaining."

Sally looked across at where her friend was watching her, a wry smile upon her face.

"Don't look at me, Newhart," she told her. "You brought the subject up."

Before speaking, Sally looked back the way the Harkers had gone. "Do they know the Robinsons?"

"Who?" Berry asked. Everyone was paying attention to what Sally was talking about.

"The Robinsons," Tina repeated. "That's the name of the farmers we're billeted with."

"Anyone heard of them?" Marcy asked, receiving shakes of head in reply. "What's wrong with them?"

Sally let out a bitter laugh. "What's right with them is more like it. The mattresses, if you can call them that, are stuffed with straw…"

"I'm pretty sure mine's got a mouse living in it!" Tina broke in with.

"…the barn they make us live in has holes in the holes…"

"…if we get hot food, we're lucky…"

"…and don't get me started on having a hot bath!" Sally ended with. "I can't remember the last time I had one."

"We live in a barn too…" Vicky began to say before Marcy laid a hand upon her wrist, shaking her head.

"I don't think we're in the same boat, lovey," she told her before turning to the disgruntled duo. "It's quite cozy in our barn," she admitted, nodding her head toward their barn behind the group.

"Do they allow you a hot bath?" Sally wanted to know.

Sophie nodded her head. "Once a week, but if we come back particularly dirty, they don't mind us having a bath instead of our cold shower—well, the bucket arrangement we've fixed up so we don't muck up the bathroom too much. Gets cold at times, but we don't mind."

"Lucky you," Tina grumbled, leaning her shoulder against her friend.

"This could have been me," Sally mumbled, though everyone heard.

"What, possibly chopping your foot off?" Tina rounded on her. "Don't forget *that* perk of the job."

Upon being reminded of the reason they'd gathered, the group fell into contemplative silence for a few minutes, a silence finally broken by Marcy clearing her throat and getting to her feet.

"Girls, let's remember why we're here." She directed her gaze at their guests. "We don't know the Robinsons, but as they're essentially Bob and Sheila's neighbors, I'd be surprised if they didn't know them. I'm very sorry things aren't very good for you, and I don't know if there's anything we can do about it. However, I am, and I'm certain Elaine is too, very grateful you were both there."

"Even if we did get off on the wrong foot?" Sally put in, with a smile, not hearing her choice of words.

Marcy toasted her, choosing to ignore that. "Even if we did start off by you biting my head off."

Tina placed a hand over her friend's mouth to forestall any argument, only letting go when Sally shrugged her shoulders.

"For which I am eternally sorry," she said.

Marcy waved her apology away. "Don't dwell on it. Suffice to say, if you both hadn't come along, things would have been even worse. So, girls, raise your glasses once more…"

"Hold on, hold on!" Berry cried. "I need a top up."

"Are we ready now?" Marcy asked, once Berry had found a bottle with some stout left in it. "As I was saying, raise your glasses. To Tina and Sal!"

By the time the sun began to set, the last bottle of stout was long dry, and everyone was finishing the last of the beer Bob had surprised them with, having taken a trip to the King's Head. Sheila had provided a kind of vegetable stew to warm everyone up, and their guests had pronounced it the best meal they'd had in a long time, with their licked-clean bowls proof of their words.

At receiving the bowls back, Sheila had pulled Berry to one side. "Is there something I should know about this pair?"

"I'll get back to you," Berry had replied, feeling she'd need to discuss Sheila's query with her friends, as what the Land Girls had confided in them might not have been meant for anyone else's ears.

The evening officially drew to a close when Midnight climbed onto Berry's lap and promptly fell asleep.

"Promise you'll let us know any news on Elaine?" Tina asked Marcy as she came out of a hug.

"We promise," Marcy agreed as their friends retrieved their bikes, and with a false start in Sally's case, the two set off on their somewhat wobbly way back to their billets.

****

Sheila popped her head around the barn door just as Marcy was climbing into bed.

"Sorry, love, there's a telephone call for you. Someone called Ethel Winter wants to speak to you."

"Who's Ethel Winter?" Vicky asked as Marcy shrugged on her dressing gown and slipped into a pair of shoes.

"My boss," Marcy answered as she trotted out.

About five minutes later, she was back, a frown upon her face. Berry came and sat on one side of her as Sophie took the other, whilst Vicky kneeled upon her own bed.

When she didn't say anything straight away, Berry nudged her gently in the ribs. "Well?"

"Well," Marcy sighed. "She's paying us a visit tomorrow."

"Why?" Vicky asked and was rewarded by Berry throwing one of Marcy's pillows at her.

"Why do you think? She knows about the accident and needs to speak to us. Er, right, Marcy?" Berry belatedly asked.

"Spot on," Marcy confirmed. "Sgt. Duncan contacted her after I'd telephoned her on Friday night. I wasn't the most…eloquent, so most of what she knows she found out from him. She wants to hear what I've got to say. Chances are, she'll want to speak to you all. Will you be all right speaking to her, Sophie?"

Sophie pasted a determined visage upon her face and nodded. "I'll be okay."

"You don't have to come in to work tomorrow. You do know that still stands?"

Sophie gave her older friend a quick kiss on the cheek. "And I appreciate it, really I do, but it's best I get right back into the swing of things."

****

The next morning, the girls were about to mount their bicycles when Elias Duncan strode into the farm's courtyard.

"Ah, I'm glad I caught you," he began. "I'm afraid I still need to ask a few questions…about the accident."

"Do you need us all, Sergeant?" Marcy asked. "You see, my boss is meeting us at the clearing this morning, and I don't know what time she's going to be there."

"He's coming to talk about what happened?" the policeman asked.

"*She* is," Marcy informed him, making certain he knew her boss was also a woman.

The sergeant had the good grace to appear embarrassed. "Sorry about that, Mrs. Gagnon, my mistake."

Marcy smiled to show there were no hard feelings and held out her hand, which he took with a smile. "Don't worry, an easy mistake to make."

"Elias!"

Everyone looked around to find Sheila striding through the kitchen door toward them. When she reached them, she quickly wiped her hands on her pinny and then shook hands with the policeman.

"Sorry, sorry. I had the window open and couldn't help overhearing. If the girls have to meet someone, why don't you let them go and come to tea tonight, Elias? It's been a while since you've been around, and surely it'll be much more comfortable for everyone to talk in the warm?"

Sheila knew her friend and knew the promise of a good home-cooked meal and good company would have him eating out of her hand. Surely enough, he readily agreed and strode off back to the village, whistling happily to himself, allowing the girls to belatedly cycle off to work.

****

By the time the four girls arrived at the clearing, Ethel Winter stood beside her little Austin Eight waiting for them. As she greeted Marcy with a handshake, nodding a hello at each of the other girls as they were introduced, her expression didn't change from one of someone who'd rather be anywhere than where she currently was. Only when Marcy introduced Sophie did her expression change as she rushed toward the slightly shocked girl, who nearly took a step backward as the unusually tall woman rushed up and grabbed her hand, not noticing the bandage wrapped around the wrist nor the wince upon the girl's face, shaking it vigorously before wrapping her arms around her.

"I can't thank you enough for what you did for poor Elaine," she told Sophie, who'd just about realized she wasn't about to be attacked. Much to Sophie's relief, she finally released her grip on her hand. "Now, I can't imagine what you went through. Are you all right? Are you certain you don't need some time off?"

Sophie shook her head and found her voice. "Honestly, I'm fine. I'd much rather be here, amongst friends."

The newcomer, who must have been in her early sixties, fixed a surprisingly fierce glare upon Sophie before giving a single nod, a smile, and a pat on her shoulder, and then she turned on her heel, hooked an arm through one of Marcy's, and the two traipsed off, immediately deep in conversation.

As the two disappeared from view, Berry and Vicky came and stood next to their friend.

"She's a ball of fire, eh?" Vicky stated.

"Just a little," Sophie agreed, wiping her forehead.

After another minute, Berry hefted her axe onto a shoulder. "Come on, let's make a start."

Berry and Vicky were on each end of a two-handed crosscut saw when the sound of high-powered aircraft engines began to make themselves heard over the rasp of the saw. Pausing in mid-saw, both looked up to try and catch a sight of whatever was making the racket, which was getting louder and more urgent as each second passed.

"Sound like a Merlin engine to you?" Sophie asked.

After a moment's thought, Vicky shook her head. "Not to me."

They looked at each other before coming to an unspoken agreement. Both left the saw embedded in the tree trunk and rushed back the short distance to the clearing where they'd left their bicycles and other gear, only to find that not only Berry, but Marcy and Ethel were there too, all with their eyes to the sky.

"There!" Marcy shouted, pointing toward two specks low on the horizon, yet getting closer all the time.

"Are they ours?" Ethel asked.

Vicky shook her head, "We don't think so. The engines sound wrong."

As the girls watched, they saw both the mysterious aircraft bank.

"They're making for Wiganthorpe!" Berry yelled, her hand flying to her mouth.

Everyone's eyes were glued to the sky, watching to see what the two aircraft were up to. All were now certain those planes were the enemy, though the patchy cloud made it difficult to make a positive identification, as they kept flitting in and out, probably trying to avoid being seen.

By now, the two aircraft could quite clearly be seen. They were single-engine planes and definitely enemy, as the hated black German cross was clear to see as they passed low overhead, plainly on a course which would take them over their village. Under each fuselage, they could make out the evil shape of a single large bomb. Without knowing they'd done it, everyone had grouped together and was edging closer to the dubious cover of some large trees. As they watched, Vicky let out a yelp and hopped up and down, pointing to somewhere behind the two.

"Do you think we should have dug some slit trenches?" Berry asked, ever practical, albeit belatedly.

What Vicky had pointed at turned out to be a flight of four Spitfires, and they'd quite clearly spotted the enemy aircraft. With the advantage of height, their dive took them overhead a mere thirty seconds after the German aircraft had zoomed over, causing the girls to all involuntarily duck their heads.

"Go get the swine!" Vicky yelled at the top of her voice, as everyone else also yelled out encouragement.

Seconds later, they were all stunned into silence as two massive explosions shook them nearly off their feet! From over the treetops, twin balls of fire blossomed into sight.

Chapter Twenty-One

Credit to Ethel, she didn't complain too much when all the girls insisted upon cramming into her little Austin Eight and being driven back to Wiganthorpe.

The couple of miles back had never seemed to take as long, even when they'd cycled in the wind and rain, and no one's nerves were helped as the chimney of dense black and gray smoke filled more of the windscreen the nearer to the village they got. As it turned out, Ethel belied her appearance and knew exactly what she was doing behind the wheel. This was just as well, as when they came to the edge of the village, the single-story whitewashed cottage that always greeted everyone had now virtually vanished!

"Hell's bells!" Ethel said, echoing everyone's thoughts.

"Watch out! Brake!" Berry yelled.

Ethel didn't question the order and immediately hit the brakes, skidding to a halt a few yards from a deep new bomb crater. Leaning over the steering wheel, panting with nerves, she managed to say, "Good call," then, "Could someone help me prise my fingers off this steering wheel?"

With some difficulty, everyone extricated themselves from the too-small car and stood staring at the jumble of rubble before them. Of the old cottage the girls had grown to know as they cycled past on their way

174

to and from work, only the back wall and a single chimney stack were still recognizable. The whole of the center of the building was a mass of brick, mangled furniture and bits and bobs.

"Do you know whose place this is?" Ethel asked.

Nobody answered, as they knew only a very few people. At that moment, a trickle of villagers began to appear now it seemed the immediate danger had passed. To their front were Bob and Sheila, closely accompanied by Sergeant Elias Duncan. As they got to the other side of the crater now blocking the road, the newcomers did exactly as Marcy and her fellow girls were doing, simply staring in shocked disbelief at the sight before them.

Berry was the first to recover her wits. Placing a hand either side of her mouth, she shouted, "Bob! Sheila! Do you know whose place this is?" Her mind seemed to refuse to use the verb, *was*.

"Paula Gibbons!" Bob yelled back. By now, he was carefully picking his way around the crater to the group, followed by the policeman and a few others.

"Are the telephones working, Sergeant?" Marcy asked Elias as, wiping his forehead, he too joined them.

"Luckily, yes," he replied. "I've called it in and asked them to send an ambulance, too."

Ethel surveyed the wreckage before them before saying, "Do you think she was in there?"

Sheila blew her nose before replying, "Nowhere else she'd be. Still—" She turned to her husband. "Bob, go and ask those others." She pointed to some other people who were tentatively picking around the edges of the destroyed cottage. "See if anyone knows where she is."

"Don't bother," came a gruff voice from behind, startling them. Turning, they were surprised to find it belonged to Muriel Lynne, from the King's Head public house. Upon her head was a tin helmet bearing the letters ARP.

"I didn't know you were our Air Raid Warden," Vicky stated.

"Guilty as charged," she answered with a grim smile, reaching up to straighten her helmet, the only item of uniform she'd had the time to don, as she was wearing a tweed skirt, sturdy black shoes instead of boots, and a raincoat. Muriel coughed, and when she replied, her voice sounded a little more feminine. "I asked everyone I came across on my way, and nobody's seen her. She's rather elderly and mostly housebound anyway, so…" She nodded toward the shouldering rubble. "If she's anywhere, she's somewhere…in there."

When no one else said anything, Berry took it upon herself to say, "We're in your hands, Muriel. What can we do?"

Taking a few moments to compose herself, Muriel took a look around, noting that in the eerie quiet, broken only by the odd crackle of flame, everyone on both sides of the crater was staring at her.

"Right, firstly, Elias. I want you to go to the end of the road and wait for the ambulance. I want someone with authority there." She waited whilst the policeman nodded and strode off before she continued, "I want everyone to be as quiet as you can. We need to see if we can hear anything. Bob, take two of the girls—Berry and Vicky, I suggest—and get back over to the other side. When you're there, we're going to listen for a few minutes. If you hear anything, anything at all, hold up a hand. If not, we'll work our way carefully in. Be careful!" she emphasized. "If I remember right, this cottage had a cellar, and I don't want anyone to fall through into it."

"Sorry to interrupt," Sheila broke in, "but if I'm right, that chimney was in the kitchen, and the door which led to the cellar was somewhere close to that."

"Do you think she could have made it to the cellar?" someone none of the girls knew shouted.

"We can only hope!" Muriel yelled in reply.

After five minutes or so, during which the last of the small fires which had started had mostly died down, no one stuck their hand in the air. From the resigned look upon Muriel's face, she hadn't expected anyone to do so.

"Right," Muriel said at the top of her voice, as she straightened up. "I don't want everyone to try searching this rubble. Bob, can you and the girls hear me?" She waited until all three had told her they could. "You and the girls start on that side. Everyone else, stand back, but be ready to move if something happens. Slowly, pick your way across, step by step. Do *not* hurry your movements, and make sure of your footing. If you come across…something…yell out, put up your hand. We'll take things from there. Make for the chimney, but remember what Sheila said, the entrance to the cellar is somewhere around it. Try not to fall in. Marcy and Sophie, you're with me. Ready, everyone?" She looked around and got nods of determination in answer.

"What about me?" Sheila asked before Muriel could move off.

"You're my eyes," Muriel informed her without hesitation. "We're going to be so close, we may miss something right down at our feet. You too…" She went to advise the middle-aged lady hovering by an Austin Eight.

"Mrs. Ethel Winter," the woman introduced herself. "I'm the Lumberjills manager."

"Sorry I don't have time for proper introductions, Mrs. Winter. Please, you heard what I asked Sheila here to do, and I need you to do the same."

Without waiting to hear if she got a yes, Muriel turned back toward the grim task at hand. "Come on, let's get a move on."

Nobody said a word for around the next ten minutes as, slowly, with the most extreme care they could get away with considering the urgency of the situation, both groups made their ways across the rubble, pausing only to put out three small fires by beating them into submission with blankets and sheets they came across amongst the detritus strewn around. No one knew quite what to expect or what they were looking for, so something that in normal circumstances would barely warrant a second glance, now took on an altogether different light.

"Did Ms. Gibbons own a cat?" Vicky suddenly shouted, breaking the near silence.

"I think she had one left," Sheila replied after a few moments thought. "Why?"

Vicky laid the blanket she'd been using to fight the fires over a misshapen, reddish lump just visible under some brick. "Not anymore," Vicky muttered, shuddering and resuming the search.

Two minutes later, Berry noticed a strangely shaped lump and, carefully dropping to one knee, began to move some rubble from the side. A few bricks here, some cups which were each miraculously still in one piece there, and as she moved the majority of a dinner plate, she saw what could only be fingers!

"I've got something!" she shouted, waving like mad.

"You're sure?" This was Bob, who was only five or so feet to her right.

To be certain, Berry moved more rubble away from the fingers until she could see a bloodied wrist. Ignoring the gore, she placed her fingers as she'd been taught in first-aid lessons but was unable to find a pulse. "No pulse!" she shouted. Quickly, Berry cleared a patch of ground so she could kneel fully down and scoop more rubble away whilst the other members of the search team made their careful way toward her. With most of the rubble around the arm now cleared and with still no movement from it, Berry decided to give a quick tug to see if she could work loose what she was presuming to be the lady they sought.

The first tug produced no results, but on the second, something gave, and caught unawares, she flopped back onto the seat of her trousers. Between her hands, she found herself holding not the body they'd been searching for, but a bloody arm which ended in a ragged, dirty stump. Someone, somewhere was screaming before the night came early for Berry.

****

Berry occupied Sheila's couch. As opposed to Sophie, she had no recollection of how she got there, only that when she tried to open her eyelids, it felt like someone was trying to stick needles into her eyes, so she snapped them shut straight away.

"Are you sure she shouldn't be in hospital?" asked a male voice that was familiar, yet not so that she could put a name to it.

"Don't be daft," said another voice, she was certain was Sheila's. "It's only a bump on the back of her head.

Barely split the skin. No, a day or two of taking it easy, and she'll be right as rain."

"Hmm." The male voice sounded rather skeptical.

Encouraged by that thought—after all, if she knew what skeptical meant, she mustn't be too bad—she tried to open her eyes again, a little slower this time. With her eyelids ever so slightly cracked open, Berry tried to make out where she was and who was there. Moving her head slightly, she thought she recognized the fireplace in Sheila's front room. So, that would make it the same sofa which Sophie had occupied not long ago. Further thoughts were driven from her mind by the thump of a body plonking itself down next to her, nearly crushing her upper left thigh.

"Berry! You're awake!" the same slightly familiar male voice exclaimed.

"Dennis?" she ventured.

"At least that proves she's still got her memory," said another voice, she was pretty certain belonged to Vicky.

"Vicky?" Berry tried to say, only her mouth was too dry and only an unintelligible croak came out this time.

"Move yourself, Flying Officer."

Sheila came into view, and Berry could just about make out the welcome glass of water she was holding. Replacing the Flying Officer, Sheila sat gently down beside her, placed a hand behind her head, and helped her hold the glass as she drank. Once empty, the farmer's wife stayed where she was.

"You gave us a nasty turn there, young lady," she told her.

With Sheila's help, she moved up the sofa until she was around semi-upright. "What happened?" she asked.

"Sure you want to hear?" Sheila asked.

Berry began to nod and instantly regretted it, the needles making a comeback. "Sure," she managed from between gritted teeth, raising a hand to her forehead and finding it wrapped in a bandage.

"I'm afraid you had the misfortune to find Ms. Gibbons," Sheila began, "or perhaps I should say, you found…a part of her."

For a few moments, Berry's head swam, and she had to swallow hard to fight off the tunnel vision which threatened to overwhelm her.

Having won her fight to stay conscious, she thought back to the last thing she remembered—and immediately wished she hadn't. With a distinct shiver, she did her best to shrug off the memory. "I take it," she started and then had to begin again. "I take it she is…dead?"

Sheila had to wipe away a few tears before she was able to answer. "Yes. We…we found the rest of her under that pile of rubble you were digging in. By the look of things, she took most of the blast. At least she wouldn't have felt a thing."

Holding on to that thought, Berry gladly accepted another glass of water from Marcy, taking it down a little slower this time. "And me?" she asked, prodding the bandage.

"If you will fall backward onto a bombsite…" Vicky told her, obviously trying to lighten the mood, though with scant luck. Berry appreciated the sentiment all the same. "Don't worry, you only knocked yourself out. You'll be fine," her friend added, coming forward to kiss her on the cheek.

There came a knock at the door, and then in rushed Harry and Lucy, not bothering to wait for an invitation.

At seeing Berry was awake, Lucy rushed up to wrap her arms tightly around the neck of the person who'd rescued her from the well in the forest.

"You're going to be okay!" she shouted into Berry's ear, nearly deafening her and then turned an accusing eye upon Vicky, who sat in a wooden chair next to the window. "You said she'd been brain-damaged!"

Marcy immediately slapped Vicky none too gently around the top of the head, "You didn't!"

"I was only joking," she protested.

"Some joke," muttered Harry, joining her little sister in cuddling up to Berry, who was enjoying the cuddles but not so much the multiple elbows which went with it. "Can I hit her too, Marcy?"

Vicky got to her feet. "I think I'll go for a walk," she said and left the room before anyone else could say anything.

Now her head was a little clearer, Berry looked around the room and found the Flying Officer whose male voice she'd heard was indeed none other than her friend Dennis Grey. In deference to her sofa friends, she didn't try to move. "Dennis! What are you doing here?" Then she noticed his left arm was in a sling.

Noticing where her gaze had settled, Dennis waggled his arm, a little awkwardly due to the sling, in the air. "Can't let you be the only wounded warrior, can I? We got shot up a few nights back, and I took a bullet through my arm."

Chapter Twenty-Two

The beginning of September came warm and with the fervent wish of every one of the girls for the future to take a boring turn.

"I'm bored," Lucy moaned, flopping onto Berry's upper legs, narrowly missing Midnight, who was fast asleep on the currently slumbering Lumberjills stomach.

"Go and get me a packet of holes, then," Berry mumbled, her face beneath her blankets. "It's Saturday morning, we've the whole weekend off, and Midnight and me aren't getting up yet."

Lucy peeled the blanket from Berry's face and tweaked open an eyelid. "How many holes do you want?"

Berry let out a groan which turned into a squeak of pain, as her movement caused Midnight to almost fall off her comfy bed and she'd dug all four sets of claws in to maintain her position. "You know," she mumbled, "I preferred it when you didn't say very much."

"Me too," agreed Marcy, swiftly followed by both Sophie and Vicky.

"How do you think I feel?" This was Harry, who matched actions to words by throwing a pillow her little sister's way. "It's like the old days—I can't get a bloody word in edgeways!"

"I do wish you wouldn't swear so much, Harry," Marcy grumbled, as she sat up, rubbing the sleep out of her eyes.

"Strange, Mr. Harker says the same," Harry agreed with a grin. "I do try," she added.

"You're very trying," Lucy shot back, sitting up and dragging a once more fast asleep Midnight onto her lap, though still managing to sit on poor Berry's legs.

"If you're really going to chat away, Lucy, then go and see if there's a pot of tea going, will you?" Berry asked as she struggled to free her legs from the young girl's bottom.

As Lucy, with a somehow still sleeping Midnight in her arms, slipped into her shoes, pulled on her dressing gown, and disappeared, there came a collective groan.

"Who's turn to say it today?" Vicky asked.

"Yours, I think," Marcy told her.

"Right," Vicky said. "Whose idea was it, agreeing to let these two bunk down with us?"

"Hey!" Harry protested. "That's not funny anymore. I don't cause any bother."

Unseen by her, Sophie had crept up behind her bed. Reaching out an arm, she ruffled the girl's hair, something she hated. "We know, but at least it's fun to hear your protests."

"Great," Harry mumbled. Kicking back her blankets, she grabbed her towel and wash things. "I'm going to get washed."

"I'm going back to sleep," Berry announced and promptly pulled her blankets back over her head.

"What's the time?" Sophie asked out loud.

Berry cracked the edge of her blankets up to look at her alarm clock and groaned. "Six thirty."

Everyone else joined in with groans of their own and matched Berry's actions. However, no one was able to get the lie-in they all craved after a hard week's work, as about half an hour later, the barn door banged open.

"Mail time!" Harry announced at the top of her voice.

"Tea's up!" Lucy hollered as she bounded in not far behind.

As no one had been doing more than dozing, there were no more protests, though which of the magic words had the effect of getting them out of their beds was up for debate.

"Where's the tea?" everyone wanted to know.

Lucy looked at everyone like they were crazy. "In the kitchen, of course."

"No breakfast in bed?" Vicky enquired.

Lucy hopped up and began bouncing up and down on Vicky's bed, causing Vicky to grab hold of the youngster before she broke her bed. "What a silly question," Lucy managed to say before Vicky decided to try and tickle her to death.

Ignoring the warring couple, Harry made her way up to Marcy and held out her hand. In it she held a battered envelope which had Marcy's name on its front, next to various addresses which had been crossed out before her current one had been squeezed into the space left. In the bottom right-hand corner was the name and address of the sender:

2nd Lt M Gagnon
Fontanellato
British Zone
Italy

Upon seeing her husband's name, Marcy collapsed back onto her bed.

"Everything all right there, Marcy?" Berry asked as

she prepared to follow her friends outside to get washed.

Marcy looked up, but whatever her face showed made Berry ask again. This time Marcy managed to convince her all was well, and Berry joined her friends, telling her before she shut the door, "Well, don't forget to wash. You don't want the tea to get cold."

Once everyone had gone, Marcy allowed her shoulders to slump. She hadn't noticed that Harry stood slightly behind her, until the girl placed a gentle hand upon her shoulder, causing her to jump.

"Sorry," Harry apologized, before coming around and sitting down next to her. "But you're not all right, are you. What's wrong? Is there anything I can do?" She looked at the envelope she'd handed to her. "Bad news?"

It took Marcy a moment to catch up, but when she did, she shook her head. "I don't know," and then added, "It's the first letter I've had from my husband since he became a POW. Well," she amended, "from the camp I've been told he's in, anyway."

"Why'd you look all downcast, then?"

After turning the letter over and over between her fingers, Marcy placed it on her lap. "That's not my husband's handwriting," she pointed at the address.

Harry shuffled along until she was as close to Marcy as possible, then wrapped her arms around her. "I'm not going anywhere."

Dear Mrs. Gagnon,

The letter began, once Harry had talked Marcy into opening it, something she did very carefully and rather reluctantly.

My name is Lt. Colonel Fawkes and it is with the deepest and most heartfelt regret, that I must write to you to inform you of the death of your husband, 2nd Lt.

186

Matthew Gagnon.

Marcy's fingers gripped the letter tightly upon reading those words, and only Harry's light but firm touch on her arm gave her the strength to get to the end of the short letter.

Matthew was a good man, always ready with a happy smile and a word of encouragement when and where needed. He died in tragic circumstances when our camp was hit by a bombing raid ~~which missed its target~~. *His hut took a direct hit, and along with twenty others, he would have died instantly. I can assure you, he did not suffer.*

Along with his comrades, he was buried with full military honors on the 20th August. I wish I could send you a photo of the ceremony and his grave, as some small condolence, but alas, this is not possible.

Please accept my personal thoughts and best wishes.

Lt. Colonel Fawkes

****

Half an hour after everyone else had disappeared for breakfast, Marcy finally made it into the kitchen. No one failed to notice she was being supported by Harry, who had an arm around her waist and was actively encouraging her to put one foot before the other.

"Not much farther," everyone first heard Harry say from the other side of the kitchen door. "Let's get a nice, hot cup of tea down you. That's it. Now, hang on to me whilst I open the door." There followed a loud thumping noise which had Bob out of his seat. He'd nearly got to the door when it crashed open, revealing Harry sagging under the burden of her older friend. Marcy's eyes were glazed, and it was doubtful she knew where she was. "A hand here, please!" Harry cried, her knees trembling.

Bob wrapped one strong arm tightly around Marcy as Berry also swiftly came to Harry's aid.

"Thanks," a relieved Harry said. "Let's get her into a chair."

"What's wrong with her?" Sheila asked, whilst unbidden she automatically poured two new cups of tea.

"If you've got it, Mrs. Harker, could you put some sugar into Marcy's?" Harry asked.

"I don't take sugar," Marcy mumbled, as her eyes nearly rolled back into her head.

"I'll get a cold flannel," Vicky announced and immediately rushed out of the kitchen, her footsteps thundering up the stairs.

Sheila had by now knelt down beside Marcy and placed her hand upon her friend's brow. "She's awfully cold, and clammy," she announced, before turning once more to Harry, who still maintained a protective hand upon Marcy's knee, even as she took her first sip from her cup.

As Vicky charged back into the room, placing a cold wet flannel upon Marcy's brow, Harry took a quick, hard look at her friend. You could almost hear her mind whirring as she thought about what to say. Eventually, she settled upon a vague half-truth. Looking up, she made certain to look Sheila in the eye. "She's had a very bad shock."

"Was it," Berry hesitantly asked, "was it anything to do with that letter I saw you holding, Harry?"

Harry nodded.

"We're being taught how to write letters at school," Lucy announced, spitting toast crumbs everywhere. "I don't know anyone to write to, though," she finished, before shrugging her shoulders and going back to her food as if nothing had happened.

"Right," Sheila managed to say, adding, "Perhaps we can find you some soldier to write to. Would you like that?"

After thinking this over, Lucy nodded enthusiastically. "Ooh, yes, please!"

Whilst this strange conversation had been going on, Harry and Berry had been trying, rather unsuccessfully, to persuade Marcy to drink some of the tea Sheila had put before her.

"If you've finished your breakfast, can you go and see if you can find Percy?" Sheila asked Lucy. As Lucy was the only one the ginger tiger didn't try to disembowel on sight, she treated him as the kitten he really was in age. She didn't need any second asking and was out the back door in a flash.

"Good thinking, dear," Bob told her with a smile, as he got up to close the door Lucy had left open. He stooped down next to Harry and, ever so gently, prised her hand from Marcy's knee. "Is there anything more you can tell us?" he asked. "What kind of bad news?" His voice was ever so gentle and full of concern, but Harry shook her head and taking her hand back, replaced it where it had come from.

"I'm really, really sorry, Mr. Harker," she told him, her gaze never leaving its place upon Marcy. "I wish I could, but it really is personal. It's Marcy's place to decide what to say."

"Honey, can you hear us?" Berry asked.

Vicky went and ran the flannel under the kitchen tap, wrung it out, and returned to place it back on Marcy's forehead. "She's got a little color back, I think."

Sheila held out her hand to Vicky and, taking the flannel from her, placed her own hand back on Marcy's forehead before replacing it once more with the flannel, and looked into her eyes. "Marcy," she began, "do you know where you are?"

Everyone waited with bated breath and, in Sophie's case, a piece of toast held in situ before her open mouth. It took another few minutes, as everyone waited to see if Marcy would react to Sheila's words, but gradually, her eyes refocused, her head straightened up, and she became aware of her location, if not situation.

"How did I get here?" she asked, reaching up to touch Sheila's hand. "And why have I got a face flannel on my forehead?"

Sophie shut her mouth with an audible snap, effectively breaking the silence which followed Marcy's words.

Strangely enough, the noise also seemed to snap Marcy back to the real world. Looking around at the concerned faces surrounding her, she ended up looking into Harry's, a face young yet old beyond her years, as she was again about to demonstrate. The girl took Marcy's proffered hand and squeezed in encouragement.

"You can do it," she whispered.

Taking a deep, steadying breath, Marcy nodded. "The letter was from the officer in charge of the POWs at my husband's camp," she managed to get out, all in one breath. "Matt was killed in an air raid which went wrong."

Into the silence following Marcy's announcement, everyone was vaguely aware of a vehicle stopping outside the kitchen door, closely followed by the blast of a horn which had seen better days. A moment later came a knock at the door, and without waiting for anyone to say anything, a head with an RAF hat on it popped into view.

Archie opened his mouth but was stopped by the unexpected sight of Marcy flying out of a seat, her hands outstretched.

Chapter Twenty-Three

Holding up his hands, Archie managed to catch hold of Marcy's wrists just in time. A moment later and she'd have had her fingers around his neck. Nevertheless, she sent him stumbling backward until he landed flat on his back at the feet of his pilot, Dennis, nearly driving him to his knees.

"What the hell!" Archie cried out, narrowly avoiding banging the back of his head on the ground.

Piling out the wide-open kitchen door, Sophie and Vicky were hard on the heels of the couple now wrestling on the ground. Making a dive, Vicky took hold of Marcy's right arm, whilst Sophie grabbed the left.

"Let…go…Marcy," Vicky grunted as she tried to prise her errant friend's fingers from where they'd managed to take a grip upon Archie's jacket lapels, as Sophie did the same on the other side.

"Leave me be!" Marcy screamed at everyone, redoubling her efforts to reach Archie's neck.

Fortunately, Bob was right on Vicky's heels and helped her finally prise Marcy's fingers free, as Jimmy Dunn did the same for Sophie, allowing Archie to scramble backward, panting as he caught his breath. Together, Bob and Jimmy hauled Marcy to her feet where she hung between the pair, hissing and spitting in anger. Slowly, painfully almost, the rage inside Marcy began to dissipate, though neither man let go of her arms.

Meanwhile, Sophie and Vicky clambered to their feet and dusted off their hands. Both had tiny cuts and multiple scrapes from where Marcy's fingernails and the hard earth had met them, but neither gave them a second thought as they went to Marcy, who now limply hung from the arms of the two men.

Berry and Sheila joined them, with Sheila briefly eyeing Marcy up before hurrying toward the barn where Harry and Lucy were stood, both having witnessed the altercation. Placing a hand on one of Marcy's shoulders, Berry gently took her friend's chin in the other and lifted her head up. Gradually, Marcy's eyes focused on Berry's. Holding her gaze for a few seconds, she seemed eventually satisfied and nodded her head.

"You can let her go now," she told Bob and Jimmy.

Bob, trusting Berry's judgment, immediately let go, whereupon Berry swiftly took up the now free hand. Jimmy, though, glanced over his shoulder and didn't let go until he got a nod from Dennis. As soon as he did, Sophie took up the free hand, with Vicky close behind.

"Would someone care to tell me just what the hell happened?" Archie, not unreasonably, demanded.

The answer he received wasn't what he'd been expecting. "Your lot murdered my husband," Marcy growled out from between clenched teeth.

"Who murdered who?" Lucy unexpectedly asked, causing Sheila to put a finger to her lips and shush the young girl into silence. No one had noticed Harry dragging the pair toward Marcy.

With Sheila's attention distracted, Harry wriggled her hand out and, stepping between Berry and Sophie, quickly moved beyond them, toward Marcy. With her arms flung behind her, she looked fiercely up at the RAF men. "Don't judge! Don't you dare judge her!"

Archie went to open his mouth and briefly stopped when Dennis put a hand upon his shoulder. Swiftly, he turned and shook his head before stooping down on one knee to address the feisty young girl.

"I wasn't going to, love, really," he assured her. "Marcy knows I like her, but that's not a good reason for trying to strangle me." When Harry didn't object, he got to his feet and stood before Marcy, who was now shaking slightly. "Marcy. Can you hear me?"

When she made eye contact with him, both Berry and Sophie unconsciously took a firmer grip upon her arms.

"You can let me go now, girls," she told them. "I'm not going to do anything."

'Really?" Dennis asked her. "Because he's due to fly tomorrow, and I don't want to have to find another gunner."

Marcy's knees suddenly gave way beneath her, and only her friends' hands kept her upright.

"Enough," Berry declared. "Maybe you can talk to her later, but right now, I want to get her inside. Sheila, mind if we take her into your lounge?" she asked the farmer's wife. Sheila was battling to keep hold of Lucy, who was trying to break free of her grip and get to her sister.

"Of course not. You take her in."

"Thanks," Berry said.

Harry let go of Marcy's waist and, grabbing one of Lucy's hands, followed Berry and Sophie as they supported Marcy so she wouldn't stumble and fall.

****

The three RAF lads were left with nearly identical

bewildered expressions upon their faces. After much silent exchanging of glances, Dennis, being the senior present, eventually asked, "Would someone care to tell us exactly what's going on? Why did Marcy attack Archie? I mean, we all know he's an ugly little sod, but that's no reason."

"Cheers, boss," Archie put in, grinning.

"Back in a minute," Sheila told him and made her way swiftly to follow the girls back inside.

Bob turned his attention back to this Dennis, using the time to choose his words. These were men who put their lives on the line virtually every night, and no matter what had happened, he didn't believe they deserved the accusation Marcy had thrown at them. True, he knew few details, other than what Marcy had told them, but based on his experience in the trenches of the Great War, he knew only too easily how accidents, or friendly fire (a misnomer if ever there was one) could happen. Thinking about it, he had to bite his lip and clamp his eyes shut. The next thing he knew, he became aware of someone catching him by the elbow.

"Mr. Harker? Mr. Harker?"

As he opened his eyes, Bob saw the one called Jimmy had his elbow, whilst his colleagues were standing by. His vision clearing, he swallowed a couple of times and eventually felt able to speak once more.

"Thanks, boys," he told them, feeling a little more like himself. "Now, what was it you asked? Oh, yes." With a sigh, he opened his mouth and was about to speak when he heard Sheila calling his name. Looking around, he saw her trotting toward them, waving what looked like a letter in her hand.

"Marcy says it's all right for them to read this," she

told him, pressing the letter Marcy had received into his hand. She addressed Archie. "Marcy says to tell you she's sorry." Then, with a quick peck on Bob's cheek, she walked more slowly back to the farmhouse.

Quickly reading the letter first, Bob fought the demons down, determined not to give in to his old memories again, before handing it to Dennis. "This will explain everything."

With his mates either side of him, Dennis held up the letter between them so they could all read it. It wasn't long, so it didn't take them much time to get through. When they'd finished, all three were distinctly gray.

Dennis handed it back. "I don't know what to say."

Carefully tucking the letter into a pocket, Bob gave a wry smile. "There isn't anything anyone can say. She's angry, so she lashed out." He stopped and thought for a second. "Did they know you were coming today?" Bob asked.

Jimmy shook his head. "We hadn't been able to see them for a while—you know how it is—and this was the first chance all three of us have had the opportunity to pop across. We thought it'd be a surprise," he finished, shaking his head.

"It certainly was, at that," Bob agreed.

"Do you think she's going to be all right?" Archie asked, looking over at the farmhouse.

Bob could only shrug his shoulders. "In time, probably, yes. Right now, everything's raw. She can't understand accidents happen in wartime. Heaven knows I lost enough mates in the last one when our artillery fell short."

The RAF men waited patiently whilst Bob gathered himself once more. This time, he needed only a few seconds. "We can't imagine what you went through, Mr. Harker," he told the farmer. "We've lost mates to friendly fire and when planes have collided, but it's not the same as what's happened to Marcy's husband."

"No," Bob agreed. "You're supposed to be safe in a POW camp."

****

"Have they gone?" Sheila asked, as the kitchen door swung open and admitted Bob.

The toot of a car's horn answered that question. Throwing a final wave, Bob shut the door and went to the kitchen, downing two glasses of water before answering. The conversation had brought back memories he thought he'd buried, especially after the rekindling of his relationship with Sheila. Despite the war, he could now see the possibility of a long and happy life for the pair of them, something he wouldn't have dreamed possible before the Lumberjills had come into his life. If things had stayed as they were, he knew Sheila would have left him (who would blame her?) and he'd either have lived out his life alone or been found hugging a shotgun barrel. The conversation he'd just partaken in hadn't been one he'd been expecting, and the memories it had brought back were ones he could do without.

A hand dropped on his shoulder. Even without turning, he knew it'd only be one person.

"Are you okay, Bob?"

Placing his hand upon his wife's, he turned and raised it to his lips. Mustering a smile, he leant his forehead against her for a few seconds. Then, cupping her face, he pressed his lips to hers. The sweet taste and sense of tranquility helped to wash away the final vestiges of the nightmares of a previous life. He wrapped his arms around her, pulling her into a tight embrace.

"I am now," he whispered into her ear. Looking over his shoulder toward where voices could be heard from the lounge, he asked, "What about Marcy?"

Sheila twisted around so she could see the hallway. "I think we'll have to wait and see."

****

"I can't find anything in this one," Marcy stated, throwing a newspaper to the floor in disgust. "Anyone else found anything?"

Both Vicky and Harry, with the dubious help of Lucy, were lying around the floor surrounded by scattered and discarded newspapers of all types and ages.

"Not a sausage," Vicky replied, whilst Harry waited until she'd finished before, with a great show, she crumpled up another and threw it over her shoulder.

"So," Marcy said, running a hand through and through her hair until it stuck out and up in all directions, "we've got newspapers going back what, four or five weeks, and there's nothing in them about the RAF bombing one of our POW camps in Italy."

Silence reigned whilst everyone waited. The door opened to admit Bob and Sheila, hand in hand. "What's going on?" Sheila asked.

Berry volunteered the answer. "Marcy's had us looking back through all your newspapers, seeing if we can find anything reported about what…well, you know, happened to her husband."

"And?" Bob asked.

"Nothing," Marcy replied, shaking her head. Looking around at her friends, despair was written all over her face. When she looked up, it appeared she'd aged ten years overnight. "You'd think something would have made it in, wouldn't you? Something. Anything. But no, nothing."

Bob took a seat next to her. Slowly, to make certain she wouldn't move away, he shuffled nearer until he was able to gather her in a one-armed embrace. Though he addressed Marcy, his eyes were locked on his wife as he knew she needed to hear what he was about to say as much as Marcy did. It wouldn't explain everything he'd gone through, but it would go some way to helping her understand why he was like he was when he came back.

"Things were the same back in the last war. You don't want to know the number of times our artillery dropped shells on our trenches, or on us when we were attacking. It's an unspoken part of war—but that doesn't make it right," he hastened to add, when he felt Marcy was about to speak. "Of course it doesn't. These…incidents, never made it into the newspapers back then for the same reasons I reckon they don't now."

"Why's that?" Marcy managed to croak out.

"Morale," Bob simply replied, absently stroking her hair back into a semblance of order. "If it got out that we were killing our own men, even by accident, how would it look in the papers? No, this kind of news never gets out. Someone high up, somewhere, will shake their head, probably down a drink or two, maybe even send off a note or two, try to make sure it doesn't happen again, but that's all."

Marcy swiped a hand across her face and held up her now rather crumpled letter. "But what about this? How did this get through?"

Unseen by either, Harry had crept up on Marcy's other side. "What does she mean, Mr. Harker?"

Bob leant around Marcy as much as he could, but

before he could open his mouth, Berry filled in the blanks. "What she means, sweety, is why did the POW camp censor *not* censor that letter."

"Censor? What's a censor?" Lucy asked.

"Someone who reads POW letters before they're allowed to be sent. Or at least that's what it means here," Berry explained.

Lucy nodded, whether she understood or not, allowing Bob to speak again.

"I don't honestly know," he admitted. "Perhaps the Italian censor thought you deserved to know the truth and his English counterpart thought the same."

"It's as good a reason as you're likely to get," Sophie put in, after everyone had thought it over for a short while.

Gradually, under as tender ministrations as Sheila had ever seen from her husband, Marcy's eyes began to droop. Slowly, carefully, he lowered her head onto some cushions Harry hastily arranged. Quickly moving out of the way, Bob lifted Marcy's legs and laid them upon the sofa. Sheila took a throw down from the back of the sofa and laid it over the fitfully sleeping girl.

"Everyone out," Sheila told everyone.

Harry plonked herself down on the floor, leaning against the sofa by Marcy's head. "I'm not going anywhere," she announced, and then, before Sheila or anyone else could object, added, "I won't make a noise, but I'm staying until she wakes up."

Forestalling her husband's undoubtedly good-hearted objection, Sheila took him and Lucy by the hand, shooed Sophie, Vicky, and Berry out of the room, and nodded her head at Harry. "If you need us, we'll be around."

Harry merely nodded her head once, as she had by now turned her full attention onto the sleeping Marcy and was patiently making a better effort of tidying her hair than Bob had done.

The last thing anyone heard as Sheila gently pulled the door behind her was Harry beginning to softly sing, "Baa, Baa, Black Sheep, have you any wool?"

Chapter Twenty-Four

Unsurprisingly, Elaine Swallow was the picture of misery, and no amount of early morning sunshine was likely to brighten her spirits. A week after Marcy's letter about her husband's death, the girls found Elaine sitting alone in a wicker chair on the terrace outside her ward, playing tag with a stone with one of her crutches. Her head was down, and clearly she wasn't much aware of what she was doing. Nurses, doctors, and other patients passed regularly before her, yet nothing seemed to catch her attention.

"Come on," Berry said to her friends, taking hold of Sophie and Vicky's hands and leading them toward their injured friend. "Whatever you do," she warned, "don't stare."

Naturally, this had the opposite effect. Vicky came to a grinding halt, though fortunately, Elaine didn't appear to have seen them.

"What did I say?" Berry hissed, letting go of Sophie's hand and stepping before her young friend. "Swallow and breathe," she told her, gripping Vicky's upper arms and staring her firmly in the eye. "Don't think of yourself. You mustn't do that! Understand? Breathe in through your nose and out through your mouth. In and out, in and out."

Gradually, Vicky got her breathing back under control, and her face returned to a more natural color.

She took in one deep lungful of air before she gave a firm nod. "I'm okay now. Sorry, Berry."

"You sure?"

"I'm sure," Vicky told her, taking her hand and squeezing it. "Come on, before she spots us and wonders what we're doing."

The thunk of a wooden cane behind Berry gained their attention. "Too late," came a quiet voice. "That's exactly what I'm thinking."

"Elaine!" Berry cried in a way-too-happy voice as she spun around.

Their unfortunate friend was leaning heavily upon her cane, with more of a grimace upon her face than a smile. Not really a surprise, Berry thought.

Without replying, Elaine turned slowly around and half stomped and half hopped back toward her seat, collapsing awkwardly into it. Placing her crutches beside her, she took a moment before turning her head to face her friends, who still stood where she'd greeted them. "Well, are you staying or not?"

Looking around her, Berry pointed toward some chairs against the corridor wall. Vicky dragged a couple over whilst Berry took one for herself. Arranging themselves around their colleague, the three friends swapped glances, waiting for someone to start up the conversation. After what seemed to be an interminable wait, Elaine let out a short, bitter laugh.

"This is going to be a short visit," she mused, raising one eyebrow.

Naturally one of her visitors said the words, "So, how are you feeling?"

Berry and Sophie both turned incredulous looks upon Vicky, whilst Elaine merely stared at her at first.

"Could be better," she finally said, lowering her eyes.

Something made Elaine's visitors follow her gaze.

There was an empty space below the left side of her nightdress where her foot used to be. Sophie's hands flew to her mouth, and she had to look away. Berry and Vicky both looked at each other before pushing themselves out of their seats and, standing over Elaine, wrapped their arms around her. It took a few moments, but Elaine slowly snaked her arms around them too, with Sophie, after a moment's hesitation, awkwardly joining the group.

This was the way they were found by a doctor in a crumpled white coat ten minutes later. Behind him stood a middle-aged woman clutching a tattered brown handbag, as well as a handkerchief—which had seen better days—held to her mouth. When no one reacted to his presence after a minute or two, he coughed a couple of times to attract their attention.

Elaine looked up and extricated herself from the arms of her colleagues. "Mother!" Waving a hand, she grabbed a crutch and, with effort, heaved herself onto her one foot. "I wasn't expecting you. What are you doing here?"

The doctor laid a hand on Elaine's shoulder. "We telephoned her, Ms. Swallow."

"Do you know what…happened?" Elaine asked.

Her mother glanced at the doctor before turning back to her daughter. "Doctor Holmes told me." With a visible effort of will, Mrs. Swallow turned her attention to her daughter's visitors, who had leaped to their feet at realizing who had turned up. "Which one of you is Sophie?"

Plainly wishing she were anywhere but where she was, Sophie put up her hand, and with a little help from Vicky prodding her in the back, she stepped forward. "I'm Sophie."

Mrs. Swallow put down her handbag, and before Sophie could react, she'd wrapped the astonished girl in her arms and was sobbing into her shoulder.

"Thank you, thank you," she eventually managed to say, once she'd stopped crying.

Automatically, Sophie replied as she patted the woman's back, "What for?"

Letting Sophie go, she dabbed at her eyes and blew her nose. With a ghost of a smile, she leant forward and kissed Sophie on the cheeks before telling her, "What for? The doctor told me everything. If you hadn't acted so quickly, my daughter wouldn't be alive!"

****

Later that night the girls, this time including Marcy, who hadn't been out since her husband's death, were sat on stools before the bar at the King's Head.

"She never said another word?" Marcy asked, nursing a brown ale.

Staring straight ahead, Sophie shook her head. "Not one word."

"And how much longer did you all stay?"

"I've no idea." Sophie shrugged. "Berry?"

Accepting her second half pint of bitter from Muriel, Berry took a sip before answering. "Maybe ten minutes. The doctor wanted to give her a check, but the whole time, she just stared straight ahead. Didn't even say goodbye when her mother suggested it'd be best if we left, nor react when we said we'd pack her things up and send them on," she added with a shake of her head.

"She did thank Sophie for saving Elaine's life, though," Vicky put in.

"Well, that's quite something," Muriel said from the other side of the bar, as Sophie shrugged.

Marcy placed a comforting arm around Sophie. "It is, and you did," she told her.

"Sometimes…sometimes, I don't know if I did," Sophie surprised them in saying. "Maybe she'd be better off dead than with one foot?"

"Don't you dare think that!"

None of them had noticed Muriel's husband Brian standing next to his wife.

"Don't you dare," he repeated. "There's many a bloke down the British Legion hall who lost a leg in the trenches, and they get along just fine. So don't you dare dwell on that thought!" Muriel squeezed him around the middle as the girls took in what he'd just told them. "From what everyone's told us," he gave Muriel a quick kiss, "what you lot did, especially you, Sophie, took guts. Not everyone would have reacted as you did. She'll get used to it, and then I'm sure she'll feel differently. It was, after all, the first time she's seen you all since…the accident. Right?"

The girls shared looks before Berry replied, "You're right."

"Sophie?" Marcy asked.

It took her a little more time but eventually, she too agreed.

"To Elaine!" Sophie raised her glass.

Everyone, including Muriel and Brian, raised their glasses.

An hour later, the girls were enjoying a game of Shove Ha-Penny. Well, three of them were. Marcy wasn't joining in but was sat at the bar, deep in conversation with Muriel. When the door opened, the movement caught her eye, and before anyone had the chance to say a thing, Marcy had shot to her feet, an expression like thunder upon her face.

"What the hell are you lot doing here?" she yelled, slamming her glass down on the bar.

As the door closed behind them, Dennis strode toward Marcy, holding up his hands, hoping to head off another confrontation. Vicky and Berry beat him to it, nearly knocking the playing board to the floor in their haste to reach their friend.

"Marcy!" Berry yelled, reaching her side in two quick jumps.

"Don't worry," Marcy assured her. "I'm not going to do anything." She turned to their RAF friends who'd stopped a few paces into the room.

Archie stepped forward. "Really? You know, we never got the chance to speak about…what happened."

For the first time in the last couple of weeks, her friends noticed a smile begin to creep onto her face. "Come in, now you're all here," she said, "and join us for a drink. I assume this is what you hoped would happen?" she asked Muriel as she turned her head.

Muriel nearly choked on her drink before recovering. "In my defense, Sheila asked me to invite you lot over, and she got your contact number from Berry."

Berry ducked, in case Marcy threw something at her. "Did it work?"

The three RAF chaps were looking at Marcy, waiting for her reaction. By the looks on their faces, they'd rather face the formidable defenses of the Ruhr than upset her friends again. By way of an answer, Marcy grabbed Archie's hand and dragged him to the bar, closely followed by his mates.

"Come and have a drink, boys." When neither of the other two joined them at the bar, she turned and beckoned to them with her other hand. "I mean it, come on. I'm not going to bite this time. Three pints please, Brian," she asked.

A few minutes later, they were all sat around the table, with Muriel on her way with a tray of drinks. "Enjoy," she told them before returning to the bar.

There were a few moments of awkward silence before Berry spoke. "So how have you three been? Sorry we haven't seen you for a while. How's the wound, Dennis?" she hurriedly added.

"You know how it is." Dennis shrugged, waggling his arm to prove there was no lasting damage, before taking a long pull on his beer. "The odd bombing raid here, some training flights there."

"All unscathed, as you can see," Archie added.

"What about you lot?" Dennis asked.

Marcy shrugged. "Oh, you know. Chopping down trees, that kind of thing."

"Never mind the trees," Archie declared. "How are you?"

At hearing this question, everyone set their eyes on Marcy. During the past week or so, all the girls, as well as Sheila and Bob, but especially Harry, had asked her the same question, often multiple times a day. At no point had she provided any other reply than, "I'm fine," which none of them believed. Berry, Sophie, and Vicky had all decided to decline Marcy's offers of help to cut down trees, believing that her concentration levels wouldn't be at the required levels to perform such dangerous work. They'd each, at some point, sat up during the night with her when she couldn't sleep for crying for her lost husband.

"I don't know," Marcy whispered, barely loud enough for everyone to hear. When no one said anything, Marcy took a sip of her drink to give her some thinking time before looking around her group of friends. "I don't, I guess." She shrugged. "And I won't for a while. So I suppose I should rely on my friends to take care of me. Tell me when I'm being silly, hold my hand when I cry…"

"…and put you to bed when you fall down drunk," Berry put in.

Marcy smiled and nodded. "That too."

Archie, with a look aimed at her from under his eyebrows, declared, "Well, I suppose that will have to do for the moment."

A while later, Dennis set down a fresh tray of drinks, then took out an envelope from his pocket and laid it upon the table. He pushed it toward Marcy.

"What's that?"

"Open it and see," Dennis told her, before adding. "Though we weren't sure about this if you were still…well, you know…" he finished a bit lamely.

"Psychopathic?" she ventured.

"Spot on!" Vicky said, ducking to avoid Marcy's swinging hand.

"Perhaps we wouldn't have put it quite like that," Dennis mused.

"That's exactly how you put it when we were talking about this," Archie told him, earning a glare from his friend.

"If no one else is going to open this…" Vicky said, reaching for and drawing the letter toward her. With one swift swipe of a finger, she ripped open the letter. A moment later, she let out a squeal. "A dinner-and-dance invitation!"

Chapter Twenty-Five

Sophie spat on her hands and rubbed them together, whilst ignoring the calluses she was accumulating. Whenever she took note of them, she did her best to dismiss her concerns, after all, what were a few hard lumps of skin when Elaine had lost her foot. A swift heft and a swing, and the first cut was made. Though the girls were always careful, they were being much more careful than they had been before…then.

Yesterday, Marcy had called them all together before they started work to let them know Elaine had been invalided out of the Lumberjills. Considering what happened to her, this didn't come as a surprise. What did, and what really upset them, was that she'd discharged herself from hospital a few days ago without telling them. Sophie swung her axe with a little more force than necessary and felt the blow reverberate down her arms and into her body. Swearing, she lowered her axe and took some deep breaths to steady herself, reminding herself that lack of concentration had caused Elaine's accident, and that was the last thing she, of course, wanted. So Elaine hadn't wanted to say goodbye. That was her prerogative. But, dammit, *she* wanted to have said goodbye, to wish Elaine all the best, or whatever nonsense words would have come to mind.

Shaking her head, she looked up into the gray sky and wondered how long they'd get away without it raining today. A few hours longer than yesterday would be nice, she thought as she brought her axe up again.

"Hey, Sophie!"

The call made her look over her shoulder to see both Sally Newhart and Tina West jogging toward her. Now seemed as good a time as any for a break, she thought, raising her free hand to wave at her friends.

"Where's the rest of the gang?" Tina asked as she came up to Sophie and gave her a quick hug hello, closely followed by Sal.

"At the sawmill. Marcy's overseeing some of the new blokes training and thought it'd be good for the others to see what goes on."

"And you didn't want to go?" Sal asked.

Sophie shook her head. "Too noisy for me. I prefer the quiet."

"Can't say I blame you," Tina said. "That's about the only good thing of this job, the outdoors."

Before Sophie could reply, Sal asked, "We've been meaning to come around and ask about Elaine, but it's been difficult to get away."

"Robinsons still not treating you well?" Sophie asked.

Both the Land Girls shook their heads. "Too many cows and not enough of us. Well"—Tina spread out her arms—"there's only us."

Sophie shook her head. "The two of you. That's all, to run all that livestock!"

"About fifty cows," Sal nodded.

"And you can manage them? Just the two of you."

Sal nodded. "Mind you, at least I knew the difference between a cow and a bull. Unlike"—she jerked her head sideway at Tina—"some people I could mention."

"Hey!" Tina swatted her friend none too gently on the bottom. "I'm a townie! I barely knew where milk came from before they sent me here."

"She sure as hell does now!" Sal added with a loud guffaw.

"None of which answers our question about Elaine," Tina pointed out.

Sophie sighed, running a hand through her already messed-up hair. "I know," she told them before treating them to a wry kind of smile. "I was hoping you wouldn't notice."

"Elaine?" Tina said again.

"She's left."

"Left? Left what?" Sal asked.

"The Lumberjills. They invalided her out after she lost her foot," Sophie finally told them.

Both her friends looked wide-eyed at one another, their mouths opening and closing in unison. Sophie noticed and held out her arms wide, which both of them rushed in to. As they cried for someone they barely knew, Sophie stroked the backs of their heads. "It's all right to cry. Believe me, I've done enough of that myself lately."

"Did you," Tina asked as she pulled away, sniffing loudly, "manage to see her?" She tried and failed to pull together a smile with the question.

"Only the once."

"To say goodbye?" Sal asked.

Sophie shook her head. "Before then. We ran into her mother and, well, she thanked me for saving her daughter's life."

"That's quite something," Tina told her, shaking her

head.

"I suppose," Sophie replied with a shrug. "Only, Elaine herself barely said a word the whole time, and then, when Marcy telephoned the hospital to ask if we could visit again, a few days ago, they told her she'd discharged herself, and they didn't have an address or telephone number to contact her. It appears her mother left false information too."

"Bloody hell," Sal swore, whilst Tina could only shake her head again.

****

"Hey, look who it is!" Berry dug her elbow into Vicky's ribs as Sophie and the two Land Girls appeared through the trees.

"Enjoyed yourselves?" Sophie shouted as she spotted her friends making their way to where they kept their bicycles and lunch boxes.

"Not a jot," Berry stated, digging a finger into her ear.

"Marcy!" Sal yelled a little too loudly, as she bounded toward her, taking her by surprise and causing her to drop her clipboard as the young Land Girl grabbed her around the middle. "I'm so very sorry to hear about your husband." She then buried her head in Marcy's shoulder and hugged her as tightly as she could, forcing the older woman to tap her earnestly on the hip when breathing became an issue.

Once she'd got her breath back, Marcy rounded upon Sophie. "You told them?"

"I didn't want them to say something to make you feel awkward," she defended herself.

Tina briefly clasped Marcy's hand before letting go. "Don't blame Sophie, please. We were chatting on the way here and, well, it kind of slipped out."

"*Slipped* out?" Marcy queried her.

"Okay, okay. I blabbed," Sophie admitted, slipping out of Marcy's reach. "In my defense, you'd probably tell them at some point anyway."

After a minute, Marcy gave a reluctant nod. "You're probably right." She faced Sal. "Thank you."

"Do you mind my asking how you're getting on?" Tina asked. "I mean, really getting on. Not what you're telling your mates."

"What do you mean?" Marcy asked, after literally taking a step back and bumping into Berry, who'd come to a surprised stop right behind her.

Sal took a step toward a startled-looking Marcy and took her by the hand. "Listen to Tina. Believe me, she knows exactly what she's talking about."

Tina's smile didn't reach her eyes, yet she still nodded. "I've some experience, yes."

Marcy went to her bicycle and took out her flask, obviously playing for time to think. A quick half cup of tea later, she closed up her thermos and, holding it close to her body, eyed Tina skeptically.

Taking a deep breath, the Land Girl let her eyes rove over the group, briefly stopping on Sal, who gave her a firm nod of encouragement, before settling on Marcy. "I'm a war widow too. I lost my husband in Norway."

"But you don't look a day over twenty!" Vicky stated after she'd taken her hand away from her mouth.

Shaking her head sadly, Tina told her, "Death is no stranger to age. We'd only been married six months. What about you, Marcy?"

"About three years," she told her, though everyone had to strain to hear her.

"Can you spare some tea?" Tina asked.

"Have some of mine," Berry volunteered, obviously hoping her new friend would carry on talking.

Accepting the cup, Tina brought it to her lips, blew on it, and then took a sip. "Lovely. Thanks, Berry." She faced Marcy once more. "It's not much, or it probably feels like it isn't, but you've three years of memories. You've probably been living in those, and there's nothing wrong with that," she hastened to emphasize, "but you've got to let your friends in. Not all at once! This lot would be too much for the stoutest heart," she finished with an evil grin.

Marcy's gaze switched back and forth between Tina and her other friends. Back and forth it went until she eventually shook her head, clamping both hands to her cheeks, and in the next minute, her legs began to shake. Before anyone could react, she'd collapsed to the ground. In moments, everyone had dropped to her side, each trying to take a hold of her hand or rest a palm against her brow.

"Will you all stop it!" Marcy shouted after a few seconds. "I'm all right. Really!" However, she brushed a hand across her eyes, wiping them clear of the tears which had suddenly sprung up. She looked across to where Tina was knelt before her, patiently waiting for her to gather herself. "How did you know?"

"Know what?" Vicky couldn't stop herself from asking, earning herself a stern look from Berry and Sal. Sophie didn't look up, her thoughts drawn once more to poor Ginger Baker.

"I didn't." Tina shrugged. "I'm no doctor, I only know what worked for me, and I only have a much shorter amount of memories than you, Marcy. They're what worked for me, though I've found you can't dwell on them. Live for today, to start with, that's another thing I've learned. It's what…I'm sorry. I don't know what your husband's name is…"

"Matthew," Marcy told her and then, more strongly, "Matt, his name was Matt."

"Matt," Tina rolled the name around her tongue. "A good name. Anyway, I'm certain he'd want you to live. It's what he was fighting for, after all. Our right to choose and to love."

****

"No, Harry." Sheila was trying to rein in a rather excited teenager and, not having much experience, was finding it a steep learning curve.

"What was that you said, Mrs. Harker?" Harry asked from where she was swinging back and forth on the gate which barred entrance to the farm from the main road.

"Please, Harry. Call me Sheila," she asked, hoping to distract the hyperactive youngster for the few more minutes it would take before the bus dropping Lucy off from school was due. "I've asked you a number of times."

Harry swung herself up and over the gate until she was now looking at the farmer's wife. "Sheila," she tried rolling it round her tongue. "Sheila, Sheila, Sheila." She shrugged. "Okay, Sheila. I'll try. Does this mean I should call Mr. Harker, Bob?"

After thinking this over for a few seconds, during which she spotted the school bus coming into view, Sheila eventually agreed. "Probably a good idea. I'm sure he won't mind. Let me tell him," she told her. "Now, hop off that gate, Lucy's about to get off the bus."

A minute later, Harry was waiting to grab Lucy from

the bottom step of her bus.

"Where've you been? The village shop's got toffees in!" she finished, setting her sister down and turning expectantly toward Sheila. "All ready!"

"Oh, the things I do for love," Sheila muttered, hurrying to grab Lucy's hand before her older sister could drag her off down the road.

Half an hour later, an exhausted Sheila pushed open the kitchen door at the farmhouse and virtually crashed into the room. Eyeing up her husband, who was washing his hands in preparation for tea, she hung her coat up on the hooks behind the door and slumped down into a chair.

"Next time, you get to take them," she stated, letting her head fall onto the table top. By way of an answer, Bob placed a steaming cup of tea before her, earning him a grateful, though tired, smile. "I knew I married you for a reason."

Bob took up the seat opposite her. "I take it they were a handful?"

"Lucy was an angel, or quite near one. As for Harry? I thought you'd wear her out, what with her helping you look after the cows."

Bob chuckled before telling her, "You'd think so, wouldn't you? It seems the cows love her or, at least, they do anything she actually asks them. It's the strangest thing you've ever seen!"

"Cows are sweeties," Harry announced as she stepped into the room, pulling out the seat next to Bob.

"Where's Lucy?" he asked.

"Getting changed," Harry said, popping a toffee into her mouth.

Sheila held the hand that had done the popping. "Do

you think it'd be a good idea to ration those, Harry?"

Harry's other hand automatically tightened around her precious paper bag of toffees. As she opened her mouth to answer, she nearly jumped out of her skin as Marcy's hand gripped her shoulder.

"I think that would be a very good idea, don't you?"

Harry spun around and, in the way of children, said the first thing which came to her mind, "Marcy! You're smiling!" then, still gripping her bag, somehow launched herself into Marcy's arms.

Whilst holding the girl in her arms, they were joined around the table by her friends, all of whom regarded the scene closely. Tightening her arms around Harry so the girl grunted a little, Marcy told them, again with her genuine smile in evidence, "I've had a good talking to and realized I've a reason to smile."

Chapter Twenty-Six

"You're sure Elias didn't object to you borrowing his car?" Marcy asked, willing her fingers to let go of the sides of her seat—and failing.

Berry noticed her friend's predicament and frowned. "You can let go, Marcy. I'm not that bad a driver," she added at the same time she jerked the steering wheel to the left to avoid a stationary telegraph pole.

"You have got a license?" Vicky asked from the back seat.

Berry whipped her head around to answer and so never noticed how close they came to running over a family of rabbits which nearly chose the wrong moment to cross the road. "Of course I have. Why?"

"No reason," Sophie squeaked from where she was huddled with her hands over her eyes.

Turning back around to face the road, Berry added, "And Elias was very happy to let me borrow the car. He's having an evening with Bob and Sheila. Whoops!"

Vicky whipped her head around. "Was that a deer?"

Berry shrugged her shoulders. "Probably. I've seen quite a few in the forest."

"You haven't driven much lately, have you?" Marcy asked as Berry leant forward over the steering wheel, the better to make out the road.

Berry hesitated before answering this time. "Not as such," she eventually admitted, pressing the horn and leaning out the window to yell, "Why don't you take up all the road?"

"Sorry!" Marcy shouted at the stunned cyclist they'd just run into a hedge. "You know…" She turned to face Sophie and Vicky. "I think that was Lucy's school teacher."

"Well!" Berry frowned as she flung the car around the wrong side of a blind bend in the road. "She should watch where she's going."

Vicky tapped Berry on her shoulder. "Never mind, just concentrate and get us to the dance in one piece."

Berry began to turn her head, only for Marcy to gently nudge her under the chin until she was once more facing the road. "Eyes on where you're driving, young lady," Marcy told her. "It's about time we all had some fun," she went on, "and I for one would prefer to get there in one piece. Agreed?"

This was the first time any of them had heard Marcy mention fun for a while. Gradually, she'd gotten more and more like her old self, though she had surprised everyone by readily agreeing to come to the dance. Whilst everyone else had been getting dressed in the barn, with some unwelcome help and suggestions from Harry, Marcy had requested Sheila's help, and the two had disappeared upstairs in the farmhouse. When she'd come down, there was a complete transformation. Her hair had been dyed brown, and Sheila had expertly styled it to resemble that of the popular movie star Deborah Kerr. The transformation was stunning, yet the only thing she said when asked about her new look was that she needed to begin a new life.

The journey took them just over an hour, not because of the traffic, as little enough civilian traffic was around these days. For one thing, most people had no fuel to spare other than for the journeys of necessity. No, what made the journey longer than it ordinarily would have been was when Vicky sent them down a country lane that definitely didn't take them toward their goal. This had led to Marcy taking over navigation duties, which caused Vicky to sulk until they were stopped by the guards outside RAF Linton-On-Ouse.

As they had all decided to go to the dance in full Lumberjill uniform, it wasn't surprising when the airman on guard looked at them with undisguised curiosity. "Can I help you, ma'am?"

Deciding it would take too long to explain to the lad that he didn't really have to address her as ma'am, Berry held out the letter Dennis had given them. Though Archie had said he'd be waiting for them at the guardroom, it had been agreed it would be best to play safe, just in case of some kind of misunderstanding. This didn't turn out to be the case, as before she'd even had the chance to open her mouth, let alone speak, Archie came bounding around the corner of the guardroom, waving a hand.

"That's all right, Groves!" he told the one on guard duty, clapping the young man on the shoulder. "They're here for the dance. Come with me, Marcy. We'll just sign in, and then I'll guide you to the mess."

Five minutes later, they were on their way, and though Vicky was no longer sulking about being taken off map-reading duties, she was now hacked off because she had Marcy on her lap. Elias's car wasn't very big, and the running board was too narrow for Archie's big feet. Consequently, he'd taken Marcy's seat to guide Berry to the officer's mess where the dance was taking place.

"Are we there yet?" she asked for the third time in less than two minutes.

"Not much longer," Archie informed her. He directed Berry to, "take the next left and then the second right. Hey, I've just realized," Archie said, turning to the others, "this is the first time you'll be meeting the rest of the crew!"

"What do you mean, the rest of the crew?" Berry asked, nearly missing her turning, causing Vicky to utter another curse as Marcy almost tumbled off her lap.

"Didn't you ever wonder where the rest of the lads were?" Archie asked, only to be met by blank stares. "We fly Lancasters...No? A Lancaster has a crew of seven, and you lot only know four..." He momentarily stumbled and had to swallow. "Well, three of us now poor Ginger's dead. Sorry, Sophie," he added, reaching a hand over the seat. She gratefully squeezed his hand with her own. "Well, the other guys are all married and declined to join us. They didn't want to...get in the way."

"Didn't get in the way of much, did they," Marcy added with a smile to show she was only stating a fact.

Marcy had forgotten who she was talking to, as Archie replied with a distinctly arched eyebrow. "Perhaps," he had time to say before hastily turning back. "Here we are, Berry, stop!"

"Where do you want me to park, Archie?" Berry asked as she came to a halt opposite the entrance to the officer's mess.

"Let's let these girls out first, and then I'll show you," Archie said. "The mess car park's around the back."

Archie quickly directed Berry to a parking spot near

the kitchens, and the two were just opening the doors when Berry froze, one foot outside. "Did you hear that?"

"Hear what?" Archie asked, slamming the car door shut.

Berry got out of the car and then ducked her head to look under the front seat, saying, "I thought it sounded like…" Without completing the sentence, she fished an arm under the driver's seat and came out with a bundle of squirming, mewing black fur. "Midnight!"

"Who?" Archie asked and then amended to, "Ah," as Berry held up her nearly perpetual companion.

Keeping a tight grip upon Midnight with one hand, Berry pulled up her jumper and tucked the kitten inside. "I guess someone didn't like getting left behind," she said smiling and stroking the top of Midnight's head, causing her to begin softly purring.

"Okay," Archie stretched out the word. "I don't think the C/O will be very happy if we try and bring this little…lady, is it?" Berry nodded. "To bring her into the mess. He's a dog person," he explained. Archie snapped his fingers. "Got it! Hold on here for a few minutes. I'll be right back."

So saying, he took to his heels, disappearing through a door marked Kitchen, leaving a rather mystified Berry alone in the car park with a once more soundly asleep kitten. "Ssh," she whispered to her furry companion. "I'm sure he'll be right back with…whatever he's gone to do."

Sure enough, she soon spotted Archie trotting out the door a little more carefully than he'd disappeared, and in his hands he was carrying a dish. When he got nearer, she saw it contained water.

"I thought she could be a little thirsty," he stated,

carefully holding the bowl right under Midnight's nose, which began to twitch.

Berry opened the car door with her free hand. "Good thinking. Put it on the floor of the passenger seat. We'll leave the windows down a little, too."

"Aren't you afraid they'll be a little, um, mess when you come to leave?" Archie ventured.

Berry carefully closed the door, leaving Midnight lapping from the bowl, before turning to address Archie. She shrugged. "Perhaps, but we'll just have to take that risk. Come on," she added. "We'd better get back to the girls. They'll be wondering where we've got to."

However, when the two of them rounded the corner and were walking up to the entrance to the mess where they'd dropped their friends, Berry saw she'd been laboring under a false assumption. Not only had Archie's mates Dennis and Jimmy found her girlfriends, but there were four other chaps in uniform with them. As the two stepped up behind them, Berry asked, "Archie, perhaps you'd do the introductions?"

"You've picked a good night," Archie informed her. "The C/O's made this an all-ranks affair, so we'd better make this quick or we'll lose our table."

"There you two are!" Marcy announced, spotting them over Dennis's shoulder. "Come and meet…oh, heck," she finished rather lamely and turned to Dennis. "You're going to have to tell us who's who again, Dennis. I'm afraid I've forgot. Sorry, boys," she told the rest of the crew with a tilt of her head.

"That's okay," he replied, laying a hand on the shoulder of one of the new lads. "This is Sergeant Teddy Cox. He's er, our new rear gunner." The girls smiled as Sophie made a point of shaking him firmly by the hand, before stepping back to clutch Marcy's. Dennis coughed and carried on with his introductions. "The twins, here, are Pilot Officer Joey Brown and Flying Officer Rupert Murdox, our navigator and wireless operator. If you have trouble telling them apart, Joey's barely over five and a half foot, whilst Rupert is a shade under six and a half. The red hair always causes confusion." All the girls, quite naturally, shook their heads. "Finally, and definitely last, this is Flight Sergeant Jerry Ryan, the finest mid-upper gunner in the RAF!"

With introductions now made, the four new chaps shook hands, and Joey told the group he'd go and make sure they'd still got a table. Dennis and Jimmy held the mess's double doors open for the girls to pass through, only to be met by the genial smile of a clean-shaven, round-faced officer. He stepped away from the two men he'd been talking to.

"Well, well, Grey!" He smiled, surveying the group before him. "It seems introductions are in order. Who do we have here?"

Dennis stood to attention before holding out a hand toward the ATA group. "Ladies, this is my boss, Wing Commander Mair. Boss, I have the great honor to introduce some of the girls of the Lumberjills. These are Sophie, Vicky, and the two who rescued me when I bailed out into that forest a while back, Marcy and Berry."

The wing commander shook each of the girls' hands in turn before saying, "I'm very pleased to meet you all. It's good to finally put faces to names. These chaps seem to talk of nothing but you girls," he said with a wink, causing Marcy and Berry to treat their friends to a knowing look and the two men in question to turn a fetching shade of red. "My thanks for helping this idiot get down from that tree." He laid a hand upon Dennis's shoulder. "I did warn him the squadron hack needed an engine service, but no, he knew better. Said it'd be okay for a quick flight to the Maintenance Unit and back. Guess who's not allowed to take a jolly now?" He winked. "Well, enjoy yourselves," he said before nodding his head and walking away. "You all look stunning, if I may say," he added over his shoulder.

Sophie looked down at her jumper and jodhpurs, before shaking her head and muttering to herself, "I take it he does mean us?"

"Seems like a nice man," Marcy eventually said after everyone had finished looking everywhere except at each other. "Shall we?" she said, offering her arm to Archie, who beamed in reply and led the way to the dining room, which was pulling double-duty as a dance hall.

"May I?" Dennis asked, offering Berry his arm. After a moment's hesitation, Berry accepted and followed Marcy, with Archie nearly bumping into a chair as he was unable to keep his eyes off the girl on his arm. "How's she doing? After, you know."

Berry regarded the back of her friend who was now leaning into Archie's side and appeared to be laughing at something he'd said. "You know, I think she's going to be all right. If you'd have asked us about this dance a couple of weeks ago, we wouldn't have come, as we wouldn't have left her on her own. But now, well, look at her. I didn't know Archie could be so funny!"

Dennis leaned in so Berry could hear over the band. "Neither did I," he told her, being rewarded with a small laugh.

With Sophie, Vicky, and Jimmy following behind, they soon made their way to a table where their crew mates were reserving their seats for them.

"Quite an entrance there, Skipper!" Teddy remarked.

Sure enough, when they'd all taken their seats, the group could see what he meant. Though there appeared to be at least two girls to each table, a multitude of uniforms amongst them, the girls stood out from the crowd by a wide margin. Not being part of the armed forces, they didn't have an equivalent uniform as such. Instead, they'd all worked hard to clean and spruce up their jodhpurs and jumpers. When Marcy had suggested the idea, no one had immediately jumped at the idea. However, by the combination of bribery and begging, she'd finally got her way.

Dennis had obviously been thinking the same thing, though his eyes were only for Berry, who was taking off her beret and making certain her hair was still in place. He got to his feet, stood before her, and with a small bow of his head asked, "May I have the pleasure of this dance?"

Chapter Twenty-Seven

"I love the outfit," Dennis told Berry as they did their best to keep in time with the music, before they both gave up and settled down to their own rhythm. They weren't alone.

Though the band was enthusiastic, this didn't anywhere near make up for their lack of expertise.

Berry tapped Dennis on the shoulder. "Is it normal for a Boy Scout band to play at these nights?"

She caught the small frown, closely followed by a chuckle. "You noticed. No," he told her with a small shake of his head, "our usual band dropped out, and this lot stepped in at the last minute."

A young lad in the back row of the band got to his feet at that moment and proceeded to perform a trumpet solo, which had nothing to do with the tune the rest of his friends were attempting to play. Everyone on the dance floor immediately stopped, turning as one to stare at the spectacle before them. A round of applause erupted as he finished with a loud wail, his instrument pointed to the ceiling. With a wide sweep of his arms, he bowed and then took his seat, the rest of the band beginning something which could have been a waltz.

"Did you see the look he got from the conductor?" Berry asked as they sorted out their arms.

"I did," he told her, as they joined the mass of twirling bodies. "I wouldn't like to be in his boots later."

"Me either," she eventually agreed on their second pass by the band. The feel of Dennis's hand gripping her around the waist and the closeness of their bodies had temporarily taken away her ability to form a coherent answer.

As the moment took their attention, with sadly the less said about the music the better once more, neither noticed Jimmy and Vicky sweeping stealthily out of the room.

****

"You're sure you don't want to dance?" Jimmy asked Vicky as they slowed to a walk once they were out of the front entrance to the mess and into the open air.

She shook her head. "I never learned."

Jimmy quickly stepped before her and took both of her hands. "I could teach you, if you like?"

"I'd rather my first dance be to a real band. If you don't mind, that is?" she asked upon seeing the airman's head droop.

For a second or two, their eyes locked, and the teenage girl and her not much older bomb aimer seemed to forget where they were and anything going on around them.

"D-did you say something?" Vicky asked, stuttering a little.

Jimmy shook his head and looked around. Still with his hand in hers, he tugged her away from the steps until they were around a corner and out of sight of the mess entrance. Because of the gathering dusk and the subsequent blackout, both almost tripped over a cat haring in the opposite direction.

"Vicky," Jimmy jerked to a halt. "Was that Midnight?"

Not waiting to answer, Vicky let go of his hand and took off after the cat.

"Never. So. Glad. Not. Wearing. Dress," she gasped as Jimmy caught her up. "Midnight!" she briefly stopped to shout.

Ignoring the two airmen who strolled past them as they neared a hangar, they both skidded to a halt. Vicky turned back to them to ask, "Have you seen a cat go past?"

From the confused expressions upon their faces, she surmised they hadn't, and once more she took to her feet, the shoes she was wearing dealing out a real pounding to the road.

"Where're you going?" Jimmy yelled after her, confusedly throwing a salute at the airmen even though he wasn't wearing his hat.

"I think I saw a tail!" she shouted back as she began to run around the perimeter of the hangar.

Concerned she might trip on the uneven grass, Jimmy put in an effort and caught Vicky up just in time to catch her as her toe caught in a divot.

"You all right?"

"Fine, fine." She waved away his concern, her head moving back and forth. "Look," she asked, "can we get inside?"

"Do you think he's inside?"

"I'm sure I saw a tail. I really am!" she implored, facing Jimmy, who'd placed a hand on either of her shoulders.

"Look," he decided, "let's check all the way around the hangar first."

Vicky gave him a look which clearly implied her thoughts on this idea. However, she eventually nodded.

Five minutes later, they were back where they'd started. "Now can we go inside?"

Jimmy nodded his head and took her by the hand. "Come on."

However, as soon as they passed through the blackout curtains and Jimmy had held open the door, Vicky found herself in a cavernous space bigger than she'd ever been in before.

"Blinking heck!" she couldn't help but cry out, causing a mechanic to drop the spanner he was carrying.

Picking it up, he looked up at Jimmy and asked, "Anything I can help you with, sir?"

Calm as you like, Jimmy asked, "I don't suppose you've seen a black cat?"

In fairness to the airman, he didn't blink in response to the strange question. "In here?"

Jimmy nodded, quickly grabbing Vicky's hand as she began to slink away. "Hold on, please. There's quite a few ways you can get hurt in here."

"Afraid not," the airman answered and then, when it appeared he wasn't needed any longer, made to move off.

"Hang on, Taggart," Jimmy asked. "Look, I'm serious. Ms. Strood here, found a stowaway in her car when she came up for the dance, and we think that it got out. She…*we*," he hastily amended when Vicky dug her nails into his palm, "last saw it heading in this direction. We can't see it outside, and it's not answering to our calls. So, as it's getting dark and we'll have little chance of finding it outside,"—he winced again—"we want to search in here."

Taggart's eyebrows flicked up, and it looked like he was about to object, only he saw the anxious expression upon Vicky's face and whistled loudly, instantly getting the attention of everyone in the hangar.

"Black cat, you say? About how big, miss?"

Vicky opened her hands, waving them back and forth a little before coming to a decision on size. By this time, about a dozen other mechanics had joined them, most of them openly curious at the sight of the strange couple in their midst, one dressed in his best blues, the other looking like she was dressed to, well, chop down a tree.

"Lads!" Taggart said out loud. "The miss and the officer here have lost a cat." Much murmuring accompanied this statement before Taggart managed to quieten them down. "It's black, about that big"—he pointed to where Vicky was still holding her hands out— "and possibly somewhere in here. Now, has anyone seen it?" Unfortunately, no one had, so he asked, "In that case, I'm sure the officer will be very grateful…" He stopped to treat Jimmy to a pointed look that meant to convey he'd better, and that this gratitude should be in the form of bottles of beer. Upon receiving a nod that his message had been received and understood, he continued, "…if we all down tools for half an hour and give this old place a good onceover."

Subsequently, for the next thirty-odd minutes, all that could be heard were various shouts along the lines of, "Midnight! Here, cat! Puss!" Vicky herself tried to look everywhere at the same time, knocking her head at least twice on the fuselage of the Lancaster bomber being repaired. All to no avail, and one by one, the mechanics drifted back to work, eventually leaving Taggart standing before Vicky and Jimmy.

"Sorry, sir, miss," he apologized with a shrug.

Vicky rapped the fuselage of the bomber they were now standing next to and slightly under. "Did anyone check in here?"

Neither the airman or Jimmy noticed the slightly manic glint in Vicky's eye, nor that she was playing with a penknife in the hand which was by her side.

"Careful there!" Jimmy told her, reaching across and rubbing his sleeve over the patch where Vicky had rubbed. "C for Charlie needs to be ready for…tomorrow," he finished rather lamely, "…and the skipper will have my hide if we knock a hole in her side."

Vicky's eyes refocused. She tucked the penknife back into her jodhpurs. "This is your plane?" This time, she reached out and carefully rubbed the palm of her hand over the large letter C stenciled upon the fuselage.

"Yes," Jimmy replied before holding out his hand and taking her around to the other side of the fuselage where a small ladder was placed to lean up against the entry to the bomber. "Put your bag down," he instructed before clambering inside and turning around to hold out his hand to help Vicky inside. "Watch your head," he advised as Vicky followed him into the shadowy interior, "and where you put your feet."

With care, Vicky looked around. In spite of the size of the bomber, there didn't appear to be many places anything could hide, let alone a cat. "Midnight!" she called forgetting her voice would be amplified inside the cramped fuselage, causing Jimmy to jerk upright and bang his head on the low ceiling. There wasn't enough height to allow anyone of anywhere normal height to stand upright. "Sorry," she told him as she did her best to hop, quite inelegantly, over the main wing spar. "Who designed this bloody thing?" Vicky muttered as she

234

made her way up to the navigator's station, calling out again.

On the alert this time, Jimmy merely winced at the noise and climbed through the cockpit, carefully looking into every nook and cranny he could.

"Any luck?" Vicky asked, though without much hope.

He shook his head, but levered himself up onto the pilot's seat so he was out of her way. "No, but feel free to take a look. Please try not to touch or move any knobs or levers, though," he asked.

Vicky moved carefully past him and poked her head down toward his bomb-aiming position, before cranking her head to one side to look up at him. "This is where you…work?"

"That's my office," he answered with a wry smile.

Being as careful as she'd been asked to be, Vicky crept down and carefully lay down upon the single green leather-pad upon which he lay when on the bomb run. Above her head were two stirrups for his feet when he was operating the front turret. "How the bloody hell do you get comfortable in here?" she asked, looking carefully around.

"You don't." Jimmy waited for Vicky to make her slow way back to where he waited before replying. Not giving her a chance to say anything, he climbed out of the pilot's seat and, in one swift, practiced movement, vaulted the wing spar. "Come on." He held out his hands to help her over. "There's only the rear to check now."

"What's this?" Vicky asked, rapping the top of a circular object the other side of the doorway they'd entered by.

She was about to lift up the lid, when Jimmy tapped

her on the shoulder. "I wouldn't, if I were you. That's a toilet," he explained, causing Vicky to wipe her fingers up and down her trousers.

They climbed past it, Vicky giving it as wide a berth as she could, eventually ending up at the rear turret. Its doors were wide open, so Vicky stuck her head inside, coming out shaking her head. Slumping down onto the fuselage floor, she put her head in her hands before looking up, her face a picture of misery.

"What am I going to do, Jimmy? Berry's going to kill me!"

Jimmy sat down beside her, reached out and took her hand. When she didn't protest, he brought it to his lips and planted a kiss on her palm. "Why Berry?"

Bum-bouncing, Vicky moved along until she could lean shoulder to shoulder. "Midnight always sleeps on her pillow," she began, but a loud coughing interrupted them.

"Pilot Officer Dunn, would you care to explain what's going on here?" came a very authoritative voice.

Looking up, both saw they were being addressed by none other than Wing Commander Mair; he didn't look happy.

Vicky looked at Jimmy, who returned the look, before both noticed the Wing Commander was giving them both a look which could freeze water.

"Anytime you'd both care to join me?" the senior officer suggested, sparking a mad scramble as the pair hastened to get down the ladder without breaking anything, including their legs. "Pilot Officer?" he prompted once Jimmy was stood to attention before him. Vicky seemed torn between being in awe of the Wing Commander and glaring up at him. Fortunately, he didn't notice. "I was telephoned by the NCO i/c this hangar that there were two mad people tearing the place apart, searching for a cat!"

"We're not mad," Vicky protested before Jimmy could open his mouth, "and we're not tearing the place apart. We *are* looking for a cat, though."

"Thank you, Ms. Strood," he acknowledged briefly before turning his attention back to the slightly shaking Jimmy. He took a long, slow look around the hangar before saying, "Well, I agree that you don't appear to have torn the place apart," he said, though the grin was soon wiped from Vicky's face at his next words. "However, I cannot have either of you disturbing the mechanics. We're…busy tomorrow night," he carefully said, "so we need every aircraft serviceable, and I won't get that if you two don't leave these chaps to do their jobs. Miss Strood, Pilot Officer Dunn, did you find your cat?"

Struck a little dumb for one of the few times in her life, Vicky could only shake her head.

"No, sir," Jimmy admitted, "we didn't have any luck."

The Wing Commander nodded before turning to face Vicky, who was relieved to find he had a sympathetic smile upon his face, though the words he said weren't of much comfort. "My dear Miss Strood, I do sympathize with your predicament. However, as you've not found anything, I must ask that you come back to the mess. I'm afraid I can't have civilians running all over the shop. This is an operational airfield, after all, and I don't want to risk your getting hurt." He quickly held up a hand as Vicky opened her mouth, undoubtedly to protest. "Firstly, your friends are worried about you, and I'm not sure how much longer the pilot officer's crewmates can stop them from leaving the mess to come to your aid. Secondly, and you have my personal promise on this, Miss Strood, I will make the whole station aware of what has happened, with instructions to catch the cat, unharmed, if and when it is seen. This is the best I can do for you. Is this acceptable?"

Vicky glanced around the once more busy hangar before nodding and allowing the Wing Commander to offer her his arm. During the next ten minutes, Vicky constantly and much to the Wing Commander's amusement shouted Midnight's name at the top of her voice. At one point, a guard patrol came running around a hedge, rifles at the ready, only to amble off, most disappointed to find there wasn't an emergency going on. Waiting on the steps of the officer's mess were all her friends.

At seeing Berry, Vicky rushed toward her, with Berry only just opening her arms in time to grab hold of the younger girl. "Oh, Berry!" Vicky cried. "I've lost Midnight!" she managed to get out before bursting into tears.

"What happened?" Berry asked Jimmy over Vicky's shoulder.

"Not sure," Jimmy admitted as he accepted a pint of beer from Dennis. "We came outside, and the next thing I knew, a cat nearly tripped us up and the chase was on!"

Marcy raised her hand and asked, "It's just a thought, but has anyone actually checked the car? You know, to see if she's really gone?"

As everyone was looking at each other, Marcy sighed in exasperation and ran off toward the car park, only to return at a slightly slower trot, shaking her head.

"Worth a try," Sophie observed.

With a shake of his head, Wing Commander Mair straightened his tie. "I have to get back to the party. Miss Strood, if I can be of service in any other way?"

Whether he was merely being polite, nobody had the chance to discover. Upon hearing his words, Vicky extricated herself from Berry's arms and took out her penknife. "Do you see this?" she asked him.

Obviously wondering if this was some kind of trick question, the Wing Commander took a few moments before replying, "Er, it appears to be a penknife."

Vicky snapped it shut. "Correct, Wing Commander. It's all I have left to remember my brother. He was killed at Dunkirk."

"My condolences," he told her.

Vicky stepped up until she was nose to top button with the officer. Tilting her chin back, her eyes seemed to blaze with fire as she told him, "Let me go on a sortie. I want to shoot down a Nazi plane!"

Chapter Twenty-Eight

"You do realize they'll phone when they find her?" Sheila informed Vicky as she picked up the telephone for the second time that evening.

With some reluctance, Vicky replaced the receiver and, with drooping shoulders, walked back through the kitchen and out the back door without uttering a word.

"I don't know what else I can say," Berry declared, turning in her seat as the rear door shut behind her friend.

"You've told her you don't blame her, and from what we can all see, you're not treating her any different. What else is there to say?" Sophie waved a dismissive hand.

"I do miss her, I'm not going to deny that," Berry answered. "It's only been a day, and despite her favorite activity being sleeping, I'm sure she'll be able to look after herself until someone finds her. Should I go and talk to her again?"

"Talk to who?" Harry asked as she burst into the room.

"If carrots help you see at night, what the hell are you eating to have hearing like that?" Bob stated as he followed the girl into the kitchen. "I was only just behind you and didn't hear a dickybird!"

Lucy looked up from her maths homework. "She's always been like that," Lucy announced, earning herself a light swat around the top of her head from her sister.

"Hey!' she protested before going back to her work when Sheila tapped her exercise book.

Harry plonked herself down next to her sister and looked across at Berry. "So who'd you need to talk to?"

Berry let her head drop onto the tabletop before replying, "Vicky. I think she thinks I hate her."

"Oh, ignore her," Marcy advised, putting down her newspaper.

"I can't!" Berry decided, pushing back her seat and getting to her feet. "I'm going to find her."

"I think she was heading in the direction of the stream!" Harry called after her.

Ever since Bob had created their outdoor shower, the girls hadn't needed to go to the stream for a wash when the bathroom wasn't available. Subsequently, whenever one of them needed some personal space away from the hustle and bustle of work, or their somewhat crowded living quarters, they'd disappear down to the stream. Normally no one would go and disturb any of them. However, in this case, no one got up to stop Berry.

"Vicky?" she called as she came within earshot of the running water, stopping for a second to see if she got an answer. When no reply came, she plodded on until she stepped around some rocks and was confronted by the sight of Vicky and nearly tripped herself up in her rush to comfort the obviously distraught girl. Before the poor girl was even aware it had happened, Berry had wrapped her in her arms. "Oh, Vicky, do stop being silly, love."

What she got in reply sounded like, "Mimble, wimble," to Berry's ears before Vicky snorted into her ear, took a deep breath, and tried again. "It's all my fault!"

Knowing she wouldn't get anywhere until Vicky

had cried her fill, Berry let her friend sob herself into sniffing silence.

Berry placed a hand on either of Vicky's shoulders and leant against her, forehead to forehead. "Look," she began, her voice soft and calm, "I don't know what I've got to do to persuade you I'm not blaming you. So"—she pulled back slightly so they could look each other in the eye—"logic dictates there must be something else wrong. Care to share?"

Vicky pulled a handkerchief out of a pocket and loudly blew her nose and wiped it before putting it away. "Am I really so transparent?" she eventually asked.

Berry kissed her on the cheek. "Only to your friends."

"Only to my friends," Vicky muttered, before stepping back and sitting back down.

Without hesitation, Berry joined her on the large mossy boulder she'd chosen. After a few minutes of silence, she nudged her friend in the side. "Well…?"

"Do you…" Vicky tried again. "Do you all think I'm being stupid?"

"Of course not," Berry assured her. "I suppose we all find it strange the way you're behaving after only a day."

They both watched a squirrel as it scampered along the tall grass beside the stream, its antics bringing a smile to each of the girl's faces, though only the one on Berry's face reached her eyes.

Vicky canted her head to the side and said, "It has really only been a day, hasn't it."

Berry nodded and flung an arm around Vicky's shoulders. "Not even that long, really. We hadn't even arrived at the station by this time."

"And they promised to call, as soon as they've found her?" Vicky asked, for probably the fifth time since they'd got back from work.

"Cross my heart and hope to die," Berry promised.

She was about to cross her heart with her hand, but Vicky grabbed it before she could complete the motion. "Don't!" she implored.

No one could mistake the desperate note in her voice. Berry let her keep hold of her hand, in spite of the pain Vicky's nails were causing her as they dug into her palm. "Suppose you tell me what this is all really about, eh?"

The same squirrel, possibly, made a reappearance and loped toward them, stopping every now and then to look up and sniff the air. Both girls watched in mesmerized silence until it stopped to sniff at Vicky's boots. Slowly, carefully, Vicky lowered her free hand, all the while keeping a close eye upon the small gray chap, until her fingers were mere inches from its furry, twitching nose. A few seconds more, and with only a slight hesitation, first one paw, then another, and another until the animal was sitting upon Vicky's palm.

Both were now holding their breath. In slow motion, Vicky brought her hand up to their eye level. Transfixed, Vicky whispered, "Isn't he gorgeous?"

Berry had only enough time to nod her head before the squirrel grew tired of the humans and, with a twitch of its beautiful bushy tail, hopped off Vicky's hand, bounded across the stream, and swept up a tree, observing the two of them for a few more seconds before disappearing from view.

"Oh, my God!" Vicky uttered, managing to rein in a squeal. "That was…amazing!"

All Berry could do was to vigorously nod her head, as she'd lost the power of speech.

Vicky finally let go of Berry's hand. "I only had one pet when I grew up," she began. "I found a stray cat in the gutter when I was walking home from school. Nursed it back to health, too," she added. "Beautiful little thing. Black as coal," she reminisced, her eyes losing focus, "just like Midnight. In fact, they're even the same size."

Sensing where this was going, Berry prodded, as gently as she could, "What happened?"

"My dad shot it."

Berry's hands flew to her mouth, her eyes popped out as if on stalks and involuntarily, her head snapped between Vicky and the way back to the farm.

"I only had it a couple of weeks," she added.

The two were still wrapped in each other's arms when Sophie appeared before them.

"Come, you two, Dennis is on the telephone, and you don't want to miss what he's got to say."

Chapter Twenty-Nine

Vicky sped out of the woods at a fair rate of knots, towing Berry, who was struggling to keep up, behind her. Crossing in front of the barn they slept in, they'd crossed the courtyard and were nearly at the kitchen door when Muriel Lynne appeared before them.

"Oh, sorry, girls," she said as her head whipped back behind her, "didn't see you there."

Sophie narrowly avoided bumping into Berry's back as her two friends skidded to a halt. "You two go on," she told Vicky and Berry, and by the time she turned her attention back to Muriel, the two were already entering the kitchen. Muriel, though, appeared as if she'd rather be anywhere than where she was. "Anything I can help with?"

Muriel shook her head and gave her a smile that looked anything but real. "No." She repeated herself after taking a deep breath. "No, I mean, I wanted to speak to Sheila, about maybe joining the ARP, but she wasn't in. Now I've got to get back to the pub. Bye," she ended hurriedly and strode on her way as quickly as possible, not giving Sophie a chance to get a word in. By the time she'd thought of something to say, the woman had disappeared from sight. Not seeing a reason to chase after her, Sophie shrugged her shoulders and hared off toward the farmhouse.

Closing the door behind her, she turned around and

stopped dead. Sitting at the table was Sheila, nursing a cup of tea. "What the…? You're not here."

"I beg your pardon?" Sheila asked, quite naturally puzzled.

She wasn't the only one. "Didn't Muriel just knock?"

"Muriel. As in, Muriel from the King's Head?"

"That's the one."

"Not that I know of," Sheila stated, shaking her head. "Why?"

Sophie went and opened the back door, poked her head outside for a few seconds, and then closed it again. Pulling out a chair, she sat down and readily accepted the cup of tea Sheila poured for her. "Oh, nothing, I think I must be going crazy."

Both were completely distracted as the hall door flew open to admit first Berry, then Marcy, and finally Vicky, who wore a huge grin. "Only something I've thought for ages!"

"Very funny," Sophie told her and then, all thoughts of Muriel forgotten, asked. "Well? What's the news?"

"They've got her!" Vicky shouted at the top of her lungs and proceeded to dance a very strange jig around the table.

"That's wonderful," both Sophie and Sheila agreed, once everyone had finished whooping with joy. "When can we have her back?"

Vicky collapsed into a seat and immediately drank down Sophie's tea in a couple of gulps. "That's the best bit. Dennis and the rest of his mates are driving over tonight!"

****

Vicky opened and closed the kitchen window once,

twice, then a third time before Bob decided to step in front of her and gently guide her back to her seat.

"Finish your meal before it goes cold," he tried telling her for the second time, and when she made to get to her feet once more, he added, "or I'll ask Marcy if she can reassign you to the sawmill."

This semi-threat had the desired effect, and Vicky, albeit reluctantly, retook her seat and silently finished up the rest of her stew.

Satisfied, Bob asked Marcy, "What's so awful about the sawmill, then? I heard Marcy threaten Vicky with the same when she kept opening and shutting the kitchen door," he explained to his wife who had a curious expression upon her face.

"It's way too noisy," Vicky answered.

"And dangerous," Berry added.

"More dangerous than felling trees?" Sheila asked, a spoon halfway to her mouth.

Marcy nodded. "People lose fingers and thumbs, and sometimes more, all the time."

"Bugger that for a game of soldiers," Bob uttered, putting down his spoon and pushing his bowl away. "Right put me off my food, that has."

"I'll warm it up for you later," Sheila told him. "Waste not, want not."

"I thought they told you they'd be here by eight?" Vicky moaned at Marcy.

Marcy finished off her own bowl before replying. Laying her spoon carefully in the now empty bowl, she sat back in her seat and regarded Vicky as one would an impatient teenager—which, she reminded herself, was exactly what Vicky was. Thus armed, she calmed herself before saying, "They told me they'd do their *best* to be here for eight. You know what the roads are like these days. I'm certain they'll be here when they'll be here."

"I hope Midnight's all right," Harry piped up and then spoiled her concern by belching loudly.

"Harriet!" her sister admonished. "At least say, 'Pardon me.' "

"You didn't—" she interrupted herself with another slightly less reverberating burp "—give me the chance. I do beg your pardon, everyone," she finally said, treating the room to a look that was in no way sorry.

This wasn't missed by Bob. "Maybe milking for the first hour tomorrow morning will teach you some manners, young lady?"

Harry opened her mouth to protest, but she stopped when she noticed Bob was serious. Any protests would undoubtedly be countered with an increase in the punishment. "Yes, Bob. I'm sorry."

"Perhaps we should send them both to bed now?" he suggested.

"Not fair!" Lucy pouted. "I didn't do anything!"

"Well, your sister did, and it's nearly your bed time anyway," Sheila pointed out. "What do you say, Harry?"

"Can I just stay to see Midnight when she gets home?" Harry pleaded.

"I don't know. What do you think?" Bob asked his wife.

"It was an exceptional belch!" Vicky announced.

"World class, I would say," added Berry.

"Best I've heard in a long while," Sophie couldn't resist putting in.

"You're not helping," Harry told them, though she struggled to keep a smirk from her face.

Things might have progressed out of hand if the

sound of a car screeching to a halt didn't interrupt things.

"Midnight!" Vicky and Harry both cried at the same time as a knock sounded at the kitchen door.

Harry beat Vicky to answering it by a second. Pulling it open, she was met by the sight of Archie holding out Midnight at the full length of his arms. Contrary to the sweet ball of fluff who wouldn't harm a flea which they were used to, this version of Midnight had all four of its legs outstretched with all her claws extended. Vicky took a step nearer and then a hasty one back.

"What the hell's that smell?"

Vicky stepped aside as Archie carried her inside, closely followed by his friends. "She's got quite a story to tell, this little one," he told the room as he stood beside the sink.

"A rather smelly one," Marcy said as she hastily stepped back after making the mistake of smelling the kitten.

Dennis produced a couple of large bottles of beer. "Firstly, charge your glasses."

"Why?" Bob asked.

"Because…" Dennis remembered just in time not to stroke Midnight's head. "If it wasn't for this little girl, I doubt if either me, Archie, Jimmy, or any of the guys would be here right now."

At hearing these words, Marcy went and stood next to Archie and took a strong grip on one of the hands which still held the squirming Midnight, whilst Vicky looked like she wanted nothing more than to do the same to Jimmy. Berry was holding her nose, and though she looked like she wanted to do nothing more than to cuddle Midnight half to death, clearly she couldn't bring herself to get any nearer to the hissing kitten than she already was.

"Here, let me play mum," Sheila announced, taking the bottles from Dennis, who immediately stepped closer to Berry. Sheila watched as the two gradually slid nearer the other before Berry made a grab for his hand. She turned to open a drawer for a bottle opener, glad the two couldn't see her smile.

"Well, what happened?" Bob asked a little impatiently.

"Yes, do tell," Vicky put in. "I really need to give Midnight, there, a bath."

"He's already had one," Archie answered.

Cautiously, Harry leaned in for a sniff, jerking back almost instantly. "I'd say he needs another."

Lucy pulled at Dennis's sleeve. "Please?"

"At least one of you has some manners," Bob remarked, though with a grin on his face in case Harry assumed he was referring to what had happened earlier. "Tell you what, Harry. You make a good job of washing Midnight there, and I'll give you a hand with all tomorrow's milking. Deal?"

Harry made a show of spitting on her hand before she held it out toward Bob, who insisted she held it out for inspection before shaking it.

"Here, you can make a start on this bundle." Archie passed Midnight to Harry before she could object.

"Move the plates, love, and you can use the kitchen sink," Sheila told her.

"Is anyone ever going to tell us what happened?" Vicky implored, a little too loudly.

"All right, all right," Dennis said, putting up his free hand. "We were on a sortie last night. Everything was going fine. We'd dropped our bombs and had turned for home. I suppose we'd relaxed our vigilance too much, as we were about to hit the Channel. Well, the next thing we knew, this little bugger popped its head out of the toilet and launched itself at Jimmy, landing upon his shoulder."

"Scared me out of my wits!" Jimmy added.

"Scared this idiot so much," Dennis continued, "he pressed the trigger for his guns. Next thing we know, this Nazi night fighter flashed over us. We figure he must have been hiding in the cloud and about to pull the trigger when the flash of the front turret scared him."

"Holy f…" Harry nearly said, earning herself a reproachful look from everyone in the room.

"What happened to him?" Berry asked.

Dennis looked down at her and shrugged. "No idea. Best guess? He buggered off in search of easier prey."

Absently and nearly regretting it, Vicky stroked Midnight. "So you were hiding in the one place we never looked!" Jimmy could only shrug.

Harry looked up as she was about to douse Midnight from the tap. "Please tell me it's only chemicals from the toilet I'm washing off?"

Chapter Thirty

"Archie handed me this, Sheila," Marcy announced, placing a shoebox-sized package upon the kitchen table. "He said they picked it up off the top of the gatepost but, in all the excitement, had forgotten it by the time they were inside."

Wiping her hands, Sheila eyed the package before turning it this way and that. Wrapped in old newspaper, with her name written in scrawled, large, black letters upon one side, nothing indicated where it had come from. Lowering her head, she jerked back straight away, a hand flying to her mouth as she fought the impulse to retch.

Her husband was at her elbow instantly. Nodding at the box, he reached out a hand, "Let me open it."

Shaking her head Sheila, a determined expression upon her face, stepped back to the table. "No. Thanks though, Bob," she told him grim-faced.

Reaching out, she took up the package and gave it a wary shake.

"You're expecting it to explode?" Harry asked, her comment glib but her eyes locked on the suspicious package.

Somewhat worriedly, Sheila merely shrugged, though she didn't let go of the package. Satisfied she wasn't about to go up in a ball of flames, Sheila placed the package back on the table, turning it this way and that before she pulled at the string it was tied up with and the paper fell away. She was left with a shoebox advertising Oxford brogues. Slowly, she slipped a finger under the lid and flipped it off.

"Oh, ugh!" Lucy announced.

Unseen by everyone, who'd been intensely watching Sheila, the little girl had edged her way in between everyone and was now standing on tiptoe so she could get a good view into the box.

"Why would anyone send you a dead crow?" she asked.

Quickly, Marcy replaced the lid before Harry could add anything to Lucy's unwanted question.

Bob raised his eyebrows toward his wife and then let his eyes wander around the rest of the girls. Sheila shrugged her shoulders. "You may as well. They're as good as family to me anyway."

Pulling his wife down onto his lap as he sat, Bob glanced around his eclectic, extended family and slowly, with a deep sigh, motioned for everyone to take a seat. The last to join them was Marcy, who'd taken a moment to put the unwanted *present* outside the back door.

With Lucy taking a place upon his wife's lap, Bob took a few moments to adjust to the extra weight. "It started not long after we took in you pair. The first thing was a fish which had gone off, together with a nasty note," he said, not wishing to say exactly what had been written, "then someone left the gate open in the field."

"You told me you'd done that!" Harry piped up from where she sat on Marcy's lap.

Bob turned a smile toward the girl. "Sorry about that, my love. I didn't want to say anything at the time."

"But now you do?"

"Remind me again," Sheila asked, reaching across to ruffle Harry's hair. "Exactly how old are you?"

"Fourteen!" Lucy announced, missing the sarcasm.

"And now the crow," Harry said, ignoring her sister. "What's it all mean?"

"Well, a crow is typically thought of as a bad omen, or a bringer of bad luck. It's certainly thought bad luck to kill a crow, too."

"Who'd want to wish you, or either of you, bad luck or ill will?" Vicky asked, glancing toward the back door.

"That's a very good question," Bob said, his face not giving anything away.

Harry then showed again how bright she was for her age, though she missed the quickly hidden looks of surprise which passed between the adults. "And you said all these horrible bits started when Lucy and me came along. So this is our fault?"

Marcy immediately wrapped her arms around Harry and dropped her head onto her shoulder, telling her, "Of course not," whilst looking at Sheila and Bob to assure her she was right in telling her this. Both wasted no time in assuring her she was.

"Of course you aren't," Sheila told her immediately, as both Bob and herself did their best to show how much the two girls meant to them by giving Lucy a single-armed cuddle whilst reaching across to lay their other hands upon Harry's squirming legs, the only part of her they could reach.

"So what is going on, then?" Harry persisted.

Before either Bob or Sheila could reply, Berry deduced, "I'd say someone's jealous; someone who doesn't like to see the two of you being happy."

****

None the worse for her adventure, Midnight had jumped into the basket of Penny's bicycle for the ride to work as if nothing had happened. Once there, she'd hopped out, skulked into the undergrowth to perform some ablutions, and then settled back in place whilst the girls spent a busy day clearing undergrowth and began the task of chopping down the trees in the second designated area.

"How long…" Vicky puffed in between swings of her axe, "Did you say…we've got, to finish this part?"

"Around a month," Marcy managed to answer, pausing to wipe the sweat from her brow.

Since the loss of Elaine, and despite Ethel Winter's assurances, they were still shorthanded. When Sophie had asked about a replacement that morning, Marcy had admitted that even before Elaine had gone, they were two girls down. This had produced many frowns and a few mutters, but nothing further, as everyone understood the difficult position Marcy was in. As she pitched in when her measuring duties allowed, this also prevented them complaining too much.

"A month?" Berry asked, from where she was taking a sip of water and looking around at the many trees that were due to be felled. "Is that all?"

"We'll do it," Marcy announced confidently.

A sudden boom of thunder cut off any immediate response, followed by a flash of forked lightning the other side of the wood.

"Axes down!" Marcy immediately ordered, not wanting anyone to be holding one, as they increased the risk of being hit.

Being in the middle of a forest, they all obeyed straight away, knowing little else could be done, except hope the storm would be over quickly and there'd be no more lightning. Whilst everyone else hunched down and drew a poncho over their heads, Berry dashed to her bicycle, grabbed up a still sleeping Midnight, and tucked both the cat and the blanket she'd been snuggled under inside her poncho before rejoining her friends.

"This is going to speed things up!" Sophie shouted over a particularly loud clap of thunder.

"Anyone got the time?" Vicky cried.

"About half four!" a voice yelled back from within the trees. A moment later the owner followed it.

"Tina!" Marcy said in surprise as the Land Girl, despite the sheets of rain now pouring down, strolled toward them.

Getting to their feet, both Sophie and Vicky rushed toward their friend who, now she was nearer, they could see was only dressed in working trousers, a jumper, and boots. Jointly wrapping her in their ponchos, they pulled her unprotesting body down to join the others.

"What the hell are you doing?"

"Hmm?"

"I mean," Marcy elaborated, "what are you doing walking around in this weather? Without a raincoat."

After a second, Tina glanced down at herself. "Well, I'll be. I could have sworn I had one on when I came out," she muttered.

Further conversation was impossible for the next minute or two, as the storm decided to expend its fury directly overhead. When it finally passed, Berry opened her poncho as the others shook theirs to get the worst of the rain off. Shaking her head, she called the others over. "Do you believe this?"

Peering in, they could see Midnight had clearly slept

through the entire storm.

"Is that kitten ever awake?" Sophie asked.

Holding her poncho open, Berry waited as Sophie took out the sleeping kitten. "You're unbelievable!"

"But so sweet," Berry replied, fussing Midnight behind the ears, eliciting a gentle purr.

Whilst Berry and Sophie walked back to their bicycles, Marcy placed her hands on Tina's shoulders and asked, "So, what are you doing out in this weather?"

Running a sopping wet arm of her jumper across her face Tina, after a few hesitant starts, eventually said, "Have any of you seen Sal? She ran off this morning, and I've been trying all afternoon to figure out where she's gone."

Chapter Thirty-One

"You'd better make yourself fit to receive visitors," Berry remarked as she strode into the barn, dumping her bag beside her bed.

"Why would I need to do that?" Marcy asked as she lolled back on her own, hands linked behind her head and her eyes closed.

Any thoughts she might have had about catching forty winks prior to tea were rudely expunged from her mind by the pillow Berry threw at her. Sitting up smartly, she found she couldn't retaliate, as her friend was now sat beside her.

"Archie's popping by."

"Archie!" Marcy said, her eyes going wide and giving away her excitement at merely hearing his name.

This wasn't lost on Berry. "Thought that'd get your attention."

Marcy play-hit her on the shoulder. "I'd wipe that smug look off your face, if I were you. I'd lay good money that was Dennis you were talking to." As Berry turned away, Marcy knew she was right.

Berry nearly fell off her friend's bed at being caught out. Unlike her own, Marcy's bed was up against a couple of bales of hay upon which were pinned a couple of photographs of her deceased husband, Matthew. Recovering her balance, Berry could only match her friend's grin.

The barn door banged open, admitting Sophie and Vicky, with a miserable-looking Tina dragging her heels.

"Any luck?" Berry asked, with Marcy snapping her mouth shut at the same time, undoubtedly about to ask the same.

"Not an ounce," Sophie answered as she too divested herself of her work bag and then began to strip out of her jumper, jodhpurs, and boots.

"I'm assuming the Robinsons didn't have any ideas?" Marcy asked Tina as the poor girl sat down hard on a bale of hay.

"The Robinsons? Hah!" she scoffed. "The only thing they're worried about is not receiving her rent each week."

"She's right there," came a man's voice, and all heads turned to see Bob standing in the once more open doorway. "Sorry for the intrusion," he said, "but I was passing the doorway and could hear you talking. Now, what's this about the Robinsons?"

"Bob!" Sophie's voice protested, though her body was nowhere in sight. "Do you mind? I'm getting changed here!"

"That's a lovely shade of red, Bob," Harry declared, even as she hurried up to the farmer and, taking him by the elbow, turned him so he was facing back outside.

"Sorry, Sophie!" he told her over her shoulder, as his embarrassment reached the tips of his ears. "Anyway, the Robinsons?"

"Hang on a second!" Sophie shouted as she hurriedly pulled on a skirt and blouse. "I don't want to miss anything."

Whether she meant to deliberately annoy everyone or not, Sophie kept them holding on whilst she rushed outside for a quick wash and brush up.

"Ready, are you?" Vicky asked, lolling back on her bed.

"Yes, thank you," Sophie answered, dropping down onto her bed and totally missing her friend's sarcasm. "Tina?"

"Firstly, they don't know where Sal is," Tina said again before adding, "and apart from missing her money, the only thing they're worried about is who's going to help on the fields, now there's only me. They seem to think it's all my fault, her running off."

"And she didn't say anything to you before? No hint she was planning anything?" Berry asked.

"Not a sausage," Tina replied. "Yes, she was unhappy, but that's her normal mood. With us all now being friends, I think she was hoping she'd be able to get a transfer to your lot. You remember how much she wanted to join the Timber Corps."

Remembering the way their initial meeting had gone, Marcy and Vicky both let out little laughs before turning them into coughs at remembering the current situation. "I don't think either of us are likely to forget it," Vicky admitted.

"Which reminds me," Marcy said and looked across to address Bob. "Whatever happened to the Land Girls who were supposed to be coming here, Bob?"

Her question was greeted by a loud snort of derision. "Don't get me started," he began. "Bloody ministry this and that. Apparently, now I've Harry helping out, they've decided I can go to the bottom of the list again; or so it seems. It looks like I'll have to wait and, by the way things are going, I doubt I'll get any official help at all."

"Hey!" Harry exclaimed. "You said I was doing a good job!"

Upon seeing the pout on her face and the way her eyes were cast down, Bob left the door and, wiping his hands upon his trousers, sat on her bed, and nudged the girl in the ribs. "And you are doing a very good job. Really! Forgive a grumpy bloke who's still relearning how to be a good man. I wouldn't swap you for anything."

Harry, now sporting a big smile, snuggled into Bob's shoulder, who happily wrapped an arm around her shoulders. Marcy told him, "You sell yourself short. You're a heck of a nice man."

"Now," Sophie cheekily added, with Bob giving her a quick nod of his head in acknowledgement.

"We do keep going off subject," Berry mentioned into the silence which followed. "Bob, the Robinsons?"

After rearranging his hold upon Harry, Bob told them what he knew. "Tina's got a very good handle on them. Money's all they've ever been interested in. Chances are, they've already been in contact with the Ministry to get a replacement in. If they don't know where Sally could have gone, then that's the truth. There's no profit in holding back any information."

"So where does that leave me?" Tina asked, dropping her head into her hands.

Bob looked Tina in the eye. "You leave the Robinsons to me," he told her. "I'll pop up and get them to show me where your things are. You'll stay with us, at least until we can sort things out."

****

"I feel a bit rotten," Berry admitted to Marcy as they both accepted their drinks from Brian, waving their free hand toward where Muriel was waving at them from the other end of the barroom, a pile of empty glasses on a tray in her other hand.

Marcy took a sip of her ale before replying, "Why's that?"

"Tina."

"I can see where you're coming from," her friend said after a few seconds contemplation. "However, it's not like we've left her alone. She's in good hands, and going on how much food Sheila was piling onto her plate when we left, I don't think she'll be in much of a state for anything other than taking to her bed by the time she's allowed to leave the table."

Marcy nearly snorted her next sip of ale out her nose and had to recover from a bit of a coughing fit before she could speak. "You make a very good point."

At that point, the barroom door opened and in came Dennis and Archie. After checking the girls were all right for drinks, the RAF men popped over to the bar and were quickly back with two pints of bitter.

"So, how's Midnight?" Dennis asked, absently kissing Berry on the cheek before taking a seat next to her.

"Told you they didn't want to see us," Berry said to Marcy, laughing.

"Don't be daft," Archie replied. "You've got to admit, it'd be strange if we didn't ask how our little observer was."

"He's got you there!" Marcy laughed too, with a raised eyebrow.

"Seriously, though, how is she? I mean, we hadn't used the toilet—never do, unless we're really, really desperate—but there may have been some chemicals left in the bottom."

Berry laid a reassuring hand upon his. "She's fine," she assured him. "Harry washed her three times before she was certain she was clean, and apart from turning the air blue with her meowing, there've been no problems. She's back to coming to work in my bicycle basket as if nothing happened."

Archie shook his head. "That's one tough little kitten. She must be a terror with the mice on the farm," he added.

Both women burst out laughing. Only upon seeing the curious looks the two men exchanged did they regain control. "Sorry, sorry. You couldn't be farther from the truth. Midnight likes comfort above all else. Now Percy, he's quite another story. We rarely see him. He seems to spend his whole life hunting, though the only evidence we have of this are little bits and pieces of tiny rodent bodies left beside our beds."

"He seems particularly fond of leaving them in Berry's boots," Marcy revealed, nudging her friend in the ribs and causing Dennis and Archie to gag on their drinks.

"Good for him," Dennis agreed, earning a glare for his trouble.

"How's the rest of the crew?" Berry asked, for a change of subject. "It's great to see you both again." She hastened to add, upon seeing both men open their mouths to comment, "Please understand, we'd simply love to see you more often, that's all."

Boldly, Archie reached across and took hold of Marcy's hand whilst Dennis simultaneously did the same with Berry's. "Is that how you feel? Because if it is, I'd love to see you any chance I can get, Marcy."

Marcy made to take her hand away, only for Archie to keep a firm grip and, ignoring anything else going on in the pub, leaned forward until his nose was mere inches from Marcy's. 'Please, I do understand you've only just lost your husband. Believe me, you have my full sympathy, and this isn't meant to sound heartless at all, but life goes on, and we'll take things as slowly as you're comfortable with. I'm only asking for you to give us a chance."

"Very loquacious, isn't he!" Dennis remarked, breaking the spell Archie had woven somewhat.

"One of us has to be," Archie replied, not taking his gaze from Marcy's.

"He is indeed," Marcy agreed, leaning in and briefly kissing a surprised and delighted Archie on the lips.

"Can I take that as a yes?" he asked, once he'd recovered the ability to talk.

"As slowly as I like?" Marcy asked to be sure.

Archie nodded. "As slowly as you like."

"And what do you have to say for yourself, Flying Officer Grey?" Berry wanted to know.

Suddenly aware he had three sets of eyes upon him, Dennis flushed, coughed, and ran a hand through his hair before recovering somewhat. With a final swallow, he was able to say, "Just because I'm this erk's boss doesn't mean I can speak as eloquently as him. However, I too would love to go out with you, on an official-type basis. If you would like to, that is?" he finished a little lamely, failing to meet Berry's eyes.

The next thing he knew, Berry had pushed her seat back, grabbed him by the sides of his head, and proceeded to give him her answer by way of kissing him all over his face.

When she finally let him go, he'd lost the ability to speak, but his wide grin spoke volumes.

Without any of them realizing it, Muriel had been working her way around the tables in the nearly empty bar, collecting empty glasses and bottles. At hearing Dennis's words because she was by now at the next table over from the group, she promptly dropped her tray, the resulting crash sending broken glass all over the place.

When they turned to see what had caused the commotion, they were confronted by a stony-faced landlady.

"Sorry," she told them. Without another word, she turned and leaving the mess behind, ignoring the concerned state of her husband and patrons, she stomped back behind the bar and disappeared from sight.

Chapter Thirty-Two

The ride past Paula Gibbons' destroyed cottage didn't get any easier, especially for Berry, who had to turn her head away each time.

Vicky pedaled harder to catch up to her friend. "Has the queasiness passed?" she asked as they turned the corner which led out of the village.

"It's not so bad." Berry gulped, tucking a blanket tighter around Midnight, it being a chilly morning. A few minutes later, she relaxed her pedaling a little. "I'm really sorry Jimmy couldn't make it last night," she told Vicky. "Dennis told me he'd pulled Orderly Officer duty."

Vicky shrugged, not an easy thing to do on a bicycle, and she only just avoided falling off. "I suppose it's as good an excuse as any."

"They're all hoping to make it over this weekend, if that helps?" Berry replied and caught her young friend's smile in the corner of her eye. "See, he hasn't forgotten you."

As Marcy and Sophie led the way, Berry and Vicky settled into a steady rhythm for the ride to work. "I assume you had a good time last night?" Vicky asked.

Careful to keep her eyes straight ahead, Berry guardedly replied, "We all did."

"*All*?" Vicky mimicked. "I suppose that explains why you kept mumbling Dennis's name in your sleep."

"I never did!" Berry protested, after she'd recovered from the jerk of her handlebars Vicky's teasing had caused.

"Yes, you did!" Sophie shouted from ahead.

"Bugger," Berry swore. She hadn't realized they'd been talking so loud. "Did I really?" she couldn't help but ask again, feeling the need for confirmation.

"You did," Marcy assured her.

They all rode on in silence for a few minutes as Berry took the time to process what she'd just found out, eventually saying, "Well, I guess I must like him, then."

"You think?" Sophie teased.

Berry and Vicky shared a smile which both knew Sophie couldn't actually see. She seemed to be getting back to how she'd been when they'd first known her. Perhaps she was starting to get over the loss of Ginger? It undoubtedly helped her to not have known him that well.

"So, what made up your mind?" Vicky asked, absently pedaling through a puddle and getting splash marks up her legs for her trouble.

Berry began slowly. "What with everything that's happened around us, especially after finding Paula Gibbons, it got me thinking. I'd decided not to even think about falling for anyone at the moment, especially aircrew, as they could be dead at any moment…"

"One way of looking at it," Vicky supplied.

"It's the only way of looking at it," Berry bluntly told her.

"And…"

"And so I decided I didn't want to end up like Paula, alone at the end of my life."

At these words, Vicky lost control and in a squeal of

brakes and a plethora of swear words a miner would be proud of, ended up on the grass verge with her bicycle half on top of her, its wheels still turning.

Hitting the brakes, Berry came to a bit more of a dignified halt than her friend, quickly joined by both Marcy and Sophie as they came to the stricken Vicky's aid. Berry and Sophie heaved the bicycle off her, whilst Marcy knelt down as her side, ignoring the dew-laden grass as it began to soak into her jodhpurs.

"Vicky! Are you all right?" she asked, placing a hand firmly on the girl's chest to stop her from getting up straight away.

Annoyed with herself, Vicky slapped Marcy's hand away and wriggled into a sitting position. "I'm fine, I'm fine," she told them, wiping her mucky hands down her jodhpurs. "Just a little embarrassed, that's all." She looked over to where Berry and Sophie were giving her mode of transport a check-over. "Anything broken?"

Lifting up the rear wheel, Sophie spun the pedals and watched as the wheel spun around before, satisfied all was well, she put it back down. "Can't see anything. What happened?"

Accepting Marcy and Berry's hands up, she dusted herself down and then playfully swatted Berry on the arm. "It's Berry's fault. When she told me she was going to marry Dennis, I lost concentration and didn't spot the pothole."

"She told you what?" Marcy asked incredulously, her head snapping around to focus on their friend, who looked like she'd seen a ghost. "When the hell did you decide that? I don't remember you talking about anything of the like last night!"

"Can I be your bridesmaid?" Sophie asked.

"Hold on, hold on," Berry implored, holding up her hands and backing away slightly. "I didn't say anything of the sort!"

"Yes, you did," Vicky objected. "You said you didn't want to end up like Paula Gibbons."

Berry appeared confused for a few moments before a lightbulb seemed to turn itself on. "Ah, I see what you mean," she told Vicky. "I only meant I can see myself getting married someday. I didn't say anything about it being to Dennis."

Vicky nodded her had once to acknowledge her friend's explanation before saying, "Well, I've seen the way he looks at you, so I wouldn't bet against it."

Berry mounted her bicycle and set off, calling over her shoulder, "That's enough of that. Time to get to work."

"Isn't that your line, Marcy?" Vicky asked before shooting off.

****

By midday, the morning discussion had been cast into memory and everyone was looking forward to Marcy calling time for lunch.

"Do you think Tina will be all right back on the farm?" Vicky asked Marcy as she strode into view. "You don't think the Robinsons will cause her any trouble?"

"No, I don't think so. Bob scared the wits out of them when he went around to get her things. Turns out, they're all mouth and no trousers," Marcy answered. "I think she'll have some explaining to do to the Ministry of Agriculture and Fisheries, but I expect they'll understand when she tells them what's happened. I can't see them expecting her to do all the work on their place by herself."

Berry leant her chin on the end of her axe handle. "Do you think she could come over to us? Bob'd find her plenty to do, I'm sure."

Marcy shrugged her shoulders. "I couldn't say."

"Could you put in a good word for her?"

After giving this some thought, Marcy shook her head. "I doubt if anything I could say would make a difference."

"Couldn't you try?" Berry persisted.

Seeing Berry wouldn't be letting this go anytime soon, Marcy sighed. "If she hasn't telephoned them by the time we get back, I'll see what I can do."

Berry bounded forward and gave her boss a quick hug.

"She said she'd telephone during the day, though, remember?" she warned her friend.

"We'll see what…"

Berry didn't get any further, as an almighty racket assaulted their ears, drawing their eyes to the skies as a Spitfire zipped low over their heads, followed a moment later by a German FW190 fighter, its guns clattering as it tried to shoot down the British fighter.

"Down!" Marcy shouted, barely in time as little puffs of dirt were kicked up as the bullets fired at the Spitfire stitched the ground a mere six feet from where they'd been standing.

A second later, there came a thunder of running feet, and they were joined on the ground by Sophie and Vicky. "Are you two okay? You're not hit?"

The two dogfighting planes had now soared into a twisting climb with the Spitfire seeming to edge slightly ahead of its attacker. All four girls turned onto their backs to watch the ballet of death being enacted above their heads. Berry and Marcy both noticed that Vicky had taken out her brother's pen knife. As they watched, the Nazi fighter's pilot seemed to lose his adversary when they turned into the sun and immediately broke off and turned back the way they had come.

Vicky just had enough time to yell, shaking her fist, "You'd better run!" before the Spitfire appeared as if from nowhere and let off a burst of cannon at the retreating FW190. Immediately, pieces flew off its wings, and its pilot must have thrown the throttle fully open as, with a roar, it clawed desperately for height, all the while with the Spitfire hanging onto its tail. Transfixed, the girls were unable to tear their eyes from the sight and, ignoring the possibility of more gunfire coming their way, sat up to watch as the dogfight came to its deadly conclusion.

The Spitfire pilot let go with another burst of fire, causing more pieces of the German fighter to be torn off. A flash of fire showed his cannon shells and bullets were finding their mark, and the next thing they knew, the canopy flew off, followed a few seconds later by the German pilot tumbling out. Everyone winced as his body glanced off the rudder of his doomed, well-aflame aircraft. Neither plane had managed to gain much height in the last few moments of the fight, so the German barely had time to pull the ripcord on his parachute before he hit the ground a few moments later. The victorious Spitfire zoomed over their heads once before climbing for height, disappearing from sight within a minute.

Without asking each other, as one the girls leapt to their feet and ran toward where the German pilot had come down. This was only a few minutes' fast run away, and before they knew it, the four skidded to a halt as they came upon the partially parachute-covered body. They all glanced at each other before Vicky stepped forward and prodded a black boot with the sharp end of her axe—which no one had noticed she'd brought with her. When she didn't get a reaction, Vicky brought the axe back and swung the butt end at the sole of the boot, knocking the leg a little way under the silk of the parachute.

A loud, large explosion on the edge of the forest caused their heads to snap around. "Must be the Nazi fighter," Berry decided, to which they all nodded before turning their attention back to their immediate concern. "Do you think he's dead?"

Not bothering to speak, Vicky tightened her grip on her axe, took a deep breath, and hooked the parachute, swiftly drawing it off the German. He was lying on his front, unmoving and unresponsive when she poked him in the side. Drawing in another deep breath, she put down her axe and knelt down by his side.

"Bloody hell!" she exclaimed as she fell backward.

Immediately concerned for their friend, Marcy, Sophie, and Berry were by her side in a moment.

"What's wrong?" Marcy asked, her eyes upon her young friend.

Instead of speaking, Vicky pointed at the German's back. All three turned and, at once, now they were very close to him, saw what had caused her reaction. The back of his flying suit was ripped open from his lower back right up to the nape of his neck, blood spilling out and soaking into the ground; his face was turned toward them, the eyes open and the back of his head gone.

Sophie turned her head and retched, whilst Marcy shook her head sadly, and Berry simply stared, unable to take her eyes away from the grisly sight. Recovering her composure, Vicky got to her feet, grabbed an end of the parachute and threw it so the dead German was covered.

"Christ," Berry muttered. "Talk about ways of putting you off your dinner!"

No one spoke for a few minutes, everyone being lost in their thoughts. Eventually, Marcy recovered her wits and said, "We need to get the police."

Everyone got to their feet, apart from Vicky, who slowly made her way to sit down beside the dead German's head. As she stroked what the others hoped was the side of his face, she looked up at her friends, though her eyes didn't appear to be focused upon them. "You go," she said to no one in particular. "I'll stay here with him." She turned her attention back to the body before adding, "He's about the same age as my brother."

Chapter Thirty-Three

"That's strange," Sheila commented as the car drew up outside her window. She turned her head to ask Harry, "Run along and find Bob, love."

Quickly finishing her glass of milk, Harry dashed out the back door, nearly running into Sergeant Elias Duncan.

"Careful there, young lady," he told her with a smile. "Running leads to accidents."

With a slight nod of her head to acknowledge she'd heard and understood him, Harry closed the back door behind her.

"Take a seat, Elias," Sheila invited the policeman. "I wasn't expecting to see you today. What can we do for you?"

Before he could reply, the back door banged open, ricocheting back against the wall and nearly hitting Marcy on the nose. Sheila opened her mouth, undoubtedly to tell her off, but any words died in her throat when she noticed Marcy was actually coming into the kitchen sideways. To her left and supported by Marcy's arm around her waist, was Vicky, with Berry mirroring Marcy on the younger girl's other side.

"What on earth?" Sheila gasped, as Vicky was virtually carried into the kitchen.

With a face normally full of color because of the multitude of freckles, they were shocked to be presented

274

with a nigh on white face, there being absolutely no color left.

Elias got back to his feet and helped the girls lower Vicky into his vacated space. "Can you make her some tea, please, Sheila?"

"What happened?" Sheila demanded as she turned to do what she'd been bid.

The back door opened again before anyone could reply, this time admitting Sophie, who placed a bucket on the floor between Vicky's knees. "Thought this may be needed," she explained.

Vicky barely had time to glance up at Sophie before she made use of the bucket.

"Good timing, lass," Elias muttered.

"What's all the fuss?" Bob asked as he appeared close behind Sophie.

Harry hurried around the farmer to kneel at Vicky's side, laying a hand upon her friend's knee as Vicky came up for air. "What's wrong, Vicky?" she echoed Sheila's concern.

Before anyone, especially Vicky herself could say anything, Bob gave his wife a pointed look. "Isn't it about the time Lucy's due back, my love?"

With their rediscovered togetherness, Sheila knew he'd rather Harry wasn't around to hear whatever was about to be told. She went and stood behind Harry, placing her hands on the girl's shoulders. "Be a love, and go and wait for your sister by the gate, will you?"

Harry, the smart girl that she was, merely got to her feet, kissed Vicky on the forehead, and made her way to the back door, though she was muttering to herself as she did so.

"In case anyone missed what she said," Berry told

them, "to summarize, she's going to get everything out of us later."

"She's probably right," Sophie agreed.

Vicky started to speak but had to make another dive toward her bucket. Everyone waited for her to finish, and then Sheila passed her a damp, cold cloth to press to her forehead. "Take your time. Elias?"

"I can only tell you a bit," he admitted. "Marcy, do you think you could start?"

Giving Vicky's shoulders a firm squeeze, Marcy pulled up a seat next to her slightly groaning friend, glancing at her before speaking. "There was a dogfight above us between a Spit and a Nazi Focke-Wulf," she began, waiting for Sheila, Bob, and Elias to nod they knew what she was talking about. "The Spit pilot got the upper hand and managed to rake the Nazi with his fire. The German pilot bailed out, but..." Marcy stopped to take a steadying breath, "his body hit the tail of his aircraft. He hit the ground not far from us, so we ran over, not really knowing what we'd find, but when we got there, he was dead. Vicky was the one who had the guts to nudge him with her axe to see if he was playing possum."

"He wasn't," Vicky surprised them by saying. She looked around the room, taking in where she was, before adding, "The back of his head was missing. It hit the tail of his fighter as he bailed out. How he managed to open his parachute, I've no idea!"

"Bloody hell," Bob swore.

Sheila had gone nearly as pale as Vicky had been when she'd been brought in. Still, she managed to take the cloth from Vicky and went to the tap to re-wet it. She came back to stand behind Vicky and wiped the cloth around her face before pressing and holding it once more to her forehead.

"Thanks," Vicky said with a weak smile.

"Vicky covered him with his parachute and stayed with him whilst Berry and Sophie went to the sawmill to call an ambulance. I stayed with her until they came."

Sheila took hold of one of Vicky's hands. "That must have been terrible. No wonder you're so upset."

Vicky pulled her hand from Sheila's before realizing what she'd done. "Sorry," she told her, shaking her head. "It wasn't really how he died that got to me," she said slowly and in a voice so low everyone had to hold their breath to make certain they could hear her. "It's that he was the same age as my brother. He could have *been* my brother!" The anguish in her eyes was heart-rending, and Sheila, acting upon instinct, threw her arms around her as Vicky broke into sobs.

Elias stood, pulled down his tunic top to straighten it, and went to the back door. "Come on," he said, opening it, "let's give them some privacy. We can talk outside."

As Marcy closed the door behind her, Harry appeared, trotting around the corner, towing Lucy by the hand, obviously in a rush to get back.

"Let me entertain the girls," Sophie told the group, striding off to intercept them.

Once Sophie had led Lucy and an annoyed Harry off to the barn they slept in, Elias opened his car door and plonked wearily down onto the front seat.

"That bit, I didn't know," he admitted with a sad shake of his head. "Was she close to her brother?"

"From what she's told us, I'd say they were very close," Berry informed him. "He was killed at Dunkirk," she added.

"That explains why she protested when the ambulance crew tried to take the body away," Elias muttered, wiping his brow on his sleeve.

"What a mess," Bob added before turning to ask Marcy and Berry, "Do you think she'll be okay?"

Both Marcy and Berry shook their heads at the same time, with Marcy adding, "I don't doubt it. She's strong, but despite losing her brother, this has to be the first time she's actually seen death close up. I'm not saying it's a good thing, but it may actually help her come to terms with his loss and, perhaps, lessen some of the anger she has toward the Germans."

This time, both the men nodded.

"That wouldn't be a bad thing. I think I'd be right in speaking for Elias when I say that in the trenches, you rarely came across a chap who actually hated the Germans."

Elias nodded, a melancholy expression upon his face. "Aye, very true. I never hated them, probably hated our generals more," he added with a wistful chuckle.

Everyone was lost in their thoughts until the kitchen door opened and Sheila popped her head out. "Come on in, you lot. Tea's ready. You'll stay for one, Elias?"

"Try and stop me," the policeman replied, following everyone else into the kitchen.

Marcy passed him on the way. "Going to tell Sophie and the girls they can come in now."

By the time Sophie, a visibly irritated Harry, and a slightly confused Lucy had joined them, Sheila was halfway through pouring out the brew from her biggest teapot.

"How you doing, lass?" Elias asked Vicky, who

seemed to have recovered some of her color. The bucket too had disappeared from sight.

"A bit better, thank you."

"Try and get that down you. It'll help take the nasty taste out of your mouth," Bob advised, pressing a cup into her hands.

"Best cure us British have ever come up with," Elias assured her.

A thin smile gracing her lips, Vicky brought the cup to her lips and, acutely aware of everyone's eyes being upon her, took a tentative sip. Only when she'd managed to swallow half down did most of her friends avert their eyes from her.

After a few moments' silence, Harry spoke up. "Sophie told me what happened, Vicky. Is there anything I can do for you?"

Everyone's eyes snapped onto Sophie, who immediately swallowed, adopting a wonderfully guilty look before jutting her chin up. "She beat it out of me!"

Harry immediately looked offended. "I did not! I only had to ask once and she blurted out the whole story!"

"Sophie?" Berry said, eventually receiving a shrug.

"Well, she did say she'd get the story out of us anyway," Sophie informed everyone, taking a long swig of her tea.

"That's true," Harry agreed.

"So what Sophie said is true?" Lucy asked from where she now sat upon Sheila's lap, before pausing and adding, "You saw a dead German?"

"That doesn't scare you?" Sheila asked.

Lucy craned her neck around, nearly slipping off Sheila's lap, before replying, "Not really." She shrugged.

"*I* didn't see him, and he is the enemy."

Vicky made everyone jump by banging down her cup on the table. "He was someone's son! He was barely more than a boy, and now he's dead!"

Ignoring the shocked stares of everyone, Vicky pushed her chair back and darted for the back door. It took a few moments for anyone to react, and then Berry pushed her seat back, much more softly than Vicky had and, without bothering to put her actions into words, shot off after their wayward friend.

"Vicky!" Berry yelled as she shut the back door behind her. She then spotted her friend's foot as it disappeared into their barn.

Hurrying after her, Berry opened the barn door, stepped in, and closing the door behind her, let her eyes grow accustomed to the dim light inside. Somewhere inside, she could hear her friend sobbing. Picking up one of the lamps they kept on a small table by the door, she flicked a match alight and carefully lit the lamp. Holding it up before her, unhurriedly so she didn't startle Vicky, Berry tiptoed toward where Vicky's bed was. Sure enough, Vicky was curled up upon her bed, still in her dirty work clothes.

Ignoring this, Berry picked up her friend's booted feet, took their place at the foot of the bed, and placed them upon her lap.

"I know this is going to sound very stupid," she began, "but how are you doing?"

Not troubling to raise her head from the pillow, Vicky snorted.

"You know you're going to make a right mess of your bed, don't you?" Berry tried some humor, getting what could be construed as a small laugh by way of a response.

"How would you like me to give you a shower? Clean you up a little, you know. Naked or clothed, your choice?" This time she received a real laugh for her troubles, and Vicky actually lifted her head off her pillow to look down at her clothes.

"I'd forgotten," she replied and then frowned. "Was I terribly rude?"

Despite the situation, Berry treated her to a big smile, but then, taking her by a hand, told her seriously, "Let's say you owe Lucy a big apology."

Chapter Thirty-Four

"Knock-knock!" Berry shouted before opening the kitchen door and entering, pulling a rather damp and visibly nervous Vicky in behind her.

"Oh, it's you," Sophie said, retaking her seat. "I thought it was a bad-joke door-to-door salesman!"

"Ha, bloody ha!" Berry replied, aiming for but missing with a swat to her friend's head. "Elias has left," she noted, looking around.

"I did try to persuade him to stay for something to eat, but he told us after the day he's had, he was in need of a quiet evening," Sheila informed the two.

Vicky asked, after glancing around the room, "Does anyone know where Lucy is?"

Bob got to his feet and stood tall, his arms crossed. "Harry took her along to the cowshed."

"Oh…fiddlesticks," she muttered. "I wanted a word."

"I think you owe her a few, my girl," Bob told her and then closed his mouth and refrained upon elaborating at seeing his wife shake her head.

Berry squeezed her friend's hand and shoved her gently toward the door. After a moment's hesitation, she returned the gesture before dashing out, letting the door bang shut behind her.

"Lucy! Harry!" she shouted as she stood in the doorway of the cowshed, wafting a hand in front of her nose.

"You'd better stand back a little, Vicky," Harry's voice shouted, momentarily accompanied by the girl herself as she kicked the door open as wide as it would go to let the cows she was leading into the shed. "Get ready to close the doors," she told Vicky in passing who barely had time to flatten herself against the wall to avoid being trampled.

"You heard her!" Lucy added as she came in behind the last cow.

"I didn't know you knew anything about cows," Vicky asked, a little bemused.

There was a muffled thump as the doors to the cowshed closed. "What's to know?" Lucy shrugged as she went to help her sister spread some hay around. "They don't need much. All they want is to be fed, watered, and milked. The only reason they're in here is because Mr. Harker reckons it's going to rain tonight."

Not really knowing how she should reply to this wisdom, Vicky instead took the pitchfork from the young girl and took over the chore. The mindless toil also gave her time to think how to broach her apology. She waited until they'd finished and Harry was putting the tools away.

"Lucy," she began, her arm resting lightly upon the eight-year-old's shoulder, "I owe you a huge apology. I shouldn't have blown my top at you like that. You didn't do or say anything wrong, and I've no excuses."

"So, why did you?" Harry demanded, appearing at her sister's side. Taking the younger girl by the hand, she led her out of the shed and back into the courtyard, forcing Vicky to quickly follow. As Harry put down the latch on the door, Lucy was waiting for Vicky, and her sister's arm went protectively around her.

It's amazing how fierce Harry can be, Vicky thought as she unconsciously took a step backward when met by a glare which would have made Hitler think twice about invading Poland.

"Come with me," Vicky asked, and walked off toward their barn, hoping the girls would follow her. On the way, she glanced over toward the kitchen window and had to stifle the impulse to grin. It seemed everyone else was crowded around the window, not trying to hide their desire to know what was going on. This had the fortunate benefit where she could see, reflected in the window, that the girls were following closely behind her. Parking herself on a log they used as a seat next to the barn, she patted either side of herself, though she had to work to hide her disappointment when Harry sat beside her and Lucy chose to sit initially the other side of her sister, before seeming to change her mind.

"Yes?"

Unsure whether the younger girl would snatch her hand back, Vicky snaked her hand slowly around one of Lucy's and was most gratified when she didn't. Deciding it wouldn't help anyone if she left things hanging any longer, Vicky began by taking out her penknife and opening it up. Both girls leaned in for a closer look at its mother-of-pearl handle.

"Wow!" Harry let out, her eyes sparkling.

Hesitatingly, as she'd never let anyone else handle it since it came into her ownership, Vicky passed the knife over. Harry turned the knife every which way before flicking the blade open. She was about to run her thumb along the edge when Vicky reached out and took it back from her. "I wouldn't do that, if I were you. I keep the blade extremely sharp."

"For a knife, it's quite beautiful," Harry declared. "Did you buy it for work?"

Vicky carefully snapped the blade into its enclosure before turning her eyes upon the two girls. "I've never told you about my brother, have I?" Lucy, possible sensing how vulnerable her older friend was at that moment, got up and hopped up onto Vicky's lap, getting an, "Oof!" and a smile for her troubles.

"Where is he?" Lucy asked.

"I don't think I've heard anything about him," Harry added.

Vicky looked up at the darkening sky, cuddling Lucy closer into her body. She spoke as if she was talking to everyone and no one at the same time.

"We're twins…we were twins," she amended with a deep, painful sigh. "I don't think we spent more than a few hours apart until he joined the Army, in thirty-nine. Silly bugger lied about his age to join up," Vicky said, letting out a bitter laugh. "Sorry about my language, Lucy," she added, ruffling Lucy's hair.

"That's all right," she replied. "You should hear Harry!"

"I have!"

"Hey!" Harry rejoined.

Vicky briefly leant her head upon Harry's shoulder. "We're only pulling your leg," she said, following up with, "but only a bit. A little less swearing would be nice." Harry nodded her head in understanding.

"Now, my brother."

"And all this explains why you yelled at Lucy?"

Vicky hung her head and nodded before looking back at Harry. "Yes. Like I said, Gary and me were close as two peas in a pod. He always looked out for me, you know. If anyone tried to pick on me at school and, because I was so small, there were always some who tried, Gary was always there to stop them. But he never hurt them! That's why I never understood why he was so keen to join the Army. He may have been the size of an outhouse, but he never laid a finger on anyone." As she spoke, tears ran down her face, and if she were aware that the two girls either side of her had leant their heads against her side, she gave no sign. She was talking to herself now. "Everyone called it the Phony War, but it can't have been for my brother, as he rarely wrote. Not," she amended, "that he was ever much for writing in the first place. Then the real war started, and I was so worried. The news only got worse, and then it all ended up at Dunkirk."

"Was he evacuated?" Harry asked.

Slowly, biting her lip, Vicky shook her head. "No, sweety, he wasn't. The Stukas got him whilst he was lining up on the beaches."

"Oh, sh…!" Harry began before she bit her lip at noticing the expression on Vicky's face. A thought struck her. "That German bloke, the one you found, did he remind you of Gary?"

Vicky couldn't speak. Wiping her eyes on the back of a hand, she nodded.

As the night drew its blanket over them, the girls cuddled into Vicky, sensing words were superfluous, that only the need to give their friend what comfort they could was important. Only when Harry and Lucy began to shiver, did it occur to Vicky where they were.

"Oh, heckers! I'm sorry, girls," she told them, straightening up. "Look how long I've kept you out.

Come on, let's get you washed and to bed, Lucy."

Lucy stood before Vicky and asked, "Are you okay?"

To which Vicky replied, "Are *we* okay?"

Lucy gave her reply in the form of a big hug that took Vicky's breath away.

Chapter Thirty-Five

"They're getting on well," Bob observed.

Sheila leaned over the sink so she could look out the window at what Bob was pointing at before going back to the washing up with a smile. "I think whatever Vicky discussed with Lucy's really done them both the power of good."

"Any idea what they talked about?" Bob asked, picking up a cloth and beginning to dry a plate.

Sheila shook her head and passed him a cup. "I haven't a clue. But I don't think I've ever seen Vicky look so…relaxed."

Bob put the cloth and cup down and, coming up behind her, wrapped his arms around his wife. "She certainly seems like a weight's off her shoulders."

"Off whose shoulders?"

"Elias! Good to see you," Bob said, kissing Sheila's neck and getting a giggle in response before striding over to greet their visitor.

The policeman swept off his hat. "Mind if I take a load off my feet?"

"Make yourself comfortable." Sheila offered him a seat as Bob went to fill the kettle. "You'll take a cup of tea?"

"Have I ever been known to refuse?" Elias smiled back as he stretched his legs out before him, crossing his booted ankles.

A short while later, they all sat around the table, hands clasped around steaming cups. "To what do we owe the pleasure?" Sheila asked.

Before replying, Elias reached into an inside pocket, taking out a piece of paper torn from a notebook. Placing a pair of half-moon spectacles upon his nose, he took in his friends' curious expressions.

"Elias?" Bob uttered, his voice lacking its natural timbre.

"I'm afraid I may have bad news about Harry and Lucy."

The blood drained from both Sheila and Bob's faces, and they reached for what comfort they could find in each other's touch. Bob eventually found his voice. "What…news?"

The policeman cleared his throat before once more looking at the paper in his hand. "You both understand I've had to carry on investigating into Harry and Lucy's backgrounds. We have to be certain there aren't any relations left they can go to."

"But," Sheila interrupted, a hint of desperation in her voice, her hand turning Bob's white as she gripped his fingers tighter and tighter, "Harry and Lucy both told us there's no one else!"

"I know they did," he replied, putting the paper down before him. "But don't you think that's strange? Surely there's someone. There's always someone. At least as far as my experience goes." He sat back and regarded his anxious friends. "You don't think it's more likely they said that so they don't have to go back?"

Bob and Sheila exchanged looks, once, twice, before Sheila, her head bowed, admitted, "You're right. We did think that, we can't deny it. You can't blame us, though," she finished, leaning her head upon her husband's shoulder.

A caring smile crept onto Elias's well-worn face. "Of course I understand. How long have we known each other?"

A quiet grin of remembrance crept onto Sheila's face, "Since you caught me creeping out for that dance when I was only thirteen."

"You were twelve, actually," Elias amended. "But you always looked older than your years."

"Hey!" Sheila protested.

"When you were a child," the policeman hastily amended, though he said it with a smile.

"What did you find?" Bob asked. "Just tell us."

"I contacted the police in the borough of London they came from and had them send me up a copy of the electoral register. I figured that if I was going to find anyone, then that would be a good place to start."

"And?" Sheila couldn't help but ask, leaning forward.

"I didn't find anything," Elias told them.

"For Christ's sake, Elias!" Bob swore, letting out the breath he'd been holding.

"Don't do that to us!" Sheila added.

Quickly leaning forward, the policeman took up his paper again. "I'm sorry, but that's not what I came here to tell you."

In a moment, the smiles of relief which had broken out upon Sheila and Bob's faces were wiped away. "You've found something, haven't you? Or rather, someone."

Elias nodded. "I think so."

Sheila grasped at the straw. "You only think so?"

She received a nod in return. "It's possible. There's a second cousin who still lives in the area, only he joined the Merchant Marine when the war broke out and hasn't been back since."

"Let me get this straight," Sheila said. "There's a *possibility*, only a possibility, that there's this relation. Only, and I'm guessing here, you haven't been able to contact him?"

"Correct," Elias agreed. "The only thing I've been able to find out is that he's been on convoy duty ever since. I had a colleague take a walk around to his place, and it's boarded up. He had to knock on a few doors, but eventually found a neighbor who told him the gentleman in question had done that the day before he took ship and had given him the key to his place to look after for the duration."

"So," Bob mused, rubbing his chin, "that would tell me there's little or no likelihood of this chap being in a position to take possession of the kids, even if he wanted to."

"And who knows how old they'll be when this all ends," Sheila added suggestively.

Everyone took a break to drink their tea in silence before Sheila put her cup down and, composing her features as best she could, asked Elias, "You know how much they've both come to mean to us, Elias. Are you…are you going to continue looking?"

Knowing how much this meant to his friends, Elias made certain he made eye contact with them both before speaking. "Listen very closely to what I say," he began, choosing his words very carefully, "and understand my meaning. If I had the time, then I would. However, I am so very busy that, taking into account the girls have a stable living environment, with people who love and care for them, I will have to reluctantly put the search to the bottom of my priority list. I'm not sure when I'll have time to follow this lead up."

It took his friends a few moments to digest what he'd just said, though when they had, Sheila launched herself at her friend, nearly knocking him off his seat in her hurry to give him a hug, whilst Bob let out a whoop of joy and pounded his old friend enthusiastically on the back.

****

Still in her work clothes, Tina skidded to a halt on her bicycle before Berry, nearly causing her to drop Midnight as she was picking up the slightly dozy kitten from her basket. From behind a hedge came a loud yowl and a squeak which was immediately cut off, and Percy stalked out with a mouse hanging from his mouth, a very satisfied expression upon his face.

"Someone's having an early dinner," Sophie remarked, reaching down to take off her bicycle clips. As she straightened, her stomach gave a loud rumble.

"And someone's ready for their dinner, by the sounds of things," Marcy teased, as she hopped off her bicycle.

Interrupting the banter she knew could go on and on, Tina waved her hands in front of her face to gain her friends' attention. "Hello! News here!"

Before she could say anymore, the ring of a small bell diverted their attention and, much more slowly than Tina had, Sally appeared in their midst.

"Well, that was going to be my news," Tina said, letting her arms flop down to her side.

"Where've you been?" Marcy asked.

"What happened?" Vicky wanted to know.

"Are you in trouble with the law or something?" Sophie put in.

"Are you all right?" Berry enquired, going over and throwing her arms around a clearly embarrassed Sally, who nearly fell off her bicycle.

"Let the girl get a word in edgewise," Marcy urged with a smile, gently pulling her friends away so Sally could dismount.

Leading the way to their log bench, Marcy didn't allow anyone to ask their young friend a single thing more until they were all seated. This was when they realized that Sally wasn't in her work clothes.

"Let's get this right," Berry began, looking between the two Land Girls. "You've actually only just got back from…wherever?"

Sally shrugged and didn't appear liable to elaborate until Tina nudged her in the ribs. "Just as Tina came in off the field, actually."

"Hold on a minute," Vicky asked. Getting to her feet, she ran to the barn door, flung it open, and shouted, "Harry? You in there?"

"Where's the fire?" came back the reply in Harry's voice.

"No fire," Vicky replied. "Can you go into the kitchen and get us something to drink?"

A minute later, Harry stomped out and threw a dirty look at the group perched on the log as she passed. "What did your last slave die of?"

"She'll be back," Vicky assured them, retaking her seat.

"Do you know what happened here?" Marcy asked Tina, who shook her head.

"Madam here wouldn't tell me," Tina informed the group, "until everyone was together."

"You're all my friends," Sally began, before adding, "plus, it's so much easier to only have to say things the once."

Berry held up a hand. "Not quite. You'll have to speak to Bob and Sheila too."

Sally frowned. "Why?"

"Because Bob went and spoke to the Robinsons, put them straight about a few things," Berry added.

Tina nodded her head. "You'll notice things are a lot better now," she told Sally whilst taking her friend's hand. "There's hot food every night." Sally's left eyebrow shot up. "We can have a hot bath at least twice a week," Swiftly joined by her right one. "The roof of the barn doesn't leak." Her hand flew up to her mouth. "And Mr. Robinson is actually pulling his weight!"

Sally had to pry her hand away from her mouth before she could say, "And all because Mr. Harker, Bob, spoke to them?"

Sophie put an arm around Marcy's shoulders and squeezed her knee. "She hasn't said so as such, but from what I gather, Marcy here had a few choice words of her own with them."

"I don't know what was said," Tina admitted, and then brightened back up immediately. "But who cares! You'll find out. Anyway, come on, what happened?"

Sally began to shift awkwardly in her seat, and no one could think of a way to ask her again. Happily, Harry chose that moment to stagger back with a tray bearing a large jug of lemonade and a stack of glasses.

"Sal! I never noticed you before," she exclaimed, putting the tray down on Berry's lap before flinging herself at Sally. A little too enthusiastically, as it turned out, as they both disappeared over the back of the log, legs flying in the air. "Sorry," Harry told her, scrambling to her feet and helping Sally up and back onto the log. "So, what happened? Where did you go?"

Sally managed to get her laughter under control as Sophie and Tina poured and distributed the lemonade, hugging Harry to her side. "I guess that's one way of breaking the awkward silence."

"What awkward silence?" Harry asked, poking her head out from beneath Sally's arm.

"Never mind," Berry said. "Go on."

"Thanks," Sally said as Tina passed her a glass. "I was homesick!" she blurted out before she could change her mind. Once it became clear that no one knew what to say, Sally finished the rest of her drink and set the glass down on the ground, where her gaze stayed. "I got homesick. I…I've never been apart from my parents before, and I got homesick. I can't even really blame the farm or the work. I'm sorry I lied to you, Tina. I didn't want you to think bad of me, so I complained about things just as much as you and hoped you'd think that was why I ran away, when all the time I was simply too immature to handle things."

"And now you're back," Sophie added.

"And now I'm back," Sally agreed. "My father's a schoolteacher and my mum works for the Women's Institute. Between them, they sat me down and got it through my thick skull that what I felt was only natural, considering how young I am."

"But won't being back here just, I don't know, bring back those feelings again?" Marcy wanted to know.

After thinking it over for a minute, Sally shrugged.

"I suppose it could, but I've got to try. I can't just sit at home and twiddle my thumbs. I've got to do my bit," she added, jutting out her chin.

"That's the spirit!" Harry blurted out, digging Sally in the ribs.

"We'll all help," Vicky put in. "Won't we, girls?"

Tina came and squatted on the ground before her friend. "And with things being better at the Robinsons', that's got to help too."

"You'll stay, then?" Berry wanted to check.

Sally looked directly at Tina. "Do you forgive me?"

"What's to forgive?" Tina replied before launching herself at her friend, knocking her backward over the log once more.

With barely a second's thought, everyone else joined them, caught up in a moment's happiness in the madness of war.

Chapter Thirty-Six

"Give me a chance, give me a chance!" Brian Lynne muttered, not troubling to keep his voice down as he simultaneously pulled down the top bolt and kicked the bottom one free of the saloon bar door. Pulling it open, he stepped back to let the patrons who'd been hammering on the door inside. "Ever heard of patience?" he asked Berry as he stalked back to the bar.

Berry threw an annoyed look over her shoulder at the girls behind her. "I did ask you not to knock so loudly, Vicky."

Vicky, with Sally on one arm and Tina on the other, pushed past Berry and headed off in the wake of the landlord. "Oh, fiddlesticks! Sal and Tina wanted to celebrate a week of relative bliss at the Robinsons, and I'm thirsty. It's been a tough week."

Marcy laid a hand on Berry's shoulder. "She's got a point. You've all worked very, very hard this week, so first round's on me!"

Upon hearing this, Vicky and her cohorts did a swift about-face, and between them, Vicky and Tina bent down on either side of Marcy and, before she could protest, swiftly wrapped an arm around a leg each, supported her back with their other arm, and carried her up to the bar. They totally ignored Marcy's near-hysterical shouts of, "Mind my head!"

"Well, there's nothing wrong with our hearing,"

Sophie muttered with a laugh and a shake of her head. She snaked a hand through Berry's arm as they stood rooted to the spot at the spectacle. "Come on. If Marcy's buying, I feel like a pint of bitter today."

Once they were all sitting around a table, Tina raised her glass. "Here's to Bob and Marcy! I still don't know what you said, but we're so glad you did."

"Here, here!" Sal echoed. "I don't feel like apologizing for how I smell anymore. It's almost become a novel experience not to feel clean!" she added, lifting up her arm and smelling her own armpit. This caused Vicky to snort some of her ale out her nose and descend into a coughing fit.

Tina rushed to the bar and asked Muriel, "Can I borrow a cloth, please?" She then cleaned up the table as Sophie pounded Vicky on the back until she finished coughing. "Thanks, Muriel," Tina said at returning the cloth.

"What's the celebration in aid of?" Muriel asked, nodding her head toward the girls.

Tina half-turned to lean on the bar top and at the same time looked at her friends. "Oh, it's all rather silly, really. We billet at the Robinsons' farm…you know them?"

Muriel nodded. "Not my favorite couple. Tend to keep themselves to themselves. I can't remember the last time I saw them in here, let alone in the village. Why?"

"Well," Tina said, feeling a little less uncomfortable at saying what she'd been thinking now she'd heard what the landlady had to say, "we'd been having some trouble with them. Things were like living in the dark ages—no hot meals, cold baths, and bad accommodation. That kind of thing." She leaned in a little. "It got so bad that poor Sal ran back home. It's all so much better now though, after Bob and Marcy had words with them. Not quite like living back home, but still, we are here to work. I've no idea what they said, but we're both a lot happier now."

"Good old Bob," Muriel replied. "He always knows what to say," she finished, before putting down the glass she'd been polishing and stalking back toward the kitchen passing her surprised-looking husband on the way.

"What was that in aid of?" Tina asked. "Did I say something wrong?"

Brian laid a hand quickly upon Tina's before telling her, "No, love, you didn't. You'll have to forgive our Muriel. She's been a bit…off, lately. You go back and enjoy yourselves. I heard what you were saying, and I know how difficult it is to be away from home. I was the same as your Sally when I first got to the trenches." Brian stopped and quickly wiped a sleeve across his eyes before finishing, "It's good she's got friends like you. Now, go on."

The landlady's strange behavior hadn't gone unnoticed.

"What's wrong with Muriel?" Berry asked, holding up her glass and using it to point with.

Tina shrugged. "Search me. She asked me what the celebration was in aid of, so I told her. When I mentioned about Marcy here and Bob having words with the Robinsons, that's when it turned…strange. Do you have any idea what that's about?"

After everyone had shrugged their shoulders, Marcy spoke for them all. "No idea. We've not had much to do with anyone in the village, really, except for when we've been in here. Even then, we've kept ourselves to ourselves."

"She's right," Sophie added. "I don't like to think about it, but the most interaction we've had with anyone, barring Bob and Sheila, was when Paula Gibbons' cottage was bombed—Oh, heck!" Sophie had suddenly noticed Berry had gone deathly white. Quickly, Sophie put down her drink and wrapped a firm arm around her friend, bringing her head to rest upon her shoulder. "I'm sorry, sweety. I wasn't thinking," she told her. "Do you need some fresh air?"

Both Sally and Tina had also put down their glasses and were looking at the pair with a mixture of concern and curiosity. "What's wrong?" Tina asked. "Is Berry all right?"

"I'm okay, Sophie," Berry told her friend, raising her head and taking a few deep breaths before turning a weak smile toward the two Land Girls. "Sophie mentioned…Paula Gibbons' cottage."

Sally frowned. "Sorry, not with you."

"You'll have noticed the bombed-out cottage as you come into the village?" Vicky asked.

"Can't miss it." Sally nodded. "Especially the bunches of flowers tied to the remains of the chimney. What about it?"

Sophie opened her mouth only for Berry to say, "I found what was left of the woman who lived there."

"Bloody hell!" Sally let out, shaking her head. "I'm so sorry, Berry. I really didn't mean to upset you."

Nodding her thanks to Sophie, who took a sip from her glass, Berry mustered a smile, a little of her color coming back to her face. "Don't be. You couldn't have known."

"Is the lass ill?" a male voice asked. Unseen by any of the girls, Brian had come up behind them.

Berry looked up into his worn, concerned face and slowly shook her head. "I'm all right, thanks, Brian. Just went back to when Paula Gibbons got killed."

Without another word, Brian turned and hurried back to the bar. Before anyone could say anything, he was back and gently pushed a tall glass of water into Berry's hands. "Get that down your neck."

Not wishing to argue, and suspecting the landlord wouldn't be satisfied until she'd done as he'd bid, Berry raised the glass and didn't stop until she'd finished the glass. Once she'd put the glass down on the table, Brian surprised her by passing on a small glass. "Now this. Nothing better for shock than brandy."

"Are you sure, Brian? Don't you want paying for it?"

Brian's concern momentarily shifted course into insult, before he recovered his composure. Glancing over his shoulder, he then turned back, leant down, and told her, "I won't tell my missus, if you don't."

So, encouraged by her friend's drink-up motions, Berry knocked the brandy back in one…and immediately began coughing. Sophie pounded her on the back as Brian took the glass off her.

"Maybe an early night would be a good idea? Eh, girls?" he suggested, pointedly looking around the group.

Never one to be shy, Vicky asked Brian as he turned to go back to work. "Is your missus feeling herself?"

The landlord chose not to answer in words, the way a hand gripped the back of a wooden chair, making it creak and groan before he let go, was all the answer they needed. Even Vicky took the hint and refrained from repeating herself. Gently releasing Sophie's grip upon her arms, Berry hurried as best she could toward the bar.

"Brian," she semi-shouted toward his departing back, but if he heard her, he ignored her. She was debating whether to nip behind the bar when Muriel appeared before her. By the way she planted herself before her, arms folded over an ample bosom, it didn't look like her mood had improved. After all she'd been through, this actually caused Berry to take a step backward. "Sorry, Muriel. I wasn't going to come behind." When all she received by way of a reply was a sharply raised eyebrow, Berry felt compelled to speak again. "I, um, wanted to thank Brian for coming over to see how I was."

Muriel glanced briefly in the direction her husband had gone before turning back to face Berry. "You'd be best to let him be. I'd say he's used up a few days' worth of interaction. I'll admit though he seems to be better lately, better than he's been for years, and that seems to coincide with you lot turning up!"

If Berry thought she was being complimented, the way the landlady all but spat out the last part of the statement stopped her dead.

"Now," Muriel told her, "if there's nothing else I can do for you, I need to run an errand." Without waiting for a reply, she turned on her heel and disappeared the same way her husband had.

Still slightly stunned, she made her way back to the table and told everyone what she'd just been told.

"I'm not sure how to take that," Marcy finally said.

"Bit of a pity this is the only pub in the village," Sally muttered.

Further comments were forestalled as at that moment Muriel, dressed in a dark coat and black headscarf tightly wrapped around her head, hurried past them, clutching what appeared to be a brown paper package to her chest. Close behind her, but struggling to keep up, came her husband. All the girls exchanged curious glances before getting up from the table as one and following the curious procession outside. By the time they stood outside, things had taken an even more peculiar turn.

They were treated to the surreal sight of Muriel disappearing into the distance, in the direction of the Harkers' farm, with Brian about to mount another bicycle, obviously with the intention of following her.

Marcy looked behind her at the King's Head; plainly he'd forgotten he was leaving the place unmanned. She made a snap decision. "Brian! I'll watch the pub!" she shouted and took the strange gesture he made over his shoulder as acknowledgement he'd heard her. Turning back to the pub, she was greeted by the sight of her companions simply standing there, rooted to the spot, so to speak. It took Marcy only a few seconds to leap into action. "Don't just sit there! Tina," she snapped, "you're with me. The rest of you, get after them!"

"I don't know anything about serving in a pub, though!" Tina whined.

"What's to know? You pull pints, you take the money, you clean up any mess! Now," she swatted the girl on the bottom, "get in there. I'll join you shortly." She turned back to the others as soon as Tina had disappeared inside. "Well, what are you lot waiting for?"

As if she were back in school, Sophie raised a hand. "We didn't come on our bikes."

Marcy slapped her forehead. "For the love of…try using your legs!" When still no one seemed to catch on, Marcy opened her mouth and yelled, "Bloody well run!"

****

The group heard the commotion just as they turned the corner before the gate to the farm. The sight before them was surreal. Brian and Muriel were, somehow, either side of the entrance gate with the bicycles abandoned on the side of the road. A strange mixture of pass-the-parcel and tug-of-war seemed to be going on, though Brian looked like he was trying to tear a brown package out of his wife's hands. For her part, Muriel was hanging onto it as if her life depended upon it.

"Let go!"

"I will not! You let go, Brian!"

Neither noticed the group approaching.

"What the hell's going on?" Vicky wanted to know after they'd been watching for a couple of minutes with no sign of the warring couple even being aware they were being observed.

"I tell you," Brian was now saying from between gritted teeth, "you can't do this! I'm not going to let you. You've gone too far!"

Muriel thrust her head toward her husband's until they were almost touching. "Why should she get all the good luck? Why should she have those children? I deserve children too!"

Making certain to keep a firm grip on Muriel's package, Brian, with a visible effort, bit down on his temper. "Please, listen to what you're saying. You don't hate Sheila. She hasn't done anything to hurt you."

"You hate me, Muriel?"

Drawn by the ruckus and unseen by the warring pair,

Sheila and Bob skidded to a halt just behind Muriel, who promptly let go of her package in shock. This caused her husband to fall backward onto the ground, and the package split open at Berry's feet.

"What the hell?" she shouted upon seeing what it contained, disgust written on her face.

She wasn't the only one—a dead, maggot-infested squirrel would have that effect upon anyone.

Chapter Thirty-Seven

"Muriel?"

Casting a quick glance toward his confused wife, Bob took a tentative step nearer, then another and another until he laid a hand upon Muriel. She didn't seem to notice, her gaze, as with most, was drawn to the multitude of maggots sprayed around the dead remains of the squirrel. He tightened his grip. "Muriel? Look at me."

Tearing his eyes from the corpse, Brian climbed over the gate and, at his wife's other side, took her by the elbow and turned her around. "Muriel? Love?"

As Muriel appeared to be incapable of speaking, Sheila asked, as she came and stood beside her husband, "Brian, do you know what's going on?"

Brian drew his unprotesting wife to his chest, then took a deep breath and faced Sheila. "You've been receiving some…nasty presents." It wasn't a question.

Sheila took a slight step backward, rubbing her chest as if she'd been punched. "You knew?"

"I suspected, before…that," he swept a hand toward the maggots and remains. "I'd noticed Muriel was somewhat…*off* with you since the children came along and you'd both told me about what was happening with them." He squeezed his wife's waist, which at last elicited some response from her. "I could tell she was jealous—heck, I'm a little jealous too," he added with a forced smile, "only I've kept things in perspective."

Sheila reached for Muriel once more. "Muriel?" She reached out and touched her erstwhile friend on the shoulder and squeezed, hard. "Muriel! Speak to me!" When still she didn't get a response, she snapped, "Muriel!"

Finally, Muriel turned her head until she was looking into Sheila's face. Her eyes were full of tears which now began to fall. The compassionate side of Sheila came to the fore, and threading her arm around Muriel's waist, she disentangled her from her husband. "Come inside. We all need to talk. Bob?"

With her husband following her, Sheila started off for the farmhouse with the compliant Muriel on her arm. Brian's head went back and forth between the threesome, the Lumberjills, and Land Girl. Making up his mind, he grabbed Berry by the arm. "I think I heard your friend shouting something at me about looking after the pub?"

"She did," Berry confirmed.

"Look, I don't know how long I'm going to be," he admitted. "Would you lot very much mind going back and holding the fort until I can get back?"

Before Berry could answer, Vicky embarrassed everyone by saying, "But I want to find out what happens."

Sally and Sophie each took the younger girl by the hand and, without a word, steered her back toward the village.

"Ignore Vicky," Berry advised, running a hand through her hair. "She's a nosey cow. Leave it with us. We'll make sure the place doesn't burn to the ground."

Looking a little apprehensive at Berry's phrase of choice, Brian took a bunch of keys from his pocket, pressed them into Berry's hand, and because he didn't have a choice, turned and ran off toward the farmhouse.

****

"There's a letter for you, Berry," Tina said in between pulling a couple of pints of bitter.

"Here? What's a letter doing for me here?" Berry asked, confused, as the group leant up against the bar, there being no room at any tables. She picked it up, and as she slit it open without paying attention, took in the now crowded bar room. "Where'd everyone come from? Looks like most of the village is here!"

She got her answer when a gentleman who looked suspiciously like their postman pounded out a chord on the piano in the corner. "Everyone got a drink? Right, we'll begin with that old favorite, 'Roll out the Barrel' " Whether he was a good pianist or not, became a moot point as he was immediately joined by every other voice, barring the girls, in the room. What they lacked in musicality, the patrons certainly made up for in enthusiasm.

"Bloody hell!" Sally said with a grin and immediately rushed to the pianist's side and joined in with gusto.

"I never knew she could sing?" Tina said, shaking her head at her young friend's antics. She then noticed all the blood had drained from Berry's face. "What's wrong?" she asked, only to be answered with a shake of her friend's head.

"Nothing," she uttered and then, a little more forcibly, "Nothing. I…just need to go outside for a few minutes."

Before anyone could say anything else, Berry had rushed outside, leaving her friends looking at her departing back in curiosity. As the door banged shut behind Berry, Marcy slapped the bar, muttered, "Sod this for a laugh," and rushed off after her friend. She found her leaning against the wall, the letter open in her hands. The ashen face of her friend, together with the letter, made Marcy's legs tremble, and she had to force herself to keep moving until she stumbled against Berry, making her aware of her presence.

"Marcy! What are you doing here?"

It took her a couple of goes before Marcy was able to speak, and when she did, all she could say was, "The letter."

Berry immediately realized what was on her friend's mind and took a hold of her friend's hand. She waved the letter and smiled. "It's not what you think. No one's…died."

Marcy almost slumped down the wall at this news. "I'm sorry. I…I saw you run out, and, well, I didn't want you to go through that alone."

"Come on." Berry tugged Marcy toward a bench outside the church wall. Once they were sitting, she put the letter on her lap and smoothed out some creases. "Honestly, it's not what you think. I wouldn't lie to you."

"But I saw the blood drain from your face!"

Berry touched her face and was glad to feel it warming up once more. "It was a shock, but a *good* shock!" She glanced down at the letter once more before offering it to her friend. "Go ahead, have a read. It's not often we get good news these days, is it?"

Marcy shook her head, declining the offer. "Good news?"

"It's from my parents. They've actually heard from my brother. The first time since the war broke out! I thought he was dead." Berry lowered her head before taking a steadying breath. "We had a colossal falling out, my family, that is."

Marcy squeezed the hand Berry still held. "Care to talk about it? I'm a very good listener."

Berry allowed her eyes to dance around the sky, taking in the velvety night, before turning her attention back to her friend. With a shrug of her shoulders, she told her, "We're a…complicated…lot. My father and mother supported the appeasement policy, and it's safe to say that my brother and I were of the complete opposite way of thinking. At the outbreak of war, they were still maintaining we shouldn't fight Hitler. My brother left home that Christmas, telling my parents he was going to join up and fight. He told me he would write to me, only I never heard anything from him after that. It took three more years before I was able to escape from my parents' clutches. They kept me very close to them the whole time, sending me off to this party, supporting that or opening this, anything to 'maintain the presence of good, patriotic citizens.' " She almost spat out the last word. "I've never made an effort to contact them again, but I've always wondered what happened to John."

"But didn't you say that letter is from your parents?" Marcy pointed out.

Berry nodded. "I know. There's not much in it, except to say that they received a letter from John"—she looked back down at the letter briefly—"about two weeks ago to tell them he was in Coastal Command, and to give me his address."

Marcy raised an eyebrow. "Nothing else? To ask how you are? And, how did they get your address?"

Berry turned the letter over in her hands before

replying, "Nothing. Well, a short line hoping I'm well and that the letter gets to me, but that's it."

"Exactly how did they know where you were?" Marcy persisted.

"I may not like them, but I did leave a letter before I snuck out, with how to contact me if they needed."

Both were silent for a few minutes, as Marcy and Berry sifted through their various thoughts. Eventually, Marcy asked, "So I assume you're going to write to him?"

Berry treated her friend to a huge grin and, springing to her feet, pulled Marcy to her feet also. "Are you kidding? As soon as we finish here tonight!"

Arm in arm, the two strolled back into the bar, immediately being swept along with the chorus of "We'll Meet Again."

****

"So what did you put in your reply?" Marcy asked Berry as they mounted their bicycles the next morning for work.

"You mean, after I'd given him a page's worth of my thoughts about him not contacting me?" she replied with a grin. "Well, I gave him a summary of what I'd been up to. Told him all about you lot!" she yelled over her shoulder.

"Did you mention that Sophie's single?" Vicky asked and then had to speed up as Sophie attempted to smack her around the back of her head.

"Of course I did," Berry shouted toward Vicky's back as she sped out of Sophie's reach. "Then I told him I needed to see him."

"Naturally," Marcy agreed. "You know, with luck, he'll get some leave whilst we're still here. I'm sure

Sheila and Bob would be more than happy to put him up."

"That'd be so great," Berry agreed in a dreamlike voice, before hastily jerking her handlebars to the right to avoid a deep hole in the road, getting an alarmed "Mew," from Midnight in her usual place in Berry's basket.

After ten minutes had passed, Sophie had pulled ahead and was happily chatting away to Vicky. "I thought she'd never leave us alone," Marcy muttered.

"I beg your pardon?" Berry asked.

"No, I didn't mean it like that," Marcy hastened to clear up. "It's only that I wanted to speak to you in private. You've got to admit, that's a little difficult to come by at times."

"Can't argue with you there," Berry agreed. "What did you want to talk about?"

"I had a rather…personal telephone conversation with Archie last night."

"Oh, ho! So that's why you came back to the barn looking like the cat that got the cream!"

"Meow?" At the mention of cream, Midnight poked her little black head out from under her gingham cover.

"Go back to sleep," Marcy urged. "There's nothing for you."

With what sounded suspiciously like a disgruntled version of "Mew," Midnight disappeared back amongst Berry's lunch.

When Marcy didn't say anything more straight away, Berry prodded, "And?"

"And we…talked."

"I gathered that," Berry answered, making another "go-on" gesture.

"And we agreed to see each other."

Berry was puzzled. "I already thought you were?"

"I meant we're going to be making it…official. You know I like him, you all do, but you've probably also noticed I've been holding back."

"We had," Berry agreed. "But we also all know why. It's quite understandable. It's not that long since your husband…died. But you're happy now? With what you've both decided?"

"Yes, oh yes!" Marcy said. "You'll all get the chance to see, this weekend. The crew's got the weekend off, and Archie's asked if we can meet them in York. Apparently, Dennis has booked a table for us at Betty's. What do you think?"

"Can't wait!" Berry smiled. "Come on, let's tell the others."

Chapter Thirty-Eight

"You're sure you won't come?"

Sophie smiled a little indulgently for, she thought, probably the third time that Saturday afternoon. Having rushed home from the morning's graft, Vicky, Marcy, and Berry had all immediately commenced rushing around getting washed and cleaned up, then deciding what to wear for their dates at Betty's later in the day. "I appreciate you're wanting to check and double-check I know my own mind, Vicky, but I promise you all, I'll be happier here than feeling like I'd be getting in the way of you bunch and your men."

"Hey! You would never get in the way!" Marcy protested, holding up first one and then another dress against herself as she tried to decide what to wear.

"I prefer the other one," Lucy told her.

Marcy let her hands flop down and fixed the little girl with an annoyed glare. "A minute ago…" she said through clenched teeth.

Lucy glared back over the top of the old *Radio Times* she was using to practice her reading. "It's not my fault I can't make up your mind!"

Unable to decide what Lucy meant, Marcy opened and closed her mouth a couple of times before turning her attention back to Sophie. "Who said you'd get in the way?"

"No one," she admitted. "It's how I'd feel, though.

Plus, I'd be reminded of Ginger, and I'd rather I wasn't. I don't think a relationship and me is a good idea at the moment."

This declaration brought silence to the barn as everyone took this announcement in, before Berry came and sat down on her bed. "All right, message received and understood. Even though you know the fellas wouldn't see it that way and I'm certain they'd also love to see you."

Sophie sat up and gave her friend a quick hug before flopping back. "I'm sure they would," she agreed. "Perhaps next time."

"In that case," Harry said, popping up, "you can give me a hand with the last milking. Bob's back is giving him some problems, so we can give him a rest."

"You cold, heartless beast!" Sophie teased. "I've spent the whole morning cutting down trees! I'm tired!"

Vicky threw her pillow at Sophie and hit her square in the face. "Me thinks the lady doth protest too much."

"Me too-eth," Harry declared. "It's all right, Sophie. The cows aren't due until about six."

Sophie looked at her alarm clock and semi-groaned. "That only gives me three and a bit hours for a nap!"

Harry kneeled next to Sophie's head and told her, "I'll make sure you're awake." With that, she ruffled her friend's hair and scuttled out of reach before Sophie's flailing arms could grab hold of her.

****

Sophie had just finished washing and changing after helping Harry with the milking, her sole thought being that a lie-down before tea would be so good right now, when Sheila popped her head around the barn door.

"Sophie, love. Are you there?" she called.

"Over here!" Sophie answered, waving a hand, and was joined momentarily.

"I wanted to let you know, tea's going to be a little later than normal tonight. I haven't had the chance to let you know, but we're going to have some guests tonight."

"I love guests!" Harry announced as she came through the door behind Sheila, rubbing her hair vigorously with her towel before throwing it over a length of string she'd set up above her bed and flopping down on top of Lucy, who let out a squeal and wriggled out from beneath her sister. From beneath the bed, came a loud, "Yowl!" followed by the appearance of a visibly annoyed Percy, who flicked his tail in his tormentors' general direction and then hopped up onto a beam and disappeared up in the rafters. "Who is it?" Harry asked, completely nonplussed.

Somewhat curiously, Sheila turned her head briefly away from the girls before telling them, "It's Muriel and Brian."

This caused Sophie to raise an eyebrow as, naturally, everyone on the farm was now familiar with the perpetrator of all the nasty little presents Sheila had been receiving. "Okay," was all she could think of to say, before adding, "Are you sure you want me around? I can have my tea in here, if it would make things…easier."

Sheila managed a small smile. "That's not necessary. You come and join us. About half an hour?"

"We'll be there!" Harry answered for her.

A little after the stated time, Sophie entered the kitchen, Harry towing her little sister in behind her. "Sorry we're a little late," she said, then greeted the guests. "Good evening, Brian, Muriel."

If the landlord showed signs of not wanting to be

there, then the amount of squirming his wife was doing on her chair merely reinforced the impression. Both simply nodded in reply.

"Do you want a hand with anything, Sheila?" she asked.

"If you could lay the table, love, that would be helpful."

"How's Bob's back?" Sophie asked as she laid a bowl out for everyone.

A creak of floorboards above their heads drew everyone's attention. "You can ask him yourself. Mind you, it'll take a few minutes for him to get down the stairs."

Harry jumped to her feet and rushed to the door leading to the hall. "I'll go and give him a hand," she said on her way, and the thunder of feet up the stairs precluded anyone saying otherwise to her.

"She's a right bundle of energy," Brian said, appearing a little surprised to hear his own voice.

Obviously wishing to lighten the atmosphere, Sophie said, "Tell me about it! We only finished milking the cows a while ago. I've no idea where she gets it from. I may need someone to fish my head out of my stew, Brian. You'll keep an eye on me?"

"I still owe you and your friends for the other night," he told her. "You can count on that."

As Sophie finished laying the table, Bob hobbled in, trying to appear not to be leaning upon Harry's shoulder. His efforts were in vain as Harry, though noticeably taller than when she'd first arrived on the farm, was walking with her knees slightly bent. To her credit, she didn't comment on this and stayed as she was until Bob had made himself as comfortable as possible in his chair.

"How's the back, Bob?" Brian asked.

Bob let out a small chuckle, wincing for his trouble. "Believe it or not, I'm actually a hundred percent better than I was this morning." As Harry took her seat next to Lucy once more, Bob mustered a smile. "Harry, I don't know what I'd do without you. I should be all right for milking in the morning, though," he told her.

Sheila immediately told him off. "Really? Let me tell you this, Robert Harker," and was rewarded by the sight of her husband swallowing hard, it being the law that when any man is called by his full name, he knows he's in trouble. "If you can touch your toes, right now, then I'll let you back to work tomorrow. If not, then you're to stay in bed. Harry and me will take care of the work tomorrow. Right, Harry?"

"Right, Sheila," Harry readily agreed.

"I'll help too!" Lucy offered.

"Of course you can," Sheila agreed, laying a hand briefly on the smallest girl's head before bringing over the pot of stew and beginning to serve up.

"Um…" Brian began and then cleared his throat when he noticed he had everyone's undivided attention. "What I mean to say is, if you need some help on the farm for a day or two, Bob, I can come around. I'm sure Muriel can manage fine at the pub during the day without me."

Though she looked at her husband as if this was the first she'd heard of this idea—which, of course, it was—Muriel nodded her head. When she spoke, though, she was obviously finding it hard to look anyone in the eye. "I can't see there being any problem with that," she managed to say.

Bob and Sheila exchanged looks before Sheila sat

down next to Muriel.

Sheila ate some of her stew, dabbed the sides of her mouth with a napkin, and laid her spoon down. "Muriel, thank you for coming tonight," she began. "I'm sure you know we have to sort things out between us."

When his wife didn't reply straight away, Brian prompted her by digging his elbow into her ribs. "Yes, yes, of course," she stammered.

As she then failed to follow up, Bob prompted, "Muriel, you've got to talk to us, or there's no way we're going to get through this. You have to tell us why."

Brian got up, knelt down beside his wife, and gripping her hand tightly asked, "Honey, Sheila's your friend, so is Bob. Just speak to us."

Sophie pushed her chair back and got to her feet. "Let me take the girls outside. This isn't something they should be hearing and, to be honest, I don't think I should be here either."

Somewhat to her surprise, Bob's head snapped up and he looked straight into her eyes. "No!"

"Pardon?" Sophie replied as she reached for both Harry and Lucy's hands.

"I want you to stay, please," he added as Sophie opened her mouth.

Sheila jumped to her feet and without a word hared out into the hall where everyone heard her pick up and speak into the phone. There then followed a quick-fire conversation before she came back into the room. "I think I know why Bob wants you to stay, Sophie. That was Elias I've just spoken to. He'll be around in five minutes." She turned her attention onto the girls. "Harry, Lucy. When Sergeant Duncan gets here…you know Elias, don't you?" she asked and got nods by reply. "I want you to take your meals and go into the barn with him."

Harry folded her arms. "We can eat in the front room. We won't be a bother." Lucy nodded her head vigorously in agreement. "Besides, Bob said to stay."

"I know you wouldn't," Sheila agreed before looking at Muriel, "but we really need some privacy, and despite what Bob just said, it would be so much easier for us if you'd do what we ask. You're okay with the sergeant, aren't you?"

Lucy mimicked her sister in shrugging her shoulders. "He's nice," Harry eventually agreed.

"Good. We won't be long," Sheila added, "and then you can both come back inside. All right?"

"All right," Lucy said as the kitchen door swung open to admit the policeman.

"That was quick," Bob remarked.

"Any quicker and I'll have to tell myself off for speeding," the sergeant said with a grin before holding out his hands to the girls. "Right, pick your bowls up and let's go out to the barn." He looked up at Sheila before following the girls out. "You know where I am if you need me."

Once the door had closed behind them, Sophie asked the question she'd been dying to ask. "Why do you want me to stay, Sheila?"

Chapter Thirty-Nine

Bob took a deep breath, taking in his friends and wife before actually addressing Brian. "I expect you've noticed how…good…things are between Sheila and me now."

Not appearing aware of the motion, Brian snaked his hand into his wife's and appeared reluctant to meet his friend's gaze, though he did eventually say, "We had noticed. We're also aware it coincided with Harry and Lucy coming on the scene."

Sophie opened her mouth to point out he was wrong, but Bob quickly shook his head. What he said next echoed what she was about to say.

"Not quite." He reached out and patted one of Sophie's hands on the tabletop before continuing. "They've merely added to our happiness. It's mostly down to Sophie here. I didn't accept their presence very well at first."

Sophie and Sheila both snorted.

Bob at least had the grace to blush. "All right, maybe that's putting it mildly. Either way, after this young lady had words with me, she… I'm not going to tell you exactly what she said. Suffice to say, she put my head right when no one else could."

"It's true," Sheila added. "Without this lass, there's a very good chance I wouldn't be here now." At seeing the skeptical expressions on their guests' faces, she quickly said, "Either that, or I'd have been found stood over Bob's body with a bloody pitchfork in my hands."

This had the desired effect, as both Brian and Muriel burst out laughing before Brian sobered up enough to ask, "That bad?"

Bob looked at his wife as he replied, "I'd have handed her the pitchfork."

Despite what had just been discussed, Muriel's almost total lack of participation in the conversation instinctively told Sophie something more was going on here than simple jealousy. If Muriel wasn't going to volunteer the news, then she'd straight out ask. "This isn't about you being jealous, really, is it, Muriel." She didn't give her time to object. "There's something much deeper here." Brian's alarmed eyebrows caught her attention. "Forgive me for asking, Brian. Is there something about you? Something you…don't like talking about? Or rather, something you don't want anyone else to know about."

All the while she'd been talking to him, Sophie had noticed the way Brian was flexing his free hand into a fist. The hand was large and quite badly scarred across the rear, she couldn't help but notice. She was trying his temper sorely, and she didn't know if she'd gone too far.

"We can't have children!" Muriel blurted out. "It's my fault, nothing to do with Brian," she added, a little too hastily for Sophie and, by the looks on their faces, Bob and Sheila too. Before anybody else could say anything, Muriel insisted, "You're wrong, though. It is jealousy. I'm jealous of Sheila having those children, having something we can't."

The way she didn't look up into anyone's eyes as she spoke meant something more was left unsaid, Sophie felt, and she didn't entirely believe her. Though Muriel had blurted out an element of the truth, it wasn't the whole truth, and if these couples were to get their old friendship back, then everything needed to come out. She said so, "I believe you, Muriel." This brought a small smile to the landlady's face, which was wiped away by what Sophie said next. "It's not the whole truth, though, is it?"

"What're you looking at?" Brian unexpectedly snapped.

Sophie's eyes snapped up from where they'd inadvertently strayed, drawn there by the way his hand had been flexing back and forth over the area, as if in protection. Her mind flashed back to what she knew about the man, automatically bringing to mind the Great War. From the way her eyes widened in realization and at seeing the tears which sprang to Brian's eyes, she was fairly certain she was right. It didn't often happen, but there were times when walking in the street, you came upon a disfigured man, a piteous relic from the Great War, doing their best to hide their face from the horrified gazes they suffered. Only, there were many kinds of disfigurement, more than one kind of cross for the poor souls to bear; shrapnel and bullets were disinterested in whom and where they struck.

Not wishing to embarrass the man, she said, barely above a whisper, "You were…wounded, weren't you." She lowered her eyes, and Brian lowered his hands to his lap in unspoken confirmation.

Neither Sheila nor Bob missed either the meaning of what *wasn't* spoken, nor where Sophie couldn't help but direct her gaze.

"Oh, Brian," Sheila uttered, one hand flying to her

mouth as she stood abruptly. Only Bob's firm grip stopped her from striding to her friend's side.

Sophie's face had lost all color. "Oh, Christ," she muttered, "I'm right, aren't I."

Bob, whilst keeping a firm hold of Sheila's arm, let his head droop before pulling her gently down into the seat next to him. "Stay put," he told her as he got to his feet. Going over to the larder, he pulled open the door, disappeared half inside, and when he turned around, he had the last bottle of elderflower wine in one hand and five glasses gathered against his chest. "We're all in need of a drink."

Once everyone had a glass before them, Brian, with Muriel leaning heavily into him, stood and raised his glass. "To all the politicians and generals, may they rot in hell!"

Everyone echoed, "May they rot in hell!"

Once everyone had finished their glass, they all sat down. Eventually, Sheila couldn't stay quiet any longer. "I don't know what to say, Brian."

For his part, Brian managed a shrug. "It is what it is, Sheila. Now you know why we've no children. I'm not, physically…able to."

Unable to help herself, Sophie put in, "Yet you, Muriel, still married him. Knowing what had…happened."

With her head now upon her husband's shoulder, Muriel turned her eyes up to look into her husband's. "Of course! I loved him, and still do."

"Yet, though you weren't able to have your own, you still craved children." Sophie got to her feet and began to pace up and down before the kitchen window. "Only you couldn't face what anyone would say if you adopted, instead of having your own," she guessed.

"Silly, isn't it." Muriel nodded. "But true. It's a failing of mine, you see. I've always hated being thought ill of."

"Was it all too much?" Sophie guessed. "When Harry and Lucy turned up and ended up staying here?"

Muriel closed her eyes before opening them and looking toward Sheila. "I won't blame you if you never forgive me, Sheila. I've been a silly, stupid, jealous woman. I...I really don't know what came over me. I hated seeing you so happy, and I went...crazy. There's no other way to describe it."

After the briefest of hesitations, Sheila held open her arms, and Muriel didn't waste a moment in rushing into them. Breaking apart after a minute or so, Sheila said, "Let's say no more about it." She led her toward the back door. "Let's go and find Elias and the girls. They need to meet their Aunty Muriel."

Even from behind, you could tell Muriel had as wide a smile upon her face as anyone had ever had. Left alone with the two men, Sophie pulled out her seat and made to sit back down before putting it back in to the kitchen table and heading toward the door herself. She was brought up short by Bob's firm words.

"And where do you think you're going, young lady?"

"Um, to go and join the others?"

Unseen, Brian had got to his feet on her other side and pulled out her seat once more. "Not a chance. Sit back down, and we'll enjoy the rest of this wine together."

Gently but firmly placed in her seat, Sophie looked across at two unexpectedly smiling faces. "You're sure?

But why?"

"She asks why," Bob said with a shake of his head.

"Unbelievable," Brian agreed, refilling three glasses and placing one before each of them. "To Sophie!"

"To Sophie," Bob replied, as the girl in question, still not sure of what was happening, raised her glass.

Once the glasses were emptied, Brian refilled them and then slumped back into his seat, his eyes upon Sophie. "I don't know how you do it," he told her, shaking his head.

"Do what?" she asked, feeling all the more flummoxed.

"Get people to talk about…" He cast his eyes briefly back down toward his lap. "About things they don't want to discuss."

Sophie could only shrug in reply and took a sip of her drink whilst trying to think of something to say. In the end, she leaned forward to look Brian straight in the eye so he knew she was serious. "I swear never to mention anything of this conversation to anyone else."

After a moment, during which she quite clearly saw his Adam's apple bob up and down as he swallowed, Brian raised his glass to chink it against hers in a toast. "I know you won't."

Bob leaned forward so he could join in before adding, "Let's finish the bottle."

****

"That's a hell of a thing!" Berry declared, with a whistle.

"Do you think anyone would mind if we add our names?" Dennis ventured, whilst waggling his eyebrows at his date.

Berry left him hanging for a beat or two more than

he was comfortable with before hooking her arm through his and kissing him on the cheek. "I've got a nail file we can use."

"What about it?" Archie asked Marcy.

Picking up her glass, Marcy took a sip before replying, "I hope you won't mind if we don't. At least, not yet. I'm quite happy going along as we are for the moment."

If he was disappointed, Archie didn't show it. Instead, he picked up Marcy's hand, raised it to his lips, and kissed the back. "I shouldn't have asked. I'm sorry, and I hope I didn't make you feel awkward."

Before Marcy could say anything, Jimmy swatted his friend around the back of his head. "Who knew you were such a sensitive soul, Archie!"

Perhaps surprising even herself, Marcy got to her feet, kissed the part of his head where his friend had swatted him, and promptly reciprocated a little harder. "And don't you forget it, Jimmy," she told the surprised bomb aimer.

With his arms around her and Marcy's around his neck, Archie stuck his tongue out and grinned at his friend, very aware Marcy couldn't see what he was doing. Unfortunately for him, everyone else could.

"Next round on you," Dennis informed him, and when Marcy opened her mouth to ask why, told her, "You don't want to know."

Marcy let her boyfriend's head go and sat back, though she was unable to tell from his face what exactly Dennis was referring to, she knew him well enough to guess he'd been fooling around. "Behave yourself," she instructed him before taking his hand and heading in the direction of the table Vicky had commandeered for them.

"About time," Vicky said, as everyone crowded around, claiming their seats next to their partners. "I've already had to get rid of two parties who wanted this table."

"Well done, you," Jimmy said to Vicky, placing a glass of wine before her and, eliciting a nice blush, kissed her on the cheek.

"Careful, you two." Berry nudged her friend.

"So what were you lot all talking about, that left me here on my own?" Vicky asked, absently accepting Jimmy's hand in hers and doing her best to ignore both Marcy and Berry's undisguised grins.

Putting down her pint of stout, Marcy pointed toward the mirror. "I take it you've seen that?"

Turning in her seat a little awkwardly, as she didn't want to let go of Jimmy's hand, Vicky peered at the mirror before turning back. "It's a mirror. So what?" she replied, shrugging her shoulders.

"You need to take a close look at it," Marcy said, blowing out her breath in exasperation.

"Can I finish my drink first?" Vicky replied.

Marcy got to her feet, took Vicky by the hand, and pulled her to her feet. "No, you can't," she told her, giving her a gentle push in the back toward the mirror.

Very shortly, the two were back, and Vicky was fairly hopping from foot to foot in barely contained excitement. "We *have* to add our names, Jimmy!" she said, grabbing her handbag and digging a hand into it. Coming up with her brother's penknife, she took hold of Jimmy's hand and dragged him to his feet.

"Wait!" he cried, as she began to drag him toward the mirror. "Before we do this, I need to ask you a question."

"What?" Vicky asked, planting her hands on her hips. "Can't it wait?"

He shook his head before saying, "I hope it'll be to your liking," and then asking Marcy and Berry, "Is she always like this?"

They both nodded before Berry informed him, "If you're going to ask her what I think you're going to ask her, then you'd better get used to it."

This caused Jimmy to look back and forth between Vicky and Berry a couple of times before finally settling on Vicky. "Because you want to scratch our names, can I assume you're my girlfriend?"

A slow smile spread upon the girl's face before she took his hand once more, a little more gently this time. "I think we can say that." She then strode off toward the mirror, penknife in one hand and a slightly dazed looking Jimmy in the other.

"I trust he'll let her do the writing," Berry mumbled.

"Why's that, love?" Dennis asked.

Berry treated him to an evil grin. "Vicky can't spell to save her life. If he's foolish enough to let her take the lead, well, they're liable to end up with an inscription along the lines of, 'Jummpy loves Vuckie'!"

Everyone was still laughing when the pair in question came back, hand in hand and both beaming. "What are you lot laughing about?" Vicky asked as she took her seat.

"Can we borrow your knife?" Berry asked, nail file forgotten, as she jumped up.

"Be careful," Vicky said as she handed it over. Berry and Dennis too disappeared in the direction of the mirror. "Why are they so eager?"

Marcy shared a look with Archie before replying, "I

think she wanted to get out of the way in case you complained when you heard what we were laughing about."

Vicky frowned. "So, are you going to tell me or not?"

Archie held up his hands. "Hey, you said it, not me!"

"Coward," Marcy told him, slapping his arm. She turned to where Vicky was still waiting. "We were saying, we hoped you'd let Jimmy do the writing."

Vicky took in what Marcy had said before she put down her drink and, slowly, informed her friend, "Sometime, when you're both least expecting it, you two are going to get tickled to death."

Puzzled, Jimmy said, "You're going to have to explain that one to me."

"I'm not the best at spelling," Vicky admitted.

Unable to prevent himself, Jimmy let out a burst of laughter before clapping a hand over his mouth as Vicky shot him a glare. "Sorry," he mumbled.

Before anyone else could say anything, Berry and Dennis came back and took their seats. "That was fun!" Berry stated.

Dennis leaned toward her and, without a care in the world, took her head between his hands and kissed her on the mouth, finally coming up for air to tell her, "And, according to the barman, there's over three hundred signatures and the like on that mirror now."

"Bloody hell!" Archie swore.

"Here's to Betty's!" Berry raised her glass.

"And their terrific mirror!" Dennis added.

Chapter Forty

"Put down your axes, girls!" Marcy shouted so she could be heard above the din of metal upon tree trunk. As soon as her three friends had obeyed and strode over to join her, she told them, "Take a seat. I've some news."

"Hitler's given in?" Vicky asked, plopping herself down on the forest floor.

"I wish," Berry put in, stretching her back before joining her friend. "My bloody back's killing me this afternoon."

"Turn around," Sophie told her, "and shuffle between my legs. I'll give your back a rub."

"Quite finished?" Marcy said, hands on her hips, but with a small smile upon her lips. "Good. Well, the more bright amongst you lot have probably been wondering why there's only us four working this patch. How come there's not more of us? Because otherwise, we're not going to clear this between ourselves in a month of Sundays, despite what I've said!"

"We haven't done that badly," Sophie broke in to say.

Marcy shook her head. "I never said we have. I was only pointing out, again, that there should be quite a few more of us working here. That's going to change shortly. I spoke to Ethel last night, and it looks like we'll get reinforcements within the next couple of weeks."

Vicky raised a hand.

"We're not in school now, Vicky," Marcy told her with a grin.

"Sorry," she said, hastily putting her hand down. "Do you mind my asking what held them up?"

Marcy sat down beside them. "Ethel didn't go into too much detail, but it appears it's a case of there being too much wood to be felled and not enough of us. You all know how hard the training is, and it's not something where you can cut corners." She hesitated before saying what was on her mind. "You all remember what happened to Elaine." Everyone let out a shudder at the terrible leg injury the girl had suffered. "Sorry, I didn't mean to bring up bad memories."

"Will they be lodging with us too?" Berry asked before letting out a groan of pleasure and leaning back into Sophie's ministrations. "Right there! Oh, yes, that's the spot!"

"Whilst Berry's reliving a date with Dennis…"

"Vicky!" Berry yelled in outrage. "I've never…we've never…I mean, Vicky, please."

Marcy shot a glare at the younger girl until she held up her hands and bowed her head, "Sorry, Berry. I got a little carried away."

After a few seconds, Berry gave her friend a small smile before saying, "Don't tease," and then settled back into Sophie's lap once more so she could resume her massage.

Marcy cleared her throat. "To get back to Berry's question. No, apparently some Pioneers will be along next week to build some huts for them down by the sawmill."

Sophie stood up so quickly that Berry fell backward and was left staring up at the sky behind her friend's back. "Hang on! Does that mean we've got to move in with them? I don't want to go," she stated.

"Me either," Vicky added, echoed by Berry as she hauled herself back into a seated position.

Marcy held up her hands to stop any further protests. "Hold on. Firstly, don't shoot the messenger. Secondly, don't worry about that. I don't particularly want to move out either." She quickly continued as Vicky looked like making further protests. "We'll be staying where we are. I like the village and the people, and Ethel agreed that as we've become such a part of the community, plus with everything we've been through, she's fine with us staying where we are until this job is done."

The only sounds to be heard for a few minutes were from the birds in the trees.

Finally, Berry shuffled away from Sophie and said, "You know, I'd forgotten we wouldn't be staying here forever."

"Forever?" Marcy asked.

Berry ran a none-too clean hand through her hair. "You know what I mean. Not forever, forever. It's just that so much has happened, it feels like I've been here forever. Leaving's going to be so hard."

"We could always work slowly?" Vicky suggested with a laugh.

"I'm very glad you were only joking, Vicky," Marcy said. "Also, don't let Ethel hear you say that. But," she added to soften her words, "I do know exactly what you mean. We'll have to cross that bridge when we come to it."

No one said anything for a few minutes. Then a drop of rain hit Sophie on the nose. As it began to rain harder, it had the effect of sparking everyone out of their own thoughts.

Marcy got to her feet, stretched her arms above her head, and let out a small moan. "Come on, everyone to their feet. There's enough light left for another hour or so. Let's get some more work done, and then we can get back to the farm. Sheila's making a rabbit stew tonight, remember?"

****

"Elias! Good to see you again," Sophie said when she entered the kitchen early that evening. "To what do we owe the pleasure?"

"Sophie," he replied, getting to his feet as she took her seat. He remained standing as they were joined by Berry, Marcy, and Vicky.

"Why's Sergeant Duncan standing up?" Lucy asked.

"He's being a gentleman," Harry answered quickly, getting an approving nod from both Sheila and Bob.

"Thank you, Harry," the policeman told the girl, before saying to Lucy, "And that's the kind of person you want to look out for. Not riffraff like Bob there," he finished, whispering not very quietly into her ear.

"Hey!" Bob rejoined. "Any more talk like that, and you can cook your own meals!"

This earned him a playful smack on the wrist with a ladle, from his wife. "Ignore him, Elias...I'd give you a hand."

After everyone had finished their stew and Elias and Sheila had finished washing and drying the crockery, everyone gathered outside on and around the log by the girls' barn, enjoying a glass of beer from the bottles the policeman had brought with him.

"So," Sophie began after savoring her first swig, "to

what do we owe the honor, Elias?"

Putting down his glass, Elias searched out and fixed his gaze upon Vicky, something which didn't go unnoticed.

"Whatever anyone says, I didn't do it!" Vicky declared, getting a laugh from everyone, though from Lucy's puzzled expression, the child didn't really understand what had been said.

"That's good to know," he teased, before saying, "I thought you'd like to know. They've buried that German pilot in the churchyard. Hold on!" he said as Vicky went to open her mouth. "Before you say anything, I was under orders not to tell anyone until the deed was done. They didn't want anyone getting wind of what was happening, so the orders were no one, other than the vicar and the burial party, was to attend."

"Poor sod," Vicky announced, not troubling to keep her voice down, as Marcy drew the girl into her shoulder.

Elias frowned. "I quite agree. However now, I wanted to ask if you, and your friends, would like to join me after tomorrow morning's service. I intend to pay my respects at his grave."

Vicky immediately said, "Count me in," closely followed by everyone else.

****

"Oberleutnant Hans Bauer," Vicky read, as she knelt down next to the gravestone. Looking down, she read on, "Twenty-one years old." Getting to her feet, she unashamedly brushed tears from her eyes before turning to her friends who, knowing how personally she felt this boy's death, were standing close by. "What kind of an age is that to die? I'm sorry, I really am, but it's such a waste."

"Here," Jimmy said, holding out a bunch of flowers to his girlfriend.

"Thanks, love," she replied, taking them with a weak smile before turning back to the Luftwaffe airman's grave and laying them at the base of the gravestone. "It means a lot to me that you came," she told him over her shoulder.

"I'd hope someone would do the same for me, if it happens," he replied.

Straightening up, she touched the top of the stone once more before taking Jimmy's outstretched hand and walking toward the lychgate. A loud "Harrumph" from the church porch made her turn her head. Dressed in faded gray tweed, they were confronted by a large, formidable-looking woman.

"Can I help you?"

The woman looked Vicky up and down before turning up her piggy little nose, obviously finding the Lumberjills slightly frayed skirt, sturdy walking shoes, and especially the sou'wester she was wearing against the constant drizzle that Sunday morning had brought, not to her taste.

"I don't think so," she eventually replied.

Both Sheila and Marcy touched her shoulder, which Vicky promptly shrugged off.

"I think you do," Vicky said evenly. "Anyone with that kind of a sniff needs to blow her nose. Can I lend you a handkerchief?"

From the look on the woman's face, you'd think Vicky had offered to perform surgery upon her without an anesthetic. "How rude!"

Vicky was only just warming up, and if the woman in question had troubled to look closely at her friends behind her, she'd have perhaps tried to make her excuses and leave—but she hadn't.

"How else do you explain such a sniff?"

"I don't have to…" the tweed woman began to say.

"I know you don't," Vicky cut her off, "but you're going to." Vicky marched up until she was nose to rather voluminous bosom. "If you've a problem with what I said, have the nerve to say it to my face, rather than trying to hide behind false excuses. So, say what you're really thinking! Either that, or don't bother to open your mouth at all!"

Jimmy, Sal, and Tina, who'd been informed of what the girls intended to do that morning and had willingly joined them, actually began to clap before noticing the glances and shakes of head from Sheila and Elias, which brought them up short.

"I…I mean, we…he was *German*!" the tweed woman eventually managed to get out, her face a quite delightful shade of beetroot by now.

Vicky didn't give her a chance to say anything else, and indeed, took one step back, reached up, and poked the woman in the shoulder. "What the hell's that got to do with anything? He's some poor boy who died hundreds of miles from home. He deserves a good Christian burial, and it's only right he should be respected!"

The church door opened behind the woman to admit the vicar into their presence. He laid a hand upon his wife's shoulder. "What's all the shouting about, dear?"

"You've met my husband?" the woman said, a little more of her previous bluster back in her sails now her husband had come along.

Vicky didn't bother to look up at him, as she was

busy trying to glare the woman's buttons off. "Not directly. Pleased to meet you, Vicar," she began, before stating bluntly, "though if this is your wife, perhaps you need to teach her about Christian values."

Tightening his grip upon his wife's shoulder, the vicar looked more curious than angry at the words the small woman had thrown at him. "Why? What's she said now?"

Vicky opened and closed her mouth, not expecting this turn of events. "I beg your pardon, Vicar?"

Before replying, the vicar bent down and whispered into his wife's ear. Whatever he said caused her to go an even deeper shade of red before she turned on her heel and, without so much as a by-your-leave, marched back into the church, even going so far as to slam the door. Rubbing a finger under an ear, when he turned back to face Vicky, he actually had a wry grin on his face.

Taking a seat on a bench in the porch, the vicar now had an understanding smile upon his face. He patted the wood beside him. "Come, sit down, and I'll try to explain my wife's behavior."

"Hi, Vicar!" Bob said as he joined them, looking at where the church door was still reverberating. "Violet's still the same, I see."

"Good to see you, Bob, Sheila," he added, briefly getting to his feet as the two sat down opposite Vicky and himself, with everyone else crowding unashamedly into the shelter. He addressed Vicky. "What happened?" he asked without further preamble.

Under his friendly gaze, Vicky cleared her throat before explaining what had happened.

"I see," he said, stroking his full, white beard and shaking his head.

"Why would she behave like that…"

"If she's a vicar's wife?" he finished, the sides of his mouth creeping up.

"Exactly," Vicky agreed, having the grace to go a little red herself.

"She's normally fine, quite the heart of the party." He stopped, as Vicky had had to slap a hand to her mouth to stifle a laugh. "Honestly! She's only like that whenever anything German is the subject."

"Really?" Bob said, not bothering to hide his surprise. "Pardon me for saying, but I always thought she was just a bit, well, and I mean this in the best possible way, stuck up."

The vicar leaned forward a little. "That too. Really, the trouble is, vicar's wife or not, she's never found it in her heart to forgive the Germans for the loss of her brother in the Great War."

Vicky wasn't the only one to turn their gaze to the door.

The vicar coughed to gain her attention back. Gently, he laid a hand over one of Vicky's. "However, if I may ask, my dear, why were you so upset?"

Grateful for the contact, Vicky squeezed back. "I…we…" She glanced gratefully at her friends as they stood watching her. "We were there when the German parachuted out. I stayed with him whilst my friends went to get the authorities. He didn't quite die in my arms, but…you see, he's the same age as my brother."

"Your brother? I'm afraid I've not met him," the vicar said unknowingly.

Vicky shook her head, ignoring the tears in the corners of her eyes. "And you won't. He was killed at Dunkirk."

After a moment, the vicar let out a sigh and leant in to give her a brief kiss on the forehead. "I understand." He looked up at the obvious concern in everyone surrounding her before leaning in close and saying, so only Vicky could hear, "If you ever need to talk, please, come and see me. At any time, I'll be here." In a more normal volume, he added, "Bob knows my telephone number, even if he doesn't come to the service as often as he should."

Bob wagged a finger at the vicar. "That's not fair. You know how busy I am up at the farm. Especially," he added, "as I haven't got my Land Girls yet."

The vicar nudged Vicky in the ribs. "It's always one excuse or another with that one."

Looking slightly red around the face, Sheila, whilst treating her husband to an annoyed sideways look, told the vicar, "I'll make sure we're a bit more regular, Vicar."

Getting to his feet, the vicar nodded before saying, "Now, if no one has to hurry away, would you all care to join me for a nice, refreshing cup of tea? I assure you, my wife will be on her best behavior, or"—he looked enigmatically down at Vicky—"I shall let young…I am so sorry, my dear. After all this, I don't know your name…"

"Vicky," she answered, holding out her hand, which the vicar gladly shook.

"Or I shall set young Vicky on to her!"

Chapter Forty-One

"Harry!" Bob shouted. "Get a move on! That one's making a break for the lane!"

Lucy, just back from school, burst into laughter.

"And you're sure your sister loves working with cows?" Tina asked, trying her best not to join in.

Beside her, Sally didn't bother to hide her mirth, nearly falling off the fence.

Untwisting the strap on her school bag, Lucy gripped on to Tina's free hand and waved her other hand above her head. "Go, Harry! Ride 'em, cowboy!"

"Yee-ha!" Sally joined in.

"Not…helping." Harry puffed as she ran past, trying to head off a cow literally ten times her size from getting to the open gate on the far side of the field. It was a closely run thing, accompanied by much cheering from her audience, but she just about made it.

"Well done, sis!" Lucy cheered.

Bob strolled over to join them, whilst Harry, hands on her thighs, got her breath back and the cow in question trotted back toward the herd. "She's going to make a fine farmer, that one," he told them with approval.

"Why's it always *that* cow?" Harry asked as she joined them, slumping back against the gate and getting her already ruffled hair further ruffled for her trouble.

"I think she likes you," Lucy said.

Harry mustered the energy to reply, "What's not to

like?"

"Break's over!" Bob announced. "Come on, you, there's feed to put out before dinner."

"See you later," Harry told them, striding after the farmer.

"My lungs ache just from watching her!" Tina said, shaking her head.

Sally nodded. "I know what you mean. I'm happier than ever we've some help on the farm. I don't think I could do that."

"How're the Robinsons with all the new girls?" Marcy asked, as she hopped off her bicycle the other side of the gate.

"Hey, you lot! Good day?" Tina asked as she went to open the gate to the waiting girls.

"Challenge you to an arm wrestle?" Vicky said as she wheeled past.

Tina shook her head. "Not after last time. I don't think my arm's recovered yet!"

"Which reminds me," Vicky replied over her shoulder as she came to a stop outside the barn. "You still owe me a beer."

"Next time at the King's Head, all right?"

"You're on," Vicky told her before disappearing into the barn.

"To what do we owe the pleasure?" Berry asked as she reached into the basket on the front of her bicycle for Midnight.

At those words, Sally's demeanor and face dropped, and she leant her head upon Tina's shoulder. "What's wrong? What did I say?" Berry immediately asked, her voice full of concern. "Go on and play," she told Midnight, setting the cat upon its feet and shooing it away. Immediately, it spied Percy stalking something in some bushes and darted after him.

Tina wrapped an arm around the younger Land Girl and squeezed before turning her attention onto her Lumberjill friends. "We came over because, well, because I'm off tomorrow."

"Off? Are you going on holiday?" asked Sophie as she bent down to untuck her trousers from her socks, and so not seeing the sad expression upon either of her friend's faces.

"Not a holiday," Tina replied when Sophie had straightened up and could see. "I'm being transferred to an agricultural college. Apparently they want me to become an instructor."

"Who's going to be an instructor?" Vicky asked, her towel over her arm.

"Me." Tina shrugged.

"And you're going away tomorrow?"

"'fraid so, Vicky," Tina said.

"This sucks!" Sally announced before throwing off her friend's arms. "I'm off," she simply said and took to her heels before anyone could stop her.

"I'll go!" Vicky announced, handing Marcy her towel and running off after the younger Land Girl as she disappeared in the general direction of the village.

After they'd watched the two disappear, Marcy asked Tina, "I didn't know she'd be so upset."

Tina looked like she too wanted to chase off after her friend, but she had a tired look in her face. "Me either," she admitted. "It's not like I asked for this transfer."

"When did you find out?" Sophie asked.

"My orders came through this morning," Tina told

them. "I don't have a choice in the matter, either."

Marcy's eyebrows shot up. "Wow, that's not much notice."

Tina shook her head. "Nothing at all. Perhaps that's why it's hit her so hard."

"Perhaps," Marcy agreed. "I don't suppose there's any way you can take her with you, is there?"

"No. I suppose I could ask about bringing her in once I get there, but I doubt it'd lead to anything."

"You don't suppose…"—Marcy eventually put voice to what everyone had been thinking—"she'll do another runner?"

"I'd thought of that too," Tina admitted. "To be honest, I can't be a hundred percent sure. If you'd have asked me a few weeks ago, just after she came back, I'd have given you even odds, but now? Maybe. I guess all I can ask is if you all will keep as close an eye upon her as you can?"

Berry, Sophie, and Marcy all gathered as close to Tina as they could, with Marcy speaking for them all. "You know we will."

****

"Slow down!" Vicky yelled as she slowly closed upon Sally.

The two of them had by now reached the outskirts of the village and were coming within sight of the King's Head. Somewhat to Vicky's annoyance, Sally ran past the public house, only giving signs of coming to a stop as they came upon the police station. Elias Duncan was leaning against the open door, a cup of tea in his hands.

"You're in a hurry," he remarked, bringing first Sally and then Vicky to a halt. "Someone after you?"

Sally jerked a thumb over her shoulder at Vicky.

"Only her."

"Well, if you hadn't run off, I wouldn't have had to chase you!" Vicky shot back.

"And why did you run off?" Elias asked.

Now she'd stopped, Sally appeared sheepish. "I…don't know," she admitted.

"Now she thinks of that," Vicky stated, aiming a playful kick at her friend.

Elias eyed up the pair before him, both bent over to catch their breath. He stood back away from the door, saying, "Come inside, you two. I could do with another cup."

Vicky took Sally's arm through hers and, just in case her friend needed a hint, pulled her into the station, nodding as they passed the sergeant.

As soon as they'd entered, the policeman closed the door and followed them into his office. "Pull up a seat," he said as he filled up the kettle and put it on to boil.

"Thanks," Vicky said with a smile, whilst Sally only nodded.

The only noise to be heard whilst Elias brewed up was his off-tune whistling and the rather labored breathing of Sally, as she got herself back under control. All the while, Vicky didn't take her eyes off her, in case she took to her heels again.

"I'm not going anywhere," Sally told her, as if she could indeed read her mind.

Elias placed a not very clean mug of what purported to be tea into the hands of each girl and took to his well-worn leather seat behind his desk. "So, care to tell me what the chase was all about?"

Vicky fixed Sally with her best glare and, when her friend didn't take the hint, prompted, "Well, you may as well tell him. It's not as if I know why you ran away!"

"If you didn't know why I was running, why did you chase after me?" an exasperated Sally wanted to know.

"Now you put it like that…" Vicky admitted.

"If you'd care to share?" Elias said.

Sally took a long sip of her tea before putting it down on the floor. "The truth?"

"It helps," Elias said.

"I'm not sure why," Sally repeated, doing her best not to look either of the other occupants of the office in the eye.

"Suppose you start at the beginning?" Elias suggested.

"I'd like that too," Vicky admitted, adding, "I automatically said I'd go after her without hearing what had been said."

Though he raised an eyebrow, the policeman still told her, "The act of a good friend."

Sally had her mouth open when this was said, but closed it and glanced at Vicky, who merely shrugged her shoulders and gave a wry grin in return. She refocused upon the policeman. "My friend, Tina…you know her?" she asked and only continued when Elias gave a nod. "She's being posted away tomorrow. Something about becoming an instructor for the Land Army."

Elias whistled in appreciation. "Well, well, that's quite something. Good for her."

"But I'll be on my own!" Sally blurted out, letting the cat out of the bag.

"Ah," Vicky and Elias said at the same time.

Vicky immediately began speaking. "Who said you'll be on your own?"

Sally opened and closed her mouth once, twice, and

then a third time, her eyes blinking rapidly.

"What are we, then?" Vicky added, going and kneeling on the floor by her friend.

"I thought…" Sally began, unable to finish.

"What did you think?"

"I thought you only put up with me because of Tina."

"You can be an idiot, Sal. You know that?" Vicky told her friend.

Sally leant forward and threw her arms around Vicky's neck, telling her, "It has been mentioned, yes."

"Look, just because you're not billeted with us, it doesn't mean you're not…with us. Sorry, I'm not very eloquent, but I think you know what I mean."

I do," Sally told her after a short pause. She took a deep breath before picking up and finishing her tea. "Come on," she said, getting to her feet. "Let's get back."

"You're going to be all right," Vicky stated, finishing off her own drink before getting to her feet and, without looking back, strode out of the office, the door banging shut behind them.

"Not lost my touch," Elias said to the empty office before making his way outside and waving toward the girls as they headed back toward the Harkers' farm.

Chapter Forty-Two

"How's Sally doing now?" Marcy asked as Berry and Sophie took a breather, one hand each on their crosscut saw.

Berry swiped a hand across her brow. It may have been a gray, musty day, with the sun now nothing but a memory, but the effort involved in sawing the trunk up was more than enough to bring up an uncomfortable sweat. "Well, she says she's doing okay," Berry replied.

"And do you believe her?" Marcy asked.

The few moments it took Berry to reply were more than enough to put Marcy on her guard. "I don't know. I really don't." Standing straight, she placed her hands in the small of her back and stretched, letting out a loud groan. "That doesn't help, I'm aware of that, but it's the only answer I can give. We've only seen her the once since Tina left, so I don't have much to go on."

"She didn't stay long in the pub, I know. Anyone know why she had to leave so quickly?" Sophie asked.

Both Marcy and Berry shook their heads.

"It was weird, I'll give you that," Marcy agreed.

"What do you think we should do?" Sophie said.

"Go around to the Robinsons'? Maybe they're picking on her again now Tina is gone," Berry suggested.

"What about asking Bob to come around with us?" Sophie asked.

"Why would we need backup?" Berry wanted to

know.

"Well," Marcy said, beginning to stalk up and down before them, "we don't really know what they're like if we don't bring along someone they know, and they may not be on the petite size."

"Who won't be on the petite size?" Vicky asked, coming up to them and adding, "Is it lunch time already?"

"No," Sophie said, "why do you ask?"

Vicky spread her arms out. "We seem to be on a break here."

Marcy shook her head. "Not really. We were discussing Sal and how she's doing. Only, we're a little worried about her. I mean, did she seem okay to you the other night?"

"Hmm, now you say it," Vicky mused, "she did run out as soon as she'd finished her first drink."

"And none of the other Land Girls turned up, even though we had made a point of inviting them when we telephoned their farm," Marcy added.

Berry frowned. "You know, I didn't think that was strange until you mentioned it."

Marcy rubbed her hands together. "That's settled, then. After we get back, we're all going around to the Robinsons'."

****

"Bloody typical," Vicky huffed. "They would have a farmhouse at the top of the only hill for miles around!"

"Stop complaining, Vicky," Bob scolded. "We're nearly there."

"Good," she grumbled under her breath before letting out a loud, "Whoop!" of surprise as the farmer effortlessly hoisted her onto his shoulders.

"Never underestimate a farmer," he said, somewhat cryptically.

"Why do you think we're bringing you with us?" Berry asked, quickly smacking Vicky's behind before dancing out of reach.

"You do know he's barely five feet tall?" Bob asked.

"Of course he is," Sophie scoffed. "Who are you kidding? I've never met a farmer yet who's anything but a walking outhouse!"

"Oh, ho," Bob laughed. "That's very nice, I must say."

"Ignore her," Berry advised. "She's only joking."

Bob turned his head to regard Sophie, noting the way her head slouched as she walked. "Perhaps," he allowed. Stooping, he lowered his head and told Vicky, "Hop off you."

Once Vicky had joined Marcy and Berry a short way ahead of them, Bob grabbed a hold of one of Sophie's hands and gently eased it through the loop of his arm. When he was certain the others couldn't hear him above their chatter, he lowered his head a little and said, "It's okay to have some fun, Sophie."

"What do you mean?" she asked, trying to pull away, but unable to break free of Bob's gentle but firm grip.

"I mean," he went on, "I've been watching you, and I know you're not making much of an effort to have fun. Look, you're not going to like what I'm about to say, but I'm still going to say it. You barely knew this Ginger bloke, so why are you so…oh, what's the word? Why's he so much on your mind?"

They walked on for another few steps until the Robinsons' farm came in sight, before Sophie finally said, "I wish it were simple to explain."

Bob raised an arm and shouted, "You lot go on! We'll be with you in a minute," before giving all his attention to Sophie. "Try me."

Still with her hand in his, Sophie looked up into Bob's kind and concerned face. "I'm a bit of a wallflower," she began and continued quickly as he made to interrupt. "No, it's true. I know I'm not pretty, and men have never paid much attention to me. Then Ginger came along and seemed interested in me. I was amazed!" She let out a small, bitter laugh. "A man, a handsome—I think so—man was actually paying attention to me. Then, what happens? The bloody war goes and kills him! So I asked myself, why should I even try to meet someone?"

Without hesitation, Bob replied, "Because life's too short not to try."

Sophie nearly laughed again, only stopping when she looked into Bob's face and saw he was in earnest. "Why are you so certain? I think I'd make an excellent spinster."

Bob actually looked slightly annoyed and didn't bother keeping it from his voice. "Now, that's just silly talk."

"Is it really?" Sophie said, beginning to turn her back as she could feel tears prickling her eyes. She was stopped by Bob's firm grip upon her shoulders.

"Look, I'm not really good at pep talks, that's more your specialty," he added, actually getting a small smile as Sophie knew what he was referring to. "However, I do know you're a very special girl, Sophie, and there is someone out there for you. Someone very special, as only someone like that would be good enough for you."

He placed a finger gently upon her lips to forestall the protest she was undoubtedly about to utter. "Believe me, they'd have me, and my good lady wife, to answer to if they ever messed you around."

Sophie immediately crushed her face into Bob's body as she allowed the tears to fall. "Give us a minute, girls," she heard him say, guessing rightly that her friends had come back to find out what was keeping them.

Bob waited patiently whilst Sophie allowed the tears to flow, only stepping back when he felt her body stop shuddering. "Okay now?" he asked, smiling down at her and when she'd run the back of her hand across her nose, she looked gratefully up at him and nodded. "Let's catch that lot up before they cause a civil war, eh?"

"About time," Vicky said, as Bob and Sophie joined them at the gate to the farm.

"Patience is a virtue, young lady," Bob told her, as he unhitched the gate and held it open whilst the girls went through, closing it behind him. Striding out, he led the way to the farmhouse front door, raised a fist, and knocked a number of times. He had to repeat this once before footsteps could be heard and the door opened.

"Bob! Bit late for a social, isn't it?"

Bob held out a hand, their host took it and quickly pumped it up and down before letting go. "Tweezil, sorry for this, but it's not really a social." He stepped aside. "The girls wanted to check how young Sally Newhart is. They've been worried since Tina left."

All four girls' jaws were hanging open. If this Tweezil was five feet tall, it was stretching the point. Bob looked between them and the man in question, a slight grin upon his face, and could almost read their minds.

Surely this wasn't someone who could hold anyone in terror. Certainly he appeared only curious rather than angry at the suggestion that the Land Girl wasn't being well treated again.

"So these are the girls which put me right?" he surprised them by saying. He matched this statement by moving toward them, his own hand outstretched and a wide grin upon his face. Going first to Marcy, as the older one of the group, and taking her hand in his, he gave it a quick shake and did the same to all the girls before stepping back to stand beside Bob. Looking up at his fellow farmer, he declared, "I'll bet you my appearance isn't what they were expecting, eh? Not the normal strapping farmer, eh!"

Marcy and Berry both took a step back whilst Vicky stood there staring at the man.

The stand-off was broken by the appearance of a woman in a stained pinny, a flour-splattered rolling pin gripped in her hand. "Who the devil are you…Bob! What are you doing here?" She changed tack, though she was still eyeing the group of girls suspiciously.

"Jenny, it's been too long," Bob said, leaning down to kiss a cheek smeared in white flour. "You can put the rolling pin down. The girls only wanted to check that Sally's all right."

"I might have known," Jenny said and turned her back without further comment and went back into the house.

"Ignore her," Tweezil said. "She's making a pie and hates being interrupted. If you want to follow me, I'll take you around to the girls' barn. They've just had dinner," he said over his shoulder.

As they walked, Marcy trotted up to join Bob and

Tweezil. "Mr. Robinson…"

"Call me Tweezil," he told her.

Marcy coughed. "Tweezil, then. A most unusual name but, wonderful, I hope you don't mind my saying." When he merely shook his head, she went on, "We'd like to thank you for treating our friends…better. We appreciate it."

Vicky had a little coughing fit at hearing this bit of diplomacy from her friend, prompting Sophie and Berry to thump her hard on the back, which brought on a real bout of coughing.

Stopping, Tweezil looked up at Marcy. "You shouldn't have. And you shouldn't have had to ask." He let out a sigh and ran a hand through thinning gray hair. Probably about the same age as Bob, Tweezil appeared to have little of the natural, after Sophie had put him right, charm of his friend and so appeared much older. "I've no excuses for what I did. I can only say that I was angry as the last of my laborers had joined up, and I was only left with my son. Then a couple of women are dumped on me and it appeared, though it actually wasn't, I was spending half my time making sure they did the job properly."

"But you're all fine now?" Berry asked, having recovered herself.

They could just make out a smile in the half light. "I hope so. Anyway, speak of the devil, here's Sally now."

Coming around a corner indeed trotted Sally, her eyes wide. "What are you lot doing here?"

After she'd managed to extricate herself from her friends, Sally took them around to sit on a couple of logs at the side of the farmhouse, leaving Bob and Tweezil to themselves. "I'll see you all back at the farm!" Bob shouted as he strode off toward the front of the house.

"So?" Sally repeated.

"We wanted to see how you were," Marcy told her.

"Yes," Sophie added. "You took off from the pub the other night as if your fanny was on fire!"

Though a little difficult to be sure, Sally looked a little sheepish and indeed, squirmed a little on the log before admitting, "I miss Tina."

"We all do," Berry said. "But why did you rush out?"

"Oh, boy, I've a feeling you're going to think I've been very silly," she admitted.

"Sounds normal," Vicky told her, grinning. "But go on anyway."

"I…I thought you only put up with me because you liked Tina."

Vicky swatted her around the back of the head, and none too gently, either. "You silly sausage! I thought I'd already put you straight on that."

Sally shrugged and rubbed the back of her head. "I thought you were only being kind. Plus, I ran away before, and because of what I said when we first met, Marcy."

On her other side, Marcy threw an arm around the girl's shoulders. "You *are* a silly sausage! That's all long forgotten and forgiven, for both. Plus, when have we ever shown favoritism? You're both our friends."

"So, no more running from our company. Understand?" Vicky told her, having to raise her voice as a rhythmic thudding noise began.

"I'll consider myself told off," Sally half shouted.

"Good!" Berry shouted, as the thudding got louder.

"What the hell's…" Sophie began to say and trailed

off as a man about her age with a full head of jet-black hair strode into view. In his arms was a pile of logs, but that wasn't what had caused Sophie to lose track of what she was going to say, as his shirt was open, displaying the most marvelously muscled chest any of the girls had ever seen.

"You ready for the night's logs, Sally?" he said as he came to a halt before them.

"Sure," Sally answered, standing up and facing her friends. "Everyone, this is Charley, Tweezil and Jenny's son. Come on, I'll show you where we sleep."

Everyone got up to follow the girl and Charley except for Sophie, who was gripping the log and staring at the man as if her life depended upon it. Berry turned back when she noticed and sat down at her friend's side, gripping her arm in concern. "What's wrong?"

Sophie tore her eyes away and, with a look of pure panic in them, told her, "I think I'm in love!"

Chapter Forty-Three

Next morning, Sophie made a point of being first at breakfast, even beating Harry, who had developed a huge appetite, which she attributed to all the time she spent outdoors working with Bob.

"So," Sophie began, helping herself to some toast and her hard-boiled egg, "What's the story with Charley Robinson?"

The kitchen door banged open at that second, and in rushed everyone else, including Lucy, who trailed in behind everyone else still rubbing sleep from her eyes. "Why couldn't I have another ten minutes?" she kept moaning, though none of the others were taking notice.

"Has Sophie asked about this Charley person yet?" Harry blurted out, taking a seat next to Sophie and digging her none too gently in the ribs.

At seeing her friend's jaw drop, Berry added, "Oh, good, we're not too late."

Whilst everyone else—including Bob, who didn't trouble to hide a grin—began making short work of the breakfast selection Sheila had put together, Sophie sat there with a piece of egg balanced upon her fork, shaking her head. "Are there no secrets around here?"

"Hey!" Marcy told her, waving her toast in Sophie's face. "You're the one who told us you thought you were in love last night."

"What's all this?" Sheila asked before asking her

husband. "Did something happen at the Robinsons' you didn't tell me?"

"Don't put this on my shoulders," he replied. "All I'll say is that our Sophie caught sight of young Charley displaying his chest."

"Oh," Sheila said, trying to put a blasé face on which fooled no one. "Is that all."

Sophie let out a sigh and admitted defeat. "Ignore them, Sheila. What can you tell me about him?"

"How much time have you got?" Sheila asked, looking up at the kitchen clock.

Marcy did the same and told her, "About ten minutes before we'll have to be off."

"Should be plenty." Sheila nodded before munching through a piece of toast and finishing off her egg, much to Sophie's obvious frustration.

"Sheila!"

"Sorry," she said, dabbing the sides of her mouth with a serviette. "Charley, well, he's a farmer, so he's in a reserved occupation, which is why he's still there. That's not to say he's happy about it at all, especially as the last of his friends who used to work there joined up six months ago. Poor boy seems to have had the stuffing knocked out of him, and he's become a bit of a recluse."

"Is that why we've never seen him around?" Sophie asked, leaning forward and narrowly avoiding putting her elbow in the butter dish.

"Probably," Bob agreed, picking up his tea. "Shame, really, as he used to be a big fixture of the King's Head darts team."

Sophie coughed, clearing her throat. "Any, um, girlfriend around? And if you nudge me one more time, young lady..." she told Harry, as the young girl drew back an elbow.

"No one I'm aware of," Sheila informed her, after barely a moment's thought. "Not much choice around here."

"Oh, good," Sophie declared, trying and failing to keep a grin from her face.

Sheila got up from the table and went down the hall toward the front room, returning shortly with something over her arm. "Stand up, Harry," she asked before saying to Sophie, "Perhaps you could speak to him tomorrow night?"

Sophie, her breakfast finished, paused with one arm half in and half out of her jacket. "What's happening then?"

"Honestly, you lot are going to have to learn to read the village notice board," Sheila muttered, with a shake of her head. "The village is having a, well, a ceremony, I suppose you could call it, for Paula Gibbons, at eight in the evening. Not everyone was able to get to her funeral," Sheila added with a slight shrug, aware the girls hadn't attended. "Now…" she returned her attention to Harry, who was stuffing the last of her toast into her mouth, "let's see if this dress I've made for you fits. Tie your dungarees around your waist for me, will you? Bob, close your eyes for a minute," she instructed her husband. "Now, I'm just going to whip your shirt off for a second," she told Harry and, without waiting for an answer, began to tug it up.

Immediately she'd done so, Harry yelled, "No! Stop!" but it was too late, and the Lumberjills stared in horrified fascination at the scars criss-crossing the poor girl's back.

"What the hell!" Berry exclaimed, shoving her chair

back and dropping to her feet before Harry, who was doing her best to tug her shirt back down. Unfortunately, Sheila's fingers were frozen to the material and it took her a few tugs before she was able to recover her dignity, by which time both Vicky and Marcy had joined Berry. Sophie sat stock still at the table, her shock at her small friend's predicament preventing her from moving.

Fortunately for Harry, Bob was in no way so hindered, and before the words had barely finished escaping Berry's mouth, he was by Harry's side and had scooped the girl into his arms. Nobody could have prevented him from marching out of the kitchen, the tearful girl in his arms, with Lucy close on their heels.

Berry, Marcy, and Vicky all exchanged glances before turning their attention as a group upon Sophie and Sheila, who was still standing stock still at what she'd done.

"Would someone care to explain what we've just seen?" Marcy demanded.

Ignoring the words, Sophie forced herself to her feet and, taking Sheila gently yet firmly by the hand, led her back to the table and put her into a chair. "Vicky, pour Sheila a cup of tea, and make it as strong as you can."

Something in Sophie's tone made the request not one to question. A minute later, Vicky placed a cup of tea in front of Sheila which would dissolve a spoon, given half a chance.

"Drink that," Sophie told her, silencing her friends with a glare that brooked no argument. Only when Sheila had put down her now half full cup did Sophie take the seat next to her. "Are you okay now?"

Sheila nodded, before hanging her head. "How could I be so careless?" she asked Sophie.

Leaning to the side, Sophie brushed her fringe aside and kissed Sheila on the forehead. "You didn't mean to."

Turning her head toward the back kitchen door, Sheila wiped a tear from her eye. "She's never going to forgive me," she muttered.

Sophie pushed the remains of the cup of tea into Sheila's hands. "Of course she will. Knowing Harry, she'll probably be angry, but when she gets around to thinking about it, she'll forgive you."

Taking out a handkerchief, Sheila blew her nose. "I hope so."

"Will one of you tell me what the bloody hell that was?" Vicky demanded, finally losing patience.

Sheila and Sophie exchanged glances before Sheila said, "Can you tell them? They may as well know now, and I don't want them asking either Harry or Lucy."

Much to the obvious annoyance of the other three, Sophie drank down half a cup of tea herself before beginning. She put her cup down and looked across at her friends sitting opposite her. "You lot remember the trouble the girls had with the McAlisters? The family they were billeted with as evacuees?"

From the way all three of her friends reacted, eyes wide, obviously they did.

Berry's head snapped around as if she could see through the kitchen door and alight upon Harry. "Those swine did *that* to her?"

Sophie nodded. "You can't blame them for running away, can you?"

"If I ever catch hold of them..." Vicky left the statement unsaid and for once, not a one of them told her to put her penknife away when she took it out of her pocket and began to flick the blade in and out.

"And you knew…how?" Marcy asked.

"Accident." Sophie shrugged. "She was taking a shower and, well, you know how unstable that thing can be."

"Poor girl," Marcy uttered, shaking her head. "How are you?" she asked Sheila.

With one more sniff, Sheila got to her feet, straightened her pinny, and planted both hands flat on the table. "I've been better." She looked at the clock. "Hadn't you lot better be off to work?"

It took another minute before Marcy slowly nodded her head and heaved herself to her feet. Looking around, she said, "You're right. Come on, we really will have to be going."

Sophie got to her feet and came and stood before Marcy. "Do you mind if I catch you up? I really want to go and see how Harry is."

Without hesitation, Marcy told her, "Take your time. Give her our love and tell her we'll see her later. Right," she said once both Sophie and Sheila had disappeared out the back door. "Let's get going. Those trees aren't going to cut themselves down."

****

Bob and the girls weren't in the barn, or the cowshed, and as neither Sheila nor Sophie had seen them pass before the kitchen window, that only left the woods behind the farm for the direction they could have gone.

"Do you think they've gone to the ruins where Berry found them?" Sheila asked Sophie as the two made their careful way across the broken ground.

"You read my mind," Sophie replied as she held a branch out of the way so it wouldn't slap the farmer's wife in the face.

A few minutes later, they could hear low voices and the occasional sob, and Sheila began to lag behind. "Come on," Sophie told her, holding out a hand. "Hanging back's going to do no one any good." She lowered her voice a little as she waited for Sheila to catch her up. "I'm sure she won't hate you, Sheila," she said, adding an encouraging smile.

This seemed enough for Sheila to pick the pace back up, and before too much longer, the two of them came across the same ruins in which the girls had been found not all that long ago. Sitting on a pile of bricks was Bob, with Lucy leaning against his side and Harry, looking much younger than her years, upon his lap. She had her head upon his shoulder and Bob was running one of his hands in a soothing motion through her hair. As they got closer, they could hear muffled sobs coming from Harry and see that Lucy was gripping one of her sister's hands in hers as if she'd never let it go.

"They're not going to judge you," was the first thing the two heard Bob say as they came into view.

Upon hearing Sophie step on a twig, which went off with a sound like a gunshot, Harry jerked her head around and, much to everyone's surprise, let go of her sister's hands, hopped off of Bob's lap, and ran toward Sheila. When she got to her, she didn't hesitate and instead jumped at her causing Sheila to open her arms to catch the girl.

Sheila immediately burst into tears, her head over Harry's shoulder, her eyes wide open and fixed upon her husband, who now had Lucy upon his lap, both of them staring at the sight before them.

"I'm so sorry, my love," Sheila wailed in between sobs. "I was so caught up in wanting to show off that dress as a surprise, I didn't think. Can…can you forgive me?"

Whatever Harry said in reply was lost to both the wind and the fact her face was buried in Sheila's hair. Hesitantly at first, Sophie sidled up to the pair until she was within arm's reach. "Harry?" was all she said before the young girl flung out an arm and, with surprising strength, probably born from dealing daily with cows many times her weight, drew her into the hug.

Eventually, Harry drew back her head, wiped her nose on her sleeve, and let out a loud sniff. To both the women's pleasant surprise, when she slithered down Sheila's body and stood on the ground, she had a slight smile upon her snotty face.

Disregarding the damp, mossy ground, Sheila dropped to her knees and held out her hands. When Harry took them, she sniffed loudly before saying, "I thought you'd hate me."

"And I thought you hated me. Which is why you…"

Sheila interrupted her. "No! Oh, God, no. I can't believe I did that to you! I would never deliberately hurt you! You've got to believe that." Harry gave her a brief nod after the barest time to think. "I could never hate you," Sheila then told her, glancing up as Bob and Lucy came to join them. She took hold of one of Lucy's hands and squeezed tight. "I love you. I love you both as if you were my own, and I'd do anything to turn back time so *that* never happened."

"Me too," Harry told her, as Lucy let go of Bob's hand and gave her big sister a huge hug.

"I'm going to get big and strong, sis," she announced, a glint in her eye no one would believe was possible for an eight-year-old. "And then, I'm going to pay those people a visit. I'll make them pay for what they did to you!"

Harry too now dropped to her knees and gripped her sister's upper arms. When she spoke, her voice was as sharp as flint. "No! Yes, you can grow up as tough as you like, but I will not have you trying to take revenge for me. I don't want that. All I want to do is to forget them."

"But the scars?" Lucy queried, in that innocent voice of the young.

Harry now stood back up, took a deep breath and undid the one side of her dungarees which was done up and then hoisted up her shirt a bit. Turning her back to the group, she looked at them over her shoulder and what she said next had both Sheila and Bob fairly bursting with pride.

"These are now a part of me. I'm sure people will come back, once we've won this war, with far worse." She made a point of looking at Bob before continuing, "They already did once. So I've got to get used to people occasionally seeing these, and not run away, and you must too, Lucy. Sheila, my mum would have been proud to know you, and the same goes for you, Bob. I can't give higher praise than that. Now, let's forget this all happened, eh?"

Bob took a step toward her, leaned down and planted a firm, lingering kiss on her forehead. "You're quite some lass," he said softly.

Everyone could see she fought the impulse to wipe the kiss away as she looked around before telling them, "I'm learning from the best. Now, you'd better go to work, Sophie, and," she added, "tell everyone that I'm fine—we're fine. Okay?" Not trusting her voice at that moment, Sophie could only nod before she turned back toward the farmhouse, waving over her shoulder as she went. "Right, I suppose we'd better get to work, eh, Bob?"

Chapter Forty-Four

"Strange," Bob muttered, half to himself as he peered through the kitchen window. "Were you girls expecting your RAF chaps tonight?" he asked over his shoulder.

"Stop fussing!" Vicky told Berry, slapping her hands away as she tried to put the beret she was wearing at what she considered the proper angle. "Not so far as I know, Bob," she answered.

He turned around and said, "In that case, how come an RAF staff car's just pulled up outside?"

"What?" Marcy, Berry, and Vicky all said at the same time, scrambling to look out the window whilst Sophie instead strode to the kitchen door and opened it to find a familiar RAF officer with a fist raised and about to knock.

"Wing Commander Mair!" Sophie said, surprise in her voice at the unexpected visitor. "What are you doing here?" she asked before she could stop herself.

"Impressive memory you have there, Miss…Baxtor," he said after a very short pause.

"I could say the same," Sophie replied and immediately stopped herself from saying anymore as she'd looked up into his face and the large frown upon his brow banished all thought of further small talk from her mind. "I think you'd better come in," she told him, stepping aside to allow the officer to squeeze past.

"Bob and Sheila Harker, I'd like you to meet Wing Commander Mair," Sophie said, making the introductions. "He's the C/O of the boys' squadron."

Hastily drying her hands from where she'd given them a quick wash, Sheila stepped forward to take the man's firm handshake, closely followed by Bob. "Pleased to meet you Wing Commander. Won't you take a seat?"

"Cup of tea?" Sheila automatically offered, to which she received a brief nod.

"Please, it's been a…trying drive." He looked around the kitchen before taking his hat off and placing it upon his lap.

"To what do we owe the visit?" Marcy asked the question upon everyone's lips and was glad she was seated when the officer lowered his eyes before looking back around once more.

I'm glad you're all here," he began, the temperature in the room dropping a few degrees. "I promise that I did try to telephone last night, but I couldn't get through."

"The line's been dead for coming on a week now," Bob supplied, recognizing the tone of voice the officer was using. "No idea why, nor when it'll be back up. We've had to walk down to use the one in the village."

"That'd explain it," Mair replied, running a hand through his hair. "Look, I wanted to let you three know," he said, making a point of catching the eyes of Berry, Marcy, and Vicky, "what's happened, even though none of you are officially entitled to know. However, I'm aware of how you feel about them, and I appreciate what you did for them, for their morale. Anyway, we had a big effort last night. All the squadrons on the base were on operations. It wasn't…pleasant. We took quite a few losses. I wanted to wait until I could confirm it, but it's beyond doubt now. Dennis's Lanc was seen losing height, with two engines on fire." Berry's hands flew to her mouth, though with a supreme effort she didn't interrupt. "Another crew on my squadron saw five chutes open before he lost sight of the crate when it flew into cloud."

"Do you know who got out?" Sophie asked the question after a brief wait, as none of her friends seemed capable of speech.

Mair shook his head before saying, "I'm afraid not."

"Where did they bail out?" Bob helpfully asked.

"Just as we were approaching the Dutch coast."

"Any chance of their being picked up?" Sophie asked.

Mair slumped back in his seat, his body language conveying what he felt the odds were for all to see. He gratefully accepted the mug of strong tea Sheila pushed into his hands.

"Drink up," Sheila told him. "You look all in."

"Thank you," he replied, and for a few minutes, the only sound to be heard was the slurping of tea. Once finished, he pushed the cup away and let out a long sigh. "I do apologize again. It's been a long night."

"I can imagine," Sophie agreed, just about stopping herself from reaching out and squeezing his hand in sympathy.

"Wing Commander?" Berry said, quietly wiping a tear away as she stood before him. "We'd like to…it's very kind of you to come all this way to inform us, it really is. Could we ask you one more favor?"

Mair smiled for the first time since he arrived. "I think I can imagine what that is—Berry, isn't it?" She nodded. "Of course I will. As soon as I know anything, I'll be in contact."

"Do you have to be off right away?" Sheila asked.

The Wing Commander brought up his arm and looked at his watch. "I should." He nodded toward the window. "It looks like it's about to rain cats and dogs out there, so I'd better make a move whilst there's still some light. These blasted taped-off headlights are the next best thing to useless," he told them, with a small laugh.

"Do you mind if I suggest something?" Bob asked.

"Go ahead," he said, getting to his feet and straightening his uniform jacket.

"You look all in. If you absolutely don't have to be back to base tonight, can we offer you a bed for the night?"

Perhaps he felt his presence could somehow bring their boyfriends back to them, and maybe the thought came to the officer's mind too. Either way, he slumped back down into his seat and let the tiredness he must have been feeling wash over his face. He looked up into Bob's kind face. "You know, that's the best offer I've had in a long time. Thank you, yes, I'd be very happy to accept. If I won't be putting you to any trouble, that is?"

"No trouble at all." Sheila smiled at him.

He looked around the room. "You all seem on the point of going out," he mentioned, "and by the look of it, for something special too."

As if she needed to gather herself before trusting her voice, Marcy coughed twice to clear her throat. "You could say that. We're going to pay our respects to a villager who was killed when her cottage was bombed a while back."

"Ah," Mair eventually said. "In such a small

community, I suppose everyone knows everyone else."

"Something along those lines," Bob replied.

"In that case, would you mind if I tagged along?" Mair asked.

Bob held out a hand. "We'd be honored."

Mair stood and stretched out his back. "I was going to ask to use your telephone, but I can use the one in the village. I'll need to let my squadron know where I am."

****

An hour later, everyone was outside, the gathering gray clouds just about holding back the rain they threatened.

"Everyone ready?" Sheila asked and upon receiving a round of nods, led the way toward the farm gate.

"Well, would you take a look at that?" Vicky said, pointing toward the tractor. The sight brought everyone up short.

Midnight was hunkered down upon one of the large wheels, her bottom wriggling back and forth, her gaze fixed upon Percy who was trotting beneath her, a mouse lying dead in his mouth. Suddenly, the small black cat who, so far as anyone else knew, had never shown any previous interest in mousing, pounced down upon the other cat's back. In the tussle which followed, fur flew until Midnight stalked away proudly with her stolen booty in her mouth.

"Well, well, it looks like our little girl has grown up," Berry declared, before everyone walked on.

As they approached the church, the vicar and his odious wife, Violet, could be seen on the road outside, greeting the villagers as they gathered before moving along to Paula Gibbons' grave. The vicar's robes were immaculate, and he had a smile and a small word for everyone, whereas the expression upon his wife's face clearly stated she'd rather be anywhere but where she was.

"Is there something wrong with that woman?" the Wing Commander asked after he'd shared greetings with the vicar and they were out of earshot.

Vicky took him by the arm. "I'm not certain I'd know where to begin. Come on," she urged as they hurried along to catch up with their friends.

Once everyone who was coming was gathered around the graveside, the vicar held up his hands until everyone was silent. "Thank you, everyone, for coming. I'll keep this short, as it's such a cold night, and the religious aspect to a minimum, just as Paula would have wanted it. Most of you knew Paula, so you know she wasn't a very religious person. That's not to say she wasn't a good, kind one, because she was. I think her greatest failing would be that she was unable to understand the cats she bred were little horrors." He made a point of searching out Sheila's face. "I'm sure Sheila Harker can attest to that. As with so many others, she is now a victim of tyranny and oppression. We shall remember her," he finished with a bow of his head.

The village formed an orderly queue and filed past Paula's grave, until it came the turn of the Lumberjills.

"Go ahead," Marcy said to Berry, who carried a small bunch of flowers.

Berry managed a weak smile at her friend before stepping forward and laying them with the others. "I'm sorry I never got to know you, Paula," she said in a clear voice so everyone could hear. "Rest in peace."

As they walked away, Marcy strode by her side. "How are you doing?"

"Okay, actually," Berry replied, patting her friend's hand. "It wasn't much, but I think I needed that."

Passing the grave of the German airman, the girls and their companions all nodded their respects before coming together before the monument to the village's fallen from the Great and Boer Wars.

"Girls," Marcy said, as they stood looking at the small obelisk-shaped piece of stone. The light was too poor to make out the names. "I don't know how long we'll be here, but let's try and make the best of it that we can." She stopped, looked up, and noticed Bob and Sheila were standing a little way away from them, both with an arm around Harry and Lucy. "Come here, you lot! And you, Wing Commander. As I was saying," she carried on, absently noting they were the only ones left in the graveyard, "we've all got to stand together, no matter what's thrown at us. To friendship!"

As the rain finally began to pour down, everyone turned their faces to the sky and echoed, "To friendship!"

A word about the author…

Mick is a hopeless romantic who was born in England but spent fifteen years roaming around the world in the pay of the late HM Queen Elisabeth II in the Royal Air Force before putting down roots—and realizing how much he missed the travel. This he's replaced somewhat with his writing, including reviewing books and supporting fellow saga and romance authors in promoting their novels.

He's the proud keeper of two Romanian Werecats bent on world domination, is mad on the music of the Beach Boys, and enjoys the theatre and humoring his Manchester United-supporting wife.

Finally, and most importantly, Mick is a full member of the Romantic Novelists Association. *The Lumberjills* is the lead book in this new series from the author of the Broken Wings novels.

Thank you for purchasing
this publication of The Wild Rose Press, Inc.

For questions or more information
contact us at
info@thewildrosepress.com.

The Wild Rose Press, Inc.

Lightning Source UK Ltd.
Milton Keynes UK
UKHW021933030223
416465UK00023B/269